T0095433

# Leland Thomson:

## A GIFT, A CELLO, AND A DREAM

CARY
FRANKLIN
SMITH

ARCHWAY
PUBLISHING

Archway Publishing books may be ordered through booksellers or by contacting:

Archway Publishing
1663 Liberty Drive
Bloomington, IN 47403
www.archwaypublishing.com
1 (888) 242-5904

ISBN: 978-1-4808-7703-0 (sc)
ISBN: 978-1-4808-7704-7 (hc)
ISBN: 978-1-4808-7702-3 (e)

Library of Congress Control Number: 2019906882

Print information available on the last page.

Archway Publishing rev. date: 6/6/2019

In acknowledgement of my three sons
whose gifts have helped them live the dream.

Dedicated to my grandchildren
and the incredible future that lies before each of them.

With appreciation to the Giver of all Gifts.

# Chapter One

"MAMA, IS THIS BLOOD GONNA COME OUTA MY SHIRT?"
"He's still moving! Shoot him again, Dearl!" Manny screamed.

The year-old boar squealed his final breath as Dearl placed another .22 slug in his head.

"Daddy, why didn't you use the shotgun?" Leland asked. "He'd been dead right then and there."

"Wastes too much meat. He'll be dead soon enough."

Winter was the best time for killing hogs. Seems the chill made them bleed out better before hanging them in the smokehouse. No one really knew why, just the way it had always been done.

Life was challenging in the Ozarks. Oh, you could go to the store in Lathrup Springs, about thirty miles away, but that killed too much of a day, took more gas than you wanted to burn and why go buy groceries when everything you needed could be caught, killed or grown for free?

Manny and Dearl lived in Pine Hollow, Arkansas, with their only son, Leland. Dearl was the foreman over the woodsmen who'd venture into the Ozarks each day to cut and haul logs for Creighton's Mill.

There were very few perks working for a sawmill. As a foreman, though, Dearl and his family got to live free in a company house. Other workers were provided what amounted to cabins they could rent, with the rent taken from their paycheck each month. Though about twice as large as the cabins, the foreman's quarters was still only a small two-bedroom, wood-framed house that Manny kept clean and orderly, no luxuries, just necessities.

In the backyard, Dearl had fenced off a section for Manny's garden. To keep away the diggers and jumpers, he buried one fence below ground level and attached another that raised the height over his head. It was Nubbin's job to scare off birds and any other critters than might try to get in some other way.

Nubbin was Leland's dog. She was a mix of questionable variety. The dominate characteristic was just plain hound, brown with black nose and ears. She used to be Dearl's dog and in those days would go with him into the woods to hunt or work. But one day when she was standing on the seat of his truck, leaning out the window the front tire hit a hole while Dearl was making a sharp turn. Nubbin (called Ruthie at the time) was bounced out the window. All Dearl could grab was her tail, which dislocated about four inches from her rump. After he had cut off the dislocated tail section, she had nothing more to do with him. She transferred her loyalty to Leland, who changed her name to Nubbin because of her nub of a tail.

Life in Pine Hollow was a combination of creativity and good fortune. An old hickory tree near the back door got struck by lightning. To deal with the problem, Dearl flattened the stump and made Manny a chopping block. The rest of the tree became wood for the smoker. Many a chicken had met their end on that stump. Other animals had lost fur, skin, scales or feathers there as well while Manny got them ready to become the evening meal.

It was too small a stump to hoist up a yearling hog onto, so Dearl and Manny teamed up to gut and clean the carcass in the yard where the pig lay. The warm, steaming entrails were piled on a board, waiting for a trip to the woods to feed the night scavengers. The skin and hooves placed in another pile to be buried out by the edge of the woods.

Dearl had no problem manhandling the hog. Though he was of nominal height, He was a strong, big-chested man. He was the type of man you wanted on your side in a scuffle. He'd never to back down in defense of his family, his friends, his company or his sense of propriety. He lived by a code that was fair, yet firm. His men respected him.

He met Manny when he came to work at the mill as a teenager. Manny's father was the foreman before Dearl. As soon as he was hired, Dearl lived in a cabin with two other men but spent most of his free time at the foreman's house. Manny was fourteen when they met and wasn't allowed to be alone with a boy. Dearl didn't mind. It gave him a sense of home he hadn't had in quite some time.

Manny's parents accepted Dearl as a part of their family. In fact, traditionally it was the father who passed his trade on to his sons. With no son of his own, Manny's dad took specific interest in Dearl and taught him the skills and management ability to lead men. When Manny's dad died, Dearl was given the job as foreman over men more seasoned and longer tenured. He had proven his ability and knowledge but had to learn personnel skills to lead men who resented him getting promoted over them. It took a while for that resentment to go away. Some got fired, some got a whipping, but most finally realized Dearl was the best man for the job.

Dearl and Leland hung the skinned and gutted boar in the smokehouse, stoked the fire, threw on some water-soaked hickory chips, then headed into the house.

"Grab a slab of bacon, Leland," Dearl said. "We need to start eating up last year's kill to get ready for when this fellow's done."

Leland took down a hunk of meat. He gave it to his Mom, then washed up for dinner. As was usual after the evening meal, Dearl churned up the embers in the fireplace and watched the embers fly up the chimney. Manny joined the three of them in the living room. Leland took his cello from the corner. He sat it between his legs, closed his eyes and lay his open hands on his legs, then, in a minute took his bow and filled the house with the deep strains of the rich baritone. Leland had the gift.

※

Bacon. The aroma of the thin layers of meat and fat filled the house. It was the contribution from last year's hog Leland had brought from the smokehouse. The sizzling strips surrendered to the flames beneath the skillet on the butane stovetop. Leland's mother forked them over and then cracked open the eggs she had just gathered from the coops out back. The routine was as right as the morning sun silently warming the frigid overnight air drifting down from the pines and hardwoods of the Arkansas foothills.

But even the lure of bacon couldn't overcome the urgings of a warm bed. Leland pulled his covers over his head and drifted back asleep. A second knock came but its muffled sounds weren't enough to wake him. The third was more of a pounding but it was the voice behind the knock, yelling his name – *Leland James Thomson!* That got him up.

Dearl was used to men doing what he told them to do as soon as he told them. At sixteen, Leland had long ago learned not to take his dad's commands lightly. "I'm up," he answered. He threw back the covers and planted his feet on the cold, wooden floor.

The winds of the Arkansas winter of 1960 had been blustery but dry. This morning they were seeping through the cracks in the bare clapboards. Later, Leland would wrap up in a heavy coat and stay warm enough to get to school, but right now, in this moment, he faced the greater challenge of the day. The warmth of his bed called back to him, and his dad's voice still ringing in his ears. He quickly pulled up his jeans over the thermals he'd worn to bed and layered on a couple of pairs of socks. He ran his slender fingers through his long, dirty-blond hair, pushing it back out of his eyes, then rambled to the breakfast table.

"I had that dream again last night," Leland said, slinging his leg over the backside of the chair.

"Which one is that?" his mother Manny asked. She was setting the plates of eggs and bacon on the table. Dearl had already taken a biscuit from the platter in the center and dabbed it into the slice of butter he'd mashed into a puddle of syrup on the side of his plate.

"The one where I'm about to play my cello in front of a whole bunch of people and then never get to."

"I wish you'd finish that dream," Dearl said. "Don't make sense to keep having the same one over and over like that."

"Well, it wasn't exactly the same this time. I had a big fight with some old man about praying before I played. He didn't like me doing it so he told me I couldn't."

"What happened?" Manny asked.

"I don't know. That's when I woke up. He sure was mad though. And his breath stank. Thank someday I'll get to play for a bunch of people like in my dream, Dad?"

"Son, we live in Pine Hollow," Dearl said. "I work for a sawmill. To the rest of the world we're trash. That's what we are. That's what we'll always be. Trash don't always get no opportunity like that."

"Dearl Thomson, don't you dare call yourself or my son sawmill trash! We're as good as anybody, and you know it!" Manny snapped. "If he's supposed to play in front of a bunch of people, then by the providence of the Almighty that's what he'll do. And being from a sawmill won't make no difference to nobody!"

Leland sopped up the remaining egg yolk with his biscuit and crammed it into his mouth. "But wouldn't it be something if I got to do that, even if for just a year?"

"Yep, it would be something," Manny said, glaring down Dearl before he could respond. "But don't talk with your mouth so full."

"Yes 'em," he said, reaching across for another biscuit.

Pine Hollow was a sawmill town. And what it was, was its only purpose for existing. Shortly after the turn of the century Samuel Grogan set up milling operations in the Ozark foothills just up from Lathrup Springs. It was an ideal location. The enormous quantity of old growth pines and hardwoods plus the saplings and yearlings struggling to reach some sunlight through the dense forest gave the appearance of an unending supply of timber. Mr. Grogan had carefully plotted the direction and intensity of the harvesting, insuring the younger trees would soon command the area once held by the older trees. And in areas where there was little new growth, he had his men plant new trees for the needs of future generations.

The mill was highly successful even past Mr. Grogan dying in the mid-twenties. His family had committed to following his intentions. They worked hard to keep everything running and then the Depression hit. As the market for lumber dried up so did the income for the mill. When the Grogans could no longer sustain the families who worked for them, the mill was shut down and deserted, leaving behind a couple of processing buildings, an office, a company store and a dozen or so houses for the workers. But it also left thousands of acres of valuable timber growing toward a future harvest.

Walter Creighton was from old money made right after the first war when his family ran a dozen or so mills east of the Mississippi. They, too, were hit by the misery of the Depression which forced them to shut down several of their mills as well. When the financial strain began to lessen and Walter was losing negotiations with banks to reestablish his old mills, he heard about Pine Hollow, Arkansas. He bought the mill in the late thirties and brought it to full-strength just before the Second World War broke out. He had expanded the facilities, built some new housing and adding a school and church.

When the war started, most of the men who worked for him joined the fight. But, instead of cutting back, he sought out the derelicts and drunks, promising them help with their demons if they would work for him to increase his sales territory into Oklahoma and southern Missouri. Later, during the building boom after the war was over, Pine Hollow proved to be a highly profitable investment, not only for the Creighton family but for the men given a new start at life and the ones who returned from fighting.

Before Mr. Creighton bought the mill and upgraded the process, the planks from the rough-cut logs would be stacked and left to air dry. Back East, kilns were being used to dry the lumber more quickly, under controlled conditions. Kilns were the up and coming technology, so Mr. Creighton had his men construct one. Now, the planks could be sent to the planer mill in less time. At the planer mills they would be scraped smooth and shaved down to proper sizes. From there they'd be shipped across Arkansas, Oklahoma and Southern Missouri for distribution to lumber yards and home builders.

Dearl had grown up in sawmills in east Texas. His dad had owned a planer mill south of Lufkin that serviced mills deep in the thickets of the Pineywoods. Dearl had quit school when he was fourteen and started working at his dad's mill fulltime. Folks would say he just had it in his blood. He felt he had had no other choice. At sixteen he was named assistant foreman, but Dearl always doubted the men respected him for what he could do and figured it was more because his dad owned the mill. A couple of years later he heard about Mr. Creighton's mill and thought it might provide better possibilities for him since he'd be out from under his father's shadow. He packed up is '39 Ford pickup, left his dad's mill and drove up to Pine Hollow.

Though the mill already had an assistant foreman over the woodsmen, Dearl signed on as a loader just to get his foot in the door. Manny's dad saw the potential in this Texas transplant and soon his background and skills bumped him above the man who had been assistant. He was now at the top of the list of those who might take over when Manny's dad stepped down.

Manny had grown up in Pine Hollow. Her dad, James Earl, had worked for the Grogans from the early days, even before Mr. Creighton bought the mill. He was a hard worker and managed the men well...when sober. The bottle was a wicked web for James Earl. But because he only drank after work and weekends, Mr. Creighton kept him employed, hoping for a day the demons might leave or be chased off.

When he was drunk, James Earl was a different man, violent and hateful. Often, he would spray abuse over both Manny and her mom. But one Saturday night, he turned physical and hurt Manny. Her mother grabbed up the girl and a few clothes and slammed the door as they walked away. In the morning, after a sleepless night of regret, James Earl went to church. Manny and her mom saw him come in the back door. Manny felt her arm being squeezed as they both expected he was there to hurt them even more with embarrassment.

James Earl walked slowly up the aisle. The pastor came down from the pulpit and stood in front of the altar. Tears streamed down James Earl's face. He threw his arms around the preacher and cried out, "I'm tired of my life. I need Jesus!"

The pastor knelt with him at the altar and spoke softly to the broken man. The pastor prayed a simple prayer of repentance and James Earl repeated his words out loud. The congregation breathlessly strained to hear each word. Then let out a collected sigh when the pastor said, "Amen and amen!" and hugged the bulky woodsman.

James Earl stood up, facing the audience. "I ain't wantin' to live like I been living anymore," he said. "Drinking lets loose something inside of me I don't want to be…maybe it showed me who I really am…I don't know, and I don't care because all that's over. Last night I hurt my family. Shoot, I been hurting them for years. It just somehow got out of control.

"Well, I don't ever want to be that man no more. I love my family and they need a new husband and daddy. The old one ain't worth coming home to. But if'n you'll both forgive me, like Jesus just did, I promise you both that old man is dead and gone."

Manny and her mom got up at the same time and rushed to the front. The tears flowed from the reunion in front of that altar, and from the people who had witnessed the transformation of a man set free from demons.

Mr. Creighton learned of James Earl's conversion that evening. He knew only God could have done something like that. Even though he had given James Earl many opportunities to dry up his life and gain a new start, James Earl always went back to his old ways. Now, it would seem, he was going to have a lot more help fighting the old man than just himself.

Dearl moved from loader to head of the woodsman. His new job involved marking the trees to be cut. He'd then direct the men to cut and haul out the timber to the mill. At the mill, logs would be sized, trimmed and cut into planks. Manny's dad oversaw the whole operation. Dearl took some of the strain off him and was even able to fully take over when James Earl was called away or unable to get out to the woods.

The whole summer following his salvation, James Earl had maintained sobriety with no regressions. Even his men who struggled, as he had before, were beginning to believe what happened to him in church was for real. Manny and her mom felt a familiar but new man had moved into the house with them. And Dearl felt more like a son than suitor of a man's daughter.

After meeting with Mr. Creighton about upping harvest production, James Earl walked by the sawing unit. The man running the large, circular saw was struggling with a log jamming the blade. It wasn't unusual for non-uniform trees to resist being quarter-sawn. James Earl ran in to help. When he grabbed the log and tried to turn it and free up the jamming, the log kicked back and slammed into his forehead. An undetected brain hemorrhage took his life a few days later. Dearl was promoted to foreman. He was eighteen. Manny was only fourteen. A year later they were married. A year after that Leland was born. Leland was now sixteen.

# Chapter Two

WITH BREAKFAST DONE AND CHORES COMPLETED, LELAND headed down the path to school. Frank Massey waited for him at the creek. Frank was Leland's age, and each considered the other his best friend. Frank's dad was the other foreman for the mill. He ran the processing operations, everything that turned the logs from the woods into lumber.

Frank was somewhat transient to the area. His dad had what might be called domestic issues. With a new wife, Frank never knew if he'd stay with them or go back to live with his aunt in Elmira. For the moment he was back with his aunt but each day he'd drive in to his dad's house in Pine Hollow, then walk to school with Leland.

By the time Frank and Leland got to the schoolhouse three other kids were walking in the group.

The milky-white paint had become useless years ago, but the old school house still served the community well. Smoke swirled from the rusty chimney pipe sticking out through the wall, staining the air. The hardwoods were barren and stark, the evergreens, dark and full, the air cold and still. The kids hung their coats on the pegs at the back of the school room then settled into their seats.

Leland was exceptional. Not in any way that one might tell by looking. He was tall and thin with long, dirty-blond hair, average in most ways, but Leland had an ability to play the cello with a grace and skill far beyond his stature, age and opportunity. Leland was a sawmill kid, which meant he was rural and poor. He was sixteen, which meant he lacked time to have nurtured his abilities to the maturity they demonstrated.

So, why could he play so well? His momma said it was the gift, a gift from God. But gifted or not, today was a school day and the old school house worked hard to capture his attention which kept drifting out the window, toward the foothills.

The mountain range formed a substantial backdrop to the school. Hefty pines and massive hardwoods peppered the landscape. Throughout the foothills, towering trees of a variety of species canopied a tight collection of small shacks. It was these shacks, the mill proper, a store, a church and the school that made up Pine Hollow. The shacks were a privilege for the families working at the mill, even though, technically they paid for that privilege through their small, weekly paycheck.

The front door of the schoolhouse stood open in spite of the chill. By afternoon, the heat from the wood stove made the air so thin and hot that the younger children had a hard time staying awake. Nubbin knew the open door was not intended for her but still looked in as she padded across the school yard. She made a slow lunge at a couple of pigeons scratching for food in the dirt in front of the steps and puffed out a huff of air from beneath the deep folds of skin around her mouth. They chose to relocate to their roost in the bell tower above the front porch. The old brown dog crawled under the porch and nestled into her familiar divot where she would nap until school was out and Leland would call her to go home.

"Whoa!" CRASH! The children's laughter poured out from the open door and through the cracks in the flooring. Nubbin miffed out a muffled bark, never raising her head off the dirt.

WHACK! The piercing jolt from a wooden pointer smacked across a desk made her jerk and scramble out from under the porch. She barked at the pigeons flapping hard to get away from the tower and into the trees. She barked again, not at anything in particular, just because it seemed appropriate. The children laughed. Miss Grubb screeched, "That will be enough, class! Hush out there, Nubbin! Leland Thomson, you get yourself down here to my desk this instant!"

Leland made the familiar trek to the front of the class and stood before the teacher's desk. "I'm sorry, Miss Ida, but I guess I sorta fell out of my chair or something."

"Leland, how can a person *sorta* fall out of a chair? You either fell out or you didn't. Since you did, and since I warned you boys sitting in the back that you would unless you sat up straight, you will be spending recess inside while everyone else goes outside."

"Aww."

"Do you understand?"

"Yes, ma'am," he droned.

"Now get back to your seat and pay attention!"

"Yes, ma'am." Leland turned back to his seat and locked in on Frank, who shrugged. He mouthed the word *sorry*. Both smiled at each other. Leland often got the accusation from Frank's mischief. This time it was Frank's foot that helped the chair topple over.

The schoolhouse was a small, one-room building. It had been freshly whitewashed twelve years before, the year Ida Mae Grubb came to be the teacher. Since that time, it had weathered hard. She had, too. The strain of commuting the thirty miles each day from Lathrup Springs—up the mountainside, through the forest, to the clearing of Pine Hollow—had taken its toll. She hated teaching in Pine Hollow. She was at a dead-end school, teaching dead-end students and only in her early thirties.

Ida had grown up there. Her daddy had worked at the mill until he lost four fingers when a log bucked as he was rough-cutting it and threw his hand into the saw blade. Before he knew what had happened, his fingers lay somewhere in the sawdust and he was looking down at four bloody nubs, too much in shock to know how much it hurt.

Missing fingers was a common trait among saw-millers. Most of the men proudly told the story of their mishap both to amaze and caution others of the dangers of the potentially mangling machinery. But Mr. Grubb took it as a sign from God to pack up and move to town. He had always feared the day would come when he'd lose a finger, and after he lost half of what he came into the world with, he couldn't face the fear of losing more. He moved his family down the mountain to Lathrup Springs when Ida Mae was in her early teens.

Lathrup Springs was an old, established town, and like most tight, southern communities wasn't open to outsiders. In fact, new folks moving to town would have to stay years just to lose the title "newcomer." Anyone who was not a local carried a stigma that always raised suspicion. To the people of Lathrup Springs, folks from the Hills were an inferior lot, and their community, though it had been there over fifty years, would always be makeshift, temporary and a necessary nuisance.

The road from town to the Hills had less to do with distance than it did with transition. Somewhere along the way was a dividing line between modern and backwards, between rich and poor, between society and clans, between acceptance and rejection. Few made the transition.

Ida's family was an exception. When they moved to Lathrup Springs, her dad told them to never mention where they came from. Her mom had insisted they present themselves as clean and mannerly as they could at all times. And though, back then, they didn't have many clothes, Mama made sure the ones they had were mended and pressed. As a result, they didn't stand out as having come from Pine Hollow, which helped Ida make friends quickly and adjust well to her new community.

With the whack still vibrating in their ears, the children sat frozen in a petrified silence. The center aisle dividing the two rows of two-by-two desks pounded from the heavy steps of the angry teacher marching to the back of the room and then whirling around and marching again to the front. She glanced from side to side. Hands were in laps, backs straight, feet on the floor, faces forward, eyes open, mouths closed. She had regained control. The wooden pointer she had slammed against her desk was tucked tightly under her arm like a swaggering field commander inspecting his troops more so than of a teacher nurturing her students.

Just to the left of the large blackboard, a potbelly stove bellowed out warm, sooty air from the front corner of the room. The area around the stove was stained a deep, blackish-gray from the smoke that escaped through weak joints in the flute pipe and settled on… well, everything. The air was hot and stale.

Each chair was occupied by a child who lived in the Hills. The ages were mixed. The younger ones sat close to the front and the older ones in the back. By most anyone's standard the children were shabby. Each child's ensemble for the day came from a selection of whatever was available. Nothing matched and nobody paid any attention. These were sawmill kids. It was how they dressed. No child wore anything that he or she had been the first to ever wear.

Several years back, a group from a church in Little Rock came during the summer and did mission clubs with the kids. They brought boxes of gently used clothing. The clothes were spread out on the floor of the schoolhouse and the moms would pick over them until they were all given out. The kids wore the clothes until they no longer fit. After that, they became hand-me-downs, being passed around until they were too worn to patch. And since everyone had this in common, no one thought anything of it. In fact, the older children found it interesting to see who might show up in something that had been handed down to them, and their mom had subsequently handed down to one of the younger kids.

"Yeah, them are the jeans I wore when I fell into the gully tryin' to get that ol' coon I shot. See the blood stains?" or "I wore that shirt Gracie Lou's wearin' the day I helped Grandma get the skunk out of her house. Momma never could get the stink out of it. Come here, Gracie Lou. See, you can still smell it." Such stories often made the wearing of hand-me-downs more a legacy than an embarrassment. They were wearing a part of each other's history, each other's lives.

Along the back wall, split into two sides by the door, hung tattered coats. With utility being more important than appearance, these coats knew no style and no gender, and even in their better days they were nothing more than a source of warmth from the cold. They, too, were brought by the church groups and given away.

From in front of her large, wooden desk, Miss Ida glared at the older children on the back row. Her long, straight dress billowed as she stood with arms crossed, swaying back and forth. Compared to the simple and well-worn clothing of the children, hers seemed out of place. The string of pearls and matching earrings she wore were fake but nice. They were her emblem, her visual that she came from somewhere else and was not a part of this society or its poverty. The tight bun into which she pulled her hair stated a snobbery she confused with refinement.

"Now!" she grunted "Are we ready to continue?" The older children on the back two rows nodded together. "Good. Elementary, you may continue your work."

The younger children fingered through their closed workbooks. Soon they found where they were working when the whack had made them slam shut what they were doing and sit frozen in fear. They quietly resumed their work scratching out their answers with pencil nubs.

Miss Ida turned and strutted back to the chalkboard. The older children glued their eyes to each step, to the swirling of her long dress and to the waggle of her pearl necklace. She took a piece of chalk and wrote: C-A-S-T-E.

"Now before our little interruption, we were beginning our lesson today about this word. Can anyone pronounce it?" she asked.

Billie Nell, a smudged-faced, freckled girl of 15, raised her hand. Like the other children in the room, Billie Nell had been born in the very house in which she now lived. Aunt Nora, not really anybody's aunt, was the mid-wife everyone called on to help with the birthing of the babies. Aunt Nora had been bringing babies into the world for as long as most folks in Pine Hollow could remember. She had even brought in the parents of the kids now in school and some of their grandparents as well.

Billie Nell was one of the smarter students in Miss Ida's class. Her strawberry-blond hair and disposition gave her a determination few of the other children possessed. Billie Nell wanted to know everything, know it first and know it best. Miss Ida often said that Billie Nell reminded her of herself at that age.

"Billie Nell?" Miss Ida offered.

"C-A-S-T-E," she spelled. "Castie."

Miss Ida reached for her pointer and poised it for another whack to silence the laughter coming from the back of the room. "No, it's *cast.* No 'e.' Just *cast.* And since we can't pronounce it, I don't expect anyone knows what it means," she sneered.

Leland raised his hand. Because of the heat in the room he was down to his jeans and a white T-shirt that had a deep smudge on the sleeve where he kept his face clean with regular wipes. His blond hair, a bit more on the brown side the longer he went between washing, was long and cut down low across his brow where it fell into his eyes.

Leland was a bright boy who usually raised his hand second to Billie Nell's and, more often than not, gave the answer Miss Ida was looking for. He was Dearl and Manny Thomson's only child. Nobody knew why they couldn't have any other children, only that Aunt Nora said Manny had such a hard time getting Leland here, she ought not to try it again.

"Leland?" Miss Ida offered.

"Wouldn't it be *caste,* like *haste?*" he asked. "I thought you said if a word ends in a 'e' then the vowel said its name."

"Well, thank you, Leland." Miss Ida had a way of twitching up her nose and tilting her head back a bit whenever she sensed the awkwardness of a challenge to something she had previously said. "Normally you'd be right, but there is an exception to most rules, and this happens to be an exception. Like I said earlier, the word is pronounced *cast.* This "e" is both silent and ignored. But what I want to know is: What does caste mean?"

From the back row, Frank muttered, "Well, if you don't know, how do you expect us to?" Again, the class laughed, but not a natural laugh, the kind of laugh that you wish you could stop before anyone would have heard you had laughed at all—the kind of laugh that usually got the desk whacked by the pointer. Frank slapped his hand across his mouth, went pale and sank deep into this chair.

"Franklin Massey! I've had about enough out of you for one day," Miss Ida screeched. Then adjusting her speech to a more deliberate and staccato pace she continued, "You may remove yourself from your desk, go to the corner chair and sit facing the wall until this lesson is finished. Then you will stay after school and write the sentence *I will respect Miss Grubb* on the board one hundred times. And *then* you will clean the board before you go home. Do you understand?"

"Yes, ma'am," Frank replied, biting the inside of his cheek. He wiped his hand across his mouth to conceal is inner fight to keep from bursting out laughing at how high Miss Ida's voice would go when she went into her hysterics. He settled into the chair at the front of the room.

Frank was not a trouble-maker but trouble followed him around. He had a sharp wit and quick tongue, which often got him attention in a way he hadn't planned. Frank's dad was Claude, the general foreman for Creighton Mill. He oversaw the whole operation from when the logs came into the mill to be rough-cut and followed them through to their final curing before the boards were shipped to the planer mill and on to the lumberyards.

Frank's life was between his dad's foreman house and his Aunt Alma's, his dad's sister, in Elmira, a blink on the road between Pine Hollow and Lathrup Springs. Claude was a disconnected man who ran through wives with a recklessness that had bored a hole deep into Frank's heart and life. After Frank's mother had died when Frank was seven, Claude began to drink heavily and take on wives with abandon. Alma became Frank's stability. Each time Claude remarried, Frank would move back in with his dad, then within a few months would be back with Alma. Flo was the current wife and worst of the step-mothers.

Flo brought two daughters into the marriage. All three of them resented Frank being there. Flo was harsh and mean; the girls, nasty and cruel. When she found out she was going to have another baby, Frank became the sole target of her frustration. The tension was constant, and Claude began to drink again. Frank started spending much of his free time back at his aunt's house. He'd stay until dark, then go home late, hoping everyone would be in bed and there'd be no confrontations.

Either because of his dad's position or guilt—no one quite knew which—Frank was the only boy in Pine Hollow who had his own car—a 1940 Ford coupe.

"That's enough class; now settle down," Miss Ida warned. "And yes, I do know what it means. But what I know doesn't help you unless you know it." Leland raised his hand.

"Leland?" Miss Ida said.

"Don't it mean how somebody fits in to where they live?"

"Well, someone did do his reading last night," replied Miss Ida. Leland glanced over at Billie Nell and twitched his nose at her. Billie Nell grabbed her pencil and threw it at Leland. Miss Ida didn't see it because she had stopped to correct something on the workbook of one of the younger students. "No, now think, Emma, how many apples did you color?"

"Four," the six-year-old answered.

"So, if you had six and took away two, how many would you have?"

"Five?"

"Quit guessing. Now sit back down and count them up. Then write that number in this box."

Without missing a beat, she continued, "For any society to maintain order and proper decency, it must organize its people into segments or castes," she said. "So, yes, in a way, Leland, that would be how they might fit them together." She wrote the words *segment* and *together* on the board. "How might that society decide who is in each segment?"

Sherry Beth, one of the younger *older* children, raised her hand.

"Sherry Beth?" Miss Ida offered.

"By how old they are?" she asked.

"Well that is one type of segmenting. But all ages usually have to fit together in a society. Billie Nell?"

"How important they are?"

"Well," she answered, "not that anyone would want to admit it, but, yes, in the big picture, some are more important to society than others." Miss Ida walked around to the front of her desk and sat on the edge. Billie Nell did a quick nose twitch toward Leland. He took his pencil poised to toss it at her. "Leland!" Ida screeched. "Don't you dare!"

He settled back and returned focus on the teacher. Ida adjusted her seat, furrowed her brow and paused as she chose her words carefully. "Everybody is important in his or her own right, but in a society, well, to make everything fit better, society must create or at least acknowledge some differences so these folks can all fit together."

"But ain't we all created equal?" Leland asked.

"Equal, but not as important, huh, Miss Ida?" Frank added. Ida turned and glared at Frank. He turned back to face the wall.

"In society, everything and everyone has its place. Since everyone can't be in the same place as everyone else, they have to be in different places. And not all of those places are as important as others. It's not that the people aren't as important, they're just grouped into those places to serve a role that supports the society as a whole. It's their role that determines how important they are."

"Like ants and bees?" Sherry Beth asked. Miss Ida looked at Sherry, furrowed her brow and slowly nodded.

"Don't you mean birds and bees!" snickered Frank. The other children puffed out a single laugh because Frank's comments usually deserved some response.

"Franklin!"

"Yes, ma'am," Frank stammered, "but I was...uh, just gonna say that there's a bee hive in the hole of that ole dead tree down by the creek."

"And?" Miss Ida asked.

"And I thought you might want to go see it and help make your point," Frank replied.

Miss Ida's eyes smiled as she brushed her hands together. "Why, yes," she announced. "Class let's go outside and have a look at this bee hive. When we get back, I want each of you to write a one-page essay on what you've learned about the caste system by looking at the bee hive Frank has told us about."

"Aw, Frank!" Leland muttered. The rest of the class groaned, except Billie Nell, who was jotting down the assignment in her notebook.

"Hey, ain't my fault."

"Grab your coats," Miss Ida told the class. "Elementary, you may leave your work on your desk and follow along and watch." She led the entire class outside, across the dirt playground and into the edge of the woods toward the creek. Soon they were all standing around the hive watching the activity. Even Nubbin found interest in the moment.

"See how these bees are organized like a caste system," Miss Ida explained. "Different members carry out different roles so the society can function. Some are building, some are bringing food in from the forest, others are caring for the young. Can anyone name the different castes of the bee hive?"

Billie Nell offered, "Workers, drones and queen?"

"Thank you, Billie Nell. Yes, workers, drones and queen," Miss Ida restated.

"And them little wormy babies," added Sherry Beth.

"Called?"

"Lava," answered Billie Nell.

"Larva," Leland corrected, getting himself smacked on the arm. "But they're all important, ain't they? What they all do has to get done, don't it? The book said in a caste system not everyone is as important as everyone else and some are more important than others. But everyone's important here, right?"

Miss Ida twitched her nose again and blew out a sigh. "Well, their *role* is important. So, they are important as a group, but not as important as individuals. You can lose larvae and the queen will make more. You can lose drones, and workers will step up to do the work."

"And can't they make another queen if somethin' happens to her?" Billie Nell asked. "Don't they feed her somethin' to make her the queen? So, she ain't all that important either, huh?"

"Well, yes, but in societies, you don't usually move from one class to another. You stay within your caste and find your own importance for being there." Miss Ida turned away from the hive and toward the back of the group. "Franklin! You put that rock down! Don't you even think…"

The rock hit just below the hive, close enough to stir up a few of the bees, and definitely close enough to cause the whole class to scramble hard for the clearing leading back to the schoolhouse.

# Chapter Three

THE HARDWARE STORE IN LATHRUP SPRINGS WAS ALWAYS cluttered with merchandise, and early in the mornings crowded with men. It was a common gathering place. Many, who had little reason other than the nickel coffee and free conversation, came in throughout the day. The morning hours, especially the early ones, brought in workers needing supplies for the day. It was noisy and busy, but the clerks maintained a high sense of awareness of who came in and who went out, who was there just killing time and who was there for business.

It was a place Dearl rarely went, but since one of his men had come in from the woods the night before having lost the sharpening files, he found himself alone in that awkward, crowded store, holding a handful of files tightly in his hand.

Though Dearl was only in his mid-thirties, his leathery skin and worry-worn face made him appear more middle-aged. His tattered jeans, muddy boots, stubby beard and mussed hair flipping out from under his sweat-stained hat clearly marked him as a sawmiller. His uneasiness with being in the hardware store made it more obvious that he was out of place.

Dearl stood silently at the counter while he watched men who came in after him being waited on ahead of him. No one acknowledged he was there. Even the men who brushed past him, headed for coffee, never seemed to notice. He pressed his lips tightly together, rubbed his hand across his mouth, furrowed his brow deeply, puffed a sigh out his nose, then set his purchase on the counter, turned and walked away. He heard muffled laughter of the men in the store as he passed through the door to the sidewalk outside and the unmistakable slur, *sawmill trash.*

✂

Back in the classroom, the kids took longer to settle down than Miss Ida wanted. WHACK! They instantly were seated, poised and quiet. She took her piece of chalk and began to write. The younger children stared at her as intently as the older ones.

When she turned to face the students, she saw the younger ones, cocked her head, raised one eyebrow, placed her hands on her hips and stared back at them. Slowly each one, without losing eye contact with her, opened a workbook and then returned to study. She raised her eyes to gaze at the back of the room before moving to the side to reveal what she had written—the words: TOWN and THE HILLS.

"Now, class, let's continue our discussion of the caste system," she began. "Often our caste is determined by the place we were born. Because of where *you* were born and who your parents are, you all find yourselves in a certain location—the Hills. It sets your life. It's your place."

Billie Nell furrowed her brow, jerked her head backward and jutted her hand into the air. "Miss Ida?"

"Billie Nell?"

"So, we're in the Hills caste 'cause we were born in the Hills?" Billie Nell asked.

"And you are in the town caste 'cause you was born in town?" Sherry Beth quickly added to the question.

"Wait. My Momma said you were born in the Hills just like us, weren't you, Miss Ida?" Leland asked.

"Humph," Miss Ida puffed. "Remember every rule has an exception."

She turned and walked back to the blackboard. Within those few steps, she felt the hot blush created by the reminder of something she had worked hard over half of her life to forget. The reminder stung.

"Well, *where* you were born *usually* identifies a person's caste, but for some, like me, it's just a place from where the journey to who you want to be begins. But we're not talking about me, we're talking about you, and in general, learning your place helps you, and everyone else, have…a better life," she stammered. She frowned then rubbed the words off the chalkboard.

"Miss Ida?" asked Billie Nell.

"Yes, Billie Nell?"

"Did moving to town erase you from being from the Hills?"

"Billie Nell," Leland answered, "you can't erase something that's already happened. But you can change how important it is to you, huh, Miss Ida?"

Ida pooched out her lips, pressed them together with her fingers, then released a slow sigh.

From the corner of the room Frank turned and added, "My daddy told me to nail a bunch of nails into a board and then pull them out. He said you can pull the nails out, but they're still gonna leave a hole." Everyone slowly turned and looked at Frank. He shrugged and grinned.

"Well," Miss Ida replied, "I guess that's why they make putty."

"Putty don't make the holes go away," Frank added. "I tried it. My daddy said it just looks like they went away, but the holes are still there."

The pause lingered uncomfortably long. A nervous but relieved smile made it across Miss Ida's face when she recognized Billie Nell's hand.

"Miss Ida, what's it like to live in town?" she asked.

"Quite nice, actually," Ida answered. She turned and paused, looking out the window. Soon she was thirty miles away, down the side of the mountain back in Lathrup Springs.

"Miss Ida…Miss Ida?" Ida drew herself back into the room, looked at the class and nodded to Sherry Beth.

"So, you were born here just like us," she began, "but because you left to grow up in town you ain't from the Hills no more?"

"Well…"

"Then it don't seem like where a person's born matters if you move to someplace else later," Leland added.

"Well, some but not most…"

"Then if where you were born don't seem to matter now, how come the people in town treat us like we're infested or somethin'?" Frank asked.

"Infected, stupid," Billie Nell corrected.

"All I'm saying," Ida continued, "is finding your place and staying in it is best. It's where we fit. And we need to fit in there as best as we can. That's called accepting ourselves."

"But it ain't us who ain't acceptin' who we are," Frank added.

"That's why it's best to stay around those who do accept you. And that's within one's place, one's caste," Ida said. "Billie Nell?"

"Well, what if I don't always like some of the ones who's around me? Do I still have to accept them?" She turned and smirked at Leland. He smirked back at her. The others laughed.

"The people part of life is always the hardest," Miss Ida said. "But it'll be easier for you if you stay in your place. It's the best place for you to be."

*Best.* The word brought a deep furrow across Leland's brow. The discussion had pressed beyond theory to a point silently personal. His eyes darted up and around, out the window then back into the room. "Miss Ida?"

"Yes, Leland?"

"It don't seem right that a body has to stay where he is just because he's born there. Why is where we start and where we end up supposed to be the same place? It wudn't for you."

Billie Nell added, "Yeah, I don't want to stay up here in the Hills all my life. I want to move to town, just like you, Miss Ida, and be a teacher."

"Well, exceptions can happen," Ida replied, "but until then, I'm just saying it's best to learn how to accept how things are. There's no shame in being from the Hills if you don't let yourself believe there is."

"Are you ashamed you were born up here?" Frank asked.

Ida came around in front of her desk and sat on the edge. "My case is different. My daddy moved us to town because he got hurt up here and found a job down there. That changed everything—my place and my future. I didn't have any say in it. But I don't see any of your daddies moving out of here. And most of you will follow along and do just what your momma and daddies do."

"I guarantee one thing, I ain't gonna be like my dad," Frank said. The room stopped. No one looked at Frank because they knew his dad. Everyone in Pine Hollow knew how difficult life had been on Frank because of his dad. Leland broke the silence.

"When you were like us, did you ever close your eyes and wished you could be someplace else?" Leland asked. "I know at night sometimes I'm just layin' there in my bed and it's like somethin' out there is callin' to me."

"From the woods?" Billie Nell asked.

"Naw, way past the woods. Somewhere further out. Don't rightly know where. Ever had somethin' calling you, Miss Ida?"

Ida looked down at the floor and drifted back into her thoughts. For a moment she was no longer in the schoolroom but in a small shanty, lying across a bed, staring dreamily through an open window. She looked beyond the trees to a place far away, a place of beauty, where ribbons streamed down from trees and little girls with swirling dresses danced in the moonlight.

"Miss Ida?" Leland pressed. "Miss Ida?"

Ida brought her attention back into the room. She said, "Leland, unless some miracle drops in your lap and gets you out of these hills, then you'd better forget that or any other silly dream about leaving.

This is your place. The sooner you accept that, the better off you—and the rest of all y'all—all will be. Don't waste time dreaming. Accept what you are."

"But wouldn't it be somethin'? Even if it was only for a year?" Leland wondered aloud.

# Chapter Four

THE THOMSON HOUSE WAS A SIMPLE, UNPAINTED, SHOTGUN shanty with living, dining and kitchen all sharing one room. A hallway led off toward the two bedrooms in the back. White smoke billowed out of the chimney, which was just a stove pipe running up from the stone fireplace. Nubbin came up on the porch and laid down in front of the door.

The soft and mellow tones of a cello spilled from within the house. On a straight-backed chair, in front of the fireplace, his head and upper body swaying with each stroke, Leland sat with an old and well-worn cello fixed between his legs. Nubbin got up and howled at the door. Dearl opened and the hound strolled in. She curled up in front of the fire beside Leland's chair and went back to sleep.

Leland played with great intensity, expressively feeling and then releasing each note. His eyes were relaxed but shut, his face tilted upwards. He painted the room with music. He drew the sound out of his soul, the simple offering of a gift that delighted the very winds that carried away what his heart expressed.

Manny stood over the sink washing the collards she clipped out of her garden earlier that day. She was a young, but dutiful woman in her early thirties. She had been only fifteen when she and Dearl married, bearing Leland the next spring. Her beauty had yet to be compromised by the strain of the life of a woman from the hills. Like the women who blazed through before her and helped settle this area, she made something from nothing, and in that something created a life for her family. She lived her sworn vows, caring for her husband and son with her very life, which she managed quite well.

When Dearl let Nubbin in he went out on the porch to smoke his pipe and sharpen his knife on a spit-moistened whetstone he held in his hand. Manny wouldn't let him smoke in the house, and since he had to be outside to enjoy his habit, sharpening his knife seemed a good secondary activity. He was a proud man but not arrogant. He knew what he was capable of doing and did it well. He had become a foreman for the mill at an age when most men were still losing fingers. Now he was the head woodsman, responsible for the crews that felled the trees and transported the logs back to the mill. He slowly released a large puff of smoke as thoughts drifted back to how the day began at the hardware store.

Leland came to the end of his song and dug powerfully into the string as he pulled back his bow. He held onto the last note with a rapid and steady vibrato that kept the sound ringing in the air. It echoed long from the body of the cello until it slowly faded away. Even after the sound was gone, he held his pause, then opened his eyes, saw his mom and grinned. Manny smiled back and shouted out at Dearl, "Mighty good ain't it, Dearl?"

"Yep, mighty good," Dearl yelled back from the porch.

"You really thank so?" Leland asked modestly.

"God's given you the gift, Leland," his mother said. "God has given you the gift. Now take off those jeans and try on these I fixed today." Leland set his cello in the corner and laid his bow against the wall. He pulled off his jeans and slipped on the ones his mother held for him. "Turn around and bend over. Let me see how that patch is gonna hold." He stuck his rear toward her. She tugged at the patch and the sides of the jeans. "OK, now, next time you go off to the creek to see some beehive, make sure you watch where them thorn bushes are. There's just so much patching these thangs'll take."

"Yes, ma'am," he replied.

"Dearl, get in here and get washed up for supper!"

Dearl dumped the tobacco out of his pipe and came into the house. "Too bad He gave it to a boy from the Hills," he said, setting his pipe on the shelf beside the front door.

"Who gave what?" Manny asked.

"The Lord. Too bad He gave that kinda gift to a boy from out here," Dearl replied, rinsing his hands in the kitchen sink.

"Dearl Thomson!"

"Well? What good's a boy that can play the chelly like that out here in the sticks? You'd think he oughta be heard by better people 'n us. And what's gonna happen when he loses his fingers at the mill?"

"Dearl!

"It's a cello, Daddy."

"Well, whatever you call it, son, you know I love to hear you play, but it don't seem right we're the only ones to hear you." Dearl walked over to Leland and mussed his hair. "I'm just sorry you ain't never gonna get to...well, you know. You're better than all this. It's all I'm sayin' 's all."

"What's wrong, Dearl?" Manny asked. He waved a dismissing hand at her.

"Thank I'll ever get to play for some of the folks out there?" Leland asked.

"Out where?" Dearl asked.

"I don't know. Just out there. I told Miss Ida that sometimes I hear something calling me from out there."

"In the woods?" Dearl asked. He slid into his seat at the table. Manny set the last dish down and pulled back her seat.

"And *Miss Ida Mae Grubb's* got something to say about that?" Manny asked.

"Yea, she said I ought not to dream of stuff like that."

"Oh, that heifer!" snapped Manny. "Ever since her pa moved them to town, she's thought she's better'n all of us put together."

"Now don't have a hissy, Manny," Dearl warned.

"Ha, Momma called Miss Ida a cow," chortled Leland.

"Settle down, son," said Dearl, "or you're gonna fall outta your seat there. Well, Manny, you know she did get a higher education than anybody else around here."

"Tenth grade is plenty high enough. If'n a body can't learn all she needs to learn by then, well, maybe she's just too dumb to start with." Manny dumped a large glop of mashed potatoes on Dearl's plate and then Leland's as he held it toward her.

"I wouldn't get myself all worked up over Ida Mae Grubb," Dearl said, hoping to calm down his wife. "I think it's mighty charitable for her to come back up here to teach our young 'uns."

"But teach 'em what?" Manny reeled. "That they ain't good as her?"

"Oh, I don't really thank..."

"Well, I do, and I thank she's just tryin' to make them feel like runts."

"Runts?" asked Leland.

"You remember that least little ol' puppy Nubbin had?" Dearl asked.

"You mean Puny? He never was good for nothin' but givin' fleas a place to live." Leland and Dearl laughed.

"That ain't my point," Manny said.

"Well, you have to admit that was about the most worthless pup she ever gave birth to," Dearl added. "'Bout the only thang he ever did was hold boards down on the porch." Dearl forked off a piece of chicken from the platter in front of him.

"Ain't a whole lot different than what her momma does," Leland said.

The tension eased as the three had a hardy laugh. Nubbin ignored their laughter and puffed out a sigh of disgusted air. "And that's what Ida Mae is tryin' to make them thank...that they ain't good for nothin' neither. Probably not even good enough to hold boards down on her porch," Manny blasted.

"Well?" Dearl cast a whimsical eye at Leland and ruffled his mussed hair even more. Leland laughed and shook his head.

"Dearl! Good is good. The rest don't matter...like where somebody's born or who her daddy is."

"Oh, Momma, you know you loved that old runt," Leland laughed.

"Well, yeah I did, and that's what matters. But Ida Mae don't understand none of that."

Dearl sat down his tea glass. "It takes all kinds to kinda round thangs out. Town folk is just like hills folk, only," he continued with a laugh, "they don't know it. And maybe they have more than we do, but you know, that don't make no matter. It ain't what you have that makes you who you are. It's what you are and what you can do. That's somethin' nobody can take away from you."

With dinner finished, Manny got up and began clearing the table. Leland jerked a look at his dad. "Daddy, thank maybe we can go into town this Saturday? Just to see what it is they have that makes them so high and mighty?"

Dearl sighed. The thoughts of the hardware store flashed quickly across his mind. "Uh, I, uh…"

"Please?" insisted Leland.

"Oh, I, I 'spect we could," Dearl stammered. "I still need to get those files."

"Thought that's what you went into town for this mornin'," Manny said.

Dearl shrugged. "We'll head down there tomorrow."

"Really? Did you hear that, Momma? We're gonna go to Lathrup Springs."

Manny darted a harsh glare at Dearl.

"Oh, Manny. It won't hurt anything to take him along," he told her. "'Bout time he saw the other side again."

Leland skipped over to the corner and picked up his cello and bow. He stood there and sawed out an Irish jig. Dearl got up, grabbed Manny by the hand and whirled her around the room, twirling, clapping and dancing. Leland grinned and bowed faster.

# *Chapter Five*

IT WAS MID-MORNING ON SATURDAY WHEN THE THOMSON'S pick-up pulled into Lathrup Springs. Though it was still chilly from the overnight frost, Dearl drove with his arm resting on the open window frame, basically because the glass had been broken out since last summer when a tree got away from one of the men. The missing window never was much of a problem except for rainy days.

Today was cold but clear. Dearl, Manny and Leland crowded together in the single seat. Manny sat beside Dearl with a blanket wrapped around her legs. Leland sat by the other window, which was still intact and solidly rolled up. His legs were cold, but he wouldn't borrow cover from his mother. He folded his arms tightly at his chest, warmed only by his coat, just like his dad.

As they came into the town square, Leland was about as wound up as a boy could get, squirming in his seat, eyes darting side to side, head jerking to keep up with the eyes. Saturday morning was a busy day in town. In fact, it was the major income day for the stores since that was the day the folks who lived on the outer regions of the community usually came in to shop.

Dearl pulled up to the curb in front of the hardware store. Manny and Leland got out on their side and stood on the sidewalk. Leland kept looking around, mouth gaping wide with excitement.

"While we're in there, might as well get me a new shovel," Manny said. "The other one's just about rusted through."

Dearl nodded. As they started into the door, he stopped. "Manny, why don't you take Leland, and y'all go look around at some of the stuff in the windows? I'll get what we need here and meet you down at the drugstore in a spell."

"Well, that's alright I guess," Manny replied. She stood for a minute looking at Dearl. She was pretty good at telling when he was uncomfortable. And though his suggestion seemed innocent enough, she could sense he was trying to protect them from what he anticipated in the store.

"Go on," Dearl urged.

"We're going." Manny drew in her eyebrows into that *something's going on and you're going to tell me about it later* look. "Well, Leland, since we're not wanted in the hardware store, let's me and you go gawk at the town folk." They laughed as they started off down the sidewalk.

Dearl took a deep breath and entered the store. The bell above the door rang to welcome him inside. The place seemed much as it did the day before. Men sat around a table playing dominos, most of them the same ones he saw yesterday. Some customers were walking around the aisles; a few waited in line at the register. A man stood behind the counter. When he heard the bell on the door, he turned to greet whoever was coming in, but when he saw Dearl his smile went away, and he quickly looked back to the customer paying for a sack of nails.

It always puzzled Dearl how quickly a friendly face could lose its delight when he entered a store in town. He walked down one aisle and across to another to where the files were racked. He picked out the same assortment he had the day before and walked back to the front. He took his place in line and waited as the merchant finished helping the customer in front of him.

"That'll be three-fifty-nine," he said.

"Here, wait a minute, Tom, I think I got exact change," the man replied.

"Good, I've been running a bit low on pennies today for some reason."

"Isn't it amazing how it is with money—the piece that's worth the least frustrates us the most."

"Tell me about it."

"Yep, some things just cause more trouble than they're worth," the customer said. Both men nodded, then slowly turned to look at Dearl and back.

"You got that right," Tom replied. He handed the sack to the customer who turned to leave. The bell rang again and the man behind the counter shouted a welcome to the next customer into his store. "Come on in. Be with you folks in just a minute." He closed his register. "Thanks again, Rusty." He then walked over to the couple who just came in. Dearl stood silently at the counter.

"Got any washers for this old faucet?" the man of the couple asked.

"Sure do. Come on, I'll show you." The three walked over to the side of the store. "Here, you look through these drawers and see if you don't find one to match," Tom said.

He walked over to another customer, "Finding everything you need?" The customer nodded. Tom stooped down and picked up a plunger that had fallen off a display, replaced it and felt the presence of the couple walking up beside him. "You get the right one?"

"I believe we did," replied the man

"Now you know if you have any trouble, just bring it back and we'll make it good," offered the store owner. He walked them over to the register and rang up their purchase. They took their sack and walked to the door as another man opened it and came in.

"Busy today, huh, Tom?" remarked the man.

"It's Saturday, what can I say?" Tom replied. "What are you in for today?"

"Needing some drill bits."

"Right here behind the counter. Got to where I couldn't leave them out. Too many loose hands, if you know what I mean." The merchant glanced a look at Dearl.

Quickly Dearl spoke, "Since I got your attention, do you thank I might…"

"Now what sizes were you needing?" Tom interrupted and directed his question toward the other man.

"Sir, excuse me," Dearl insisted.

The two men ignored Dearl's presence and questions. "Need an eighth and a quarter."

"Got 'em."

"Sir, I was standin' here before this man came in. Reckon I'd be next," Dearl said.

"Be with you in a minute, Sawmill."

Dearl glanced down at the floor, then up. He wagged his head as in disbelief and rubbed his chin. He held his breath, then sighed. The man came back to the counter.

"That'll be seventy-five cents," Tom said.

"Ha, two bits for three bits," the customer said, laughing. "That's a good one. Two bits for three bits." The merchant laughed too as the man received his merchandise and turned to leave the store.

"Much obliged," Tom shouted after him. "Now, have any trouble with 'em, bring 'em on back and we'll make 'em good."

The bell rang. Dearl and Tom both looked at the door. It closed as the last customer left the store. Tom looked back at Dearl, who was now staring harshly at the merchant.

"Now, what did you want?" Tom asked Dearl.

"Need a shovel," Dearl replied, tightening his lips so he didn't say more.

"Well, what kind of shovel? Rounded, square, sharpshooter? Hurry up, what kind do you want?"

"Uh, round will do."

"On the back wall. Go on back there. You'll find it." The merchant pointed to the back of the store.

Dearl squinted at the man, sighed, then turned and walked to the back of the store where a teenage boy was restocking merchandise.

The boy heard Dearl approach and jumped up to help him. From the front of the store, he heard Tom clear his throat. He looked at Tom who wagged his head. The boy squatted back down and resumed restocking.

"Lookin' for a round shovel," Dearl told him.

"Over there," the stock boy said, motioning with his head without even looking directly at Dearl.

Dearl picked out his shovel and carried it back to the counter. Tom was standing at the end of the aisle as if he had been watching him the whole time.

"Ain't got no place to hide a shovel if that's what you're worried about," Dearl said.

"Never can be too careful with folks like..."

"And I'll be needin' these files, too," Dearl interrupted as he laid his selection on the counter. "Now these I could hide."

The merchant blew out a loud puff and stared deeply at Dearl. "Don't like folks carrying small things like that around the store. Sometimes they just walk off with 'em."

"Happens a lot, huh?" Dearl asked.

Tom wiped his mouth. "Alright, you got money?" he sneered.

"Just tell me how much," Dearl returned.

"Four bucks for the shovel and two bits a piece for the flat files. Rat tail is a quarter."

"Four bucks for a shovel? Ain't that a might much?"

"Well, if you don't have enough money..."

Dearl drew in a slow breath. "I've got the money. Just seems a bit high. At that price, I'd 'spect it's a good one, then?"

"Good enough," Tom replied.

Dearl handed the man his money. The merchant set it into the register and handed him his change, then slammed the drawer shut.

"What if I have any problems with it?" Dearl asked.

Tom glared at Dearl. "It's a shovel," he snapped. "You shouldn't have any problems if you use it right. If you don't know how to use it then maybe you should get somebody to show you."

Dearl tightened his grip on his shovel. He could feel himself trembling inside. A swat across the man's forehead would make him feel better, but he decided against it. He squinted his eyes, breathed out slowly and walked to the door. He stopped, turned and said, "Amazing how losing a few fingers can change a man, idn't it?" Dearl said as he left. Tom fumed.

He glanced back inside as he passed the display window. Underneath the sign announcing *Grubb Hardware*, he saw Tom storming back to the teenage stock boy. By the merchant's gestures, the boy was getting reamed for not noticing the files in Dearl's hand. Dearl shook his head, tossed the shovel into the back of the pick-up and the files onto the seat. He headed down the sidewalk to the drugstore.

# Chapter Six

Dearl couldn't help but notice his reflection in the store windows as he made his way to the drugstore. He wasn't looking at appearance as much as he was image. What did Tom Grubb see in him that he didn't see in himself? He looked past his clothes at his posture—erect, proud, confident. He stopped and leaned in to look at his eyes—clear, honest, sincere. And yet the merchant saw him as…less.

He thought of his responsibilities at the mill, the men who answered to him, who trusted him, who respected him. He thought again of the man at the hardware store, and the stock boy in the back. *I'm a man just like the rest of 'em. Maybe even more of a man than they are. Their pants go on the same way mine do. They pull up their boots the same way I do. They sure ain't seein' what I see. Sure, I'm sawmill but I ain't trash.*

Manny and Leland were browsing about mid-way back in the drugstore as Dearl walked up. The drugstore was long and narrow with rows of shelves lining the walls. Down the middle of the store was a bin with glass shelves displaying breakables—porcelain, ivory and glass animals, flowers, cups and hummingbirds. About halfway back was a soda counter with a long bar behind a row of round, swivel seats. An older lady busied herself with a sink full of dirty glasses and spoons. At the counter on the first stool sat a heavy man appearing to be in his early sixties, enjoying a sundae. At the very back of the store was the pharmacy where the druggist stood, grinding pills into powder with a stone pestle. Manny and Leland saw Dearl long before the bell jingled as he opened the door. Leland grinned as his dad came up to him.

"Help you?" the pharmacist called to Dearl from the back of the store.

"Naw, just in to get a cone," Dearl replied.

"Carrie Lee," yelled the pharmacist, "hurry up and pay attention. You got some customers."

The soda jerk wiped her hands and turned to help the Thomsons. "I guess I's so busy I never heard you folks come in. Get something for you?" she asked.

"Yes'um, in a minute," Dearl answered. The gesture of quick and ready service from the pharmacist to most would be a sign of courtesy. Dearl knew it was an attempt to get them in and out in as short a time as possible. And to get them away from the displayed merchandise.

"Well, how's the sights been, Leland?" Dearl asked.

"Daddy, I never knew there was so much purty stuff all in one place like this. Wish I could buy it all." Leland tossed up a teddy bear that went wide and brushed against a blown-glass wind chime, which, in turn, did what it was made to do and clinked louder than any of the Thomsons or the pharmacist were comfortable hearing.

"Hey!" yelled the druggist. "Boy, you break it, you buy it. That's store policy."

"Son be careful with that," Manny urged. "We ain't got money for any of this frilly stuff, especially not the broken kind."

Dearl glared back at the pharmacist. Manny caught a quick look at Dearl. "What's wrong, Dearl?" she asked.

"Nothin'." He quickly shook his head. He looked at her and forced a smile.

"Well, got a nickel for a cone?" Manny sang.

"I think I can manage that. Ready for a cone, son?"

"A cone?" Leland's forehead pulled toward his brow as his head cocked back. "What's that?"

"Manny, this boy's definitely been in the sticks way too long," Dearl said.

"It's ice cream in a cup you can eat." He held up three fingers to Carrie Lee.

"Vanilla, chocolate or strawberry?" she asked.

"Make 'em all vanilla," Dearl replied. "We can get fancy next time."

Carrie Lee quickly handed back an ice cream cone. Dearl handed it to Leland. "Here, now see how you like this."

"Whooee!" he shouted. One lick had Leland convinced this was far superior to most anything he had ever had.

"And don't forget you can eat the cone," Manny reminded him.

Leland looked at the little tan waffle holding his ice cream. He smelled it and took a bite. His eyes went wide, and his face joined in a huge grin. "Look at this, I'm eatin' the cup," he said. "I like this."

"Thought you might," his dad said.

"Hey, they ought to make all your dishes like this Momma, so you don't have to wash 'em. We can just eat 'em too."

"That *would* be somethin', now wouldn't it?" Manny replied.

They were sitting together in a booth at the end of the counter, finishing their ice cream when the man at the first stool spun around, got up and came over to their booth.

Ralph Watkins was a rotund, thin-haired, short man. His beige, cotton suit, thin string tie dangling under his heavy neck and flat-brimmed, straw hat easily placed him from some place another than Arkansas. He carried an air of deeper south aristocracy; yet when he spoke, he bore no accent that would hint at southern roots. He was as much out of place here as were the Thomsons.

"You know, I've been listening to your conversation," Ralph began, "and with this being the boy's first time to have an ice cream cone,

I was wondering if you'd permit me to let him also try a cherry soda? Always been a favorite of mine since I was his age."

"You accustomed to getting in the middle of other people's business, mister?" Dearl started toward the man. Manny touched her husband's arm.

"Sir, thank you but we're just fine," she soothed.

"What's a cherry soda?" Leland asked.

"One of the better ways to experience that vanilla ice cream you're enjoying so much," Ralph responded.

Leland fidgeted in his seat and jerked his head in frustration until Manny gave in. "Oh, Dearl, I guess the man's just being neighborly." Dearl looked at Ralph, then at Leland, at Manny then back at Ralph and said, "Your nickel."

"Alright!" shouted Leland.

"Madame," Ralph called, "a cherry soda for my young friend." Carrie Lee dried off her hands again, took a glass from the drain and began mixing the syrup and carbonated water with the ice cream.

Ralph squeezed himself into the bench beside Leland. "This weather is something, isn't it?"

Dearl looked deeply at Ralph. "I reckon," he said slowly.

"Freezing last night and barely needing a jacket today. And look at you folks, ice cream cones in the middle of January."

"Some reason you thank we ought'n to be doing this?" Dearl questioned.

"Oh, I meant no offense. It's…I'm just amazed that an ice cream cone sounds like a good thing to do even though it's the middle of winter."

"It's more or less what we thought," Dearl replied.

"And along with that cherry soda, I believe I'll have a vanilla cone myself, please," he ordered.

"Yas, suh," Carrie Lee responded.

"Back east, once winter sets in, you don't get many days like this to enjoy ice cream cones. This is more like desert winter. Some of the deserts I've been in you could freeze to death at night and nearly burn up in the daytime. All has to do with the angle of the sun they say."

"Round here we just kinda say it's how the good Lord felt like doing things," Manny added.

"Reasonable way to look at it, I suppose," Ralph replied.

"You've seen a desert?" Leland asked.

"Why, son, I've seen lots of deserts. Not much to see, though. Nothing to get very excited about."

"I ain't seen much a nothin' 'cept the Hills," Leland said.

"From the Hills, are you?" Ralph asked

"Got a problem with that, mister?" Dearl glared.

"Oh, by all means, no. You folks have some beautiful country up there."

"We thank so," Manny responded.

"Now, son, surely this is not your first time to come to town, is it? How old are you?"

"I'm sixteen," Leland replied. "I've been to town before. But that's about it. Ain't been in here. And ain't never been nowhere else."

"Sixteen? Mercy, I'd been clear around the world by the time I was sixteen."

"The whole world?"

"Pretty much. My daddy was into land development back east and thought himself something of a big game hunter. He'd go to..."

"I know, he'd go to other countries and kill their animals," Leland answered proudly.

"Well, that takes a bit of the romance out of it, but yes, that's essentially what he did. He took me with him on quite a few adventures."

"Where'd you go?" asked Leland.

"Oh, well, places like Africa, India, Thailand. I don't remember all the places."

"Africa? India? Thailand? Did'ju hear that, Momma?"

"I heard, Leland."

"Now, let me understand this better. You're sixteen and Lathrup Springs is as far as you've ever been in the world? Now why *is* that?"

"It's just the way it is up in the Hills," answered Manny, again touching Dearl's arm as he leaned forward. "We kinda just keep to ourselves. Don't need to go no place else. We just come into town when we need to. And we don't always brang the young 'uns.'"

"But don't you believe in letting your kids broaden their horizons? Let them see what's around the next bend in the road? Improve the breeding stock?"

"Don't rightly know what good any of that might be, but we do jist fine with how thangs are," said Dearl.

"Well, I consider myself quite fortunate to be among the sights you're getting to see on this venture into town, young man. Tell me, what do you think of your trip thus far?"

"Done seen some mighty purty thangs and getting' to eat my cone," Leland replied. "And this cherry soda is real good."

"Well, Poppa, you're gonna have a hard time keepin' this boy up in the Hills now that he's had a cherry soda."

"He dudn't have to stay in the Hills if he don't want to. Ain't nobody's stoppin' him. When he's a man, he can make up his own mind."

"Uh, my apologies, sir. I mean no disrespect, I assure you." Dearl waved Ralph off.

"You mean, I might could live in town someday, Daddy?" Leland asked.

"We can talk about this later," Dearl dismissed. "Mister, it's different being from the Hills and all. Disrespect is somethin' you kinda count on when you come to town."

"Boy, if I could live in town, I'd 'spect lots of people could hear me play my cello. Thank maybe they'd even let me play it in here?"

"Oh, Leland," laughed Manny. "You'd knock down half of this stuff just tryin' to use your bow."

Ralph looked at Leland with curious disbelief. "Cello?" he asked. "*You* play the cello?"

Leland grinned and nodded. Dearl slowly leaned toward Ralph. "I'm trying not to take offense, but just how'd you mean that to come out?"

"Again, I'm sorry, but I just wasn't expecting to hear that your son, or anybody around here, could play the cello. I'm rather fond of the instrument myself. Son, do you play well?"

"Momma says I got the gift," Leland grinned.

"The gift?" Ralph puzzled. "And what is this gift you have?"

"I... uh... uh don't know," stuttered Leland, "ain't never been asked that before."

"It's from God," Manny said.

"From God?" Ralph dripped, "Well, then, that must make you... appreciate whatever it is you're able to do." Ralph took his napkin and wiped his mouth. He pressed his hands on the table to push himself out of the booth to leave.

"Don't thank a boy who plays the cello with a gift from God's gonna be any good, do you?" Dearl asked.

"Oh, I would never say he's not good. I'm sure he plays well, and you all enjoy him playing very much."

"Sounds like you're judging him by what he looks like," Dearl said. "Goes on a lot 'round here. But maybe you oughta hear a 'body play before you decide if he's any good or not."

"Can you come out and hear me?" Leland asked.

"Well, that sounds interesting," Ralph replied. "But tell me, young man, how is it you came to take up the cello in the...uh..."

"Hills," reminded Dearl. "It was supposed to be mine. Belonged to my Great-uncle Willie Jim. He died and left it to my Uncle George. Uncle Willie Jim had tried to get Uncle George to learn it when he was a young 'un. He played it a little, but Uncle George never did take to it much. So, he gave it to me just to get it out of his house, I guess. We just left it in the corner gatherin' dust 'til one day Leland picked it up and started playin' at it. Sounded like a couple of cats fightin' 'til Uncle George came over and tuned it up for him and showed him how to hold it. Played him a song. Then he just took right off."

"Your Uncle George?" asked Ralph.

"Well, yeah, but, no, Leland. He just took right off and started playin' that thang."

"So, Leland plays by ear?"

Leland looked up at Ralph, scrunched his nose. "Naw, I use my bow. How could I..."

"Not important." Ralph raised his hand. "Well, Leland, you keep up the work, son."

"So, you still don't thank he's any good?" Manny challenged.

"Good? That's...that's such a subjective term. What's good to one may not be *as* good to another. And without any instruction I'm not sure..."

"Didn't need none, I tell you," Dearl interrupted. "Sorta like he already knew how to play. Just needed the chance to do so."

"It's God's gift," said Manny.

"God's gift?" Ralph sighed. "Well, back to that. Would you look at the time? I really need to run. But it has definitely been interesting meeting you folks. Maybe I'll get to hear you play sometime, son."

"You could come on out to the house," Leland offered. "I could play for you right now."

"Oh, I don't know. I'm not sure now is a good time. I wasn't planning on staying in town this long. And I really need to be moving on."

"How long *will* you be stayin'?" Leland asked.

"Seems I'm stuck, uh, staying here until Tuesday. My car needs a part that won't be delivered until the bus comes through on Monday night."

"Then come out tonight," Leland insisted.

"Tonight, oh, I don't know."

"It'd mean a whole lot to the boy if you could come out and hear him play," Manny said. "He's never played for nobody that really knew much about the cello before. And ever'body round home's done heard him plenty."

She poked Dearl in the ribs. "Uh, if you'd like, I suppose you could follow us on up," Dearl plodded. "We're 'bout done here, I guess."

"Well, I really don't believe I can make it out there tonight. But I guess I could drop by…say, tomorrow evening," Ralph said.

"Then you'll come tomorrow?" Leland grinned.

"Sure, why not. This isn't what you would call an exciting place, contrary to how you've experienced it, young man. Why don't you give me the directions and I'll see you tomorrow?"

Ralph took out a pad and began to write. "Head out 69 till you get to the Pine Valley cut-off, take a right and follow the dirt road up the hill for a spell till you come to a Jasper creek. When you cross over the bridge, turn down the next road you come to."

"Whoa, slow down a bit," Ralph begged. "I'm having a hard time keeping up. Turn left or right?"

"After the bridge, it don't matter," Dearl continued. "It's the next road. There's a big ol' oak tree right there. Foller that road on a spell till you come to Elmina. Go on through; then keep on till you come to a big rock on the side of the road."

"A big rock?"

"Yeah, that just lets you know you're on the right road. You cain't miss it. It's a real big rock. Keep on till you find yourself in some pretty thick woods. In a bit you'll be at Pine Hollar. When you get there, take the first right. If you miss that you'll have to ask somebody where the Thomson place is."

"OK, I hope I've got it. Now what time do you want me there?"

"Better make it when there's still daylight. Ain't as easy to get there in the dark when you don't know where you're goin'." Manny answered.

"I'll be there before sundown."

"On at least by dark thirty," Dearl replied.

"Dark thirty?"

"Right before it starts getting dark. Got about thirty minutes from the sun goin' down and dark startin'."

"Dark thirty. Well, what a chance encounter with you folks. Here, in the last few minutes, I've learned new expressions, made new friends and been introduced to a cellist who has the gift. I can't wait to see what our next meeting holds. Until sometime between sundown and dark thirty tomorrow then..."

Ralph folded the paper with his directions and slipped it into his chest pocket. He licked out the rest of his ice cream, downed the remainder of his drink, tipped his straw hat and left the booth. He stopped at the counter, laid a few dollars by the register and said to Carrie Lee, "This should take care of all our refreshments." He turned again to the Thomsons and nodded.

Dearl, Manny and Leland watched him make his way out the front door. "Ain't that something how he turned about," Manny said. "Didn't thank he was interested at all in hearin' Leland; then he just sorta swung around. Kinda makes you wonder why he got so interested, don't it? Makes you thank the Lord's up to somethin'."

"Naw, sounds like he's just a lonely man who needs to be around some friendly folks for a spell," replied Dearl.

"Well, mighty nice of him buyin' our cones," said Manny.

"Oh, I could'a handled it."

# *Chapter Seven*

THE HOUSE WAS QUIET. NUBBIN AND LELAND HAD BEEN ASLEEP for some time. Dearl sat on the front porch smoking his pipe and whittling away a stick. Manny dried and put away the last bowl, draped the dish towel over the edge of the sink and joined Dearl. She sat on the steps, leaning against the side rail and looked up at her husband. "You gonna tell me *now* what was going on in town this morning?"

"You asking or telling?"

"Dearl Thomson!"

Dearl took a long drag on his pipe and blew the smoke high above his head. He stared a minute at the ceiling. The muscles in his jaw began to tighten. He swallowed hard then began, "Oh, I had a rough time at the hardware store." He paused.

"And..."

"I didn't like it."

"What happened?"

"Manny, you just don't know how bad some of the folks in town treat us men when we have to go down there. It's like we're dirt. They look at me like I'm some ol' stray dog with the mange or fleas or somethin'."

"Dearl, what are you talkin' about?"

"I went to the hardware store on Friday and Tom wouldn't even wait on me. Like I wudn't even there. All these other folks came in and he was so friendly and helpful to all of them but flat out ignored me. Like I didn't matter."

"Tom?"

"The owner."

"Oh, Dearl, I'm sorry."

"Weren't you're fault none."

"What'd you do?"

"Left. Either that or steal the stuff. He wudn't gonna wait on me."

"Dearl!"

"I know. I wouldn't have stole nothin'. But I was mad enough to." Dearl tapped out his pipe against the heel of his boot, took his knife and reamed out the hole, then set the pipe on a small table beside his chair.

Nubbin pressed her nose against the screen door and nudged it open. She slowly walked to the edge of the porch staring intently into the darkness. The hair between her shoulder blades bristled. A low rumble vibrated in her throat.

"What's she lookin' at?" Manny asked.

"Prob'ly a 'coon or 'possum. What is it, Nubbin?" Dearl whispered to the dog. Nubbin's ears perked high. She growled louder.

"Now don't you get her all riled up."

"She's purty much already riled," Dearl said. Nubbin tore off the porch and lunged into the bushes down by the bend in the driveway, her deep bark a definite sign she had found her prey. From the bush scurried a fat raccoon, Nubbin right behind. The varmint beat her to a long-limbed live oak and shot up the tree just ahead of the gnashing teeth of the hound. Nubbin's bark turned into a howl.

"You want some fresh coon?" Dearl asked.

"If you shoot it, you clean it," Manny answered. "I ain't goin' to bed with coon stink all over *my* hands."

"Well, I have to shoot it now. Can't let ol' Nub thank we don't appreciate her for treein' that thang." Dearl reached over and picked up his rifle. He pulled back the bolt to insert a bullet in the chamber.

Manny never liked Dearl leaving a gun on the porch, but that was one argument she knew was needless to make. The compromise: he'd never leave it loaded.

The moon lit up the limb the raccoon held to. POP. The small crack of the .22 placed a well-aimed bullet in the head of the raccoon. He let go of his perch and fell, brushing across a limb that sent him tumbling on top of Nubbin before he hit the ground. The dog yelped and jumped back, then growled and nipped at the raccoon's fur to see if there was any life remaining in him. He was dead.

"Got 'em," Dearl announced, bounding off the porch to claim his prey.

"What's goin' on," Leland drawled out, standing at the door.

"Oh, Nubbin found a coon and Dad shot it," Manny answered. "Go on back to bed."

"A'ight," Leland said and was gone.

Dearl held the raccoon high by his tail as he came back to the house. Nubbin jumping up to nip at the coon. Dearl laid the animal on the bottom step and leaned his rifle beside the railing. He got his knife and began the process of dressing and skinning the raccoon.

"Dearl, don't you dare do that here at the front porch," Manny insisted.

"Guess that wouldn't be best." He grabbed the raccoon and started for the back.

"No, wait. Just leave him there a while and let's finish talkin'. You can clean him later." Dearl set him back down, got his rifle and placed it behind his chair. Then he sat down.

"I still want to know what happened *today*," Manny said.

"Oh, same thing, except this time I spoke up and made him pay attention to me."

"What happened?"

"I got my stuff, but he watched me like a hawk. Guess he reckoned me a thief or something 'cause he just got out in the aisle and stood there, watching. The boy in the back was gonna be helpful till Tom made him stop. I just don't know why some folks gotta be that way. You'd thank they'd have been raised with better manners than that. Or at least some descent courtesy."

"They thank they've always been better'n us down there."

"You know what really got me?"

"What's that?"

"His right hand."

"What about it?"

Dearl held up his hand and pulled down four fingers. "No fingers."

"So, he used to be a sawmiller?"

"Worse than that, Manny, it was Tom Grubb!"

"As in Ida Mae Grubb?" Manny closed her eyes and spit the words out of her mouth.

# Chapter Eight

Dearl had an early Sunday meeting at the Mill with Mr. Creighton and Claude Massey. Mr. Creighton owned the milling operation and Claude was plant foreman. Claude was responsible for the output of lumber each milling process produced. He had supervisors that helped but everyone knew Claude was in charge. Dearl was foreman of the forestry concerns. Claude was senior to Dearl in rank, responsibility and attitude.

Dearl had a hard time respecting Claude. A product of a rough childhood, a war and the depression, Claude was a difficult man, arrogant and demanding. He only had one way for work to be done—his way. Though he was usually right, being right was often a club with which he'd beat men into submission. No one questioned or challenged him. And Claude drank. He drank hard.

Mr. Creighton tolerated Claude because of the output he could command. He never drank on the job but would head toward the beer joint in Elmina before going home each night and stay until he was just ready to pass out. Somehow, he'd get home and into bed. The next morning, he'd wake up, hung over, but he'd go to work, work hard all day and then do it all again at quitting time.

Aunt Alma was more responsible for raising Frank than Claude. The first time she took the boy in to live with her was the day she went over to visit after Claude's wife, Frank's mom, had died. She found Claude passed out in bed and Frank filthy, hungry and half naked, running around in the yard. She told Claude she'd keep the boy until Claude could straighten out his life. Alma reared Frank by her standards and with limited exposure to his father. She was a good mother to a thrown-away child. Her husband, Elmer, resented Claude for his drinking but accepted Frank as his own son up until he died when Frank was ten.

When Frank was twelve, Claude married a woman named Flo who brought two young daughters into the marriage. Feeling outnumbered, Claude asked Alma to let Frank come back and live with them as soon as everything got settled. He had done this once before, when Frank was eight. He married a local lady, but that marriage lasted only a year.

Alma agreed to allow Frank to return to his father with the insistence Claude would quit drinking and keep Frank in church. Claude had a hard time with the second promise but did cut back on his drinking. This time he seemed to be adjusting well to his new family.

"Claude tells me," began Mr. Creighton to Dearl, "that if you could get more work out of your men in the woods, he could get greater output from the men in the mill."

Dearl frowned. "Well, sure, that makes sense, I guess. I don't see why I'd do that, though. I'm working the men pretty hard as it is and still able to keep 'em safe."

"No, we appreciate the work you're doing. Just wondering if you can do it a little more." Mr. Creighton always talked with a smile. It made some people more comfortable with him, but it always made Dearl suspicious.

"Well, yes sir, but I don't like to push the men harder than I thank they can handle. Thangs can get purty crazy out there. How 'bout telling me why it is you want me to do this?"

"Basically, it will help us improve the bottom line," Mr. Creighton said, smiling. Mr. Creighton was short and round. He had short, stubby fingers that usually got lost in the other man's grip when he'd shake hands. What was left of his hair was a yellow-white mat that he'd comb over from one side to the other. And he smoked an ever-present cigar.

"Is that what this is all about?' fired Dearl. "Makin' more money?"

Claude snapped, "Dearl, what the heck do you think we're doing this for, our health?"

Mr. Creighton held up a hand and redirected back to Dearl. "Dearl, every business has to watch the bottom line. That's where we get the money to keep the mill running and expand things when we need to." Dearl felt the same stinging glare he had gotten at the hardware store. He looked over at Claude and saw the intensity in his eyes, trying to stare Dearl into submission. His face tensed as his neck tightened.

"So, I'm gonna push my men and machines to the point of tearin' somethin' up or hurtin' somebody just so there's more money bein' made?"

"No," Mr. Creighton said calmly. "I want you to tell us what you need in order to get more logs out of the woods. That's all. Do you need more men? Do you need more equipment? We don't want anyone getting hurt. Or anything being destroyed."

Dearl leaned back in his chair. His face relaxed. "Yeah, I guess."

"You guess what?" Claude said, with a bit more volume than to the point at which things had settled down.

Dearl's eyes drew into slits as he glared at the foreman. "You tell me how many more logs you want, and I'll tell you what I need to get 'em to you."

"All right then," said Mr. Creighton. "Claude, get Dearl some numbers and then, Dearl, you get me your needs, and we'll be just fine. Everybody alright?"

"A'ight," said Claude, eyes locked in a glare with Dearl.

Dearl looked away to Mr. Creighton. "Yes, sir."

※

The screen door slammed back against the wall. "Miz Thomson, come quick, Aunt Nora needs you!" Billie Nell yelled in one breath. Manny appeared from the back bedroom.

"Billie Nell, what's going on?"

"Aunt Nora sent me to get you. Sara Beth's mommas got another baby inside and Aunt Nora needs you to help her get it out."

"Twins?"

"Yes, 'em. We gotta hurry!"

The two shot out of the door and down the steps, across the lawn to the road. They ran down the road, past the schoolhouse, across the creek and up a trail to a small dog-run house nestled in the trees. The kitchen and living area were on one side of the open breezeway and the bedroom was on the other. Everyone slept in the same bedroom. Sara Beth and her two younger sisters were sitting in the breezeway when Manny and Billie Nell reached the house.

"Hey, Sara Beth," called Billie Nell. "Yur momma still alright?"

"They won't let us in," answered Sara Beth. "We heard a baby cry, then a lot of yelling. Miss Thomson, you gonna help my momma?"

"I hope so, Sara Beth," Manny said. "You girls know how to pray?"

"Yes, 'em."

"Then you pray with Billie Nell and I'll go help." Manny went into the bedroom. Sally, Sara Beth's mom, lay propped up on the bed, sweating and straining. Aunt Nora was at her feet watching for the second baby to crest.

"Can't get this one out," she said to Manny.

"What do you need me to do?"

"Clean up that first one," the midwife answered. "I can't leave Sally."

In the rush of delivery, Aunt Nora had hurriedly wrapped the little girl in a towel and placed her in the crib. Manny unwrapped her and began to wipe her gently with warm, moist rags. The umbilical cord was leaking so she took a string and tied it off closer to the navel. She trimmed off the excess. Once the baby was clean and tended to, she swaddled her and placed her back in the crib.

"Anything happening over there?" she asked.

"This baby musta turned sideways," Aunt Nora said. "I've been waiting on the head to crest and out popped this foot."

"Where's the other one?" Manny asked.

"In there somewhere. I need them to come out together or get this baby turned around."

"What are you gonna do?"

"Push it back in, then try to move that baby around in there till we can get it to come out right." Aunt Nora gently pushed the exposed foot back inside and began to massage Sally's tummy, trying to get the baby to turn around. "There's a knee," she said. "If I can push it back up top…got it. I thank it slid around." She reached across Sally and felt a bulge. "Bet this is the head. See if I can get it headed back the right direction." She pushed the bulge. "It's moving! Manny, look down there and see if anything's showing up."

Manny shouted, "There's hair!"

"Good," said Nora. "Now push, Sally, push!"

Sally strained, yelled, grabbed another breath, held it and pushed hard. Manny cradled the baby's head in her hand and guided it out. Soon she held a crying, slippery baby girl. "Sally, y'all shore do know how to make baby girls. Got yourselves another one." Aunt Nora handed Manny a towel. She wrapped the baby in it and laid the bundle on Sally's tummy.

"Manny, you do the cord," Aunt Nora ordered.

"Sure," she replied. Manny took the string and tied the umbilical, then cut it off. She took the baby girl to the crib and began to clean her up. Aunt Nora moved over in time to deliver the afterbirth and clean up Sally. She then helped Sally get positioned to nurse the first baby.

"Can the other girls come in?" asked an exhausted new mother.

"Billie Nell!" called Manny. "Bring those girls in to meet their new sisters!

"Sisters?" said the trio through the wall.

The three girls rushed into the room. Sara Beth ran over to the crib to look at the baby lying there. The other two ran over to their mom. Billie Nell stood at the door.

"Ain't much to look at, are they?" Sara Beth said.

"Sara Beth!" snapped Aunt Nora. "All babies are beautiful. Some just mo' beautiful than others. And these had a rough time comin' out, so don't you be disparagin' of 'em none."

"Yes, ma'am."

"Now bring that other one over here and let's let it eat a while," Aunt Nora said. Sara Beth, as the oldest, was well experienced in picking up babies, helping get them fed and changed. She slid her hands underneath the newborn's bottom and neck and lifted her gently, cradling the baby in her arms. She waited beside her momma's bed until Sally could adjust the first one so there was room to fit in the second.

"Sara Beth," said Manny, "I thank you know more about tendin' to babies than most folks."

"Got company coming," Billie Nell announced as Willa and Faye, Sally's twin sisters, came into the room. Even though nearing eighteen, they were considered a bit slower than other girls much younger.

"Good, family," said Aunt Nora. "Ladies our job is 'bout done. Y'all can take care of the rest." Manny collected the soiled towels and sheets and took them to the kitchen. Aunt Nora looked over the two babies, both nursing, checked Sally and said, "I'll be back 'bout dark to see how everybody's doing. Now Willa, you and Faye keep checking things. If anything changes come get me, now. You understand?"

"Yes 'um," the twins answered.

Manny sent Billie Nell to the well to draw water while she went to the kitchen and got a fire going in the stove. A large pot was heating up when Billie Nell came in and poured the pot nearly full. Manny put in the soiled sheets and towels and let them boil. After several minutes she rinsed them in the sink and hung them across the porch rail to let them dry. Aunt Nora came outside. "Manny, I need to talk to you."

"Sure, Aunt Nora."

"Manny, I'm getting too old to keep doing this. If you hadn't come over when you did, I might have lost one or both of them little ones or worse lost Sally. I want you to take over for me."

"Aunt Nora, I don't know enough to start birthing babies like you do!"

"I ain't asking you to, just like that. I want you to help me for a while. Then I'll help you, and when you feel like you can do it without me, I'll quit."

"Do you thank I can do it?"

"Girl, I watched you do it just now. Who taught you to tie off the cord and cut it like that?"

"Never thought about it. Just knew how it needed to be done, I guess."

"See, you've got the gift."

"The gift?"

"Yep. I done seen it. You got the gift."

"Huh, imagine that. Me and Leland both got gifts. It felt really good helping in there. Real natural. Like I belonged in that room doing that."

"And with Leland 'bout grown and you not havin' a bunch of little ones to take care of, God's made it so you can take over for me. Now, talk this over with Dearl." Manny was still thinking about having the gift when she suddenly caught what Aunt Nora had said and what it meant. She loved Leland but regretted she and Dearl had not been able to have more children. Thought she had been cheated. Thought God had let her down. "Manny," Nora said, "you talk this over with Dearl, you hear me?"

"I will, but don't worry, he'll agree," Manny said. "Billie Nell lets you and me head back. I was thanking some berry cobbler would be nice for tonight when that man from town comes over. Wanna pick some berries with me?"

"Shore do," Billie Nell answered. "You gonna teach me how to make the cobbler?"

"I reckon I could. You're gonna have to fix it for Leland one of these days. It's one of his favorites."

"I know."

"Send for me when you need me next, Aunt Nora," Manny said. "Me an' Billie Nell are going berry pickin'."

"I will, child. Next one coming is Annie Mae. Ain't quite sure when she's due but ought to be coming soon enough. I'll come by next week and we'll talk about it. Save some of that cobbler for me."

# *Chapter Nine*

"U H, OH, NOW I'VE DONE IT," LELAND GROANED, SLIPPING THE slingshot into his back pocket. The robin lay on its back; his right wing and feet were still moving. Leland looked around, then slowly walked over to the bird. "Augh! Momma's gonna kill me fer shore. Stupid bird! I didn't think I'd hit you."

Manny and Billie Nell were picking wild blackberries from a patch just over the ravine from where Leland was standing over the robin. He glanced toward them, then back to the bird. It had stopped moving. He gently nudged it with his foot and...nothing. He unbuttoned his shirt, reached down, picked up the bird and stuffed it inside. Again, he scanned the woods for his momma and Billie Nell, before running off toward the house.

"Thomas! C'mere, cat! Thomas! Kitty, kitty, kitty." An old, yellow tomcat came out from under the porch and slowly trotted over to Leland. "Here, I've got you a fine, fresh bird to eat," Leland said, tossing the robin toward the cat. Thomas stopped in front of the bird, sniffed, looked at Leland, then turned and walked away.

"Hey!" he shouted, "get over here. Eat this bird, you varmint. Momma's gonna kill me. And if'n she does, I'm comin' after you, you stupid cat!" Leland got the bird and threw it in front of Thomas again. This time the cat sidestepped the bird and strolled back into the shadows under the porch. "I'm dead."

Leland snatched the bird and stuffed him back into his shirt. He glanced around and ran back into the woods. As he brushed past a big oak, he faced his momma and Billie Nell coming down the trail. He never slowed.

"Lookie here, Leland," Billie Nell said. "Me and yur momma got a whole mess of berries."

Leland raised his hand as he ran by as if agreeing with how good they were going to be. "Leland Thomson, you get back over here and look at these berries!" Manny scolded. "And you tell Billie Nell they look nice."

He stopped and backed up toward them, glanced over his shoulder and said, "They sure do look nice. Mighty big and juicy."

"Here, have a bite," Billie Nell offered.

"Uh, alright," he said, sticking his hand toward the bucket.

"You get your hand out of that bucket!" his mother yelled. "Where'd that blood come from? Did'ju cut yourself or somethin'?"

Leland pulled his hand back. "What blood?"

"On your hand there."

"Oh, I, uh, shot a bird and it must have bled on me."

"Better not've been a robin," Manny challenged.

"Uh, didn't tell me his name," he said, laughing nervously.

"Leland James Thomson!" Manny roared. "What's that in yur shirt? If'n you shot a robin…"

"I'll be right back. I… uh…left my slingshot in the woods."

"It's in yur back pocket," offered Billie Nell.

"My other one," Leland said. He ran off down the trail, glancing back to see that Manny and Billie Nell were headed toward the house. As he hit the rise to the ravine, he took the bird out of his shirt and threw it as far as he could off the trail into the bushes.

The shadows had grown long. Manny and Billie Nell busied themselves in the kitchen with preparations, awaiting the arrival of their guest. Billie Nell washed berries. Manny gathered pans and ingredients for the cobbler.

"Now wash 'em real good, Billie Nell. Especially since Leland stuck his filthy hand in there."

"Yes 'um. Will we use all of 'em in the cobbler?"

"Purty much, I reckon. We'll set aside enough for one and see how many we got left over. Might be enough for some fried pies."

"Ms. Thomson, who is this man that's coming out here?"

"You know, I don't remember him saying what his name was. We met him at the drug store in town."

"And he's coming all the way out here just to hear Leland play his cello?"

"That's what he said. Beats all, don't it?"

"Yes 'um, beats all."

Dearl sat in his truck and stared at the office window. Mr. Creighton and Claude shared a drink to celebrate their victory. Dearl felt his temples grow hot and lips purse. His breathing became slow and deliberate as he tried to relax. He liked his job, would never leave, but had to fight the urge to walk away. Like his father, he planned on working here until he got too old, but he didn't need this strain. His own expectations were high enough; he didn't need another man placing demands on him beyond those he placed on himself.

"Mr. Dearl," Ernest Jones said softly. Dearl didn't hear him. "Mr. Dearl!" Ernest said louder.

Dearl turned and saw the old, black mechanic standing beside his door. "Hey, Ernest, how you doin'?"

"Oh, I's doin' good, Mr. Dearl, but Mr. Elwood ain't doin' so good."

"What's the problem?"

"Well, he done got his truck stuck in a ditch comin' out of the woods Fri'dy. He said somethin' broke when he wuz trying to git it out so he just left it there."

"And we're just now finding out about it?"

"Yes, suh. I was gonna do some work on the truck this mownin', but the truck wudn't nere. I done went over to his house and he told me what'd happened. Said I could take care of it. Cain't get it by myself."

"Alright, Ernest," Dearl said. "You get in. We'll go get Elwood and head out to the woods."

Ernest climbed into the back of the truck. "Ernest, get up here with me! You ain't no dog."

"Yes, suh," the mechanic said, hopping out of the bed and opening the passenger door. "But I might be needin' some tools."

"We'll stop by your shop first. Then we'll get Elwood."

The mechanic's shop was simply a tall garage, opened on both ends so Ernest could get whatever he was working on inside and out of the weather. He could fix anything, and what he couldn't fix, he could rig it so it would work until he could get a part to make it right. The mill provided him with all the tools he used, nothing power-driven, just hand tools requiring all the strength his mighty back and arms could muster to break off rusty and dirty nuts from trucks or equipment coming out of the woods. When he wasn't working on the trucks, tractors and cranes, he was maintaining the machinery within the mill. He generally worked daylight to dark, six days a week.

Dearl pulled into the shop. Ernest got out and quickly grabbed a toolbox, shovel, pry-bar, jack and blocking wood. He tossed it all in the back of the truck and then placed his hand on the rail to jump in. He looked up and saw Dearl watching him out the back glass, got down and slid back onto the seat inside the cab.

Elwood Kelly was a middle-aged man, as far as logging was concerned. He was early forties and well-worn. He came outside when he saw Dearl's truck pull up in front of his house. Though it was chilly outside, he wore trousers held up with suspenders; no shirt, no shoes.

"Elwood, get dressed," Dearl shouted from inside the pick-up. "Seems you left a truck in the woods."

"Well, you said if'n it was gittin' dark jest leave it till later," Elwood said.

"Well, it's later. Come on, we're going back to get it out," Dearl strained.

"Don't you thank the two of you can do it without me?" Elwood asked.

Stubbornness was not a characteristic Dearl dealt with lightly. He pushed open his truck door. Even before his foot hit the ground, Elwood had opened the screen door to go back inside. "Give me a minute and I'll be right out," Elwood said."

When Dearl had to ask the same thing a second time, most men were smart enough not to question the command. They knew Dearl had reached his limit with them. Elwood went back into his house to change.

"Mr. Dearl, I be gittin' in the back now?" Ernest asked, opening the door.

"Ernest," Dearl said sharply. "I don't care if Elwood gits back there but you're staying up here with me. 'Cause if you ain't up here, I just might be killin' him before we ever get to the woods."

He closed the door. "Yes, suh. I'm stayin'."

Elwood drove a logging truck. Driving in the woods required unique skills. Not only were there no roads, but the trails he drove down were narrow gaps cut out of the forest and an obstacle course of stumps and large limbs he had to negotiate. When there was a steep ditch, the men would make a bridge of logs laid long-way across the ditch. Since the back tires were tandem, they would easily track across the single log, a bit of each hanging off on each side. The true skill was running single front tires with no margin for error on narrow edges of log. You went slowly, hung out the door to watch the tire on your side. If it aligned the other would. On Friday it didn't.

All three men saw the log truck dipping low into the ditch, strad-dling the log bridge. Dearl knew Elwood hadn't told Ernest the whole story of what he would find when he went to get the truck. It would be a long afternoon.

It was just after dark when Ralph Watkins drove up to the Thomson home. The truck he had borrowed from the repair shop in Lathrup Springs looked quite at home in the Hills. Ralph, however, still didn't fit the profile.

Pine Hollow wasn't much more than a clearing in the woods with a few shanty houses scattered about. It was a community of necessity, built to keep workers closer to their jobsite. Prior to that, the daily drive up the mountain would cause most of the men to find work elsewhere.

Sawmill communities have a lifespan equal to the population of trees within a short distance. Since Pine Hollow was in one of the thickest forests in Arkansas, it had had a longer lifespan than most. Most of the men employed with Creighton Mill worked out in the woods, cutting and hauling. The rest worked at the various mill operations.

The mill at Pine Hollow was a processing plant that stripped the bark from the trunks and then rough-cut them into planks determined by the original size of the tree. It was the job of the sawyer to call out the way he wanted a log cut. The block setter set the saw to the specifications the sawyer ordered, then pushed the log out for cutting. Most of the work was mechanized but still required expert eyes to make sure everything went as planned.

Once the logs were turned into planks, they were stacked and placed in kilns for removing the moisture in the boards. When they had dried to the level desired, they were taken down to the planer mill. At the planer mill the rough boards were trimmed to final dimensions and shaved smoothed for shipping to retailers.

Since the saw mill was the beginning stage in the finishing

process, there was more refuse there than at the other mill. The bark and sawdust generated by the large circular blades were carried away from the mill on a conveyer belt and dumped into a ravine. Usually overnight the constant fire within the mountain of debris turned the pile into a powdery heap of grey/black ashes. The smell of smoke was always in the air.

Out in the forest the woods foreman would mark the trees in the area chosen for cutting. The paint he smeared on each tree would lead the men to which ones to take and which to leave. It was the foreman's job to see that the forest was not stripped bare but selectively harvested. After the cutting and clearing were completed, another crew would return in the spring to plant new trees. The limbs from the trees were left on the ground to compost back into the soil to nourish the new plants.

Dearl was the head woodsman in charge of the logging crews. He'd guide them to the area he had marked the day before and they would spend the day cutting, loading and hauling the logs back to the sawmill. Each job required specific skills. Some men felled the trees, others would strip off the limbs, others, still, would load the trucks. The drivers would haul the logs away and additional men would unload them back at the mill. Then the drivers would return for more. Because of the danger of saws, axes, falling trees, loading equipment and trucks, each man carried a heightened awareness of the danger involved.

Manny, Leland, Billie Nell and Nubbin stood eagerly on the front porch. Ralph got out of the truck and walked up the steps. He tipped his straw hat to Manny and Billie Nell and shook hands with Leland.

"Well, the directions were right on target," Ralph said.

"Glad you made it," Manny replied.

"Is your husband not here?" he asked.

"He'll be in soon," Manny answered. "Had a meetin' at the mill this mornin', then some problem out in the woods he had to tend to."

A horn sounded from down the driveway. "There's Daddy," Leland announced.

Dearl drove up and parked beside the other pick-up. He got out, covered with the dirt and grime of having dug Elwood's log truck out of the mud.

"'Spect I'd better git cleaned up before I shake hands," he said.

"Go right ahead," Ralph answered. "No hurry."

Dearl went around to the back of the house and stripped down on the porch. He then went directly into his and Manny's bedroom. It was his customary entrance to avoid tracking in on the front part of the house that Manny tried to keep presentable. Everyone else went in the front door.

The house was plain and rustic. And though it was small, it had a cozy family feel that made Ralph instantly comfortable. The fireplace glowed warmly. Nubbin trotted back over and lay in her spot in front of the hearth. Leland's cello stood in the corner.

"I have to admit you do live out of the way," Ralph said.

"Yes, sir," Manny answered. "While Dearl cleans up, d'you wanna have a bite of desert? Billie Nell and I made a fresh juice-berry cobbler. I was just putting on a pot of coffee. Would you care for some, sir?"

"You know, I believe I would," he answered. "A cup of coffee would be just the ticket if it isn't too much trouble."

"Oh, no trouble. I'll be just a few minutes."

Manny went over to the stove and checked the fire under the kettle. Billie Nell followed her. "Billie Nell, get the bowls and start serving the cobbler."

"Yes, ma'am."

Ralph walked over to the cello. "So, here's the famous cello," Ralph said. "How old is it?"

"Don't rightly know," answered Leland. "Oldern' me."

Ralph laughed hard. "Well, let me hear you play, son," he said.

"Cobbler and coffee first," ordered Manny. "Then we'll wait for his daddy to get in here."

Billie Nell set the bowls on the table. Manny placed the coffee cups beside each bowl and waved Leland and Ralph to join them. She poured the coffee.

"Dearl," she called. "You 'bout ready?"

"Yep, I'm coming," he announced, coming into the room. He joined them at the table, spooned in a bite of cobbler and began, "That Elwood Kelly is dumber than a stump. You know how backwards things get when you're on one side of the truck telling somebody on the other side which way to move somethin'? Ever time I told him to go to the left he'd say, 'Which left, mine or yours?' I kept tellin' him when I told him which way it was, I was talkin' about his not mine. But he just kept on askin', 'Which right, mine or yours?' Then of all thangs he'd move it the wrong way anyhow. Aggravated me to death. He couldn't figure it out the whole time. Me and Ernest spent half the afternoon fightin' his stupidity. I finally just started tellin' him backwards before he'd move the way I wanted."

"Must be a challenge working with such *backward* thinking people," said Ralph, amused at his pun.

"Oh, it does have its moments," Dearl answered, laughing as well.

# Chapter Ten

THE MEN GATHERED IN THE LIVING AREA WHILE MANNY AND Billie Nell cleared away the bowls and coffee cups. Since the living room, kitchen and dining room were all one room, it wasn't like anyone left one to go to another. They just moved where they were sitting.

"Now, I was just wonderin'," began Manny, "why you decided to come on up here to listen to Leland? Why was that? Mister..."

"You know, come to think of it, I don't think in all the talking we did at the drug store we ever formally introduced ourselves. My name is Ralph Watkins. I know Leland here, and I know your names from listening to you speak to each other. Now who's this young lady, Billie Nell?"

"That's Billie Nell Goodman," Leland answered. "She lives just on the other side of the gully."

"Someone special to you, Leland?" Ralph prodded.

"Well, everyone thanks we'll get married someday."

"Well, well, and what do you think?"

"Be alright, I guess."

"It shore 'nough better be alright, Leland Thomson," Billie Nell bristled, smacking him with a dish towel.

"Why, Leland, I do believe you've been spoken for," laughed Ralph.

"Yeah, I reckon."

"Well, Manny, why did I come? Let's say I'm a man who loves music, especially music played on classical instruments like the cello. And there was something in the way your eyes lit up when you told me about Leland. It just piqued my curiosity."

"Well, we're mighty proud of him," Dearl added. "And most everybody up here done heard him plenty. Why you came don't make me no matter to me. Just glad you took the time to come."

"Well, if my coming is any encouragement to a young cellist, then I, too, am glad I came."

"More coffee, Mr. Watkins?" Manny asked.

"Please, it's Ralph."

"Don't count much on her callin' you that right off, Mr. Watkins," Dearl said somewhat quietly. "Kind of the way it is up here."

"I understand."

"Do you want any sweetnin' or colorin', Mr. Watkins?"

"I'm sorry, what?"

"Want any sugar and cream for your coffee?" informed Dearl.

"No, this is just fine, Mrs. Thomson."

"But you can call her Manny," Dearl said. "And I'm Dearl."

Leland got his cello from the corner and brought it over to the chair in front of the fireplace. He settled it between his legs, tightened the bow and then began to tune. He ran his fingers up and down the neck in crisp and clear arpeggios. After several minutes of feeling the music from his fingers, he looked at Manny, then at Dearl. Dearl nodded.

"Go ahead, son," Dearl encouraged. "Play that one you played for your momma and me the other day."

Leland opened his hands on his lap, closed his eyes and began to mumble. After a few seconds—that seemed much longer to Ralph—he stopped, turned his face upward and with eyes still closed began to play *A Mighty Fortress is Our God*. From the first note it was obvious Leland had instantly lost himself in the music. The air bore the gentle waves of beauty and strength coming from each note and with them a power that overwhelmed Ralph.

He watched intently, pressed forward in his chair. He watched Leland's bowing strokes, his fingering, his hands rolling out his vibrato. A short distance into the piece, Ralph slowly closed his eyes and leaned back in his chair. He tilted his head back and folded his hands across his protruding belly. He smiled as a tear traced its way down the side of his face.

When Leland finished the song, the final note still ringing throughout the room, he slowly opened his eyes. Dearl held his hand up for him to wait and nodded toward Ralph. Leland furrowed his brow as he looked at their guest. "Did he go to sleep?" he whispered.

Ralph wiped the tear and opened his eyes. He brought his hand to his lips and breathed out a sigh. "Oh, Leland, son, don't stop. Please continue."

"Well, I'm done."

"And we were worried, thinking maybe you'd gone to sleep or somethin'," Dearl added.

"Oh, no. No, no. Just lost in this wonderful, magnificent rhapsody."

"Rap sodi? I thought it was *A Mighty Fortress*," Leland said.

"No, Leland," Ralph laughed. "Rhapsody means you've captured me and taken me someplace far beyond where we are. Into another realm. Someplace wonderful."

"Huh? Where?" He looked around the room. "Weren't you here all the time?"

"Just play, dear boy, just play."

Leland looked at Dearl. "Go on, play somethin' else, son."

"What?"

"Whatever you like," Ralph urged.

Leland stared at the floor, reaching deeply within to find another song to play for Mr. Watkins. As he thought, his fingers ran up and down the neck in mindless, yet perfectly tuned arpeggios. Ralph watched the boy incredulously. *What is connecting him to what he is doing?*

"Well, there's this song they did at church this mornin' that's kinda been buildin' up and wantin' out," Leland said.

"Wanting out?" Ralph asked.

Dearl waved at Ralph to dismiss the intrigue and smiled. Ralph knew this was not a day to analyze but to enjoy. Leland closed his eyes, set his hands in his lap, palms up, and began to mumble again. In a few seconds he stopped, turned his face upward and with eyes still closed began playing *Great Is Thy Faithfulness*.

Familiarity with the hymn allowed Ralph to listen, not with technical scrutiny of notes and rhythms but with openness to enjoy the expressiveness of a young boy playing a song from a place so deeply within, that few have ever discovered it could even be found. Ralph closed his eyes and settled his head back on the chair.

When Leland finished the song, Ralph remained fixed. Leland dropped his eyes and looked at him. Manny crossed over from the kitchen and stood by Dearl. Billie Nell looked over from the table. All looked at Ralph. After several long seconds, Ralph opened his eyes and paused, staring now at the cello. A few seconds more and he slowly brought his head up and looked at Leland.

"No one ever taught you?" he whispered.

"Sir?" Leland asked.

Ralph cleared his throat. "No one ever taught you?" He strained to speak clearly.

"Like school?"

"No, this."

"How to play?"

"Yes."

"No, sir."

"No lessons, no instruction?"

"No, sir."

"Leland, your finesse, your touch, your articulation..."

"My what?"

"The way you play…"

"Told you he was good," Dearl added.

"Sir, that word is far and away much too inadequate for what I just heard," Ralph said.

"He ain't good?" Dearl asked.

"I'm not sure there *are* appropriate words," Ralph responded. "But *good* is just one of the lesser qualifiers. He is so far beyond *good*."

"Better'n good," Dearl snapped his fingers and grinned proudly, "now that's right up there with purty dang good." Leland set his cello over in the corner and turned back to Ralph.

"Son, can you read music?"

"Read music? Like I can read a book?"

"Have you ever seen a sheet of music?"

"Seen a hymn book. Does that count?"

"And you can read the notes? Is that where you got this song?"

"Naw, we sang it at church this mornin'," Leland said.

"And you remember the notes from off the page?"

"All them dots and stuff? Didn't pay no attention to that, just the words. We just all sang along with Miz Gertie."

"I know that hymn," Ralph began, "and when you played it, you played so much more than what is on the page of any hymnal. Where did your arrangement come from?" Leland stared blankly as Ralph rambled through his thoughts for an answer. "Why did you play it the way you played?" Ralph asked clearly.

"Oh," Leland brightened. "Don't know."

"You don't know?"

"No, sir."

"Leland, I need some help here."

"Yes, sir?"

"Where did the notes you played come from? How did you know which notes to play?"

Leland paused. He knew the answer but wasn't sure how to tell

Ralph in a way he might understand. He wiped his hands across his mouth, then slowly dropped his fingers against his chest and began to tap it. He looked at Ralph and smiled.

"Well?" Ralph prodded.

Leland tapped harder on his chest, now pointing with his finger.

"Your heart?" Ralph asked.

"Mr. Watkins, I don't thank he can tell you what yur wantin' to know," offered Dearl.

"He can't, meaning you aren't allowed?" Ralph directed back to Leland.

"Oh, no sir, just don't know how," Leland responded. "Ain't never had to before. Nobody's never asked me to."

"What *can* you tell me?" Ralph asked.

"Songs go in here and stay till they want to come out," Leland answered.

"Into your heart? And what happens to them until they want to come out?"

"Stuff, I guess," Leland offered.

"Stuff? What are you talking about, *stuff*?" Ralph quizzed. "I mean, are you thinking about how you would like to play the song, what notes, what style, what embellishment?"

"Ain't sure what you just said, but I don't thank down here. It's just where the song goes and waits 'til it's time to come out."

"Now, let me see if I get this. You sang this song in church just this morning and without reading the music or studying it or even thinking about it, have just sat down and played this incredible arrangement for me for the first time?"

"Yes, sir."

Ralph sat back in his chair and brought his hands to his mouth. He pulled down his bottom lip, turned and looked at Manny and Dearl.

"It's the gift, Mr. Watkins," Manny offered.

"A gift indeed, Madam. An unbelievable gift."

"I thank I'll be havin' another cup of coffee," Dearl announced.

"How 'bout you, Mr. Watkins?" Ralph nodded slowly and moved back to the table.

Manny poured up the coffee and sat the cups around the table. She brought back the cobbler and Billie Nell took the bowls out of the drying rack, wiped them off and set them back on the table.

"Now Leland," Ralph began, "I need to know a little more about what happened tonight."

"You do?"

Ralph spooned in a bit of cobbler. "Now, you said this song was in your heart, *wanting* to come out. What did you mean?"

"Well, when I hear a song, I sorta hear some other stuff, too, I guess. It all kinda swarms around in my ears and then it goes in my heart. I can feel it in there."

"You can feel the song in your heart?"

"Yes, sir."

"What does it feel like when it wants to come out?"

"Kinda warm a little at first. And then if I don't hurry up, it sorta gets hotter, kinda. It's like the song starts wanting to get played. So, I have to let it out."

"You can feel the song trying to get out of your heart?"

"Yes, sir. It's kinda like one of them volcanoes Miss Ida told us about. You know where the hot lava just bubbles around inside the mountain until it comes out and spews all over the place?"

"And that's how these songs are inside your heart? They build up until you play them?"

"Yes, sir."

Ralph laughed deeply, yet nervously, for he was breathing rarified air in that small shanty.

"One last question," Ralph said. "Does that happen with *any* song you hear?"

"Purty much, I 'spose. Probably not all songs, just those that swirl around in my head when they go in."

"Do the songs you hear at church do that?"

"Not all of them. Some do."

"What I'm asking is, is it only hymns that work this way inside you?"

"Don't know. Ain't heard much else."

"He can play Irish jigs he heard Floyd Whittington play on his fiddle," said Dearl.

Ralph drew back then turned to Dearl. "Mr. Thomson, may I come back again, please? It would mean a great deal."

"Well, don't see why not."

"Tomorrow?"

Dearl spun a quick look at Manny. "Well...alright," he said. "But I thought your car was getting fixed and you had to head on back?"

"That won't be until Tuesday. Is dark thirty tomorrow acceptable?"

"Dark thirty's fine."

Ralph got up, shook hands with the Thomsons and Billie Nell. He stopped at the door and turned. "Just so you know, Leland, I'm going to bring something with me that I think you'll enjoy."

"What's that?"

"I want you to listen to some cellists whose music I believe you will find quite interesting."

"You're gonna bring 'em out here?"

"No, I'm going to bring a recording of them playing."

Leland smiled. Ralph knew now was not the time to try to explain recording technology. "But before I go, could you play me that song one more time?"

Leland closed his eyes and played. Ralph closed his eyes and wept.

# Chapter Eleven

It was approaching evening, the next night. Leland and Billie Nell played with Nubbin in the front yard as they waited for Ralph to arrive. Leland tossed a stick down the driveway. Nubbin ran after it and brought it back. "Here, let me throw it," said Billie Nell. She took the stick back beside her head and whirled it past the last tree where the driveway curved.

As Nubbin shot down the driveway, Leland heard his dad's truck coming up the trail. "Nubbin!" he shouted. "Stop!" But the dog, focused on the stick, never heard the command. She skidded to a stop just in the opening around the corner. All Leland and Billie Nell could hear were tires scraping into the dirt, a thud and a yelp.

Racing down the driveway, they found Nubbin lying on her side just under Dearl's front bumper. "Dad! Back up!" Leland shouted.

"Leland, I'm sorry, son. I never saw her."

"It's alright, Dad."

As Dearl pulled back from the dog, Leland slipped his hands underneath Nubbin and picked her up and carried her to the truck. Billie Nell opened the tailgate and Leland scooted onto the ledge holding his dog. Billie Nell slid up beside him. Dearl slowly drove them the rest of the way to the house.

"It's all my fault," offered Billie Nell. "I shouldn't have thrown the stick so far."

"Ain't nobody's fault," Leland strained. "It just happened."

Leland took Nubbin into the house and laid her in her usual spot on the rug in front of the fireplace. Nubbin was unconscious but still alive. Leland and Billie Nell sat beside her, stroking her head and side.

"There's Mr. Watkins," Manny said, peering through the kitchen window. She let the curtain above the kitchen sink go, wiped her hands and started for the door. "Now prob'ly ain't the best time for him to show up."

Ralph sounded his horn. Dearl came down from the porch as Manny stood at the door to welcome him inside. Ralph opened the trunk and took out a suitcase.

"What happened? You get kicked out of your hotel?" asked Dearl.

"Ha, oh, no," he responded, "just a little equipment I'll need tonight." The two men came into the house. Ralph carried in a stack of record albums under his arm.

"Hey, Mr. Watkins," Leland said, solemnly as Ralph came into the house.

Ralph took the case and set it on the table. "Leland, I do believe that dog sleeps more than any dog I've ever seen."

"Well, he got a little help tonight," Dearl replied. "I hit him with the truck when I came in."

"Hit him? Dearl!" Ralph said

"Weren't none of his fault, though," Leland offered.

"Yeah, it was mine," answered Billie Nell. "I threw the stick too far, and…"

"Okay, Billie Nell," shot Leland. "I told you ain't nobody's fault. Now don't you be sayin' that again."

"Do you need to take him to the vet?" asked Ralph.

"He's just a dog, Mr. Watkins," Dearl answered. "He'll either be alright or he won't."

"But…" Ralph began.

"Way it is out here, Mr. Watkins," Leland said. "He ain't bleedin' so he'll be alright in a while. What'd you bring?" He left his hound asleep on the rug and walked over to the table where Ralph had placed the records and equipment.

"Well, let me set all this up first and I'll show you." Ralph opened the suitcase to show a record player. He pulled out the cord and plugged it in. He set a record on the spindle and rubbed his finger under the needle. He flicked off the lint and rubbed it again until he could hear the scratch through the speaker.

"Is that what I'm supposed to listen to?" Leland asked.

"No, I want you to listen to this record, Leland," Ralph began. "It' a recording of a man named Bolognini playing a very famous cello piece by a very important composer named Bach."

"Box?" Leland asked.

"No, Bach," Ralph corrected, emphasizing the harsh, guttural ending sound.

"Bauck," Leland repeated. Some name; sounds like you got something caught in your throat."

"Sounds like a chicken to me," Billie Nell added. "Baak, baak, baak." They all roared with laughter.

Ralph laughed politely. "Bach was a famous German composer from the eighteenth century whose works are still enjoyed and appreciated today. I want Leland to listen to this recording and then see what he can do with it after he's heard it. Let's see how broadly the gift can be applied."

Ralph switched on the player. *Suite One from Bach's Suites for Cello* began to play. Everyone gathered around the machine and watched the record revolve, everyone but Ralph. As they watched the rotations, he watched Leland.

Leland's focus left the record as his body began to bob and sway. He closed his eyes and began to follow the music with his head moving from side to side. His right hand, though hanging at his side, began to follow an invisible bow sliding across the strings, his left tracing across an invisible neck. Ralph smiled approvingly. At the end of the piece, Ralph switched off the record player. "Well, Leland?"

Leland stood there, then exhaled through his nose as though he had been holding his breath for a long time. He began to nod. "Mighty good," he said. "That's one mighty good song."

"Do you think you could play it?"

"Not the way that fellow did."

"No," he laughed. "Of course, that would take years of training. No one would ever expect you to play as he did. But...why don't you go ahead and see what you can do. Just do the best you can with it."

"Can't right now."

Ralph pulled back. "Oh, did the gift not work with this type of song? You can't remember it? Is it too difficult? Too long?"

"Naw, just not right now. Ain't ready to come out yet."

"Ah, I see." Ralph grinned nervously with a smile that really meant I don't see, but I'll say I do because I don't know what else to say.

"Got some of that cobbler left over, Mr. Watkins," Manny offered. "Want me to get you some?"

"Thank you, Manny, but I'd really rather wait to hear Leland play."

"That could be a spell," Dearl said. "And a bowl of cobbler with cream would sure help *me* pass the time."

"Well, then, sure, cobbler sounds just fine."

Ralph, Dearl, Manny and Billie Nell all sat around the table enjoying their cobbler and coffee, laughing and talking. Leland sat on the sofa watching the fire. Time passed, but Leland didn't interact. He got up and moved over to the fireplace and sat beside Nubbin, stroking his dog, watching the embers drift up from the burning logs.

"Dog still breathing?" asked Dearl.

Leland nodded and continued stroking Nubbin's head. Then he suddenly stopped, quietly got up, walked over to his cello and brought it over to the chair in front of the fireplace. Everyone at the table stopped, turned and watched him. Ralph turned his chair around and scooted it closer to Leland.

Leland again stared into the fire, set his cello into position, then turned to Ralph. "Now it ain't gonna come out the way that fellow played."

"Leland, that's perfectly understandable," Ralph offered. "But, son, the notes do need to be the same. Feel free to interpret the notes however you feel, but you must play the same notes."

Leland closed his eyes, placed his open hands in his lap and began to mumble audibly. He turned his face upward and with his eyes still closed began to play the same piece, perfectly, never questioning a note. His interpretation, though, was fresh. It was smoother, more melodic, expressing more drama than Bolognini had played.

Ralph listened for a couple of minutes, then noticed his heart racing and his hands beginning to shake. He realized he had stood up at some point so quickly that he sat back down hard in his chair. He leaned back and nearly tipped over. He brought the chair under control and abruptly stood again. He staggered to catch his balance, knocked his chair over and fell across it, trying to pick it back up. Leland stopped.

"You alright, Mr. Watkins?" Dearl asked as he reached over to help Ralph back up. Ralph simply lay there staring at the ceiling, laughing. Dearl looked at Manny and shrugged.

"Mr. Watkins, you alright?" Manny asked.

Ralph slowly looked over at them, nodded, then looked at Leland. He took Dearl's hand and got up. "Leland, you said you couldn't play it like Bolognini. Son, that was the understatement of the year. Your interpretation is far superior to his. I don't understand this." He set his chair back upright, then began to pace quickly across the room and back. "What is going on here?"

"Well, you just played it for me on your record player and I played it back to you," Leland answered. "Remember?"

"Then you fell out of your chair," added Dearl. "Did you hit your head or somethin?"

"Yes, no, but I *just* played it for you, son. You can't possibly be playing it back like this after listening to it just once."

"How many times should it take?" Dearl asked.

"This is impossible. This can't be happening."

"Am I doing something wrong, again?" Leland asked.

"He didn't know no better, Mr. Watkins," Manny pleaded.

"No, you don't understand. I have just witnessed in this very room perhaps the single most miraculous demonstration of musical ability...ever. No one on earth can listen to a piece one time and then play it perfectly, and in fact...play it better than what they just listened to. No one."

"Ain't that what Leland just did?" asked Dearl.

"Leland, you listened to Bolognini for the very first time and not only played what he played, the exact notes he played, without seeing the music, but interpreted far more from the piece than he did. How did you do that?"

"I don't know. I just played it the way it wanted to come out."

"Come out? What is going on inside that head of yours?"

"I told you, stuff."

"Is that why you close your eyes before you play? To hear the stuff?"

"Naw, I was just prayin'."

"Praying?"

"You do know what prayin' is, don't you, Mr. Watkins?" Manny asked.

"Of course, but why..."

"I guess you need to know this, but when Leland was born, he had the thumbprint of God on his head," Manny said.

"Thumbprint?"

"See that white spot in his hair?" Dearl said, pointing at Leland's head. Leland tilted forward to show a small white streak of hair on the top of his head.

"Well, no, I guess I never noticed."

"Out here folks believe that's where God touched him before he was born. And that's where he got the gift from."

"To play the cello?"

"That's what we believe," Dearl answered.

"So...the prayer is for..."

"It's just what I to do before I play," Leland answered.

"Pray."

"It's what makes the stuff come out."

"Stuff? Stuff? You keep saying *stuff*. What is the stuff you hear?" Ralph insisted.

"I don't know!" Leland announced. He eyes showed his frustration with the questions. "I just sorta hear stuff, like how the notes want to be played. Then when it wants to come out, that's how I play it."

"Mr. Watkins, y'all are both gettin' mighty worked up there," Dearl said. "Thank we mite oughta settle these things down a bit?"

"Yes, I'm sorry. This is all so incredible. How long?"

"How long what?" Leland asked.

"How long can you remember a song you just heard and still be able to play it?"

"I guess from then on. It sort of goes back somewhere inside and just stays in there."

"You mean if I asked you to play this song again in, say, a month, you could still play it just like you did for me tonight?"

"S'pose."

"What about six months?"

"Don't know that that makes no matter."

"It doesn't matter how long from today you play this piece, you will still be able to play it just like you did for me tonight?"

"Prob'ly so. Songs don't usually change the way they want to be played."

"Unbelievable. Absolutely unbelievable."

"You keep sayin' that like you thank the boy ain't tellin' you the truth, Mr. Watkins," insisted Dearl.

"No, I just don't know what to think or do with what I have just experienced, Dearl. That's all. You must understand, something like this just doesn't happen. I'm having a difficult time sorting all this out. I don't know what to think."

"Well, do you at least thank I might could finish the song now?" Leland asked. "It's kinda wanting to come on out and get done."

"Oh, by all means play, my boy, play."

Leland closed his eyes and began playing exactly where he left off. Ralph was too shocked to even close his eyes; he just stared at the boy. His lips quivered as he tried to smile, then he dropped his mouth open and cocked his head in disbelief. He smiled again, took out a handkerchief and wiped the sweat from his brow. He rolled the handkerchief and pulled it up to his mouth. He then clasped his hands tightly together and began to cry.

When he finished playing, Leland sat frozen in the moment. Ralph, barely breathing, sat still as well, looking at him. When the final ringing sound of the last note dissipated, Leland opened his eyes, looked down and grinned at Ralph, who managed another nervous smile in return.

"Well, Mr. Watkins," Dearl asked. "What do you thank about our boy?"

"Mr. Thomson, I really don't know what to thank, uh, think," Ralph answered. "This has been an amazing night. Please, you must allow me one more trip. I need to get an additional piece of equipment and desperately ask your permission to return tomorrow evening. May I, please?"

"Mr. Watkins, someone who enjoys Leland playing as much as you seem to, is always welcome here. Just come on back anytime. You ought to know that by now."

"Tomorrow?"

"Tomorrow's fine."

Ralph gathered up his equipment and loaded it into his car, laughing all the while. Dearl, Manny, Leland and Billie Nell watched as he drove past the corner and headed back down the hill to town. They all turned and went back inside.

"I wonder if he hit his head a bit too hard when he fell out of his chair," Manny said. They all laughed.

"I like playing for Mr. Watkins," Leland said. "He sure likes listenin' to me."

"Well, we like it, too," Manny said.

"Alrighty then," Leland said. He picked up his cello and began to play a jig. Billie Nell began to clap as Dearl spun Manny around the room. Nubbin opened her eyes, raised her head and looked up at Leland. She then closed them, yawned and went back to sleep.

# Chapter Twelve

THE TUESDAY EVENING SUN SHOT A BEAM THROUGH THE WEST-
ern window and onto the chrome latch of the recorder. It bounced
up into Ralph's eye as he opened the latch and took out a microphone
and cables. Usually calm, now his trembling hands made it hard to
attach the cords and screw on the cables. The words under his breath
were best left unspoken. "Sir?" Leland kept asking, believing his mum-
bling was some attempt to make conversation.

"Alright, Leland," he announced, "I believe I've finally hooked
everything up. Ready to give it a test?"

"Yes, sir," Leland said. "What do you want me to do?"

"Well, just have a seat and I'll show you how this thing works."

Leland positioned himself in his chair, facing the large microphone that was bent toward the belly of his cello.

"Now, just play some arpeggios so I can get a sound check."

"Sir?"

"Uh, your warm-up exercises where you move your fingers up and
down the neck when you're getting ready to play."

"Oh," Leland replied as he began sliding his fingers across the
strings in a blur of sixteenth-note runs. Ralph turned on the recorder
and adjusted its receptivity.

"Okay, that's good for now. Let's listen to how well you recorded."

He rewound the tape and then pushed play. The first few notes were distorted until the point where Ralph had made his adjustments. Soon the vibrancy of Leland's arpeggios was sharp and clear.

"What do you think?" Ralph asked Leland.

"Is that me?"

"It certainly is."

"Ain't never listened to myself before, at least not when I wasn't playin'. What are you gonna do now?"

"I want to make a recording of what happened last night."

"How you gonna do that?"

"No, no, I mean I want to repeat what we did last night and make a recording of it." Leland creased his forehead as he made a half-smile at Ralph. "Remember, last night I played a recording for you and you played the piece back to me?"

"Yes, sir."

"Well, I want to do the same thing tonight, but this time I want to record the whole thing on this tape recorder while it happens."

"Oh, me playing and everything?"

"Yes."

"Hold on," Manny said, "your daddy just drove up and he'll be comin' in in a minute. Want some coffee, Mr. Watkins?"

"Not just yet, Manny. Maybe when we're through."

"What we got here?" Dearl asked as he came through the door.

"Daddy, Mr. Watkins is going to make a tape recordin' of what we did last night."

"How's he gonna do that?"

Ralph hung his head, laughed, and then looked up. "I'm going to repeat what I did with Leland last night, but this time I'm going to record the whole thing on this tape recorder."

"How come?" Dearl asked.

"Last night was quite remarkable. I thoroughly enjoyed hearing Leland play, and I believe some friends back in New York would enjoy hearing him as well."

"And they're gonna be listenin' to Leland through that thang?"

"Yes."

"Can they hear us now?"

"No, I'm recording it now, and once I get back there, I'll play it for them," answered Ralph. "I'm not sure they would believe me if I just told them the story."

"You prone to lyin', Mr. Watkins?" Dearl asked.

"No, not at all, it's just that what Leland can do is...well...hard enough to explain and would be even harder for other folks to believe."

"I don't know, Dearl," Manny began, "reminds me of when the Talbert's heifer had that two-headed calf. And then that reporter from Lathrup Springs came up here and took its picture and put it in the paper. Caused all kinds of commotion. All them town folks coming up here, poor thang died from all the attention."

"Yep, I remember."

"I assure you, Manny, this is nothing like that," Ralph said. "Leland is not a freak of nature. He has, as you say, a *gift*. I would like to share that *gift* with others so they can appreciate him as I do."

"By lettin' them listen to him play out of your recordin' machine?" Manny asked.

"Yes, if you don't mind."

"Well, I just don't know. Dearl, you okay with all that?"

"I reckon," Dearl answered.

"But I still don't want people to start coming out here just to look at Leland like they did that calf," said Manny.

"Oh, Momma," Leland added.

"Manny, I can assure you, the people who will be listening to this recording would not dream of coming out here. I can guarantee you, that's something you need never to worry about."

"Well, I guess it'll be alright then," Manny conceded. "But we ain't gonna put Leland in some pen so folks can come look at him." They all laughed as Leland settled into his chair and positioned himself to play.

"What are we gonna do first?" Leland asked.

"Well, first of all, I'd like you to play the song you played for me last night."

"My church song?"

"Oh, no, the Bach."

"OK. Now?"

"Let me get the tape cued up and then I want to introduce you."

"Who to?" Leland asked, looking around the room.

"To the people who will be listening to this recording," Ralph answered. "Manny, Dearl, everyone will need to be quiet while we record this."

"Me, too?" Leland asked.

"No, you, we need to hear." Ralph switched on the recorder. "Gentlemen, I would like to present to you, Mr. Leland Thomson, cellist. He will be playing *Suite One of the Unaccompanied Suites for Cello* by Bach." Ralph nodded, but Leland was watching the tape on the recorder go around. "Leland," he whispered, "go ahead."

Leland nodded, closed his eyes, held open his hands and began to mumble inaudibly. Ralph began to perspire. Though Leland couldn't see him, Ralph rolled his hand for Leland to hurry and begin. With his prayer finished, Leland lifted his face upward and with eyes still closed began to play. Ralph smiled and hummed out his sigh strongly enough that Dearl and Manny turned to look. *Sorry,* he mouthed.

At the end of the piece, Leland held his last note long, then relaxed. He opened his eyes, popped a quick grin and looked to find Ralph. Ralph held up his hand as he turned off the machine. "Now we may speak," he announced.

"How wuz that, Mr. Watkins?" Leland asked.

"Fine, Leland. Just fine."

"You gonna play it back so we can hear it?" Dearl asked.

"No, I'd like to continue recording if you don't mind."

"Naw, we don't mind none."

"Now, Leland, I'm going to play another piece by Bach, and I want you to listen to it as you did the piece last night. Then I want you to play it and I'll record the whole thing."

"OK, but it may take a while before I can play it back, you know," Leland reminded him.

"I know. I'm just going to let the recorder run to document that time lapse."

"Huh?"

"Here we go. Now let me explain what I'm doing."

"Thank he got it straight now," said Dearl.

"No, not Leland," Ralph said. "Remember, the men I'm going to play this for." He switched on the recorder. "In this experiment I am going to play the second *Suite*, have Leland listen to it, then in a short time he will play it back. We are using no music other than this recording. He has never seen the Bach *Suites* nor had even heard about Bach or this work prior to my coming here. He has never been taught to play and cannot read music."

Leland nodded, laid his cello beside him and faced the record player. Ralph started the music. As *Suite Two* began, Leland strained to hear. Ralph turned up the volume. Leland's eyes darted around nervously. Soon, he closed them and the tension on his face relaxed. His head swayed as he followed the movement of the notes on an invisible neck board of a cello. When the piece ended, Ralph switched off the player but left the recorder running. "Now, Leland, what did you think of that?" he asked.

Leland opened his eyes and stared off into the corner of the room. He slowly nodded. "I like it. Real good."

"Can you play it for me?"

"Nope, not yet."

Ralph cleared his throat. "Soon?"

"Reckon so."

Ralph leaned toward the microphone. "The music isn't ready to come out yet. I'll explain later."

Dearl leaned toward Ralph, "Who you talkin' to?"

"Hmm, actually, the men listening to this tape recording."

Dearl looked around the room. "I thought you were tapin' it so they could hear it later. Where they at?"

"In a room in a conservatory in New York."

"And they can hear you all the way from here to New York?"

"No, they'll hear this recording when I play it for them."

"So why are you talking to them now? Why don't you just talk to them when you get there?"

"Well, I was...you're right. I'll just wait and talk to them when I get there."

"Hey, y'all," called Billie Nell through the screen door.

SHHHHH! Everyone shushed at Billie Nell.

"Come on in, Billie Nell, but we can't say nothing," Manny whispered. She came in and joined Manny at the table. Leland reached over, picked up his cello and positioned it. He held it a minute, then closed his eyes, held out his open hands and began to pray. He stopped, turned his face upward and with eyes still closed began to play, perfectly.

Ralph quickly looked at the recorder to see if it was still running. If the meter that indicated sound was passing through the microphone was telling the truth and if there was enough tape to capture the moment, he knew he would astound the men in New York. He smiled with great approval that Leland was doing exactly what he had done the night before, and, yes, he was indeed capturing it on tape.

# Chapter Thirteen

THE SCREEN DOOR SLAMMED AS LELAND AND BILLIE NELL left. Since it was dark, Manny had insisted he walk her home. Neither argued. Ralph and Dearl gathered up Ralph's equipment and loaded it in his car. Manny stood on the porch and called out to Ralph, "Want some more cobbler before you leave, Mr. Watkins?"

"Oh, why, yes, Manny," he answered. "I have to admit I'm still somewhat lost in the moment though. Tell me, did this night really happen or am I dreaming?"

"Ain't sure what you're talkin' about but you were awake all the time, that's for shore," she said, handing him a bowl of cobbler.

Ralph sat down at the table. "Thank you. Now, I need some help understanding this ritual Leland goes through," Watkins began.

"What do you mean?" asked Manny.

"You talkin' about him prayin', Mr. Watkins?" Dearl bristled.

Manny snapped, "Mr. Watkins, I don't know what you believe about prayer, but out here…"

"Manny, Dearl, no, I mean no offense. Please, I know I've touched a nerve and probably shouldn't even bring this up, but this is more important than you might realize."

"Well, it's mighty important to us, too," Manny fumed.

"No, please, again I'm sorry," Ralph pleaded, "but I need some help understanding why Leland does it each time he plays and how necessary it is."

Dearl began, "We don't fully know. When Leland was a little boy, whenever he'd sit down to play, he'd hold his hands out, you know, open like he does, and pray for God to bless 'em. We asked him why he did it, and he just shook his head and said 'cause,' like that should be answer enough. And that was it."

"I may need a little more," Ralph prodded.

"The boy has a reason that goes beyond explainin'. He just does, alright?" Manny sliced her hand through the air in front of her, cutting off any further discussion.

"Manny, I really need to know. I'm going to have to explain this to folks who aren't going to accept *because* as an answer. I hope you can appreciate that."

"I'd appreciate it if we'd just have our cobbler. We're done talkin' about it, and I ain't gonna say no more about it," she snapped.

"Dearl?" Watkins pleaded.

"Want some coffee to go with that cobbler, Mr. Watkins?" Dearl consoled.

Watkins received the cobbler from Manny as Dearl poured them both a cup of coffee. He settled back and ate. Manny forced a southern smile at him, and he smiled back.

The evening was pleasant, but with Watkins' question still hanging somewhere south of being answered, he was not as in touch with the general conversation as usual. Leland came in from walking Billie Nell home and saw them all sitting in front of the fireplace.

"Hey, Mr. Watkins," Leland greeted. "I didn't know you'd still be here."

"Just had some things to talk over with your mom and dad," he replied. "But we're all finished, and I need to be getting back. Leland, come on out to my car with me. I need to ask you something."

"Sure."

Ralph leaned against the hood of his car. "Tell me about what you're doing before you play," he asked.

"What about it?" Leland asked back.

"Tell me what you're doing."

"You mean tuning up?"

"No, after that."

"Arapahoeing?"

"It's arpeggios. But no, after that."

"Prayin'?"

"Yes, praying. What are you doing?"

"You know...prayin'."

"Yes, but what's going on?"

"What do you mean what's going on? You know what prayin' is, don't you, Mr. Watkins?"

"Yes, I know about praying, but, OK, why specifically do you pray before you play?"

"'cause."

"Leland, I need more of an answer than that," Watkins insisted. "I'm going to go before a very prestigious committee to see if I can have you play at Carnegie Hall. I must tell them everything. They are going to want to know about your prayer habit.

"It ain't just a habit, Mr. Watkins."

"Leland, son, what's going on when you are praying before you play? Why do you do it and it is necessary?" Watkins strained.

Leland reached down, picked up a rock then threw it at a tree down in the brush. He leaned over against the car and said, "If I don't, I cain't."

"You can't what?"

"I cain't play." Leland looked down at the ground and wagged his head. "I have to. It makes what's in my heart come out."

"The music?"

"The whole stuff, Mr. Watkins. I know when it wants to come out, so I just thank God and out it comes."

"And if you don't thank Him..."

"Ain't never not wanted to."

"But what will happen if you don't?" Ralph pried.

"I don't know."

Watkins got off the car and stood in front of Leland. "Son, I don't understand and I'm afraid I'm risking too much not to find out, so I have to ask. Why would your God give you a gift like that and then make you have to go through that ritual before you can use it?"

"He ain't makin' me," Leland strained. "It's just what I gotta do. It's what I wanna do. He gave it to me; don't that make sense?" He moved away, back toward the house.

Watkins sat in his car for a minute before starting up. *Explaining a backwoods prodigy is going to be difficult enough,* he thought. *To explain this prayer ritual…* Ralph's mind drifted away to the committee back in New York as he drove past the rock, across the creek and back onto the blacktop then off toward Lathrup Springs.

# Chapter Fourteen

RALPH HAD NOT BEEN BACK IN THE CONSERVATORY FOR ALMOST a year. The unplanned stop in Lathrup Springs had interrupted his return from the Berkley School of Music where he had been guest lecturer for the past two semesters.

The New York Conservatory of Music was old school. Traditions that shaped everything from the curriculum to the performance expectations, even to the protocol by which students could address their instructors had been in place and not changed for the past seventy-five years. The musty smells in the hallways were reminders of the past.

The Chancellor's office was quite large. Two of its walls were lined with shelves overflowing with books and stacks of music. On the other two were pictures and plaques recognizing moments of grandeur in the Chancellor's long history with the conservatory. A Steinway rested proudly and prominently under a bank of windows overlooking Central Park. In the center of the room was a seating arrangement of four sofas facing a common table filled with journals, well-used ashtrays and empty coffee cups. Today it also held the recorder Ralph had used to capture the experiment with Leland.

As one of the regents, Ralph had spent many hours around that table, churning out the business of the music school, ruling over disputes, maintaining the status quo. But now, he knew he would be challenging all he had fought so hard in the past to avoid—crossing the forbidden lines of non-conformity, venturing off the traditional path.

Sitting across from him was the chancellor, Ernst Steinman. He was a deliberate man, even to the detail of how distinctly he would pronounce his name. Each letter was a word of its own so that the final "t" of Ernst was never lost on its way to Steinman. Once president of the conservatory, he was appointed Chancellor at his retirement. Among other responsibilities, Steinman was now chairman of the Board of Regents. Smoke from his pipe added seasoning to the room.

To Ralph's left was George Chadwick. Perhaps because of his British roots, he brought enough aristocracy into a room to intimidate even the most challenging intellectuals into keeping their conversations simple and to the point. On Ralph's right was Raleigh Peterson, the youngest of the men, yet their equal in knowledge and beyond them in insight.

Though there was no published dress code for faculty or regents, all four of the men wore similarly styled brown-tweed jackets, white shirts and narrow, black ties. The only variety was in the color and texture of their trousers.

From the adjoining office entered Mrs. Knudson, Steinman's secretary, carrying one her tray a carafe of coffee and a pot of hot water along with tea bags, a pitcher of cream and a bowl of sugar. With no acknowledgment she sat the tray on the table before the men, turned and left the room.

With fresh coffee in his cup, Ralph directed the conversation away from mundane matters of the school to the subject of Leland. "Gentlemen, I would like to share with you the reason for my having requested this meeting."

"Well, enough for the weightier matters of weather and week-end activities then," Steinman said. "Watkins, I have to admit the assertions you made in your letter are incredible to say the least."

"Incredible, yet true," Ralph replied.

"I do believe we will be the ones who determine that," Chadwick challenged. "Let's get on with it."

Ralph reached over to the recorder to switch it on. "Wait a

minute," Peterson said. "Let's rehearse some of the things you assert before we listen to your tape. You're saying this boy from …Arkansas… plays the cello well enough for you to request this listening session? That in itself is quite incredible. I thought the fiddle and banjo would be the only instruments they would be familiar with down there."

"Mr. Peterson, as I told you in my communiqué, this sixteen-year-old boy from Arkansas, whose name is Leland Thomson, is the most magnificent cellist I have ever heard in my entire life. And I believe you will find him so as well."

Chadwick leaned forward and set his cup on the table. "Mr. Watkins, we know the caliber of cellists you've heard. We've had most of them play here at the Conservatory and beyond that, through our partnership with Carnegie Hall, we've heard world class performances. We have hosted the best of the best. But a bumpkin from anywhere, with no formal training, a sixteen-year-old boy, can hardly be placed among…well, even the best in some public-school programs, much less the best you have ever heard. Preposterous!" He lifted his cup and sat back in the sofa. "Surely, you have forgotten yourself, sir?"

Ralph stood and walked over to the window, turned and began. "Gentlemen, is it ability or circumstance that makes the world aware of the truly gifted…be they athletes, artists, mathematicians or musicians? Is there a young man somewhere in the African bush who can run faster than any other person on the planet and no one will ever know it, because no one, save only a few gazelles, will ever see him run? Is there a lady living somewhere in the congestion of a New York or Boston or any other city, who has a better grasp on resolving world issues than any politician we have elected to any office of our country, who will never be listened to because she is a woman?"

He continued, "Is there a child, within whom lies a gift, who could so astound and enhance the world of music yet remains unknown due to never having held an instrument in his hands through which he could express that gift. Or could there be one who had been given the privilege to discover the gift, but was hidden away in a Pine Hollow,

Arkansas, far removed from anyone who might recognize his ability to play? I believe Leland Thomson to be that one."

Steinman waved Ralph to return to his seat. "Such passion. Then by all means, stop the soliloquy and let us hear the boy. Words cannot convince what the ear must determine."

Ralph switched on the tape recorder. The men listened to Leland playing the *First Suite*, gazing off into the distance, fully appreciating the music they were hearing. After a couple of minutes, Ralph stopped the recording and sat back.

Peterson looked sharply at Ralph. "What are you trying to pull, Watkins?"

"Do you want us to believe this is your bumpkin from Arkansas?" Steinman asked. "I hear far much too much maturity for any sixteen-year-old. Who is this you've recorded?"

"I assure you, it is Leland Thomson, a sixteen-year-old boy from Pine Hollow, Arkansas," Ralph asserted. "Now let me show you the demonstration of his talent…gift…that places him beyond any other cellist I have ever heard. Let me fast forward a bit."

Ralph stopped the tape and began to play at the beginning of the *Second Suite*. After a few measures, Chadwick rose from his chair and challenged, "What is this, Watkins? How dare you? Do you think you can deceive us so easily?"

"Excuse me?"

"Sir, I agree with Chadwick," Peterson asserts, "that most definitely would be a recording of Bolognini playing and not your little hillbilly."

"What kind of joke is this?" Steinman demanded.

"This is no joke at all. What you are hearing is indeed a recording of Bolognini playing the Suites. What you are listening to is the second part of the recording session. The first night I played a recording of Bolognini playing the *First Suite*, then after a few minutes Leland played it back for me. It was incredibly perfect and far more expressive than Bolognini had played. I returned the next night to see if he could do it again and this time, I captured it on tape. What you are listening to is that second night. Yes, I am playing Bolognini, but let me fast forward a bit more."

Ralph leaned over to adjust the recorder. "The whole session is recorded. You'll notice there is a gap that is the actual time between Leland hearing the piece and then playing it. Here, I believe this is the end of the second suite. You will hear the transition."

"What is that conversation in the background?" Peterson asked.

"Leland's parents and a young friend were in the room. We carried on normal activities while Leland focused on what he had heard."

The tape went silent. "What is going on now?" Steinman asked.

"Just listen."

Leland began to play. After only a dozen measures, Chadwick interrupted, "Now you want us to believe that this is this Leland lad?"

"This is Leland," Ralph answered.

"This, coming from your boy from the boonies?" Peterson quizzed.

"Again, this is Leland Thomson."

Peterson crossed his arms and pressed back into the sofa. "This has to be some hoax. No one can do this. Beyond your assertion of how he is doing it, no sixteen-year-old can play this well. Not even Bolognini captured the heart of Bach as does this cellist. This cannot be your boy or any boy. I hear years of training, technique, maturity, depth..."

"Mr. Watkins, surely you do not expect us to believe we are hearing what you suggest we are hearing." Steinman added.

Ralph leaned over and turned off the player. He settled back into his seat, smiling. "Gentlemen," he said in quiet excitement, "what you are listening to is a live recording made of an actual event. The night before this recording, I played the *First Suite*. Leland listened intently and then he played it back. I was so amazed, so challenged with what I heard, I returned the next evening and made this recording. I went through the same procedures as the night before, but this time I recorded the experience. It is that simple. I can understand your bewilderment. Even now, hearing it again, I feel the same astonishment I felt in that small house. But I assure you, gentlemen, the cellist you are listening to is a sixteen-year-old boy who lives in Pine Hollow, Arkansas, named Leland Thomson."

"But he plays..."

"He plays magnificently," said Steinman. "Your recording of Bolognini was the first time he ever heard the suites played?"

"Yes."

"And he's playing without seeing the music?"

"He can't read music."

"This is incredible," asserted Peterson. "And how do you account for the greater depth of expression than Bolognini? Bolognini is a premier cellist."

"Stuff," Ralph said.

"Stuff?" bristled Chadwick.

"He says that whenever he listens to music, he hears more than what he is listening to. It's like he feels inside how the music wants to be played."

"Feels the notes?" asked Peterson. "Extraordinary. But surely, he has had to have heard these and memorized them. No one can perform what he has just heard and then play it perfectly. Regardless of how well he plays it, that just..."

"Remarkable? I assure you, he had never heard them."

Steinman stood and walked over by the window. "So, by simply hearing this played, he, without hesitation, played it perfectly from memory?"

"There was hesitation. He always..." The pause became uncomfortable. Ralph knew this was the moment he dreaded, even more than dealing with three highly intelligent musicians' disbelief in the fact of Leland's playing. "He prays before he plays. That was part of the silence you were listening to."

"Prays?" retorted Chadwick.

Ralph sighed. "It's connected to his family's belief that this ability is a gift from God. He acknowledges that gift each time before he plays."

"And that's where he believes the music comes from? From God?" Peterson challenged.

"It's within him. Gentlemen, Leland does have a gift. I saw the gift in operation and am fully convinced. I'm not particularly fond of the God part, but, for the life of me, I can find no other reasonable explanation."

"We all know of wonderfully gifted musicians, but gift or not, one cannot play previously composed pieces he has never heard nor seen and play them perfectly after hearing them only once. Gentlemen, I still fear we are being put on," Chadwick said, slamming his hand on the table.

"Mr. Watkins?" Steinman directed.

"Gentlemen, you know me," Ralph answered. "My reputation can withstand any scrutiny by which you may choose to examine it. But if you think for one moment..." He rose to his feet.

"Mr. Watkins," Peterson began, "you have to admit, what you are presenting to us is almost...no, not almost...*is* beyond belief. Were it not *for* your reputation, we would not even be having this conversation. We would have dismissed this claim outright. And if someone else brought this to us and if you were sitting where we are, you would be questioning the whole matter as adamantly as we. Please sit back down and let us work through this a bit more."

"I agree," Ralph said, returning to his seat. "I am amazed and have been ever since I made this discovery. I have never been as enraptured as I was the first time I heard Leland play. I turned to look at his mother and all she said was, 'It's the gift.' That is the only explanation that makes any sense. I assure you, what you are hearing is coming from a source deeper than what can be taught."

Steinman walked over and sat on the corner of his desk. "Now, Mr. Watkins, are you suggesting an innate wisdom, a predisposed knowledge? That the boy was born with this ability somehow encoded?"

"I don't know where it came from. All I know is, it's there, just as you have heard. No tricks, no mirrors, no hidden recordings. All real, very, very real."

"Too real if you ask me," Chadwick snorted.

"Might I take our discussion into a more...metaphysical realm?" asked Peterson.

"Such as?" replied Steinman.

Peterson walked over and closed the door to Mrs. Knudson's office. He returned and stood behind the sofa. "Have we courage to entertain the notion that we might be embracing some semblance of reincarnation?"

"Oh, come now, Peterson," Chadwick challenged. "Let's not lose our sense of reason in fishing for explanations."

"No, hear me out. What if—that's all I am saying—what if, somehow, in some cosmic redistribution in the afterlife, Bach was reassembled into this backwoods hillbilly?"

"If that is what you are suggesting, then I say absurd!" Chadwick responded.

"Absurd, yes, I agree, but what if?" Peterson returned to his seat. "How else can you account for a totally untrained bumbling hick to be able to play the works of Bach, which he has never seen nor heard, and play them as though he has known them all his life?"

"Mr. Peterson, I do believe you're stretching this a bit out of shape?" Ralph challenged.

"No," said Peterson, "since we all take the fact that we cannot derive any reasonable, physical explanation to this ability, then why must we not at least consider the metaphysical. He says God gave him the gift. Could some power out there have done so?"

Chadwick added, "As much as it frightens me horribly to even for a moment suggest that Peterson's proposition could be worthy of consideration, I confess it does actually let this whole matter somehow make sense."

"That Leland is a re-embodiment of Bach?" Ralph laughed.

"What other possibility explains it as well?" replied Peterson.

"And that satisfies your mind rather than the simple belief that God may indeed have touched the boy?" Ralph said.

"Gentlemen," said Steinman, "I will not say that I agree with the conclusions drawn from this discussion, but I admit I *am* intrigued by the implications. However, in the interest of...propriety...I suggest you return from this trip to the shadowy frontier and consider the hazards of your implications. We are either on the verge of the sublime or the precipice of the ridiculous. I recommend we not compromise ourselves, our reputations nor the reputation of this conservatory by taking this matter outside of these chambers."

"Thank you, Mr. Steinman. But in the meantime, what about Leland?" Ralph asked. "Is my reputation still sufficiently intact that I might be able to premier Leland through the auspices of this conservatory?"

Steinman walked over to Ralph who stood to face him. "Though questioned, your reputation remains intact. So, with your assurance your boy can reproduce before an audience what we have just heard on tape, then, yes, Mr. Watkins, we can arrange for a concert by your protégé. You may select the repertoire and the manner appropriate to showcase your discovery."

"All in good taste, of course," quipped Chadwick. "We don't want this turned into some carnival hawker bringing God into the venue."

"Of course, I'll see to that," Ralph replied.

"Gentlemen, your calendars?" Steinman said. The four men opened and examined their schedules. "How soon do you feel the lad would be ready?"

"As soon as we can put everything together. Remember, Leland comes ready. Could we say, two or three months?"

"On April eleven the chamber orchestra will present Bach's *Brandenburg Concertos*," Steinman suggested. "I would think it appropriate to the evening to include your Leland playing the *Suites*. That should work well. All agreed?"

"Agreed," said Chadwick.

"Yes, agreed," added Peterson.

"The eleventh of April it is," said Steinman. "Mr. Watkins, the ball, as they say, is in your court."

"Thank you, gentlemen," Ralph said. "I will begin to make arrangements right away. And, by the way, as you consider this further, there remains the *gift* aspect. I know your reincarnation theory sounds plausible to you, but consider the possibilities that the One who gifted Bach could also have turned His attention on Leland, perhaps pouring the gift out from the same container? Just a thought. Good day, gentlemen."

# Chapter Fifteen

ANNIE MAE TUCKER WAS THE WIFE OF DEARL'S PUSHER, TOM. It was the pusher's job to make sure the loggers did their work. He was in charge of the site at which the logs were being cut, hauled and loaded onto trucks. It was the highest position a black man had risen to at Creighton Mill. Annie Mae and Tom lived in the squatters' shacks up past the Mill. The squatter's shacks were simply one-room huts, with a roof, wooden walls, wooden floors, one door and a single window. They were crude cabins with no electricity, no running water and no plumbing. A wood stove in the corner served as both a heat source and a cook top. There was one double bed, a well-worn sofa and a small table with four chairs around it. A coal-oil lantern hung from the exposed rafters, serving as the only source of light during the evening.

Mr. Creighton provided housing for most of his employees. It was considered part of their pay, which, of course, they never saw. The other "privilege" was shopping at the company store. It had most essentials for life in the Hills. No luxuries, only necessities and limited choices of those necessities at best.

No money ever exchanged hands at the store. Employees or family members simply signed their bill and the amount would be deducted from their take-home pay the following week. For many, their pay envelope often had an I.O.U. from the company store instead of money, since what they bought used up most of their income. Some rarely received money and were months behind in what they owed the company store.

Annie Mae kept their hut clean and orderly. She also worked her garden, raised her pigs and rabbits, kept her cow milked each morning and cared for her two young children. Tom was a hunter and regularly brought home squirrels, raccoons and turkey when one would wander too near where he was working in the woods. When resources got sparse, he would take a Saturday and hunt bigger game. Since there were no hunting seasons in the Hills, he'd go after whatever he could track, stalk or happen upon. He and Dearl often hunted together.

Annie Mae was pregnant with their sixth child. Only two were still alive. The first had died at birth. The second died a few days after being born, and the third died when it was two. Their two girls were Hope and Grace. Hope was the first to survive after the first three had died. Tom had decided to make the having of babies a spiritual matter and began to pray regularly for their health and welfare from the moment they realized Annie Mae was pregnant. The name Hope came out of their deep desire to have a baby and "hoped" God would let the baby live. Grace's name came from the pastor speaking about God's grace being a present. When Grace was born just before Christmas, they declared her a present from God.

Tom was hoping the next child would be a boy and that he also would survive. Aunt Nora had helped with all the other babies and knew that Annie Mae always had a hard time giving birth. She had suggested she and Tom not try anymore, but when Hope and Grace were born healthy, their church convinced them to try again since God was surely blessing their efforts. If the baby was a boy, they were thinking of naming him Blessing.

Her birth pains began about midnight. Aunt Nora had fallen a few weeks before and told them she probably couldn't make it, especially at night, and for them to get Manny. As Tom approached the Thompson house, he could hear Nubbin barking inside.

"Shut up, hound," Dearl yelled. He opened the door and saw Tom standing at the base of the steps. "Tom?"

"It's Annie Mae, Mr. Dearl," he said. "Baby's a-comin'."

Manny came to the door. "Tom, let me get my bag and we can go get you that baby." Tom grinned. Manny had already started dressing when she heard Nubbin. It wasn't his varmint growl, so she knew it was probably Tom. She had been over at their house earlier in the day checking on Annie Mae and felt she should be delivering soon. Tom took her bag and led them both out into the darkness, down the path toward the Mill.

"You need me to come along?" Dearl asked.

"Naw, go back to bed. We'll make it just fine," Manny answered.

"Aw-right then," he said. "Now, Tom, don't try to come to work tomorrow. You stay home and take care of that wife of yours and that new baby."

"Yas, suh," Tom replied. "Much obliged."

The path from the Thomson's home to the Tucker's was treacherous in the dark. Manny knew Tom had made the trip almost every week and could probably handle the trail blindfolded. With no moon tonight, it was almost that dark. She held his arm as he guided her up and down the small gullies and through the trails until they could see the faint light of the lantern hanging on the porch.

"Tom, I'm hopin' this one's a boy," Manny said. "Not that you ain't done good with your girls."

"If'n it pleases the Lord," Tom said, "I'd shore like that, too. Done spent the better part of the day askin' Him for it."

"Well, the baby's already what it's gonna be, but I'll be joinin' you in that prayer."

Annie Mae struggled through the contractions. She tried to stay as calm and quiet as she could so as not to wake the girls who slept on pallets on the floor. The intensity was increasing to the point she was ready to yell when Manny and Tom walked through the door. "Hang on, Annie Mae," Tom said. "I got Miss Manny for you."

"Tom, can you get me some light in here?" Manny asked.

"Yas 'em, and then what you gonna want me to do?"

"Come over here and help keep Annie Mae calm while I get everything laid out. Now, Annie Mae, you remember what we talked about earlier?"

"Yas'em," Annie Mae groaned.

"Now there's nothin' for you to do but get through all of this. When it's time to push, I'll tell you so we can get that baby out of there." Manny laid out towels, her string and knife. "Tom, git me a butcher knife," she said. Tom handed her the large knife. She made sure Annie Mae could see it, then placed it under the bed and told Annie Mae it would help *cut* the pain. Manny knew it wouldn't, but Aunt Nora had used that to help get Annie Mae through the other deliveries. She had suggested Manny do it as well to make Annie Mae calm down and think her pains were not as strong as they really were.

Manny sent Tom out back to the rain barrel to collect a pan of water while she started a small fire in the wood-burning stove. Tom returned and set the pan there to heat the water. Annie Mae was crying. The two girls began to stir. "Annie Mae, I need you to breathe and relax as much as you can," Manny offered. "It won't be much longer, but I don't want you to get all worked up. It'll just make it harder for me to get that baby out."

"Yas 'em." Annie Mae was struggling. This made six times she had been at this point and knew what to expect, but the intensity was making it hard for her to do what Manny was asking.

Manny checked her and saw the curly black hairs of the baby's head. "Won't be long now," she announced. "Head's comin' out. Why don't we try pushin' when the next pain comes?"

Annie Mae strained through the hurt. "Good, that got things going," Manny said. "Let's get that baby the rest of the way out and see what it is." Annie Mae pushed, sweat pouring off her brow. Tom wiped it away with his hand, then wiped his hand on his trousers. As he took his hand back, a smaller hand grabbed it. Hope stood beside him looking at her momma.

"Momma's fine, Hopey," he said. "She's just havin' your little brother."

"A brother?" asked Hope.

"Well, we don't know yet," Manny answered. "But it won't be long now."

Annie Mae pushed again, hard and firm. "He's out!" Manny announced.

"He?" all three asked together.

"Yep, baby's a he. Tom, you done got that baby boy."

"Hallelujah!" Tom yelled, waking Grace. He picked her up off the pallet, grabbed Hope and danced them both around the room, tears streaming down his face. "Thank you, Jesus. Thank you, Jesus," he said over and over.

Manny laid the baby on Annie Mae's tummy and tied off the cord, cutting him free. She quickly wiped him clean with a warm, moist rag and then wrapped him in a towel and placed him in his mother's arms. Annie Mae unwrapped him and looked at him naked. "Just wanted to make sure he was a boy," she said. She kissed him, cuddled him tightly, then wrapped him back up and began to nurse him.

"Is he alright?" Tom asked.

"Yep, he's all there," she said.

"Everything looks alright to me," Manny replied. "Got a name for him, Tom?"

"Gonna name him Blessin'," Tom answered. "Blessin' Tucker. Now ain't that a name?"

"That's a real good name, Tom," Manny said. She found her thoughts rush back at the house, sixteen years ago. Dearl paced in the living room while Aunt Nora took Leland and placed him on her stomach. She remembered looking at him, seeing the promise, seeing the hope of a mother in the face of her baby, her flesh, her bone, her blood. Her life would live on in his.

When Aunt Nora had told Manny not to have any more children, her warning had fallen on deaf ears. She heard the words but never absorbed what Aunt Nora was saying. The only thing that mattered was Leland was here. And in that moment, he was there, and she was his mother. On another day, he being the only child might matter, but not then, not that day.

"Just one thang to do," Tom said. He lifted the little boy from Annie Mae's side and held him high above his head. "Lord, we shore do thank You for this fine baby boy. Thank You for gettin' Annie Mae through this and for Miss Manny coming to help. Lord, we gonna call him Blessin' 'cause You done blessed us again with another baby, and You done made that baby a boy. Lord, please let him live and help him grow up to be a good man. I know Annie Mae'll be a good momma for him but help me be a good daddy. A boy needs a good daddy. Amen."

"Amen," Annie Mae agreed.

"Tom, that was a mighty fine prayer," said Manny. "God surely done blessed you both." She gathered up the soiled sheets and towels and washed Annie Mae and helped her get resettled in the bed. She checked Blessin' and placed him back in his mother's arms. She gathered up her bag and said, "Well, guess I'm 'bout done here. I'm gonna head on back home now. Annie Mae, I'll check back on you sometime in the morning and see how you and little Blessin' are doin'."

"Thank you, Miss Manny," Annie Mae said.

"Thank you, Miss Manny," repeated Hope and Grace.

"Now you girls help yur momma real good, okay? And help her take care of that little brother of yours."

"Yas, um," the girls answered.

"Thank you, Miss Manny," Tom added. "Need me to walk you back to your house?"

"No, I'm fine, Tom. You stay here and enjoy your family. I can make it back by myself. It's breakin' daylight anyhow."

# Chapter Sixteen

THE EVENING SUN WAS BEGINNING TO SET OVER THE HILLTOP west of Pine Hollow. It had been about a month since Ralph Watkins had recorded Leland. Night was coming fast as Dearl, Manny, Leland and Billie Nell seated themselves at the table for dinner.

Though people from the Hills were poor by anyone's standard, they were never without resources for meals. Gardens, woods in which to hunt game and a willingness to share with others provided more than enough for most families. For the Thomsons, a hutch out back held a family of rabbits that provided occasional meat, a pen kept a pig being fattened up for the annual slaughter next winter, a yard full of chickens were roosting in the coop behind the pigpen. They gladly provided eggs and meat on a regular basis. Manny was the gardener and kept her family supplied with a vast assortment of fresh fruits and vegetables. Tonight, chicken and dumplings filled the bowls as the Thomsons and Billie Nell laughed through the day's events.

"It was Frank," answered Billie Nell.

"Frank Massey?" asked Manny.

"Yeah, but Miss Ida don't know," Leland added.

"Couldn't she tell the snake was dead?" Dearl asked.

"Well, she didn't really care to find out," Billie Nell said. "But if it weren't dead before she opened her desk drawer, it *was* purty soon right after."

Nubbin stirred from his sleep in front of the fireplace. He trotted over to the window and began to bark. "What on earth?" asked Manny. Everyone got up and rushed to the front door just as a late model car came into the clearing.

"Who in blazes is that coming out here so late in the day?" Manny asked as Dearl opened the screen and walked out on the porch. The others followed closely behind. Nubbin brushed past them all to be the first one to the car.

"It's that Mr. Watkins," said Billie Nell.

"I was wondering if he might ever be showin' back up here again," Manny said. "Wonder what he's been up to."

Ralph got out of his car and grabbed Nubbin by the face. "Who's a good dog? Well, hello there, Thomsons, Billie Nell. Glad Nubbin remembers me. Sorry to just drop in on you folks unannounced, but with no phone, it's kind of hard to get in touch with you."

"Well, now that you're here, come on in," Dearl announced. The two men shook hands aggressively. "You still findin' somethin' wrong with us up here just 'cause we ain't got no phone?"

"Oh, no, I'm not being critical, just apologizing for dropping in without you expecting me."

"Well, we sorta been expectin' you ever since you left the last time," Manny replied.

"Is the welcome mat still out then?"

"Manny, thank we got enough vittles for one more critter?" Dearl asked.

"Always plenty. Come on in, Mr. Watkins. Billie Nell, get Mr. Watkins a bowl of dumplin's."

"Want some tea with your supper, Mr. Watkins?" Billie Nell offered.

"Why, thank you, Billie Nell." Ralph sat at the table feeling as comfortable as if he were family. With a bowl of food set before him, they all began to eat. "Tell me, what's been going on with the Thomson family since I've been away?"

"Manny done birthed a baby all by herself," announced Billie Nell.

"You birthed a baby? Now what does that mean exactly?" Ralph asked.

"You know how babies are born, Mr. Watkins?"

"Yes, of course, but..."

"Well, ain't got no doctors up here so Aunt Nora's been the one helpin' the women have their babies for, I don't know, thirty-forty years," Dearl explained.

"And how did that bring *you* into the birthing of this baby, Manny?"

"Well, Aunt Nora fell and hurt her hip, so I had to do it."

"My, my, how is it you've learned to do this?"

"Aunt Nora's been showin' me. Said I had the gift."

"Well, there you are. Another gift. How interesting! Now, tell me about this family you helped?"

"Tom and Annie Mae Tucker. He's Dearl's logging pusher."

"Now that's a new one."

"He makes sure the men I send into the woods do what they're supposed to do," Dearl explained. "And if they get lazy, he *pushes* them to work harder."

"Aren't most of your loggers colored?"

"Yep, why?" Dearl asked.

"Manny, you helped with the birth of a colored baby?"

"Yes, sir. Why?"

"Well, shouldn't they have their own mid-wives, one of their own kind?"

"Mr. Watkins, there ain't but one kind up here in the Hills," Manny fumed. "They's just women havin' babies. It ain't no us and them. It's just us all. We take care of each other."

"You got a problem with accepting folks who might be a different color than you, Mr. Watkins?" Dearl asked. "Cause if you do..."

"No, no, not at all," Watkins replied. "It's just, where I come from…let's say people don't have the same…courtesy for others you do up here. I find it refreshing."

"I take it that means you're awright with it then?" Dearl asked.

"Well, yes, yes, of course. Just wish I could bottle it up and take it back with me," Ralph said, taking a large spoonful of dumplings into his mouth.

"Like that recording you made of me?" Leland asked.

"Something like that," Ralph answered, laughing.

"Mr. Watkins, you are one different sort of fellow," Dearl said. "Now, what brings you back to Pine Hollar?"

*Uhmm*, Ralph held up a finger, took his dishtowel-napkin and wiped his mouth. "Well, you know the recording I made of Leland during my last visit? I played it for a committee of three very important men in New York who represent The New York Conservatory of Music. They were so impressed we were able to schedule a performance at Carnegie Hall."

"You've been all the way to New York?" Leland asked.

"Yes."

"And you're already back?" Billie Nell added.

"I'm back."

"But that's clean across the whole U.S.A.," Billie Nell challenged.

"Only halfway across," corrected Leland. "Don't you ever listen to Miss Ida? You got California on one side and New York on the other and Arkansas right in the middle."

"Leland!" Billie Nell strained.

"Who is this Mr. Hall fellow?" Dearl asked.

"Hall?"

"You said Karnie Hall or somethin'."

"Oh, no, Carnegie Hall. It's a concert hall in New York City, where musicians and singers perform before large and often very important audiences."

"He ain't got no room bigger than a hall?" Dearl asked.

"No, not hallway. A hall, a rather enormous room, auditorium actually, and smaller venue rooms."

"And he built this big o' room in his house so people could come over and play their music for other folks to listen to?" asked Manny.

"Well...sure, why not. Mr. Carnegie was a philanthropist. He was a wealthy man who set up a foundation to build and maintain a beautiful facility dedicated to the performing arts. Carnegie Hall is one of the most prestigious concert halls in use today. Performers from all over the world dream of playing Carnegie Hall. A call to play there is considered the pinnacle of a musician's career."

"Leland, maybe that's who's been calling you," Billie Nell suggested.

"What did you say, Billie Nell?" Mr. Watkins quizzed.

"She said..." Leland offered.

"I can say what I said, Leland. I said maybe it's this Mr. Carnegie who's been calling Leland," Billie Nell responded.

"Calling?"

"Aw, I was telling Miss Ida about somethin' calling to me from out there," Leland said. "I couldn't explain it to her. Guess 'cause I couldn't explain it to myself. It's just that I've had this dream, not like a night time dream, but somethin' inside me that's told me I had some place I was supposed to go to, someday, out there somewhere."

"Now, Mr. Watkins, Mr. Carnegie's hall sounds mighty nice, but what does that have to do with Leland?" Dearl asked.

"The men I met with listened to the recording and have agreed to grant Leland the opportunity to play at Carnegie Hall. It would be in conjunction with the New York Chamber Orchestra. It would be a very great honor. And I would like to take him there."

"Oh, I don't know about that," Manny stated. "Dearl?"

"Ain't so sure about this one, Mr. Watkins," Dearl said.

"Well, I had hoped to be able to better explain the proposal to you before I asked, but now that I have, please hear me out, and please think carefully about what I'm asking. The three men I told you about are as amazed at Leland's talent as I and have scheduled Leland to play on April the eleventh."

"In New York?" shouted Leland.

"Yes."

"You done did that without askin' us?" Manny snapped.

"Well, yes. What I had hoped to do was see if I could get everything set up before I told you about it, in case it didn't work out. I didn't want Leland to feel rejected."

"Because he couldn't play in some place he ain't never seen or heard about before?" Dearl asked. "Mr. Watkins, we don't rightly see how what some men in New York do or don't do could make Leland feel anything here."

"My point is," Ralph offered, "they did. They want Leland to play and have scheduled a date for him in less than two months. He'll not be doing a full concert, only one piece from *The Suites* by Bach that we've been experimenting with. Now, my question to you is: May I take him to New York so he can play at Carnegie Hall?"

"Well..." Dearl pondered.

"Dearl!" Manny reeled.

"Dearl, are you open to me taking him there?" Ralph prodded.

"Not really," Dearl answered.

"No? But, Mr. Thomson, I..."

"If there be any takin' to do, I reckon we'd do the takin' ourselves," Dearl responded.

"You're saying you would drive all the way to New York so that Leland could play this concert?" Ralph quizzed.

"We can *all* go to New York?" Leland asked.

"Don't see why not," Dearl said. "That alright with you, Mr. Watkins? The whole bunch of us going? Might be a good vacation. Ain't never been that far before, but I 'spect we could make it."

"Well...this creates an interesting twist I wasn't expecting. But what if I make the arrangements and you all go with me," Ralph answered.

"Even better," Dearl said.

"Oh, Leland," Billie Nell said, leaning over and giving him a peck on the cheek. "I'm so proud of you."

"Can Billie Nell come, too?" Leland asked.

"Do you mean it? Would that be alright, Mr. Thomson?" Billie Nell squealed.

"I reckon Manny would like another female going along with us," added Dearl. "Okay with you, Mr. Watkins?"

"By all means. Now I do have some arrangements to take care of. Instead of a party of two, we now seem to have become a party of five."

"Leland, we're going to New York!" Billie Nell shouted. "Can you believe it? Won't Miss Ida thank we're something now! Bet *she* ain't never been to New York."

"Yep, we're shore somethin' now," Leland said.

"And maybe you get to meet this Mr. Carnegie and find out why he's been callin' out to you," Manny added.

Leland smiled, got up and walked over to get his cello. He sat down and began to play an Irish jig. Dearl and Manny got up and danced across the living room. Ralph looked over at Billie Nell who was clapping to the beat. He got up, bowed, took her hand and followed Dearl and Manny, twirling and spinning Billie Nell around the room. Nubbin just slept soundly in front of the fireplace.

The house was quiet. Dearl had undressed and lay in the bed watching Manny brushing out her hair. "Why do you do that?" he asked.

"Do what?"

"Brush your hair so many times."

"It's just what women do, Dearl."

She continued. He watched. "You countin' or somethin'?"

"Yeah, and every time you say somethin' I have to start all over, so hush up."

The moon shone brightly through the window frame, setting a beam across the foot of their bed. Dearl continued watching as Manny removed her housecoat and laid it across the chair in the corner of the room. She walked over to the window and stood silent, gazing out into the darkness, her form silhouetted by the moon. She pulled the curtain over to block out the light. Dearl watched her make her way to the bed in the dark. He pulled back the covers as she slid in. He left his arm lying across her side of the bed, and as she lay back against it, he pulled her over to his chest. "Manny, we gotta let him do this."

"I know. I'm just thankin' what if he don't come back, Dearl? He's all we got. I just can't thank about him not bein' here."

"But he's sixteen. He and Billie Nell's gonna be gettin' married before long. He ain't gonna be here much longer anyway."

"I don't mean in the house. I mean here in our lives, in the Hills. Right down the road. I want to see him and Billie Nell. I want to birth their babies then hold them in my arms. I don't want him to go away. If he goes away, he won't be Leland no more."

"Oh, Manny…"

"Don't, oh, Manny me, Dearl. He's my only baby. We ain't havin' no more. I always thought we'd have a bunch of young 'uns."

"You know what Aunt Nora said…"

"I know, and I ain't sayin' I don't accept that. I'm just sayin' I don't wanna lose the only one I got. That's all I'm sayin'."

"Leland is Leland. That ain't gonna change. You ain't gonna lose him."

"Dearl, you know how a bird won't have anythin' to do with her young uns after a human touches them? They just don't smell the same to 'em. The momma knows somethin's different. That's what's gonna happen to Leland, and I know it."

"Manny, you ain't no momma bird. They don't love their babies. They're just doin' their job. You love Leland and Leland loves you.

Ain't nothin' gonna change that. Lettin' him go find whatever's callin to him out there don't mean we're gonna lose him. He'll be back… someday."

The darkness became heavy as Manny softly whimpered, her tears pooling on Dearl's chest. Dearl rubbed his hand across her arm and held her tightly. He looked up at the ceiling, felt the hot sting in his throat, and soon a droplet trickled down from the corner of his own eye.

# Chapter Seventeen

THE DRONE OF THE JET ENGINES KEPT A CONSTANT BUZZ IN THE air. Ralph sat asleep; the cup of coffee on the tray before him rippled from the vibration and turbulence. Billie Nell sat beside him, absorbed in a stack of magazines. With each fascinating page, she'd breathe out a long, slow "ooh." Leland occupied the window seat, forehead pressed against the glass. He kept trying to get Billie Nell to look at the things he saw, but she only replied with "uh, huh" and returned to her magazines.

Across the aisle, Dearl mirrored Leland, forehead pressed against the window, pointing out things for Manny to look at. Manny sat petrified in her seat, staring straight ahead, shaking her head sharply to each of Dearl's insistences that she look outside.

The attendant stopped by and asked if anyone needed anything. "I need to go to out back," Billie Nell answered.

"Out back? Haven't heard that one," the flight attendant laughed. "We have lavatories in the aft of the plane."

"Huh? What's a lavatory?"

"We call the outhouse a lavatory," she whispered. "They're in the back of the plane."

"OK, but any idea how I get over Mr. Watkins?"

"Sir?" the stewardess touched Ralph's arm and he jerked awake. "I'm sorry, sir, but the young lady requests use of the lavatory."

"Oh, I'm sorry, Billie Nell," he said, grabbing his coffee, setting up his tray and stepping out in the aisle. When Billie Nell passed by, Ralph sat back down and leaned over to Leland. "Leland, we need to discuss something about when you play."

"What's that?" Leland asked, never looking away from the window.

Ralph pursed his lips and released a sigh through his nose. "It's your habit of praying before you play." Leland sat back in his seat and looked at Ralph. "Son, is there any way you can play without doing that?"

"Not pray?"

"Oh, you can pray. Just do it before you go on stage, you know, instead of when you're sitting there ready to play?"

Leland stared hard at the back of the seat in front of him. "I don't know. It don't feel right."

"I think in this case it might help matters, for me at least," Ralph began. "There are going to be a lot of people there who might not understand what you are doing or why. They may not like waiting for you to play."

"So, you don't want me doin' what I do all the time, the way I always do it, because folks won't understand?"

"Is that alright?"

"Well, I ain't never done it that way before."

"You've never played Carnegie Hall before either. First time for a lot of things, don't you think?"

"I don't know. It don't feel right."

"Well, let's just see. You never know."

"What if I can't play?"

"Oh, let's just wait and see, OK?"

"Mr. Watkins?" Billie Nell asked.

"Oh, Billie Nell, here, let me get up."

As Billie Nell settled back into her seat and magazines, Ralph rested his head back on the headrest, closed his eyes and soon returned to his nap. Leland looked out the window, but this time without focusing on anything he saw. Now he simply stared out into the space, forehead wrinkled, lips tight.

Dearl leaned across Manny. "Leland, look at how little everythin' is down there. Now I know what it's like to soar with wings like eagles."

"Well, I'd a whole lot rather be scratchin' down there with the hens right about now," Manny snapped.

# Chapter Eighteen

THE GRAND HOTEL HAD NEVER SEEMED MORE GRANDIOSE TO any guests than to the foursome from the Hills of Arkansas. Ralph had checked them in and gotten them get settled into their room. He and Leland left to attend a rehearsal at Carnegie Hall.

"Manny, would you look at the size of this room. It's bigger'n our whole house," exclaimed Dearl.

"Shore is fancy and all. Kinda makes you not want to touch anythang," replied Manny

"But Mr. Watkins said to make ourselves at home," Billie Nell said.

"Well then, 'spect we ought to start touchin' stuff," Dearl said, reaching for the curtains. Manny and Billie Nell began to run around the hotel room laughing, touching lamps, chairs, tables, floral arrangements, pictures, any and everything. Dearl opened the curtain, and the skyline of New York loomed before him.

"Whoooo, you gotta see this," he said. They all stood at the window with mouths gaping wide until Manny began to feel the same swirling in her stomach she had experienced on the airplane. She backed away, found the corner of the bed and sat down.

Andrea Cacucci was a tall, slender man in his fifties, yet his flowing, white hair made him seem much older, especially to Leland. Even standing at a high table marking the lighting order with a technician, he projected absolute command. He showed no warmth in his face, yet in his eyes Leland could sense a deep kinship.

Ralph and Leland walked up to the table. Cacucci remained focused on the lighting issues. When he had completed the assignments, he looked down at them. Ralph began the introductions.

"Maestro, may I present cellist Mr. Leland Thomson. Leland, this is Maestro Cacucci."

"Well, Mr. Watkins, so this is your find from the backwoods of Arkansas," Cacucci began. Ralph smiled and nodded, urging Leland to extend his hand to the Maestro.

"Mr. Thomson, I've heard remarkable things about you, most rather...implausible, I must say," he said stoically. "But in a moment or two we will see, won't we."

"Mr. Maestro, I'd rather you just call me Leland. That's what everyone else calls me."

"So, we add familiarity to implausible. Very well, *Leland*, let's go meet the chamber orchestra."

Cacucci escorted Leland on stage. Ralph followed but stopped at the back of the violins. Leland was captured by the size and magnificence of the concert hall. He never even saw the orchestra. He was drawn back by the sounds.

Most of the musicians were warming up, playing different parts of their music, not even on the same piece, some running arpeggios, some talking, some sitting quietly. Cacucci took his baton and tapped the stand. The strange music faded away and now every musician looked at Leland. Leland, however, still faced the auditorium.

Cacucci looked around for Leland and realized he had wandered over to the edge of the stage where he stood, rapt by the vastness of the room. Cacucci stepped off the riser, took him by the arm and returned him to face the orchestra.

"I know you have heard about our guest cellist for tonight's performance," he began. "Ladies and gentlemen, I would like to present to you Mr. Leland Thomson, cellist."

The chamber orchestra tapped their legs in a polite yet muffled applause. Leland looked around and grinned. "What a turnip!" whispered the bass player. Beyond Leland's hearing, a violist said, "boonie." The principle cellist spoke a bit louder, "Look, a real live hillbilly." Cacucci glared sharply. Leland glanced over nervously at Ralph who smiled back with a calming assurance that settled Leland for the first time since they came into the hall.

"Well, there are many questions surrounding this young man," Cacucci began, "and I, for one, would like to have a few answered. Mr. Watkins, I know you've just made it here, but would you be so kind as to have Leland play for us?"

Leland shot a look at Ralph who again smiled at him and nodded for Leland to get his cello from the wings. Leland slowly walked past Ralph, who stopped him and placed his hand on Leland's shoulder. "This is alright. Just imagine you're back home and Nubbin's asleep in front of the fireplace. You can do this."

Leland came back, cello in hand. Cacucci set a chair in front of the orchestra. Leland took his seat, tightened his bow and began to flow across the strings in strangely disjointed arpeggios. In his confusion of being in such a strange place, he had forgotten to tune. Puffs of disgust came from the cello section.

"Let's tune, shall we?" Cacucci pointed to the principle violinist who drew out an "A." Leland stopped, set his bow in his lap and listened. When she stopped, Leland picked up his bow and tuned his strings. Cacucci pointed to the violinist again. She played her "A." Leland stopped, set his bow in his lap and listened. Cacucci looked over at Ralph who said, "That's fine. He has it in memory now."

When Leland finished tuning, he looked over at Ralph, who nodded that he look at Cacucci. The Maestro presented the floor to Leland. Leland looked back at Ralph. "Just begin the *First Suite*," he mouthed.

Leland closed his eyes and began to mumble inaudibly. Cacucci darted a glare at Ralph, who smiled a tight grin that indicated his embarrassment, shrugged and said, "It's OK, give him a moment to settle down." Leland turned his face upwards, and with eyes still closed began to play Bach's *First Suite* with great expression, sensitivity and movement.

The orchestra froze in rapt attention. Even the cellists, who had been carrying on their own conversation to this point now strained to watch the young boy play. Cacucci closed his own eyes and felt himself being carried away by the brilliance of Leland's playing.

# Chapter Nineteen

WATKINS HAD LEFT DIRECTIONS FOR DEARL, MANNY AND Billie Nell to get to Carnegie Hall from the Grand Hotel. It was but a six-block walk one way, then one block over to the right. *Shouldn't be too complicated for a man who made his living finding his way through forests,* Ralph had thought.

What he hadn't taken into consideration was the length of time it might take three people to dress in the finery he had provided and then cover the short distance seeing things they had never even imagined.

"Would you just look at how fast everbody's walkin' around here?" Manny kept saying as they made their way to Carnegie.

The orchestra was already warming up when Dearl opened the door to the opulent foyer. The lobby at Carnegie was more spectacular than even the Grand Hotel. Each sparkling light on the chandeliers reflected off the marble walls and floors. Giant mirrors gave vastness to the depth and width of the narrow entry. The doors had yet to open and the patrons were shuffling around in the foyer. With so many present, the room was quite crowded.

"This must be Mr. Carnegie's hall that Mr. Watkins was tellin' us about," Manny said as she and Billie Nell swirled about on the shiny floor. "Sure, a lot of folks in here."

"Would you look at the hide that woman's wearing," Dearl exclaimed. "Don't get too close; you might get it all over you."

"I'd sure hate to try and eat wearin' that thang," said Manny. "You'd get hair in everythang on your plate."

"Do you thank we'll be seein' Leland before he plays?" asked Billie Nell.

"No. Mr. Watkins said we'd just be in the way," Manny answered. "They must be havin' a lot of people playin' tonight, so I guess it's gonna get crowded in there. 'Spect he didn't need us to add to it."

Dearl looked from one end of the lobby to the other. "Well, this is some place," he said. "Why don't they have any chairs to sit on in here? Some of them older folks gonna get mighty tired standin' until this thang's over."

"Where's Leland gonna play?" Manny asked. "They ain't even got him a chair. Looks like they ain't ready at all for this thing to start. What time did Mr. Watkins say, Dearl?"

"Oh, 'bout now, I reckon."

"Look," said Billie Nell, "them doors are opened on the side of this hall and the people are leavin'."

"Well, ain't that somethin'," replied Dearl. "Guess they just got tired of waitin' and gonna leave."

"I thank we're supposed to go with 'em," suggested Billie Nell. The three followed along with the crowd. As they entered the expansive auditorium of the main venue, Manny staggered. "Whoa, now this place can make a person dizzier than riding a spinnin' jenny."

"Well, don't look up; just look at where you're goin'," Dearl offered.

"May I see your tickets, sir," asked a uniformed usher.

"Tickets?" Dearl reeled.

"Yes, sir. I need to see your tickets to see where your seats are located?"

"Do reckon we have any tickets," Dearl said.

"You know, Dearl, the ones Mr. Watkins gave you," she replied.

"Uh oh, I plum forgot 'em. I flat left them back at our hotel room."

"Oh, Dearl!"

"You'll need a ticket to be seated, sir."

"But our boy..."

"There's Mr. Watkins," Billie Nell announced. "He's comin' over here."

Ralph walked up to the usher and asked, "Is there a problem?"

"Mr. Watkins, I believe I've done messed things up pretty bad. Seems this officer here won't let us in without our tickets."

"But I gave you your tickets in the room, remember?"

"I 'spect I left 'em in my other pants back at the hotel room when I was puttin' on my fancy duds. Ain't I a sight?"

"I believe that says it quite well," laughed Ralph. "Well, we'll take care of this another way. Officer," he winked at the usher, "these folks are with me and will be joining me in my box."

"Sure thing, Mr. Watkins. Enjoy the concert, folks."

Ralph led them off to a side stairwell, then down a hallway that took them to his box seats. Manny and Dearl kept turning toward each other.

"I don't know about this," Manny said to Dearl.

"Well, seems strange to me too," Dearl replied.

"Could I help with anything?" asked Ralph.

"Well, we was just wonderin' how big this box is and if we're all gonna fit into it," Dearl answered.

"Ha!" burst Ralph again. Their host opened the door, welcoming them inside. "I believe you'll find these accommodations...fitting. Now you go on and get comfortable," he continued. "I'll join you in a few minutes. And, Dearl, I must say, yes, you look rather dashing in your tux tonight."

"Cleaned up right nice, didn't I." Dearl walked over to the banister and looked out into the grand expanse of the hall. "Whoooo." He backed away quickly. "Now I'm the one gettin' dizzy."

Manny grabbed his arm and pulled him into his seat. "Oh, Dearl, you done flew all the way out here nearly hangin' your fool head out the window of that airplane, then went outside our hotel room and looked over the fence hollerin' at the folks down below, and now you can't handle bein' up here in Mr. Watkins' box?"

"Close your eyes, Mr. Thomson," suggested Billie Nell.

Dearl closed his eyes as he sat into the luxurious seats. "My head's still a swirlin'."

The house lights flashed, and the house quieted. "What's wrong with the lights in here?" Billie Nell asked.

"I don't know, but it sure got everbody's attention," replied Dearl.

"I wonder when Leland's gonna play." Manny said.

The size of the crowd was overwhelming for a boy from the Hills. Actually, it would be quite overwhelming for anyone from anywhere, for in that auditorium sat those whose prominence went beyond airs and prestige, whose status was accompanied by years of discriminating appreciation for fine music. This was Leland's test, the moment Watkins felt would give notoriety to an obscure wunderkind. For himself, it held his own credibility in a balance so fragile that innumerable unknown factors could send it in directions that even he wasn't prepared for it to go.

Leland stood in the wings, watching the people as they found their seats and began to read their programs. He could read their lips and understand the common questions of who this boy was and... Arkansas?

Watkins placed a steadying hand on Leland's shoulder, wishing for one in return from anyone who might sense the pressure he also felt in that moment. Cacucci unwittingly obliged as he brushed past, coming in from the Green Room. Not the comforting hand Ralph longed for, but still welcomed, Cacucci patted him on the back and cantered out a brisk, "Well, here we go, Watkins."

"Leland, I'm going to sit in the box up there with your family," Ralph said, pointing to his family. "Are you okay with that?"

"Sure, I guess," came a weak reply.

"If you need me to, I'll come down here for when you play."

✄

"Everyone excited?" Ralph said as he entered the box and found his seat.

"All but Dearl," Manny said. "He's done gotten himself light-headed."

"Is there anything we need to do for you, Dearl?" asked Ralph.

"Naw, I'll get better. Just this place's makin' me kinda dizzy."

"It's a spatial disorder. The room is too large for your eyes to adjust to and it's causing dizziness as they try to focus. It happens to a lot of people. You'll acclimate to the room soon."

"Ain't sure what you just said, but the longer I sit here the better it's gettin'."

"Good. How about you, Billie Nell?"

"Uh, oh, now they're goin' out. What's wrong with the lights in here?" Billie Nell asked.

"They use the lights as signals to tell everyone what's going on," Ralph explained. "They flash them to tell us there is five minutes before the concert begins. When they dim, it's time to start."

The audience applauded as the concertmaster walked onto the stage.

"Well, ain't that somethin'?" Manny whispered. "How come they's clappin' for that woman comin' in late?"

"Concertmaster," Ralph replied. "She's the concertmaster. She's the first violinist, the principle player of the chamber orchestra." Ralph looked into blank eyes. "She comes in when it's time to begin and gets the orchestra tuned and ready for the conductor."

The concertmaster sounded a concert "A." The chamber orchestra matched her note and began tuning their instruments. "Whoa, that's about the awfullest racket I ever listened to. I thank I can play that good," Dearl complained.

"They're tuning, Dearl."

"Oh."

The concertmaster took her seat and the orchestra faded into silence. As they did, Cacucci entered the stage. The audience applauded his entrance. He bowed, then presented the orchestra. As he stepped on the riser and took his baton, the orchestra took their positions and began to play.

"Whoooo, yeah, now that's aw right," Dearl said.

"Dearl, we need to be quiet during the concert," reminded Ralph.

Manny hit Dearl on the arm. "Sorry, Mr. Watkins," he whispered.

The orchestra ended its first movement of the concerto. Dearl, Manny and Billie Nell burst into hearty applause. Ralph quickly grabbed one each of Dearl's and Manny's hands, cleared his throat, gaining the attention of Billie Nell. She stopped. Cacucci turned and looked up at Ralph's box. Ralph smiled a request for forgiveness and waved for Cacucci to continue.

He whispered to his guests, "Please don't applaud until everyone else does. Wait for me. When I applaud, you applaud."

"This concert stuff is mighty confusin'," Dearl whispered.

"What does applaud mean?" Billie Nell whispered back.

"Ain't quite sure, but whatever it is Mr. Watkins does, that's what we'll do," Manny suggested.

At the end of the concerto, Cacucci stepped off the riser and moved toward the audience as they applauded. Manny, Dearl and Billie Nell looked quickly at Ralph who joined the audience. They began to clap as well. When the applause subsided, Cacucci said, "Thank you for your warm response. The heart of any musician beats for the approval of his or her audience."

"Now, I know because some of you have already asked me personally, you are likely wondering about tonight's premier performer, Mr. Leland Thomson. I assure you, he is beyond any simple answer. He is not a diamond in the rough, for not even a finished diamond shines like this young man. He is beyond the word prodigy, for he is being presented at a level at which most prodigies have already arrived after years of performance.

"At sixteen, Mr. Thomson is a cellist without peer. He is beyond categorical relevance. Simple words cannot enhance or embellish what you are going to hear. He is, by simplest explanation, a gift. And it will please me greatly to share this gift with you later in the evening."

He continued, "But now, let's let Bach speak again from the instruments before you." He turned to the orchestra, raised his baton and released the *Brandenburg Concerto No. 3 in G Major.*

The chamber orchestra concluded its final movement. The audience responded. Dearl, Manny and Billie Nell turned to look at Ralph again, who nodded and began to applaud. They all joined in.

"Bravo! Bravo!" shouted Ralph.

"Why they yellin'?" Billie Nell whispered.

"Don't know but it seems like the thang to do," Dearl answered.

"Bravo! Bravo!" copied Dearl, Manny and Billie Nell.

Ralph laughed heartily at his friends and continued to applaud.

# *Chapter Twenty*

"WHERE ARE THEY GOIN'?" BILLIE NELL ASKED. "IS THE CONcert over?"

"Ain't Leland gonna play?" asked Manny.

"This is called intermission," Ralph responded. "The orchestra is going to take a break."

"A break?" Dearl wondered. "They been sittin' the whole time."

"They use a lot of energy playing as they do," Ralph explained, "and we've been sitting quite a while, too. I for one would like to stand and stretch my legs. They'll be back for the remainder of the concert in a few minutes; then Leland will play."

"Come to thank of it, my legs could use a bit of stretchin' too," said Dearl.

"Well, Manny, how do you like the concert thus far?" Ralph asked.

"You know, it ain't my kind of music," Manny replied, "but it's real good. Those orchestra folks sure know how to play them thangs."

"Yes, they do." Ralph stood to stretch. "You might want to get up and walk around, too, Billie Nell. How's your light-headedness, Dearl?"

"I thank I done got used to thangs in here."

They all left their chairs and walked back to the railing. "Since we have a few minutes, let me point out a few things about this wonderful concert hall," Ralph said as he began his lecture on the history and architecture of the building. He told them of the construction of the building, the acoustics and the exquisite chandelier. He gave them a quick synopsis of some of the musicians who had played there, the conductors, the pieces performed, none of whom bore more significance to them than the one they were waiting to hear.

"There go them lights again," Billie Nell announced.

"Meaning?" Ralph quizzed.

"We got five minutes to sit down," she beamed.

"Yes. Shall we take our seats?"

"Where's all the orchestra people?" whispered Billie Nell.

"Well, most are simply backstage, off to the side. Some are in the Green Room," Ralph explained. "They can sit around and enjoy refreshments while they take their break. There are also TV monitors broadcasting what's going on out on the stage to help them know how much time they have before they need to return."

The house lights dimmed, and the murmur of the crowd died down. Maestro Cacucci walked back on stage to the thunderous applause of the audience.

"Maestro Cacucci is going to introduce Leland," answered Ralph.

Cacucci took the microphone. Ralph leaned forward in his chair and squirmed. Dearl placed his hand on Ralph's arm. "Hang in there, Mr. Watkins."

"Ladies and gentlemen, when we look back on our lives, evaluating how we have spent our time, we will find much of it mundane, routine and ordinary. For the next few minutes, however, I am confident you are going to experience a performance that will be bookmarked into your memory as one you will recall with incredible delight. You are among the privileged few to hear the premier performance of a young cellist, who fits none of the criteria imposed upon those whom most of us appreciate in the music world. But now, playing the *Unaccompanied Suites for Cello* by Bach, I present to you, Mr. Leland Thomson."

The seasoned audience applauded politely but not with overwhelming excitement. They had heard many premier performances and like most who had been given that honor, very few had their playing reach the level of their introduction.

Leland stood by the curtain listening to Cacucci's introduction, his legs and hands trembling. From out of the shadows a calming arm slipped around Leland's shoulders. "Ready, son?" came a comforting voice. Paul Perski was the principle cellist. Leland obviously didn't know him but remembered that Paul had been the first person to come up after rehearsal to tell Leland how much he had appreciated his playing.

"Yes, sir," Leland replied. "'bout as ready as a body can get, I guess."

"A bit nervous?"

"Naw, just a little skerd."

"I remember my first time to play here. I was terrified."

"Naw, I ain't skerd cause of playin', it's just…"

"Maybe this will help," Paul said as he pulled a vintage cello from its case and handed it to Leland.

"What's this?"

"Leland, tonight is a special night. You are a special young man. I want you to play a very special cello. This cello means a great deal to me. It gives me great joy when I play it. I would like you to use it for your premiere."

"I don't thank I should be playin' somebody else's cello. You sure it's alright."

"I would be honored, and I even think Mr. Stradivarius would be happy to have you play it as well."

"Did you ask him?"

"No, he's been dead for a few hundred years."

"I ain't playin' no dead man's cello," Leland exclaimed.

"Leland, trust me, it's alright."

"What do I do with my cello?"

"It'll be right here on this table," answered the cellist. "Leland?"

"Sir?"

"Play the joy out it, my friend."

As Leland left the wings, he pulled the cello up under his arm, grabbed his bow and walked out to his chair. The murmur from the crowd caught Cacucci unprepared and he turned to look at them, then at Leland. No one had shown Leland how to carry a cello, a mistake he knew would be forgotten before Leland even finished his first measure.

Leland calmly walked up to Maestro Cacucci and shook his hand, something Ralph had insisted he do. Cacucci left the stage. Leland took his seat, tuned, looked backstage at Cacucci and Paul, who both nodded for him to play. He turned and looked up at his family in Ralph's box. Dearl, Manny and Billie Nell waved. Ralph nodded. Leland looked at the audience, then at the floor in front of him. He shook his head slowly, then began the *First Suite*. The tension in Ralph's body relaxed as Leland played beautifully and with tremendous expression. Cacucci smiled, knowing nothing he had said in his introduction would be taken as hyperbole. Paul Perski stood solemn, his eyes welling as even he felt the joy of how Leland performed.

The audience lost its breath, captured by the brilliance of his playing. As Leland opened the gift and presented his piece, they knew they were in such virgin territory that even the air was refreshed and alive with molecules never before breathed—that is, if anyone even dared to breathe, not wanting the faintest hint of sound they make to invade the space of such music. No one looked away, no one acknowledged anyone else in the room, no one dared a thought for fear that even a thought could dishonor the moment. The *Suite* was being played as Bach had heard it in his head even before he wrote it on paper. It was being played as he probably had hoped one day to have heard it played. It was being played as no one had played it before, with an exquisite emotion that would now define the piece.

But suddenly Leland stopped. He held a final note that was not the last note in the *Suite*. The note lingered as if refusing to bring conclusion to the magnificence of the remaining music. When the sound slowly faded away, even after it could be heard no more, the audience sat in stunned silence.

Leland opened his eyes, but instead of the wide-eyed grin that usually followed his play, his eyes darted fiercely around the room. The audience still held its breath not knowing how to respond. They had heard magnificence. Do they acknowledge it? The piece is not finished. Do they wait in silence? A few released nervous coughs. Cacucci looked up at Ralph. Ralph looked at Manny.

"Somethin's wrong," she said.

"Wrong, what do you mean, wrong?" Ralph asked.

"It's in his eyes," she continued. "He can't do it no more."

"No, he must. He's just begun. He has to finish the piece."

"If the boy cain't, he cain't," quipped Dearl.

Ralph waved his hand to get Leland to look at him. "Go ahead," he mouthed. "Play."

Leland shook his head and dropped his eyes to the floor in front of him.

"He's gotta pray," Manny said.

Ralph shot out of the box, down the stairs and was quickly back stage standing beside Cacucci.

"What's going on, Watkins?" Cacucci demanded.

"I'm not sure, but I believe it's my fault."

"Yours! Then you had better straighten it out. Not only is Leland not finished, there is more concert remaining. I'm going to have to remove him."

Ralph walked on stage, took the microphone and announced, "Ladies and gentlemen, permit us a moment before Leland continues his performance." Ralph set the microphone down and walked over to Leland.

"Cain't do it no more," Leland said. "It don't want to come out. It just stopped. I cain't play no more without prayin'."

"Leland, I'm sorry," began Watkins, "I was trying to take away from you something that is the greater part of why you play than I was willing to accept."

"It's a gift, Mr. Watkins."

"I know it is. Go ahead and acknowledge the gift. Pray, my boy, pray."

"You mean it?"

"Yes. I can't force you away from who you are just so I can get you to perform the way I want you to perform. By all means, pray, son. Then play like you've never played before."

Ralph took back the microphone. "Ladies and Gentlemen, again, I apologize for this interruption of Leland's performance. But there is something you need to know about this young man. He considers his talent a gift. Now I know that being gifted is not usually enough justification to play in great halls like this, but tonight it is. Leland has never been taught how to play. As difficult as this is to imagine, he plays with no musical education whatsoever. He has never had a lesson. When he discovered the cello, the gift came attached, so that from the first moment he set it between his legs, he could play.

"There is a part of Leland's story that no one has mentioned tonight. It probably would have been harder to explain had you not first heard him play. But tonight we...I... tried to separate him from his gift. I wanted to showcase him in order to display the music, not the gift. But I now realize his gift is a much greater part of his ability to play than I wanted to acknowledge. The gift was discovered through the songs he heard in church. From these hymns came the fullest expression of the gift.

"We learned by experiment that there was a direct transfer of that ability to encompass other types of music...thus, the *Suites* you are hearing tonight. But because we did not allow him to honor the gift, he seems to have used up the energy of that transference. Leland is drained and feels he cannot play any longer...unless he acknowledges the Giver of his gift. If we could permit him a moment...a moment of prayer...he will continue."

Leland looked slowly from the audience to focus upon his hands cupped in front of him. He bowed his head, closed his eyes and began to mumble. The audience began to mumble as well but not in prayer. They sounded their restlessness through faint coughs, a gentle laugh and a rising murmur. After only a few seconds, as if seeing a bird lift off his hands and soar into the air, with eyes still closed, Leland's face followed the unseen image until it seemed to stop mid-way above the audience and the ceiling. He smiled at it and nodded. Without opening his eyes, he positioned Paul's cello and began to play. But instead of the second suite he played the hymn, *Great Is Thy Faithfulness*.

Cacucci took Ralph's arm and demanded, "What is the meaning of this, Mr. Watkins? This is a hymn, not the *Suites*. What is going on here? You cannot turn this into some religious meeting. What's next, an altar call?"

"Trust me, Andrea. You'll get your *Suites*. Just give the boy what he needs to do in order to bring all of himself into this moment."

From the Green Room, the orchestra watched the monitors. They saw Paul Perski walk out from the wings onto the stage with Leland's cello. He sat in his chair and began to play counterpoint to Leland's melody. Soon others from the orchestra filtered in and took their seats. Without direction or music, they began to improvise around Leland's and Paul's playing. Cacucci stood in the wings watching until from somewhere deep within him he knew his place was on the riser. He walked out, took his baton and though unnecessary, waved his stick with the movement of the music. He, too, joined the song.

Leland, with eyes still closed and heart pouring out the music, never knew the orchestra was there. He played on as though it were just the cello, the gift and himself.

# *Chapter Twenty-One*

THE AUDITORIUM FINALLY CLEARED EXCEPT FOR MANNY, Dearl and Billie Nell. Watkins had told them to remain in their seats following the concert so they wouldn't get lost in the crowd and he'd know where they were.

"Well, Daddy," said Manny, "I thought that was right nice."

"Yep, the boy did himself proud," Dearl added.

"Well, I still thank it was rude for all these people to start yelling at him after he got done," Billie Nell puffed.

"Oh, it didn't seem to bother nobody but you, Billie Nell," Manny said. "The way they said it and the look on their faces made you thank that weren't no bad thang. Now where is that Mr. Watkins? Somebody's gonna come in here and make us get out in a minute, and we ain't gonna know where to go to."

Principles and season ticket holders filled the Green Room, awaiting the chance to be seen standing close to Leland more so than to imbibe in the free libations, typical aggrandizing after a good performance. Watkins, fully recovered from his spiritual introspection, beamed as he moved Leland through the crowd, making introductions and telling a now much-condensed version of the story about getting Leland from Pine Hollow to Carnegie Hall.

Steinman, Chadwick and Peterson moved together through the room. Their matching tweed jackets reflected their independent conformity. Ralph saw them coming. He took Leland by the arm and drew him into the tight circle they had made, blocking all others. Everyone watched. To be congratulated for a performance by the Regents was extraordinary. Rarely did they even come into the Green Room after a performance, feeling it more of a social experience than sincere gratitude for the level of play just performed.

"Gentlemen, Leland Thomson," Ralph introduced.

Each man shook hands with Leland in turn. "Remarkable, young man," said Peterson.

"Outstanding. Simply outstanding," added Chadwick.

"Young man," began Steinman, "I mean this sincerely. It is my honor to meet you tonight. You are, without a doubt, the most exceptional cellist I have ever had the pleasure of hearing."

"Well, thank you," Leland said, then turned to Ralph. "Mr. Watkins, have you seen my folks?"

"Augh," groaned Watkins, "I forgot your parents. Gentlemen, please excuse me." He spun and rushed from the reception back out onto stage. There was Leland's family, still sitting in the box where he had left them.

"There he is," pointed Billie Nell.

"Folks, I'm sorry to have left you so long, please come around to these side steps and let me take you to the Green Room."

Manny, Dearl and Billie Nell got up and made their way to the side of the stage. "Why would they name a room by the color it was painted?" asked Dearl.

"Don't rightly know," answered Manny. "In a place this big you figure they're gonna run out of names for all of 'em after a while. Maybe colorin' 'em helps keep 'em straight."

Since Leland clearly was the main attraction, Watkins had no problem slipping the three into the room without fanfare. They hadn't been in the room long until Leland noticed and flashed a wide-eyed grin. He looked quickly at the Regents and said, "Them's my folks." He walked away, slipping through the crowd and finally was back together with his family. Manny hugged her boy and Dearl stood by patting him on the shoulder. "Mighty fine," Dearl kept saying, "mighty fine."

"What did you thank, Billie Nell?" Leland asked.

"Oh, Leland, you was good and you know it."

They stood in their own group while the finest of New York City elite moved away from what now seemed an unwelcome circle. No one intruded, and all stood back merely to watch, unable to imagine such roots producing the caliber of cellist they just heard. Watkins whispered into Cacucci's ear and the maestro nodded. The two men walked over to the Thomson family. "Maestro, may I present Leland's parents, Dearl and Manny Thomson, and this young lady is Miss Billie Nell Goodman."

"It is an honor to meet the parents of such a remarkable young man," Cacucci said.

"Well, thank you, Mr. Maestro," Dearl replied. "We thank a lot of him, too."

"No, it's …" Watkins began his correction, but was quickly cut off by a sharp hand from Cacucci. "Again, it is my pleasure to meet you," he said. He turned and stepped into another conversation as if to prevent any further awkwardness with the family.

"Well, Dearl, Manny, what did you think of your boy playing at Carnegie Hall?" Watkins asked.

"Wudn't all that bad," Dearl answered.

"All that bad?" Watkins bristled, "Do you realize …" He abruptly cut himself off, knowing that they indeed had no reason to see this venue as anything other than a large room, and Leland playing there as anything more than what they have heard him do on any given day back in Pine Hollow. And again, he was humbled. "Yes," Watkins said, "it wasn't bad at all, was it?"

# *Chapter Twenty-two*

THE FLIGHT TO LITTLE ROCK, THEN THE LONG DRIVE BACK TO Pine Hollow had taken its toll on Billie Nell. Even though she slept most of the ride, the strain of the trip had not let up. She slept so soundly, it was nearly noon when she walked into the kitchen.

"Well, did Miss Hoity Toity finally decide to get up?" her mom said, as she sat slouching deeply into a worn and dirty sofa. She was haggard. Her stained and wrinkled house coat draped over ragged pajamas. She squinted from the smoke drifting up from the cigarette dangling from her lips. Her hair was straight but scattered around her head. Dishes were piled high in the sink. "'Bout time. This place is a dump. Get it cleaned up."

"Momma, you wouldn't believe New York," she said. "It's like living in the woods, except instead of trees there're buildings ever'where. Tall ones, reachin' all the way to the sky."

"So, now you're some high-falutin' priss? Not around here. Start cleaning this place up, I said!"

"I will, I just want to tell you all I saw. I'm about to bust."

"Girl, if I hafta get up, it's your tail that's gonna get busted."

"But…"

"You heard me!"

"Yes 'um." She knew the routine, only the house had never been this bad. She usually kept it more orderly, but since she had been gone a week, things had built up. She got the dishes out of the sink, drew up a pan of water and set it over a fire on the stove.

"Make me some coffee. Hadn't had none since you been gone."

The lid on the drip-o-later was stuck. She got a knife and pried it loose. The grounds were covered by hairy strands of mold. The soured stench gagged her. She took the grounds outside and dumped them in the yard. She poured most of the water from the stove into the sink and washed the two halves of the coffee pot. She dried them, connected them back together and filled the top section with coffee. She poured in the rest of the hot water and set the coffee maker aside while it dripped. She methodically washed dish after dish, scraping hard to get the dried food off. Soon they were all washed, dried and put away. She wiped her hands on the dishtowel and moved over to the living room.

"Where's my coffee," her mom demanded.

"Sorry, forgot." Billie Nell took out a cup, measured out the sugar and milk and poured in the coffee. She set in on the table in front of her mom.

"Now can I tell you about my trip?"

"Not with this house looking like it does. Yur daddy's done had a fit ever' night you been gone, gittin' madder and madder that we let you go."

"But it was good to go. Please let me tell you."

"I ain't tellin' you again. Get this house cleaned up before yur daddy gets home!"

Billie Nell jerked around and started picking up clothes strewn about, taking them to the bedroom. The screen door slammed hard against the front of the house. She jumped, then slowly stepped back into the living room as her dad walked through the door.

"Well, finally it's starting to look decent around here," he growled. "'Bout time you got home."

"Hey, Daddy."

"Is that coffee any good?"

"Just made it," she said.

John Goodman was one of Dearl's loggers. He ran the loading truck. After the logs were cut and hauled to the clearing, John would snatch them up with his picker and place them onto the trailers for the truckers to transport to the mill. Dearl gave him that job because it kept him away from the other men. John would spend the day sleeping in his truck until time to load, then he'd get onto his lift and pick up the logs. He was usually alone until a truck came up. He'd load it in less than thirty minutes then the truck would leave. He had very little contact with the other men.

No one in the milling community considered themselves John's friend, nor did he consider any of them his. He was contentious and opinionated. He emasculated the black men by calling them boys or using racial slurs and denigrated the women with constant sexual suggestions. He had fought with nearly every man for one reason or another, most of the times he lost. Billie Nell was the only reason Dearl tolerated John.

"Daddy, want to hear about my trip to New York?"

"Never should've let you go off like that."

"But Daddy, it was real good."

"Thank you're somebody now 'cause you done been to New York City? Just like that high and mighty Dearl Thomson, showing off and lettin' you go with them. Like he's done got rich."

"Daddy, it weren't like that."

"So now you're all better'n us and all."

"No. I don't thank nothin' like that."

"Don't you smart mouth me." John whacked Billie Nell across the side of the face with the back of his hand. She spun around and fell against the table, bruising her eyebrow on the edge. John grabbed her, turned her back to face him and drew back his hand. She twisted out of his grip and ran out the front door.

"You get back in here and get his house cleaned up," he yelled at the door.

Dearl and Manny were sitting on the porch when Billie Nell came running up the driveway. Dearl tapped out his pipe and got up just as she hit the steps. Manny stood as well. Billie Nell buried her face into Manny's shoulder and wept bitterly.

"What's wrong, Billie Nell," Dearl asked. She sobbed louder. He looked at Manny who motioned him to wait. Soon, the crying stopped, and Billie Nell pulled back. Her eye was swollen and bloodshot. The imprint of John's hand was still visible on her cheek.

"Who did this?" Manny asked. Billie Nell shook her head.

"Billie Nell, did John do this?" Dearl asked. She looked at him then slowly nodded. Manny took her into the house, got a wet rag and began to gently wipe her face with the cool moisture. They heard the door of the truck slam shut. Dearl started up and tore out of the driveway, scattering rocks and dirt across the yard. Within a minute he was sliding to a stop in front of the Goodman house. Before the dust settled, he was pounding on the door. Billie Nell's mom answered.

"Nelda, better get John out here."

"He ain't here." Dearl stared at her with such intensity she had to look away. "John, Dearl wants to see you."

"Hey, Dearl," John chirped as he came to the door. "What brings you by?"

"Figure you know. Need you to come on outside."

"I'm alright right here. Why don't you come on in and we can sit and talk?"

"'Cause I didn't come to talk and you know it."

"Now, Dearl, I ain't sure what yor all riled up about."

"For starters, Billie Nell's moving in with us. Nelda, you pack me up some of her stuff. She and Manny'll come back tomorrow and get the rest of it."

"Hey, you ain't got no right takin' our daughter away just like that!" John shouted.

"You gave me that right when you whacked her across the face." He ripped through the screen door and grabbed John by the shirt. He pulled him outside and threw him off the porch and into the yard.

John lay on the ground crabbing away from Dearl. Dearl reached down, pulled him up and slammed him against the truck. He wadded two fistfuls of shirt into his hands and jerked John up to his face.

"If you ever so much as breathe the same air she's breathing, much less say anything to her, look at her, come near her I'll finish this. I promise. But if you ever lay a hand on her again, it will be the last thing you ever do on God's green earth. Do you understand me?"

John started to say something but looked into Dearl's eyes. Dearl tightened his grip and drew him closer to his face. "Do you understand me?"

"Yeah, I understand. Go on take her. I don't care. You can have her. She ain't worth nothin' no how."

The blow knocked John across the hood of the truck and rolled him onto the ground in front of it. Dearl walked back up the steps to the screen door, which hung loose on its hinges. Nelda stood there in the opening with a bag of clothes. John lay stunned and groggy on the ground.

"Nelda, did you hear what I told John?"

"Yeah, I heard."

"Billie Nell's gonna live with us from now on. John ain't gonna have nothing to do with her ever again."

"What about me?"

"That'll be up to Billie Nell. And until she says she wants to see you, you ain't gonna see or talk to her or get around her either. You understand what I'm sayin'?"

Nelda nodded submissively.

"How the two of you ever raised somebody like her I'll never understand."

Dearl snatched the sack out of Nelda's hand and got back in his truck. John sat up in the dirt shaking his head to regain his senses. Dearl started up the motor then leaned out the open window. "One more thang, John. Two weeks and you're out of here. Cause me any more trouble and you're fired on the spot."

Manny took Billie Nell inside and boiled some water for tea. By the time the tea was ready Billie Nell had stopped crying and was back to normal. Manny saw the transformation and realized how many times Billie Nell must have had to make that switch.

"Billie Nell, this has happened before hadn't it?" Billie Nell nodded and smiled.

"I wish there was some way you could have let us know this sooner. Stuff like this can mess your whole life up. Once or a couple of times you can just get over it and go on but when it keeps on happening you need healin'."

"But I ain't sick."

"Healin' covers a lot more than just being sick. A cut or a broken bone or a bruise on the face or on the heart all need healin'."

"Is this gonna mess me up from being a good wife to Leland?"

"Not if you don't want it to. Remember when you had the chicken pox. Well, you ain't got it no more. And you ain't contagious no more neither. Your well. And your gonna get well from this. God's good at gettin' folks well."

"But don't tell me I gotta forgive Daddy. 'Cause I cain't. He don't deserve it."

"No, he don't deserve it, but you're gonna have to forgive him. Someday. If you wanna get well, you gotta forgive."

"Manny, I cain't."

"Maybe not today but you're gonna have to. If you don't then you ain't never gonna get over this."

"But you don't know what he's done to me."

"He ain't gonna get away with all that. Dearl'll see to that and God's gonna make him pay. But holding stuff against somebody only hurts you. It'll just fester up inside you and make *you* sick."

"But he don't deserve..."

"No, he don't, but forgiveness ain't about him. It's about you and God workin' things out inside you. You gotta let go of it. Remember that story Ida Mae had you and Leland read last year about that man that had that big dead bird draped around his neck."

"Yeah?"

"Well your dad is that big dead bird. But you're the one livin' with the stink, not him. A skunk don't care how much he stinks. It's the one that gets sprayed that has to deal with it."

"Yeah, but I don't ever want to see him again. How am I gonna forgive him?"

"You go tell God you forgive him."

"That's it?"

"Well, you gotta mean it. God knows what's goin' on inside of you. You cain't lie to Him. But if you cain't say it to God it ain't real."

"Then what? Do I gotta go tell Daddy I forgive him?"

"Tellin' somebody like John ain't gonna do no good. He'll just turn it around on you and try to hurt you even more. You just gotta let it go."

"How do you let somethin' go like this?"

"Ever time you even thank about what your daddy did, you gotta remind yourself you done forgiven him, then you gotta thank about somethin' else. You cain't think about it or it'll come right back."

"What will?"

"Ever'thang you done been feelin'. Thank about it and it'll all come back, just like before."

"I don't thank I can do this."

"You can."

"Why're you so sure?"

Manny closed her eyes and sighed. She opened and looked at Billie Nell. "My Daddy was a lot like yours. He drank and would come home and beat my Momma. I tried to stop him one time and he hit me so hard it knocked me out. When I came to, I ran away to my Aunt Gertie's, til my Momma came and took me back home. So, we're kinda alike, you and me, only I didn't know what to do with all the hurt till after me and Dearl got married."

"Your daddy was like mine?" The tears again flooded her eyes.

Manny bit her lip that had begun to tremble. He was, then he found the Lord and got all changed. But what He did hurt for some time after.

"You ain't forgot about it?"

"People ain't made that way. You don't just forget. Time helps though. I thought about it all the time back then but now I hardly never thank about it."

"So someday I might not be thanking about all this?"

"Well having a good husband helps."

"Like Leland's gonna be?"

"Yep."

# Chapter Twenty-three

NINETEEN-SIXTY WAS AN EVENTFUL YEAR IN PINE HOLLOW. The small sawmill community nestled in the Ozarks of Arkansas saw its favorite son, Leland Thomson, leave for a year-long tour playing cello along with the New York Chamber Orchestra. His premier concert at Carnegie Hall set in motion a whirlwind of excitement and obligation. The schedule consisted of performances almost every night, every week, each month for the entire year. There was little time for Leland to write much less to take a break and go home for a visit. And since the only phones were at the mill office and in the Creighton's home, calling was not an option.

His mom, Manny, had taken over the midwifery from Aunt Nora. Aunt Nora had been the midwife for Pine Hollow for over forty years, but a fall this past winter left her with a broken hip. Manny took over right before Leland left. Her only instruction was the brief on-the-job training Aunt Nora had given whenever she observed Manny needed help. Aunt Nora said Manny had the gift and God would help her get the job done.

For Manny, the year turned into a particularly busy one. Back in March a late-season Canadian cold front blew in and met with some moisture that had swirled around a low coming up from the Gulf. The snowstorm dumped over a foot of snow and knocked out the little power most of the houses used. Everything shut down till the snow melted.

Not that any of the couples needed any encouragement but with little else to do in dark houses, heated by the warm, romantic glow of their wood-burning fireplaces, the baby birthing business reached an all-time high. Five couples were now pregnant. Rita Gay and George Rutledge, Sally and Luke Johnson, Gustine and Leonard Roberts, Linda Lou and Otis Taylor, and Irma and Rufus Colton.

With five ladies about half-way along, Manny began meeting with them weekly to discuss the birthing process, their pre-natal needs and the care and nurturing of babies. They'd all gather at her house and usually spend a couple of hours around the kitchen table each Saturday.

Billie Nell took care of the refreshments. Manny let her sit in on the discussions to strictly observe. Since she now lived with Manny and Dearl, any questions she had could be asked later, after all the other ladies left. Though she and Leland were not even engaged, much less married, everyone knew they would be soon and the inevitable would surely follow.

"Miss Manny?" asked Rita Gay, "I don't know if I can do all this."

"Do what?"

"You know, this…having this baby."

"Well, Rita Gay, I ain't sayin' it ain't gonna be hard, but you can and will," Manny answered. "I'll get you through it."

"Little late to be thankin' that now, don't ya thank, Rita Gay?" chided Sally.

"Well, I guess you should know, huh, Sally?" Gustine snickered.

All the ladies laughed. Sally already had three girls and an extra set of twin girls. This one came out of nowhere, at least that's what she said. The twins were born last January. She didn't think she could get pregnant so soon but there she was. She didn't really need the classes, having had so much experience, but Manny's rule was everyone came, no exceptions. She knew the experienced mothers could help her get the newer ones better prepared.

"Thank y'all better find out what's causin' all that?" Rita Gay snapped back. "If not yur gonna hafta get a bigger place." Again, the laughter roared.

The laughter was good. A lot of tension built when the reality of child birth got serious. If Manny couldn't get the ladies distracted with a funny story, she'd welcome interruptions to break the spell.

"Wait a minute," Linda Lou said. "I thought if you were usin' your own milk you couldn't make another baby."

"Don't know nothin' 'bout that but I ain't been feedin' the twins my milk," Sally said.

"Well, they ain't starvin'," Gustine said.

"Naw, they just weren't handlin' mine like the others did," Sally answered. "They were real colicky, so Aunt Nora told us to get a goat."

"A goat? How they gonna nurse from a goat?" Rita Gay asked.

"Milk the goat and give it to the twins instead of me, Rita Gay," Sally answered.

"Oh."

"The goat milk settled 'em down just fine. But then they started buttin' their heads into ever'thang." They all laughed.

"Miss Manny, what do we do if you cain't get there in time?" Irma had sat quietly as long as she could. She was the worrier. This was her first. She and Rufus were still considered newly-weds and she was the youngest of the group. Because she got pregnant so quickly, some suspected they might have jumped the gun. It was embarrassing since she was Preacher Dutton's daughter. He was the black preacher of the church at Pine Hollow, a part-time position. Full-time, he worked at the mill. He and Ernest, the mill mechanic, were brothers.

She had assured her daddy they had waited but everyone in the family was nervously counting the months. She probably got pregnant on their wedding night, Manny believed, and if so, everyone knew about when the baby should be due. But she was getting bigger, quicker than the other ladies were. Sally said it was probably twins. "I did the same thang," she told Irma. "I blew up like a dead hog with the twins." That would be fine with Irma, except that usually meant twins came early, which would give more fuel to the suspicion they hadn't waited. She asked Manny to be ready to explain all that, just in case.

While the ladies discussed everything, often in graphic detail, Dearl and the men sat outside and talked about things of manly importance: hunting, dogs, trucks and work. Having kids was the wife's job. Theirs was to keep working at the mill and make sure the roof didn't leak over the place where the wife wanted to put the baby bed. To them, everything else should continue on as usual. To the ladies, having a baby placed them in the midst of an identity change.

All of the men worked at the mill. Sawmilling was life in Pine Hollow. Most of the men worked under Dearl, out in the woods, cutting and hauling the logs. Luke, Sally's husband, used to work at the mill proper. He was apprenticing under his dad to become a sawyer. The sawyer determined the cuts to be made and oversaw the set up and processing of each log, which was critical to the accuracy of the cuts. Luke's job was to keep the saw blades sharp and aligned and learn the other responsibilities when time and work-load allowed.

The tradition of son following dad was long-standing. In a community like Pine Hollow, unless you moved away, you worked in the mill. And unless you just couldn't get along working with your dad, you usually apprenticed under him. If you were good enough, you would be expected to take over his job when he died, retired or got hurt. If you weren't good enough, you were assigned another job.

Dearl would survey the timber and mark the ones to be cut each afternoon. The following morning he'd meet with the men and coordinate them and their machinery to get to the right places to harvest the day's logs. He usually marked just enough trees for what the men could cut and haul.

Each man had an assigned job. Though one could probably do any other man's work, rarely did they mix skills in the woods. Mainly it was for safety. Each job had its own risks that usually had to be learned in time and often by mistakes.

"So what'cha hear from Leland?" Luke asked. He had missed

the birth of the twins by being too far out in the woods to get back in time. Since they didn't know there were two babies inside Sally, and not knowing they should expect them to come early, nobody was prepared for them when they did come. He'd make it for the next one, he had promised everyone, especially Sally. Luke and Sally were hitting their 30s.

Luke looked up to Dearl more than any other man. His dad had been a rough one. He worked in the mill stacking rough cut lumber and forking the stacks into the kilns. Luke had successfully learned his dad's skills, but he couldn't work with his dad. His dad complained about everything Luke did. He either did it wrong or too slow or too carelessly or not the way he wanted it done. He couldn't be pleased.

Luke had never had trouble with instructions or completing an assignment, but his dad went on like he was *dumber than a stump*, he'd often say. One day Luke had had enough and stormed out of the yard. Dearl was driving by and stopped. He knew of the strain. When Luke asked Dearl about working for him, Dearl told him to get in. He took him directly to the woods and made him his own apprentice.

As the women talked of motherhood, Dearl and the men found other topics more appealing. "What do ya hear about Leland these days?" Luke asked.

"Don't hear much," Dearl said. "We get a card ever' now and then so he can tell us where he's been but not much 'bout what he's up to."

"Where has he been?" Luke asked.

"Heck, 'bout anywhere you can name, at least in all the big cities. He's done been from one side of the country to the other and I don't know how many places in between."

"When's he comin' home?" Luke asked.

"I ain't got no idea. When we see him, I guess."

# Chapter Twenty-four

NIGHT TIME BROUGHT CRITTERS AND IMAGINATIONS ALIVE. Flo had just left Aunt Alma's house. With the kids still in the car out front, she poured her disgust of Claude into Alma's ear. "I've had it," she said over and over. "I've had it, and I'm taking the kids and going to California." Her tears were more from uncontrollable anger than hurt. She sped off into a dark night with the full moon casting long shadows across the gravel roads.

Alma waited until she became guilty for holding the story captive to her own thoughts. She woke Frank. "You need to go tell your dad that Flo left him and took the kids to California."

"What?" the groggy reply came from the sixteen-year-old. Soon he was dressed and sped off to Pine Hollow.

The roar of the dull-black, 1940 Ford coupe broke the silence of the mid-summer's night as it ground out rocks and spit them up in a heavy cloud of dust. The saplings alongside the road bent to the force of the car sucking their air behind it. The young driver wrestled frantically with the wheel to keep the car as close to the center as he could. Frank struggled to keep himself planted behind the steering column as his car bounded from ditch to ditch. To each attempt he made to correct his skid the car groaned. Where it wanted to go and where its driver wanted it to go clashed in strong disagreement. He brushed back his long, dirty-blond hair from in front of his eyes, repositioned his hand tightly on the gearshift and clenched his teeth while down-shifting to slow his car and maintain control.

"Peterson Curve! Go wide, cut in short," Frank shouted and narrowed his eyes. "Brake. Brake. Brake! Slow down you piece of junk. Slow down!" He crammed the gearshift into second and popped the clutch, hoping the engine could help slow the car.

His instructions were deliberate but far from appreciated by the coupe. He missed the short side of the curve and cut deeply into the ditch. The rear-end came around. He spun the wheel into the direction of his skid but the force of the line he had taken threw him back to the far side of the road. The coupe tilted and jerked as Frank steered into the opposing ditch, then back to the other side.

He chewed his words and spit them through his teeth, "Get-back-on-the-road!" The tires scratched at the gravel until they bit into solid hard pack. Frank took aim but the car slid into the right-hand ditch. As it lunged to free itself, it caught a row of mailboxes leaning into the path of the right rear bumper. Mail, boxes and a stand of saplings and briars growing underneath the posts filled the air with debris. A stump raked the underside of the chassis and tore lose the muffler, leaving it dragging behind the car and the motor rumbling deeply. The rear license plate, hanging by a couple of strands of bailing wire, lost its grip. It stayed behind in the ditch.

Chewing up the gravel and dirt, the Ford emerged out of its dusty cloud loudly rumbling down the narrow road. It shot past thickets of tall pines and scruffy undergrowth finally approaching the clear-cut meadow of Pine Hollow.

Though Claude lived in the foreman's house in Pine Hollow, Frank lived with his Aunt Alma at Pine Valley. Aunt Alma was his dad's oldest sister. When his mom, Lou, short for Louise, died during childbirth of a brother or sister he never knew, Aunt Alma took him away from Claude. Claude's method of dealing with torturous memories was drinking. So, after Alma came over to visit and found Claude passed out on the couch and Frank lying in his crib—dirty, hungry and crying, she took Frank home with her.

When the drinking eased up, Claude found another wife. Soon after they were married, he moved Frank back in. After a few months Claude took him back to Alma. When that marriage dissolved, he met Flo. She came along shortly after he had sworn off drinking after a revival meeting Preacher Dutton had led at the church. Everyone knew it was too soon, but he married Flo as quickly as she said yes. She brought two daughters with her, both being younger than Frank. With his dad in such a generous mood with his new family, Claude brought Frank back home.

But living with Flo was hard on both of them. She gave Frank chores instead of her girls and beat him when he refused. She even tied him to the bed when he said he wanted to go back to Aunt Alma's. The day Claude came home found Frank chained to a tree out front, he decided to pack him up and send him back to his sister's. Flo was furious and refused to release her anger. After a few days Claude went back to drinking.

The tires cut deeply into the gravel as Frank slid past the sign announcing *Creighton's Mill*. The dust overwhelmed the Ford. He crammed the car into reverse and popped the clutch. Gravel peppered the underside of the coupe. He fishtailed wide as he skidded back onto the main road into the mill town. The un-muffled engine roared, then popped as it strained to slow the coupe. He slid the car to a stop in front of the first house in the row, the one with the white-washed, picket fence and two unruly rose bushes. He shut off the engine and ran into the house. The screen door slammed hard against the outside wall as he stormed through the living room, down the hallway and into Claude's bedroom.

"Dad! Hey, Dad!" he yelled.

Claude was a short, stocky man in his mid-forties still hung-over from last night's binge. He lunged for the shotgun that leaned against the wall beside the bed, grabbed the grip and BLAM! The blast ripped a hole through the ceiling above the window, knocked the flimsy curtain off its hanger and rattled the chickens roosting in the coop in the back yard. Chickens squawked and dogs barked from nearly every house in the row.

Frank scrambled back into the hallway and stumbled onto the floor. "Dad! It's me, Frank! Don't shoot!" He pressed his face firmly against the corner of the wall and floor, his rear unprotected and sticking in the air. "Dad!"

"Fr...Fr...uh...Frank!" Claude stammered. "Mercy boy, I nearly blew your dang fool head off." He pulled his leg from under the covers, not realizing he was half-way off the bed and tumbled to the floor. Frank came over cautiously and helped him up.

"You alright?"

"What'da ya mean busting in here in the niddle of the might," Claude slurred. "Y'know better'n nat. Ever heard a'knockin'?"

"I did," Frank fired back. "And been yelling since I got out of the car."

"Well, I didn't hear." Claude squinted at the alarm clock, shook his head and strained to look again. He groaned and sat back down on the bed, grabbed his head then fell back onto the pillow.

"Dad!"

Claude lifted his eyebrows until his eyelids popped open. "What?" His eyelids began to blink, gave up the lift and closed.

"Dad, it's Flo. She took Jack and left."

Claude shook his head till he was back in the moment. "Swhat? Shwere she'd go?" He pulled himself up on his elbow, then pushed up with his hand, continuing to shake his head. He sat on the side of the saggy bed, staring at the floor, blinking his eyes. "Okay, I think I'm awake."

"After you came in and passed out on the bed—well, she'd already packed up the car—she got Jack and the girls and just left."

Claude got out of bed and staggered toward Frank, his eyes wide and intense. He grabbed him by the shoulders. "How you know that?" Claude spit fumes into Frank's face.

Frank pulled back. "She stopped by Aunt Alma's and told her. Said she was tired of you coming home drunk and was going to California." Claude stepped back rubbing his temples. He turned and faced the bed. "Aunt Alma made me come over here to tell you. Didn't thank it should wait till mornin'."

Claude spun around and rushed out the door. He brushed past Frank and knocked him against the dresser. He slammed into the wall then stumbled down the hallway to the bedroom used by Flo's two daughters and their son, Jack. He flipped on the light and stood at the doorway looking into the empty room. He walked over and took the pillow off Jack's bed, held it to his chest then threw it across the room, knocking the lamp off the dresser, sending the room back into darkness. He fought his way back down the hallway and into his bedroom. He opened the closet door only to be met by a few empty hangers left on the side of the rod Flo had used. He sat back on the bed, his glassy eyes empty and dark. He reached over and saw the empty pillow beside his. He grabbed it and threw it against the wall. His shoulders drooped as he stared lifelessly at the floor.

Frank stood at the foot of the bed rubbing the back of his shoulder from its collision with the dresser. "What you gonna do?"

Claude slowly looked up at him, anger and hurt glared from reddened eyes. "Get 'em back," he said dryly.

"You goin' after 'em?"

"Don't 'spect her to come back if I don't."

"Youn't me to go with you?"

"Ain't nobody runnin' away from me—nobody," Claude said, positioning the hurt within his heart.

"Dad, youn't me to—"

"Mr. Claude? Is you okay?" The distinctive voice of Ernest Jones rang out through the open front door. Ernest was the chief mechanic for the mill.

"What? Who's there?" Claude shouted.

"It's Ernest, Mr. Claude," Ernest said.

"What do you want, Ernest?" Claude snapped.

"Is you okay?"

"Yeah. Yeah, I'm okay."

Ernest stood bare-feet at the front screen door. His had hastily pulled up over-alls barely covering his undershirt. "We heard a shot."

"Frank woke me up," Claude yelled from his bedroom. "Grabbed my gun 'fore I knew it was him."

"'Ja hit him?" Ernest asked.

Claude breathed deeply and blinked his eyes to regain focus. "Naw, missed."

"Well, maybe next time," Ernest laughed along with the others who had joined him in front of the house. "Need anythang?"

"Naw, y'all just go on home."

"You sure?"

"Go on home, Ernest!"

"Yes, suh." Ernest stepped off the porch and he and the twenty or so folk gathered there made their way back to their houses.

Claude got up, took his clothes from the chair that he had tossed them toward when he got in and sat back on the bed. After several attempts to connect the leg hole with his foot, he threw his pants across the room. He looked at his trembling hands, brought them to his eyes and began to cry.

"Do you want me to go with you?" Frank asked slowly.

"What? Who's there?"

"Dad, it's me, Frank. Do you want me to go with you to find Flo?"

"I got enough to deal with without a nag along, uh, tag along."

"Thought you might—*sigh*—never mind."

Claude looked up. From the light spilling in from the window, he saw Frank close his eyes, heave his chest high, exhale and then slowly turn to leave. "Aw, heck, boy, just do what you want. I don't care."

"When do you want to leave?"

Claude got up and staggered against the chest of drawers. The pictures on top crashed to the floor. He held on until he regained his balance, bent over to pick up the pictures and drove his head into the wall. "Gosh dang it! What time is it?" he snapped.

Frank squinted at the alarm clock, "'bout one-thirty."

"Can't do this now," Claude said. He turned and made his way back to his bed. "Leave in the mornin'. They cain't get that far ahead. Gotta get s'more sleep." He laid back on his bed, pulled the covers to his chin and closed his eyes.

Frank headed back down the hallway. He felt his way into the living room. He adjusted the cushions on the couch and lay down, his eyes too wide to close and his heart racing to fast to relax. In the quiet of the mill town stillness, Frank stared at the ceiling and listened to the faint sobs of his heartbroken dad.

# Chapter Twenty-five

SUNLIGHT SPILLED INTO THE BEDROOM THROUGH THE HOLE above the window. Claude lay on his side, his face away from the bright light. Frank called out from the kitchen, "Dad, breakfast." He went to the door to Claude's bedroom. "Dad! Wake up. Breakfast."

Claude rolled to his back. He looked over at the empty side of his bed, then up at Frank. "Wudn't a dream, wus it?"

"Nope. Ready for breakfast?"

"Yeah, gimme a minute." Claude slowly pulled up his trousers and staggered off into the kitchen. Frank handed him a cup of coffee. He sat at the table and stared at the plate in front of him.

"Frank?" a voice called from the screen door.

"Ernest? That you?"

"Yas suh, got that oil ya wanted."

"Thanks, just put it down on the porch."

"I could put it in yo' car for y'all."

"Well, alright, if you don't mind, appreciate it," Frank replied. Ernest took the jars of thick, black oil and made his way to Frank's car. New oil wasn't that expensive but in a car like Frank's it wasn't going to stay in the engine very long anyhow. Frank's car was a smoker. The billowing, blue fog that followed the car meant it burned nearly as much oil as gas. New oil just wasn't worth it, so Frank would get used oil from Ernest. Ernest put the jars into a heavily stained, wooden crate in the corner of the trunk.

Claude ate his breakfast without saying a word, emptied his coffee cup and pushed away from the table. "Dad, you want…" Claude waved his hand. He headed down the hall to the bathroom. He splashed water into his face, brushed his teeth and brushed back the sparse crop of thinned hair with a wet rag. He went back into the bedroom and closed the door. He opened the top drawer on the chest and felt around in the back. The sock he and Flo had kept extra money in was gone. He slammed the drawer closed, grabbed his fedora and headed back into the kitchen.

Frank had brewed another pot of coffee and was pouring it into a thermos when Claude came into the kitchen. "You 'bout ready," Claude growled.

"Yep, got us some coffee for the road," Frank replied.

The screen door slammed behind them as they left the house. Ernest slid out from under the back end of the old Ford. He had a roll of wire and a pair of pliers. "Saw ya muffler was draggin' the ground, so I tied it up for ya. Ain't got time to put it all back together so it ain't gonna be as quiet as it was but least it won't be fallin' off."

Claude squinted in the morning brightness. "Where's my car?"

"Flo took it," Frank replied.

Claude turned toward the truck with *Creighton Mill* painted on the door, parked beside the house. "Well, the truck ain't mine so we cain't take it."

"My car's ready to go." Frank said happily.

"Ain't sure this heap'll make it, boy," Claude said. "California's a long way from Arkansas. Just keepin' oil in the thang's gonna take more'n we got to eat on."

"Ernest put me some in the trunk. Ought to get us pretty far down the road." Frank closed the trunk lid and turned down the locking handle. He slid into the driver's seat. Claude threw his bag into the back and settled into the passenger seat.

"Thanks again, Ernest," Frank yelled out to the mechanic. "We'll make it, Dad."

"Gotta stop by Creighton's house'n tell him what's goin' on."

The coupe roared as Frank cranked its engine. He let off the gas and it loped in a well-tuned rumble. "Well, at least it sounds strong enough. That Ernest is one heck of a mechanic to keep this heap running like this," Claude said.

"He ain't done nothin'. I did it. He just watched me. He don't tell me nothin' unless I ask. Said I'm nearly as good as him."

"Humph."

"I mean it. Gonna do a ring job when we get back."

They pulled up at the large white house just as the Creighton's were leaving for church. Frank honked as he pulled into the white-rock drive blocking their Buick. Mr. Creighton slammed on the brakes and was out of the car by the time Claude was just opening his door.

"What's the meaning of this, Massey?" he demanded.

The house never did fit in with the other houses in Pine Hollow. Where they were shanties and shotguns, some little more than shacks, the Creighton's was like a mansion. The stately, two-story, white-clapboard house with a wrap-around front porch and manicured lawn looked more fitting for a house in Lathrup Springs than Pine Hollow. Many of the loggers' wives worked at the house, both inside and out, keeping everything tidy and presentable.

"Got a problem, Mr. Creighton," Claude began.

"And it can't wait 'till tomorrow?" Mr. Creighton replied. "We're heading off for church."

"No, sir, it can't."

"Alright then, what is it?"

"Flo's done took off and left me. Done took our young 'un with her."

"Took him where?"

"California."

"Mercy, Claude."

"Yeah, I know, but I gotta go find her."

"And then what?"

"And bring her back home, of course."

"She might not want to come back. Ever think of that?"

"Don't make no matter. Me and Frank are gonna go and get her and the boy and they're all coming back with us. Just need some time off."

"How long you gonna be gone?"

"Shouldn't be more than a couple'a weeks."

"Alright. But no more. I need you back here running things."

"Sorry, but I gotta do this."

"I said alright."

"My job'll still be here when I get back?"

"You just get on and get back here. We'll manage."

Claude tipped his hat to Mr. Creighton and got back in the car. He rolled his hand at Frank who started up the coupe, pulled out of the drive and back onto the road.

The old Ford roared as it sped down the row of shanties, past the company store and back to the main road. Two small children turned from watching the embers explode and shoot upwards from the burn pile. Frank glanced over and saw the embers rise high on the hot currents. The smell of smoke blew in through the windows. In return, the Ford billowed out its own smoke from the dangling tailpipe, fogging the road, obscuring the car as it sped off. The children waved goodbye.

There was only one church in Pine Hollow. It was a mixture of denominations, sort of a blend of Baptist and Pentecostal. Ernest's brother, Preacher Dutton Jones was a *hollerer*, at least that's how the people described him whenever anyone who didn't already know asked. He'd yell and pound the pulpit and pace back and forth across the stage, then he'd bend over and whisper so quietly you'd have to strain to hear, but somehow loudly enough to still be heard in the back of the auditorium. Never were many sleepers in a service where Preacher Dutton was preaching.

But let the worship time begin and this wild-eyed prophet would melt like a stick of butter in a hot skillet. Somehow the songs just changed his temperament. Where, in a message he'd glare the devil out of you, when the singing started, he'd tear up so badly sometimes he'd just have to sit down and cry. You never knew what might happen on any given Sunday. The test of it being a good Sunday was how much crying and yelling he did, how much of his pants' legs he was stepping on at the end of the service, and if his shirt tail was hanging out from under his belt. He definitely got into the service both in body and spirit.

The Creighton's went to church down in Lathrup Springs. They were Methodists. They liked the predictable. They knew the program would be followed and everything done in order. Church was much tidier there than in Pine Hollow and the people more like the Creighton's than not. The services were stale, worn out and lifeless. But they fit the Creighton's expectations.

On the way back to Pine Hollow, Mr. Creighton said, "I need to stop by the Thomsons before we go home." His wife was listening but unresponsive. She rarely had an opinion contrary to his.

Seeing the big blue Buick pulling up to the house was enough to have Dearl, Manny and Billie Nell out on the porch even before the engine was turned off. The Thomsons had already been to church and were just finishing up lunch.

"Mr. Creighton?" asked Dearl.

"Got a problem, Dearl," he began. "Somewhere we can talk?" Dearl nodded toward the tool shed.

"Manny see if Mrs. Creighton wants to come in?" he asked. Manny and Billie Nell started walking down to the car.

"Oh, she's alright," Mr. Creighton answered back. "We'll be just a minute."

Mrs. Creighton got out of the car and the three ladies stood beside it and shared their visit.

Mr. Creighton began, "Claude had to take off for a few days."

"What?" Dearl reeled.

"I know. He couldn't have picked a worse time since we have all that new equipment coming in this week, but Flo left him last night and took off to California with the girls and their kid. He wouldn't be much use to us anyway. He's gone to try and catch up to her and get them back."

"I might be tempted to just let her go."

"You and me both, but his pride's been hurt. He and Frank left out this morning."

"He's already gone?"

"Afraid so. He met me when we were on our way to church this morning."

"How long's he gonna be gone?"

"He said a couple of weeks."

"Crud," Dearl said. His eyes darted back and forth, then peered out from underneath a deeply furrowed brow. "Let me thank about all this this afternoon. We'll figure a way. Don't worry about it. It's my problem. You and Mrs. Creighton just go on and enjoy the rest of your Sunday."

"Thanks, Dearl, we'll do that. See you in the morning. Let's go Momma," he called out to Mrs. Creighton. It was a strange name to use since they had no children. But for one reason or another it had become her pet name. They loaded back into the Buick, turned around in the yard and headed home.

# Chapter Twenty-six

"I NEED SOME GAS," FRANK SAID. THE TRIP WAS WELL INTO ITS second day and had droned on for nearly three hours since their last stop. They had hooked up with Route 66 in Oklahoma City. It would give them a relatively straight shot to Barstow, California. From there they'd have to go on intuition or luck. Claude slept most of the way, turning often to seek out a more comfortable position. He stirred and rose up.

"Where are we, now?"

"I don't know. Somewhere between here and there I'm thanking," Frank said, intending the joke that Claude missed.

"Man, I've been asleep a long time...and hungry. Got any money?"

"Nope. Used the last you gave me on gas this morning."

"Well, that was perty much the end of it, then."

"What?"

"I ain't got no more. Flo took the extra I had in the sock drawer. Just brought what I had on me. Next town we come to, we better find a store or somethin' and see if they've got some work. Guess we'll have to earn our way to California."

As the Ford pulled into Tucumcari the downtown was rolling up its sidewalks. Woodman's Hardware was the first store to catch Claude's eye. "There, that one should do. Just go in and see if the owner has anything you can do."

"Me?"

"Yeah, you. Just go on, I said."

Frank pulled into a parking space at the corner and left Claude in the car. Through the window, he could see an older man walking toward the front door carrying a chain of keys. He looked friendly, a bit over-weight, upper sixties. He stopped and clicked off a row of lights. The store went dark. He flicked another switch and a sign above the awning illuminated the words *Woodman Hardware*. As he opened the door Frank said, "Evening, sir. You Mr. Woodman?"

"Sorry, son, I just shut her down for the night," he said.

"Yes, sir, I know. Weren't needin' nothin' to buy."

"You weren't?"

"No, sir. Ain't got no money, no how."

The merchant from the store next door walked past. "Goodnight, Sam," the man said.

"See you tomorrow, Manuel," Mr. Woodman replied. He turned back to Frank. "Don't do charity, son."

"No, sir. Ain't wantin' none. Thought maybe we could do some work to earn some gas money. Maybe sweep up for you? We'd take anythang you thank might be fair."

"Don't know. Where you from?"

"Pine Hollow."

"And that would be…"

"Arkansas," Frank said proudly.

"So, where are you headed?"

"California. My dad's wife done left him and took off with their boy. We're goin' to get him back."

"Just like that?"

"Well, we gotta get there."

"Without any money?"

"We had some, but it all ran out."

"Well, I guess the store could use a good sweeping. Come on in. Broom's in the back."

"Let me get my dad. He's in the car."

Sam reached in and switched the lights back on. He watched Frank through the window go back to the car. He found it curious that Frank stood there, looking around, and then disappeared around the corner. As Frank rounded the corner, he saw a large man pushing Claude out through the open door of a pool hall. Claude stumbled across the sidewalk and landed on the hood of a parked car. He turned and raised a clenched fist at the man. The man tossed Claude's fedora onto the sidewalk.

"What happened now?" Frank yelled, running across the street. Claude jerked his arm back as Frank grabbed it to help stand him back upright.

"Idiots wouldn't give a guy a drink," Claude said, reaching for his hat.

"Thought we didn't have no money?"

"Don't."

"So, you thought you'd go in there to bum a beer?"

"Needed a beer. And bummin's what you do when you don't have no money."

"Got us a job sweepin' up the hardware store."

"Us? I ain't sweepin' no floor. I'm a foreman. I run a sawmill. I tell other people to sweep. You get in there and do the sweepin'. How much he gonna pay you?"

"Won't know till we're done."

"Boy, don't never accept a job without knowin' how much you're gettin' paid. You ain't got no negotiatin' power. You just have to take whatever they give you."

"Figure'd anythang's better'n nothin'."

Mr. Woodman stood at the door and opened it when Frank and Claude came in. "Much obliged, Mister," Claude said, tipping his hat.

"This is my dad, Mr. Woodman. His name's Claude. We'll do you a real good job."

"Claude, you and your boy can come on to the back," Sam Woodman said. He turned the *open* sign to *closed* and led them back to a small broom closet in the storeroom. In the corner was a large cardboard barrel of red sawdust and beside it a trash bin.

"Just take a bucket of this red sawdust and sprinkle it on the floor. It keeps the dust from getting stirred up. You don't need too much, just a bit, so sprinkle it lightly. A little goes a long way."

"Thank we can handle it, Mister," said Claude.

Sam stared hard at Claude, turned to Frank and said, "I'll be in my office, son, upstairs. Might as well finish up some paperwork while I wait. Just holler when you're done, and we'll settle up then."

"Yes, sir," Frank said. He took the bucket and began sprinkling the floor sweep down the aisles. Claude sat on a stool in the broom closet. Frank came back with the empty bucket and tossed it into the barrel. He grabbed two brooms and handed one to his dad. Claude looked at it, leaned his head against the wall and closed his eyes. Frank sighed. Claude never said a word.

Frank went to the front of the store and began sweeping toward the back. The floor sweep worked well, no dust. He kept a good motion, stretching to catch anything hidden underneath the toe-kicks of the base cabinets. He felt eyes watching and looked up to see Mr. Woodman nodding from the window in his upstairs office. Frank was just finishing up the last aisle when Claude came out of the storeroom. "Ain't you done yet?" he asked.

"Would'a been if I'd had any help."

"Told you I'm a foreman."

"This job don't need no foreman, just peons."

"Ain't no peon," Claude snapped. "Missed a spot." He grabbed Frank's broom and brushed it under a counter. "You gotta bend down and reach under stuff. It ain't gonna just jump out in front of your broom. If you don't, see, you leave stuff."

Frank glared at his dad. "Why don't you keep that broom and help me finish up?"

"Naw, you're doing good enough. Just bend your back." Claude went back to the store room and resumed his position on the stool.

Frank looked down each aisle as he walked back through the store. He looked up at the window. Sam was standing there looking down at him. Frank waved at him and offered the room for inspection. Sam nodded, then waved him up.

Mr. Woodman was back at his desk when Frank opened the door. "Took you a little longer than I expected," he said.

"My help...uh...wudn't any help. Wanta come check it out?"

"No, I can tell from up here you did a good job." The two left the office. The noise of footsteps on the stairway stirred Claude. He quickly adjusted himself and walked out of the storeroom.

"'Spect we'd be settlin' up now," Claude said, "or do you need to do some *inspectin'* first?"

"Should, I?"

"Not unless you ain't much of a trustin' fellow."

"I believe Frank, here, has done an acceptable job."

"If not, I'll do it again," Frank offered. Claude coughed and shook his head at his son.

"Won't be necessary," Sam said. "Here's five bucks. That ought to get you something to eat and some gas."

"Five bucks?" Claude snatched the bills out of Sam's hand. "That ain't bad." He walked to the front of the store. Mr. Woodman had left the key in the door. Claude turned it and walked off down the street.

"Mr. Woodman, I'm real sorry..."

"Frank, you can't go through life apologizing for other people. Here, take this. And let's keep it just between the two of us." Sam held out another five-dollar bill. Frank's eyes widened and mouth dropped open as he stared the money. "I could always use a good worker like you, so if you ever want to move out here to Tucumcari, you've got a job."

"Thank you, sir. And I would...if I ever move out here. Thank you again."

✄

Large trucks were a common sight in Pine Hollow. The loggers drove old converted box trucks that had the boxes removed and pipes welded onto the frame to hold the logs in place. Some pulled trailers, but most were simply one-unit trucks. But the two, shiny new semis pulling into the compound in the middle of the afternoon drew out a large crowd.

The tarps covering the flatbeds concealed a new ripsaw, planer machine and crane assembly that would provide another lifting mechanism to move the logs around inside the mill. The goal was to increase the output of the mill. Instead of adding a hoot owl shift to the schedule, Claude had convinced Mr. Creighton they could increase the milling capacity, hire a few more men and get the same effect. Claude's greater concern was how much additional time he'd have to put in to get the new shift started up. Being salaried he knew he'd have to work more hours without any extra pay.

Ernest was the first one out to meet the lead truck. With Claude gone, Ernest was brought into the meeting earlier that morning with Mr. Creighton and Dearl. And since Ernest would be the man in charge of assembling the new equipment, he needed some say as to how and where it was unloaded.

The land had been cleared for the additional machinery. A new shed had been laid out. The support posts were in place, but the joists were not up yet, which meant the tin roof was not up, nor the cross beams to support the new crane. Those could be finished later. Now, they just needed to position the pieces in the location Ernest had scratched out on the dirt floor.

The trucker wheeled his rig around in the clearing and backed it into what would be a covered shed when the tin was in place. He loosened the ropes holding the tarps and pulled the canvas onto the ground. He methodically stretched out the tarp, straightening its wrinkles and began folding it into a tight bundle. Dearl and Ernest, usually patient men, stirred like caged cats, anxious to get their hands onto the new equipment. The trucker's myopic steps to unloading unsettled them both.

"Cain't you just drag that away and fold it up later?" Dearl asked.

The trucker stopped and glared at Dearl. He was a large man with the sleeves torn off his untucked, button down shirt. The arms exposed were nearly as large as Dearl's thighs, which Dearl hadn't noticed until the man turned to face him. Dearl backed away and nodded. He walked over to Ernest and the two stood still, watching the man work.

Mr. Creighton drove up in his Buick. Though the office was only a couple hundred yards away, he preferred driving to walking. Too much walking left him winded, which was the usual result to any exertion. He was a heavy, short man.

He slid the car to a stop. His wide grin was interrupted by the cigar clenched tightly in his teeth upon which he puffed veraciously as he emerged from the car along with a cloud of smoke. "Well, here it is," he announced proudly. "A bit earlier than I expected but I guess we can deal with that."

"Yep," Dearl answered. "Just waiting for it to get unloaded."

"When will we be up and running?"

"Uh, not really sure about that," Dearl said. "Figure we need to get the roof on first, then we'll get everything set up."

"Well, whatever you think."

"Gonna have to double up since Claude took off, you know. Probably have to pay some overtime. It'll take me out of the woods for a while."

"Dang it. What will you do?"

"I can put Luke in charge of the woods, I guess, and pull some of the men in and probably get it up in a few of days."

"Alright then, get on with it."

"Yes, sir."

"All right you lookers, quit standing around and watching me. I've got it unwrapped. Now it's yur job to get this stuff off my truck!" the trucker ordered.

"Yas, Suh," Ernest replied. "Tommy Boy, git that rubber-tired fork-lift over here and git this down!" Ernest was suddenly in command. Dearl smiled. Within an hour all the machinery was off the trailer and into the marked-off area. The trucker took his bill of laden to Dearl who pointed toward Ernest. The man looked back at Dearl, shrugged, then walked over to the mechanic. Ernest looked at him, then at Dearl and smiled. He took the pen and signed his name in large letters on the line marked by an X.

When Frank left the hardware store, Claude was nowhere out front. He stopped, shook his head and yelled. Sam could hear him from inside the store. Frank walked around the corner, across the street and up to the open doorway of the pool hall. Claude was sitting at the bar holding a half-gone bottle of beer. Two empties were still on the counter in front of him.

Frank went back to the car and sat on the fender, his feet on the bumper, his elbows on his knees, his chin resting in his hands. The flicker of the streetlights coming on caught his attention. Again, he yelled. He scooted up onto the hood and laid back against the windshield starring up into the warm, New Mexico sky.

# Chapter Twenty-seven

"Manny, I sure do miss Leland," Billie Nell said. "I ain't enjoyin' him bein' gone and tourin' and all."

"You and me both, girl," Manny said. "And we still got some time before he'll be comin' home. Mr. Watkins said he'd be gone for a year and we're just now 'bout halfway."

"I want me and Leland to have a family but I ain't sure I wanta make a baby right away," Billie Nell said.

"Where'd that come from? Ain't nobody said you have to have one right away. Let's get the two of you married first and then just let it happen. Lord knows when it's right."

"Miss Ida said I might could start helpin' her with the young 'uns this next school year. She thanks I might could be a teacher someday."

"She did, huh?"

"Yep."

"What do you thank about that?"

"Kinda scared. I really thank I'd like to be a teacher but ain't sure if I'd be any good at it."

"Billie Nell, there ain't nothin' I've seen you do, that you ain't good at, once you been learned to do it. Just wish it was somebody other'n Ida May Grubb doin' your learnin'."

"So, you thank I oughta?"

"That's up to you. But as far as thankin' you wouldn't be any good, that's the devil talkin'. You love school and I thank you'd love teachin' those young 'uns."

"Then I'm gonna."

"You said anythang to Leland about it in any of those letters you write him?"

"Uh, not really."

"Well, you know you cain't thank just for one no more. Y'all both need to decide what's best."

"What if he don't thank I should?"

"Oh, I'd bet he'd be okay with it. He just ought to get to help you decide, that's all. You gotta talk to him about it. Cain't go off just thanking about yourself no more."

"How'm I gonna talk to him about it? We don't even know where he is?"

"Just put it in the next letter."

"Okay. Sure hope he's alright with this, though."

Claude slept most of the day. The overnight binge had nearly put him in a coma. After the money Mr. Woodson had given them had run out, after buying a drinking buddy a bottle, the buddy pretty much opened his tab to include Claude's needs. Claude staggered back to the car around two. Frank had moved inside and was asleep on the seat. Claude banged his open hand onto the hood until Frank awoke and managed him into the back seat. Frank lay back down on the seat and quickly was asleep again.

Around six, a car pulled up beside the Ford. The uniformed officer shined his light through the window and called out, "Hey, anybody in there?"

Frank rose up. "Yes, sir," he answered, rubbing his bleary eyes.

"No sleeping in your car in town. Get up and move on."

"Yes, sir. Sorry."

"Where you heading?"

"California."

"Haven't been drinking have you?"

"No sir. I ain't old enough. My dad has but he's asleep in the back."

"Well, I my shift's about over and I don't want to mess with it, so go on and get out of here."

"Yes, sir. Thank you, sir." The Ford fired up. The loud rumble from the dislocated muffler made the officer jerk a quick glare back at Frank. He sighed and pursed his lips, shook his head and waved for Frank to back up and leave.

With exhaust forcing its way around the muffler the engine had a mellow drone. Frank began to fight hard to keep from drifting back asleep. He glanced back at his dad, crumpled up in the small backseat, dead to the world. He tightened his lips and shook his head, then stared back down the road.

The unloading went smoothly. Mr. Creighton smiled at Ernest's efficiency of getting all the right boxes into the areas he had designated. Ernest had been Mr. Creighton's chief mechanic for fifteen years. His brother Dutton came to the mill eleven years ago to be Ernest's helper but was longing to spend more time at his church. In operating a milling camp, when new equipment is brought in, the chief mechanic has priority over time and manpower until he gets everything assembled and running. There was no reason to start bringing in the extra logs until he had the mill capable of processing them.

It was a stretch for Mr. Creighton to hire Ernest. Ernest had been given a medical discharge after getting wounded while serving in the Army during the Korean War. All he could present were his discharge papers, a documentation of his purple heart and a letter of commendation. Ernest had served as a tank mechanic which kept him generally far removed from actual combat. One day a call came in for a detail to go to the edge of "Napalm Ridge" and retrieve a disabled Sherman tank. He and two other men got into a truck and rambled into the war zone and found the tank. It had thrown its track.

While they were working on the tank a helicopter came low over their heads, scraping the crest of the hill and dipping sharply to the ground. The engine was dead, but they heard the whirling as the blade continued to rotate. With no power or control it slammed hard into the ground. The impact jarred the earth as well as the three men working on the tank.

Ernest never said a word but jumped up and ran down the ravine to the Huey. He rushed in to drag out three of the four men inside. He would have gotten to the fourth except some sniper off in the distance kept firing at the chopper until he finally hit the fuel tank. It exploded and the flames fully engulfed the copter. Ernest's forearms still bore the crinkled scars from his injuries.

After all the men were rescued and subsequently transferred from the M.A.S.H. unit, the commander stopped by the hospital and presented Ernest with his Silver Star. He told Ernest he'd receive a letter of commendation when he was discharged and would get his Purple Heart at a later date.

Ernest gave the medals to his mother when he got back home but kept the letters. When Mr. Creighton asked for any references for recommendation, Ernest showed him what he had. Mr. Creighton swallowed hard, looked at Ernest and said, "The job is yours, son."

When it came to mechanics, Ernest was a natural. He explained his abilities as having a knack for being able to know what the machine was supposed to do and then fixing anything that kept it from doing that. He never used drawings or schematics. He simply *thought it through*, at least that's how he explained it.

The new shed was a duel project. While Ernest was assembling the machinery, Dearl and his crew were hoisting beams until the roof's framework was in place and secured. They then positioned and nailed down the tin. When Ernest fired up the new rip saw for a test run, he glanced up and the last section of tin was being fitted in place.

It was early morning, still dark, when they pulled out of Kingman, Arizona. Claude had decided it would be easier on the two of them and the Ford if they went through the desert at night instead of the heat of the day. He had driven them to Kingman and Frank would take over from there.

Claude settled back onto the rear seat and soon settled into a rhythmic snore. Frank fixed his eyes down the long highway to California. The sign welcoming them came unexpectedly fast, even though Frank had been looking for it as soon as they left Pine Hollow. Frank watched it come and go and was well into Needles before it hit him: they were there—at least in the state.

"Uh, Dad?" he tried. "Dad!"

"Huh?"

"We made it."

"Made what?"

"We're here, in California."

Claude raised up off the seat. "Don't look a whole lot different than Arizona."

"Well, the sign said we're here."

"You know I didn't thank this old heap was gonna get us here."

"Nothin' like a Ford, huh, Dad?"

"Guess so. But we still got a ways to go. Wake me back up when we get to Barstow."

"Alright."

It was nearing noon when the Coupe pulled into Barstow. Claude was up and sitting in the front seat. The urge to go had hit an hour or so ago and the stop at the roadside park stirred him enough that he didn't need to sleep any longer.

"Pull into that café there," Claude said. "We still got enough to get us a good meal and maybe somebody in there's seen 'em."

"Just find a seat, boys," a cheerful waitress called out. "Menus are on the table. Somebody'll be with you in a minute."

"Thank you, ma'am," Frank replied.

The waitress laughs, "Hey Gracie, the kid called me ma'am." Gracie joined her, laughing, shaking her head. Gracie walked over to the table and began clearing off the last customer's debris. She was early 20s but the years getting there gave evidence of a hard upbringing. She had been making her own way since she was fourteen. She was polite but seasoned, her white uniform showing the effects of an already long day.

"Worthless busboy," she said. "Excuse the mess, boys. He never can keep up with the mid-day crowd. This'll cost him," she said slipping the tip into her pocket. "Now, what can I get you two?"

"Yes ma'am," Frank began, "can I get your meatloaf and mashed taters?"

"You can have whatever you like, pumpkin, just stop calling me ma'am, alright? I'm not that much older than you are."

"Yes, ma'am, uh, sorry."

"Look," she said sliding into a thick southern accent, "That may be okay back in Mississippi or Alabama or wherever *you all* came from but out here in Barstow…it just doesn't fly. If you get my drift."

"Yes, Ma…." Frank stopped as quickly as he could but not fast enough to stop the glare.

"Now, Pop, what about you?"

"You'll have to excuse him, uh, lady, he ain't never been this far from Arkansas before. I'll have the same thang. And brang us a couple of teas."

"Tea?"

"Yeah, y'all got tea out here?"

"You two just don't look much like tea drinkers," she said heading back to the kitchen.

"What was that all about?" Frank asked.

"Probably some California thang."

"Thank Flo came through here?"

"I'll see if Gracie knows when she gets back."

"Miss Manny!" Sara Beth screamed. She stood at the door shuffling from one foot to the other. "Help, Miss Manny!"

"What is it, Sara Beth?" she asked, pushing back the screen door.

"Momma's bleedin', you know, down there, and she told me to go get you."

"Alright, Sara Beth," Manny said. "Billie Nell, grab my bag and come on. 'Spect I'm gonna need you to help with the kids."

"What's the matter?" Billie Nell yelled as the screen door slammed behind them. She ran to catch up with Manny and Sara Beth.

Manny pulled her close and whispered, "Sally's probably losing the baby."

"What?" Billie Nell jerked away from Manny and stopped. "I ain't gonna go over there."

"Hush. Just come on. I'm gonna need you there."

"I don't wanna see that."

"And I don't want the girls to, either. So, I'm gonna need you to keep them away. Alright?"

"Alright," she said, getting back in the trot toward the house. "Just don't make me see nothin'."

Sally was sitting in a rocker on the front porch, tears streaming down her cheeks. She stared blankly down the trail as Manny and the girls came up. Blood dripped from the back of the rocker and pooled onto the floor. "Reckon I'm losing this one," she said as Manny walked up on the steps. "It's my own fault, you know." Her voice was somber and without emotion.

"Billie Nell, round up the girls and the twins and take them over to Annie Mae's. Then watch all the kids there and tell Annie Mae to get over here. Hurry!" Billie Nell stood looking at the blood. "Do you hear me? Go on!" She snapped back, went inside and gave one of the twins to Sara Beth. She took the other. They disappeared down the trail toward the Tucker's.

"Sally, when did this start?" Manny asked.

"'Bout a hour ago, I guess. Started hurting like the devil, all crampy, then I felt something warm. I knew what it was. It's my own fault."

"Well, let's get you back to bed. Wait here and let me go put some towels down to soak up." Manny left Sally and got her bed ready. As she pulled back the covers, she noticed the spotting stains on the sheet.

Sally walked slowly back into the house and over to the bed. "Let's take off that gown and put something else on," Manny offered. Once covered and repositioned in bed, Manny began to examine to see if she could tell anything. She mashed on Sally's tummy and her fingers sank in too deeply. The womb that once was tight and full of potential now was losing its life. What had been in it was now coming out.

Manny pulled back and looked at Sally. Sally's vibrant eyes had gone cold. The joy was gone. The spark had died. "Sally, I sent the girls to the Tucker's and told Billie Nell to send Annie Mae over here. She ought to be showin' up soon."

Manny didn't have to explain why she wanted Annie Mae to come. Sally knew. Annie Mae and Floyd had lost three children. Manny felt if anyone would understand that kind of loss, Annie Mae would. She was also hoping Annie Mae might have some insight into what to do.

"Miss Manny?" Annie Mae called from the yard.

"Be right there," Manny called back. She met her on the porch and explained what was going on. Annie Mae began to tear.

"Aw, Miss Manny...Miss Sally," she moaned.

"I need you to help me, Annie Mae. I don't know what to do. Ain't never had nothin' like this happen."

"Don't do nothin'," Annie Mae said. "God'll take care of it."

"No, I thank it's already too late."

"No, not to fix it. Just take care of it."

"So, I don't do nothin'."

"Naw, ma'am, it's done been done."

"Manny!" Sally screamed. "Help me! Somethin's goin' on!"

Manny rushed back in. Annie Mae stood at the door. Manny pulled back the sheet and watched some stringy afterbirth material oozing out. Along with it, the beginnings of a new life now cut short. She quickly pulled together the towel holding the remains, wrapped them up and set them on the edge of the bed. It was a boy. With the five girls Sally and Luke already had, the thought of them losing a little boy would make a tragic loss even worse. Not only were they losing a precious live but the prospects of Tom passing on his legacy through a son who could apprentice with him, share his life with him, learn to be a man from him. There was nothing left to do but clean Sally up and get her to rest.

Sally just stared at the ceiling. Her body now numb offered no resistance nor help as Manny moved her around on the bed. Sally's eyes were becoming hollow and distant. Manny wanted the words to bring her back. None came. She heard Annie Mae praying on the front porch.

"Lord, from our side ain't no reason for this to happen. But from yur side there most prob'ly is. Wish we knew, but since we don't, we just ask You to be merciful to Miss Sally. Lord, help her heal up both inside and out. Amen."

"Amen, Annie Mae," she said. She turned back to Sally and stroked her hair, and repeated Annie Mae's prayer. "Lord, help her heal up on both the inside and outside."

"It's my own fault," Sally said.

"Why on earth do you keep sayin' that?" snapped Manny.

"'Cause she don't know it's God who decides thangs like that," offered Annie Mae. Manny waved her to come in. She shook her head and slowly walked inside the house.

"I didn't want this 'un," Sally said. "I just had the twins and wudn't ready for another'n. God took it away 'cause I didn't want it."

"Ain't 'cause you didn't want it," Annie Mae said. "Me an' Tom beat ourselves up somethin' fierce ever' time one of ours died. He blamed me and I'd blame him. Then we'd blame ourselves. But ain't nobody to blame. You hear me. You ain't big enough to make God do what He don't want to do. And God ain't punishin' you 'cause of somethin' you said or thought. He's bigger'n that."

Sally looked over at Manny, "Is that what you thank, too?"

"Yeah, it is."

"Then why?" she screamed. "Why didn't *He* want this one?"

"Maybe He did," Annie Mae said. "Where do you thank the angels in Heaven come from?"

The moment froze as Sally looked deeply into Manny's eyes. Her lips began to quiver. "So, God done used me to make Him another angel?" she said. Fresh, new moisture began to well up in her eyes.

"Sounds good to me," Manny said.

"Then I'm gonna reckon that's just what He did." Sally closed her eyes. Tears began to trace down her cheek. Manny felt her own tears release and trickle from her eyes.

"You want me to stay with her a while?" asked Annie Mae.

"Yeah, I do. She needs to rest so I need you to keep her in bed. If she needs to go to the bathroom, help her but then get her back in here. I reckon she ought to stay in bed 'til she feels like gettin' up. Keep her drankin' lot of water."

Manny gathered up the towel holding the still-born baby. "What you gonna do with that?" Annie Mae asked.

"Don't rightly know, just cleanin' up."

"Tha's their young un. They're gonna want to bury it somewhere. Yur 'sposed to bury your dead."

"You're right. I'll put it over here in the corner till Luke gets here."

"I'll see that nobody messes with it."

"I'm gonna run over to the mill and see if somebody can go get Luke out of the woods. He needs to be here. You just stay till he comes. Billie Nell is gonna take care of your young'uns till you get home. Alright?" "Yas 'em. We's alright. Mighty alright. God All mighty alright." Annie Mae began to sing, "Precious Lord, take my hand, lead me on help me stand…" Sally closed her eyes and soon fell asleep. As Annie Mae continued to sing, she took up a wet rag and went back to the porch to clean up the rocker. Manny disappeared down the trail.

"Here you go, two meatloaves with mashed potatoes and two teas," Gracie said, placing the steaming plates in front of Claude and Frank.

"What's this?" Claude asked.

"It's your tea."

"No, it ain't."

"Yes, it is."

"No, it ain't."

"You specifically asked for two teas. I even questioned you about it."

"Well, this ain't what we wanted."

"Yeah, there ain't no ice in it," Frank added.

"You wanted iced tea?" Gracie asked.

"Of course," Claude snapped. "What'd you thank we wanted: coffee tea?"

"Next time you need to order *iced* tea."

"Now ain't that the stupidest thang," Claude said.

"You ain't in Texas no more, boys," she twanged.

"It's Ar-kan-sas, ma'am," Frank strained each syllable.

Gracie glared at Frank, turned to walk away. Claude grabbed her arm. She spun back slicing through him with piercing eyes. "I'd like to apologize. We've just been on the road for a long time. Guess we done used up our manners, before we got here."

"How many did you start out with, one a piece?"

"One a piece, funny." He felt her pulling away and let her go. "If you wouldn't mind, we'd like some *iced* tea with our dinner."

She returned with two iced teas and set them on the table. As she turned to leave, Claude grabbed her arm again. She spun around and pulled at her arm. Claude held tight. She glanced back over her shoulder at a large man standing behind the counter. Claude quickly let go. She began to walk away.

"Wait, Gracie. I'm lookin' for a woman."

"Not available."

"No, she's from Arkansas. Just wondering if maybe she came in here in the last couple of days. She'd of had three kids with her: two girls and a little boy? Did you see her?"

"You a cop?"

"No, her husband. And this is my son, Frank."

A Hispanic busboy came by. Gracie stopped him. "I had to clean this one up, Jose. You understand what that means?"

"*Si, Senorita.*"

She turned back to Claude, "What'd you do?"

"Me? I didn't do nothin'. She's the one runnin' off. Just got up in the middle of the night and took off. Took my young 'un with her. I didn't do nothin' I tell you!"

"Whoa, fella. I know you came a long way out here, but did it ever dawn on you she might not want to be found?"

"She can tell me that after I find her. Now did she come through here or not?"

"Whether she did or didn't, do you actually believe I would tell you? You've got way too much anger in your eyes."

"Gracie, please!"

"No, I'm sorry. This is not my problem. Here's your bill. Pay up front when you get through."

"Ma'am, if you know anything, please help us," Frank said.

She shrugs and turns to walk away. Claude stands up and grabs her by the arm again. She looks over at the large man behind the counter.

"Let her go, Mister," he called out.

Claude turned to the other patrons, never letting go of Gracie. "Excuse me, folks, but a lady might have been through here a couple of days ago with three young 'uns: two girls and a little boy. Did anybody see them? She's my wife and I need to find her."

"Alright, that's enough," the large man said. He stormed from behind the counter and walked toward Claude, a baseball bat dangled from his hand. He pulled Gracie's arm out of Claude's grip and spun Claude around to face him. Claude turned back to the people.

"Leave me alone! I know she's been here. Somebody in here knows it."

The man placed the bat alongside Claude's face. Claude went still. Frank rushed over to stop the man but a couple of men sitting at the next table grabbed him and held him back.

"Walk with me outside, friend," the man said. "Give me any problems and I'll crease your head and drag you out. Either way you're leaving. Don't make me hurt you, mister."

"Curtis," Gracie said, "he hasn't paid."

"Give me your wallet. How much was it, Gracie?"

"Oh, two dollars."

"Here's three. He's a big tipper." Curtis pressed Claude's wallet into his chest and pushed him outside. Frank followed with the two men on either side of him. Curtis shoved Claude out the door. Claude stumbled and fell on the sidewalk. Frank pulled away from the two men and ran over to his dad.

"You okay, Dad?" he asked.

"Yeah, I'm alright. Let's get out of here. We'll find 'em ourselves."

# Chapter Twenty-eight

CLAUDE WAS NOT A BIG MAN BUT WHEN CONFRONTED BY SOME-one bigger and that person armed with a baseball bat, he could easily be shut up and redirected. The smaller, Hispanic man calling to him from the side alley offered no threat. Claude stood and looked at him. Frank had already gotten into the car.

Jose still had on his long apron he had been wearing inside when Gracie chewed him out at the table. He, too, was a small man, mid-thirties. The holes worn in his ragged jeans caught the light from the street lamp. "*Señor*," he called to Claude.

Claude waved him off and reached for the door handle. "*Señor!*" he said again, motioning Claude to come to the alley.

"What do you want, Mexican?"

"*Señor* I remember your wife and children."

Claude rushed over to the man, grabbed him by the collar and pressed him against the wall. "Where! When!" he shouted. Frank had left the car and was pulling his dad back before his drawn-back fist could make contact with the busboy's face. "When? Tell me quick, boy."

"She was here maybe two, three days ago. She tried to get a job, but they need no more waitresses."

"Where's she now?" Claude yelled, reaching again for Jose's shirt. Jose backed up a step. Frank stuck his arm between them and nodded for Jose to answer.

"*Señor* Stanton. He owns a farm just outside of town. He was inside having dinner and told her she could work for him. She followed him off in her car. That's all I know."

"You better be tellin' me the truth, Mexican."

"*Señor* please. I try to help."

"Then tell me how I get to this farm."

"It's down the road to Victorville, about eight miles out is sign to Stanton Farm. That's where you turn and go down that road."

"Where's the road to Victorville?" Claude asked.

"At the light turn right."

"Alright then," Claude said, "get in, Frank, let's go."

"Señor it might be better to wait for morning."

"I ain't waiting for nothing. She'd better be there. And if you're lyin' I'm coming back here."

"I don't know if she is still there, *Señor*, but I'm not lying."

Claude got behind the wheel. Frank became the passenger. He fired the engine and squealed the tires as he peeled rubber from the tires and left it in streaks on the street in front of the café. Claude said nothing as he squinted at the roadway with the sun cutting through the edge of the windshield. The black and white sign saying Victorville was another thirty miles ahead made him kick the speed up another ten mile per hour.

Right where Jose said it was, the sign to Stanton Farms loomed just off the road. "Well, the Mexican is right so far," Claude said.

He turned onto the gravel road, slowed the coupe and stopped. The long driveway was lined on each side by barbed wire that seemed to pull together somewhere in the distance. His heart was beating strongly enough within his chest that he knew Frank probably heard it. He sat still, staring blankly into the horizon.

"Dad?" Claude didn't move or respond. "Dad!" Frank repeated. Claude blinked and turned to Frank. Frank recognized the fear. He'd felt it many times when he was uncertain as to what might happen after he had said or done something inappropriate. Or when he'd stood in the room waiting for the yelling to begin or the strap to swing. Or when he'd nearly run his car off the road several times sliding around corners at full speed. He knew fear, but he'd not seen it this close and coming from his dad's eyes.

Claude looked back down the road, let off the clutch and slowly rolled the Ford toward the farm. Frank saw the muscles in his dad's jaw tighten and release and his lips purse, then let loose. Claude was nervous. The arrogance by which he ran the mill was gone. The cockiness with which he dealt with Jose was absent. He was just a man unsure of what lay ahead. All he knew was he was going to beg his wife to come back to him, knowing he offered her nothing that might counter the reasons upon which she left.

Ivan Stanton was a life-long Californian, tanned, tall, with a sandy-blond crew cut. His family had run farms further up the San Fernando Valley. Back in the Valley, they had grown a variety of crops but typically sustained their livelihood with Roma tomatoes, almonds and grapes that were morphed into raisins.

Ivan had always been interested in livestock. After a falling out with his dad, he left the farms and moved to Bakersfield where he found work with an oil drilling operation. His work ethic and ambition quickly moved him up in the company. When he retired at fifty-five, he took his several million in stock and bought the Goodson's farm, expanded its capabilities and brought in cattle, sheep and goats. Now, seven years later, the operation was productive and profitable.

Claude pulled up in front of the main house. The original house had been moved a hundred yards up the side of a ridge. In its place was a southern-style plantation house. Tall, white columns framed the large, wrap-around, front porch. Ivan made an impressive exit from the front door on to the front edge of the porch. He handled his sixty-two years very well. His tight, athletic body pressed large chest muscles against the inside of his t-shirt, much as it had done when he played defensive end with Fresno State. Beneath, he wore jeans and cowboy boots. His arms were thick and powerful, his gut taunt.

When the engine stopped, Claude slowly opened the door and stood beside it. "Hey, name's Claude Massey. This is my son, Frank. We're from Arkansas." Claude said politely.

"Not hiring," Stanton replied.

"No," he laughed, "we're not lookin' for work." Out of the corner of his eye, coming from around the corner of the house, he could see a group of men walking toward him. He shifted his weight and leaned toward the inside of the car. Stanton looked over at them and held up his hand. They stopped. Claude glanced over at the men, then back at Ivan. "I was told that maybe my wife might be out here."

Stanton stared hard at Claude.

"She was lookin' for work. Her name's Flo. She's got her girls with her and a boy, Jack. He's our young 'un.

"She said you'd be coming." Stanton said.

"Then she's been here?" Claude took a step away from the car toward the porch. Ivan held up his hand. Claude stopped and backed up.

"She was here, but they left three or four days ago," Stanton said.

Claude stared hard at the large man. He glanced over at the ranch hands watching from the corner of the house, then back. "Uh, don't thank she could of done that. Ain't been gone long enough."

"Wouldn't be calling me a liar, now, would you?"

"Uh, sir, I'm just lookin' for my wife and our boy. If she was here and left, just tell me."

"She was here. She's not here now."

"Did she say where she was goin'?"

"Let's see, believe she said Fresno. Or was is Sacramento? Or maybe San Francisco?"

Claude knew he was lying. He felt strongly she was there but was slowly realizing he may never know. He couldn't force this man to tell him the truth and was not going to be able to look around to see for himself. "Which one?" he asked.

"Not sure."

"She wasn't sure where she was goin' or you're not sure what she said?"

"Doesn't matter. You might as well go on and leave." Ivan dismissed Claude with a wave.

"Listen, Mister," Claude challenged. He slammed the door to the car and started toward Stanton. Frank quickly got out and followed, more to stop his dad than to help take on the rancher.

"No, you listen," Ivan said stepping down from the porch. He met Claude at the mid-way point in the yard. Claude looked up as Ivan towered over him. "She came out here to get away from you. And as long as she's under my roof that's the way it gonna stay."

"Just who do you thank…wait, she's here?"

"Get back in your car and go home to Arkansas. She doesn't want to see you."

"I'm not leaving until I talk to my wife!" Claude yelled. "Flo! Flo, you in there?" He stepped aside to go around Ivan. Ivan caught him with a massive forearm and knocked him backwards, onto the ground. Frank dove onto his dad.

"No, mister," Frank plead, holding up his hand toward the man.

"They're my family," Claude said. "What gives you the right? I don't care what you or them or anybody else says, I'm takin' them home with me."

Stanton pulled Frank off his dad and tossed him aside. He reached down and lifted Claude to his feet, then grabbed a fist-full of shirt front. "You are an irritating man, Massey. She doesn't want to see you and that's the way it's going to stay. Can you understand that, or do I have to beat that into your hard head?"

Claude looked up at Stanton, his eyes draining out tears. "I ain't a fightin' man." Ivan relaxed his grip. Claude drew in a trembling breath, "I cain't leave without hearin' it from her."

Claude spun around and kicked the ground. Ivan started for him, but Frank jumped between. Ivan stopped. The pressure within him built up from his lowest gut. Claude spun around and started to run to the door. He screamed, "Flo, please. Just tell me yourself if ain't gonna come back."

Ivan clinched his fist and drew back to connect with Claude's jaw. Before he could swing away, the screen door opened behind them. "No, Mr. Stanton!" Flo yelled. Stanton stood down. A tall, slender, plainly dressed lady stepped out from the house. Her long, auburn hair caught the sun as the wind blew it into her face. She brushed it back. In her arms was a small boy. At her side were two young girls, nine and eleven.

Claude began to move toward the porch. Ivan grabbed him on the shoulder. Claude tried to push it off. Eight ranch hands watching from the side of the house quickly moved in front of the porch. Claude wasn't getting through.

"Just stay there, Claude," Flo said. "I don't want you hurt."

"Flo, baby, I'm sorry. Please just come on and let's go back home. I'll make it all better. It'll be alright, I promise."

"I ain't goin' back, Claude."

"Cain't we talk even about it?"

"Ain't no talkin' to do. I ain't goin' back and I ain't gonna be yur wife no more."

"But I'll quit drankin'. I can do that. I've done it a bunch of times. It'll be differ'nt this time."

"Claude! You and Frank git in that car and leave. I ain't never goin' back with you. Never! Do you hear me?" She turned and pushed the kids back into the house.

"Flo! Don't leave me!" Claude sobbed.

"She already has," Stanton said.

"Stay out of this!"

Ivan fisted up quickly and placed a solid lick against Claude's temple. Claude crumpled onto the ground, stunned but still conscious. Frank quickly stepped over in front of Stanton. "Son, you better back away," Stanton warned.

"Sir, we're done. Just don't hit him again. We'll go on and leave."
He pulled his dad up and walked him to the passenger side. Frank then slipped in behind the wheel.

"When he gets some sense back in him, you tell him if he ever comes back here things are going to get a lot worse. You understand me, son?"

"Yes, sir. We won't be back. I promise." He fired up the Ford and backed into the yard. When he stopped to engage first gear, they both look up at the porch. Flo's silhouette was clearly visible behind the door. They drove off with her watching through the screen. Out the rearview mirror Frank saw Mr. Stanton dismiss his men and head up the steps. Flo came out onto the porch and hugged him.

When Frank got back to the highway, he stopped and looked at his dad. Claude was slumped in the seat, moaning. Frank looked back behind them through the mirror. The blue smoke was hanging low in the ditches. He breathed hard, then turned the coupe left, toward town and opened her up.

Stanton's foreman pulled Flo's car around from the garage. She came back out of the house carrying a suitcase and Jack. The girls followed closely behind, dolls in hand. Behind the girls was Mrs. Stanton, then Ivan. The other ranch hands came around to the front. They all hugged as the foreman loaded the suitcase into the trunk. With all the kids fitted into the back seat, Flo got behind the wheel, waved at the foreman, then drove off down the long driveway. When she got to the intersection, she turned right and disappeared down the highway toward Victorville.

"Dad?" Frank asked. Claude strained to open a swollen eye. "Hurt bad?"

"Don't matter none."

"What we gonna do now?"

"Go home."

"Just like that?"

"Yeah."

"You sure? We're so close."

"Ain't never gonna be close to her again."

"But what about Jack?"

"She can have him. I don't want nothin' that has anythang to do with her again."

"But..."

"But nothin'. She never was worth nothin' no how. Should'a never come out here in the first place. Stupid idea."

"Dad?"

"Shut up, Frank. Just drive. You hear me? We're done talkin' about it. Just drive."

The coupe rumbled as it passed back through Barstow. The noise caught Gracie's attention. She looked out the window of the café. Claude looked over. She waved and smiled. The insincerity was obvious.

Manny was coming through the gate to the chicken coop when Billie Nell came out the back door. The young rooster she squeezed tightly under her arm had no idea why Manny's other hand held such a strong grip on his neck. "You want to do this?" Manny asked.

"No, go on ahead," Billie Nell said.

Manny released her hold from under her arm and swung the rooster in a tight circle with her hand still gripping the neck. With a quick flick she snapped the neck and threw the rooster on the ground. He flopped around, trying to get up, but with no place to go and no longer any connection with his brain helping control his actions, he soon lay lifeless on the grass.

Because most of their meat was from the animals they raised or from game Dearl would bring back from hunting, they had a processing table in the backyard to keep fur, hair and feathers from getting all over the kitchen. It was made from a thick slab of a hickory tree crosscut from a wide stump. Dearl had placed a barrel beside it where Manny could scrape off the uneatable residual matter which he would carry off and burn or scatter in the woods for the night varmints.

Manny set the chicken on the slab and began to pluck off the feathers. Billie Nell reached in and grabbed a handful and ripped them out as well. When the bird was clean, Billie Nell went back inside, took the pan of hot water from the stove and poured it into a large bowl Manny had left out. She grabbed a couple of hand towels and brought everything outside. She knew the routine.

Manny slid her knife down the belly and opened up the gut to remove the entrails. When Billie Nell placed the bowl on the slab, Manny set the bird in the water and began to wash the carcass clean. She dumped the water on the ground for Thomas the cat to enjoy and carried the bowl and chicken back into the house.

Until that point no words had been spoken. Usually the two ladies were non-stop chatterers, but the heaviness of the day had silenced them both. Billie Nell got out a larger knife and began to cut up the chicken. Manny smiled at her helpfulness. Manny washed her hands and then selected out some potatoes to boil.

Billie Nell was about halfway through with the chicken when she stopped and turned to Manny. "Alright, what happened today?" Manny had not seen her face so serious. She turned, leaned back against the counter, wiped her hands with a dishtowel.

"Ain't gonna be able to answer that one," she said.

"Why not?"

"'Cause I don't rightly know myself."

"Sally lost the baby?"

"Yeah."

"Why?"

"Don't know. Somethin' went bad wrong and the baby didn't make it."

"Why?"

"Might as well quit askin' why, 'cause ain't nobody on this side of heaven got a answer to that."

"Thought the Bible said there's a reason for everythang?"

"Yeah, so?"

"Then there's gotta be a answer to this."

"Not that we might ever know."

"And you can live with that?"

"Don't see I've got much of a choice not to."

"But what if that happened to me?"

"That ain't gonna happen to you, Billie Nell."

"But it could, couldn't it?"

"Well, I guess."

"Then, what if it happened to me?"

"Suppose somewhere under heaven there'd be a reason."

"But we might never know what it is?"

"Prob'ly."

"They gonna get over this?"

"Sally and Luke? Yeah, in time."

"Don't thank I could get over this hap'ning to me and Leland."

"But for the grace of God, don't see how anybody could."

Billie Nell took in a deep breath and blew it out slowly, nodded her head, turned and finished cutting up the chicken. It struck Manny hard that Billie Nell was thinking the same things she was. Billie Nell's words became hers. Her mind began to ask the questions. *But for the grace of God...how does anybody get over somethin' like that?* Manny filled the pot with water, set in the potatoes and placed the pot on the stove. Dinner would be ready when Dearl got home.

# Chapter Twenty-nine

THE ROADSIDE PARK WAS CROWDED. EACH PICNIC TABLE HAD a family camped around it. Trucks lined the roadway with truckers asleep in their cabs, the drone of their diesels provided a lulling sedative to a long day's travel. Claude was waking up in the backseat of Frank's car. Frank was stirring the fire to rekindle flames for making coffee.

"How long you been up?" Claude asked, dragging himself out of the coupe.

"Not long. Just about got some coffee brewed up."

Claude took in a deep breath of air, thickly stained with diesel fumes and burning fires. He coughed. "Man, you'd thank being out here in the middle of nowhere the air would be fresher."

"Soon as the coffee's ready, we can load up and go," Frank said. "How you feelin'?"

"Like I been run over by a Mack truck. My head's killing me. Where are we, anyway?"

"Arizona. Ain't sure where on the map, though." Frank poured up the coffee into their thermos and doused the flames with the remaining brew. The embers shot upward. He stood there and watched them sail off into the morning sky.

"Put out that fire and let's go," Claude said. "The sooner we get back the better."

"Dad, ever wonder about where these sparks are going?"

"Don't matter, none. Just pour some water on it and let's go home."
The water killed the flames but shot up more embers. Frank stirred the mixture and soon the pit was dead. Claude was sitting in the car. He honked the horn.

"Hey, fool, knock it off!" the people from the next campsite yelled.

Luke had asked Dearl to help him bury the baby. He brought Manny and Billie Nell with him. Luke had dug a small hole in the back yard beside a young oak tree. When the Thomsons walked up, Sally, Luke and the girls were standing around the tree looking into the hole. Sally had wrapped the baby's remains in a blanket and placed him in the ground.

"Dearl, Manny, Billie Nell," Luke said, nodding to each. "Thanks for comin'."

They just smiled back. Manny went over to Sally and slipped her arm around her waist. Billie Nell stood by the girls, Dearl beside Luke. Dearl held his Bible under his arm.

"Don't know what else to do," Luke said.

"That's why I brought my Bible," Dearl answered. "Maybe God's got somethin' to say."

"I'd like to know what?" Sally said, the raw edge of her weary, bitter heart showing through. Annie Mae's thoughts about God populating Heaven with babies to make angels lasted only a short time.

"Sally!" Luke whispered loudly.

"Well, let me read what I found," Dearl said. He opened his Bible and read: "*My heart is sore, pained within me: and the terrors of death are fallen upon me. Fearfulness and trembling are come upon me, and horror hath overwhelmed me. And I said, oh that I had wings like a dove! Then I would fly away and be at rest. Then I would wander far off and stay out in the wilderness.* Now, I ain't never lost a child, but I've stood right where you two are standin' when I lost my Ma and Pa, and this is how I felt then."

"Yeah, I'd say I pretty much feel that way, too," Luke said. "What did you do?"

"Let me read a bit more. *As for me, I will call upon God; and the Lord will save me.*"

"We done been saved," Luke said, "all but the youngest ones there. And been baptized, too."

"Ain't talkin' about that kind of savin'. Talkin' about the kind that pulls you out of the water when you're drowning."

"Oh, yeah, I get what your sayin'. I nearly drowned when I was a kid. Needin' to breathe and can't get out from under the water. Yeah, that's kinda like what this feels like."

"We can't take away the hurt," Dearl said. "And, Sally, we can't make you not be mad at God. Girls, we can't make you not be sad. But God ain't through yet. This young un didn't make it but his little life wasn't worth nothin'. Somehow God's gonna show you how much He loves you by helpin' you go through this. He ain't gonna leave you out here. That's all I'm sayin'."

Luke nodded. Sally just stared down at the hole. The girls hugged onto Billie Nell. Dearl prayed, "Lord, we ain't got sense enough to know why stuff like this happens. But I guess if we don't know why, the best thang we can do is trust that You do and leave it at that. I know that's easier for me to say than for Luke and them to do it, so hug them tight and heal up this chunk of life that's done got torn out of their hearts. Amen."

"Amen," Luke said.

"Amen," Manny said, tightening her hug on Sally. "Amen." Sally just stared into the hole.

"Manny, you and Billie Nell take the girls on back into the house. We'll call for you in a minute," Dearl said. Manny pressed against Sally side. She turned and followed. Billie Nell herded the girls away from the tree.

Dearl took up the shovel leaning against the backside of the tree and dug down to scoop up a load of soft dirt. He looked at Luke. Luke took the shovel from him and sprinkled it lightly into the hole. Tears streamed down his cheeks. He stopped, set the point of the shovel onto the ground, leaned against the handle and began to tremble. Dearl slipped his arm across Luke's shoulders as the big man shook and sobbed.

"Want me to finish?" Dearl asked.

"No, I'll do it," he said, wiping his nose across his sleeve. He shoveled in another load, and another until the hole was rounded over. He patted it down then tapped in a wooded cross he had made. He stood and looked at the small grave.

"I'll get the girls," Dearl said.

Everyone again stood around the tree. The rounded heap covering the baby brought a measure of comfort rather than seeing his blanket and knowing he was wrapped inside.

"Levi," Sally said solemnly. "We're gonna call him Levi, after my dad."

"Levi," Luke said. "That's a fine name. Levi."

"Mr. Dearl, is Levi gonna go to heaven?" Sara Beth asked.

"Speck he's already there," Dearl answered. "God's got a way to take care of little ones like him."

"So, he ain't under this dirt?" asked one of the younger girls.

"His little body is but Levi's gone."

"Good," she said. "I was gettin' worried about leaving him out here in the yard."

"He's fine, Sara Beth. Don't you be worrying about little Levi. He ain't here; he's with the Lord," Manny said.

"Okay, then."

Dusk brought a breath of coolness to the dry heat of the desert. The glare of the fading sun was behind them as they rolled toward home. Frank spun the radio dial to find anything that might break the monotony of the long, empty drive. After a few crackles Hank Williams came through. The loneliness from which he wished to die latched onto Claude's heart. He turned his face toward the vast spaces and swallowed hard.

Frank saw his dad's shoulders shake. He knew the silent cries would never be heard. "Dad?" he asked. Claude ignored the call. Frank drove a bit further. "Dad?" he tried again. Claude shook his head. The dark of the desert began to spill over onto the road. Frank turned on his lights, but the darkness in the car didn't change.

Claude said, "Stop up here so I can pee."

Frank pulled the Ford off the side of the road and turned off his lights. Claude got out, took a few steps into the ditch and relieved himself. Back in the car, Frank asked again, "Dad?"

"What?"

"You gonna be okay after all this?"

Claude jerked toward Frank, his non-swollen eye pierced through the darkness between. He puffed his lips and nodded. "Just keep on driving. The sooner we get back the sooner I can get my life back." The coupe droned on. "Done lost too much work, lost my family, lost everything."

"Not everything," Frank said. "You still got me."

"Boy, you don't know nothing. If you ain't got it all you ain't got nothing at all. I don't want just you. I want everything back like it was."

The words stung deeply. Frank said, "But Flo ain't coming back. It won't ever be like it was."

"I don't want Flo. I want what I had."

"Yount me to move back in with you and help take care of stuff."

"I don't want some snotty-nosed kid! I want a wife. Wives are important. They make you get up in the morning and go do things, then make you feel glad you did it. They make you feel necessary."

"Well, maybe you can find another wife." Frank sapped.

"Frank, it ain't that easy for somebody like me. I'm getting too old and ugly to find some woman who'd give a rip about me."

"Well, what about me?"

"What about you?" Frank held his breath then blew out a sigh as he looked out his window into the blackness. Claude continued, "This ain't got nothing to do with you."

"Why do you thank I came on this stupid trip in the first place? I don't care nothin' about Jack or Flo or any of the rest of 'em."

"Well, why did you come, then?"

"So, I could be with you, like it used to be before they ever came along."

"Yeah?"

"Dad, why did you kick me out when you married Flo?"

"Me? You were the one causing trouble. You and that attitude of yours. If you'd of behaved you could have stayed."

"I was twelve years old."

"Shouldn't have bothered you so much then."

"She came in and started throwing out everything that belonged to us. It was her house, her couch, her dishes, her beds, her floors, her air to breathe. The whole place was hers. It wasn't even yours and hers, just hers. Then she'd beat me. She chained me to the bed and beat me. Did you know that? She beat me, Dad."

Claude looked away and shook his head.

"You knew it and let her do that?"

"That's the way it is when you bring a new wife into an old house. You just have to put up with stuff. Yeah, I knew what she was doin'. That's why I sent you to Aunt Alma's."

The sting in the air silenced the conversation. They drove on through the night. Claude pulled his hat over his eyes and slept. Frank just stared down the narrow highway.

Ernest finished hooking up the last of the equipment. Dutton carried off the packing and stabilizing timbers to the burn pile. The secondary rip saw with its overhead pulleys was operational. Mr. Creighton drove up as Ernest walked out of the building.

"Got it all done, Mr. Creighton," Ernest said.

"Mighty proud of you, son," Mr. Creighton said. "Now if we could get Claude back here and help us get us get the operation back up to speed, we could start using all this new stuff."

"He'll be back soon, won't he?"

"Maybe in a couple of days. So, let's just leave all this here and get back to what used to the old normal till he's home."

# Chapter Thirty

THE TRUCK STOP CAME AS A WELCOME RELIEF TO THEM BOTH. Frank was fighting staying awake. Claude was shivering in the New Mexico night. The car needed gas. Frank pulled into a parking space.

"Thought we needed gas?" Claude asked.

"We do, but we don't have enough money for gas and food, so I'm gonna see if I can work for a couple of hours to earn enough for a tank of gas."

"Good idea. You do that. I thank I'll just look around." Claude watched Frank go into the store. He got out and walked around back where a couple of truck drivers were downing a six-pack. "Got an extra for a needy traveler?" The bigger of the two took out a brew and tossed it to Claude. He popped the top and downed the beer in one gulp.

"Man, you're either mighty thirsty or pretty bad off," the trucker said.

"A little of both right now," Claude said.

"Gotta name?"

"Does it matter?"

"I'm Chuck and the brute here is Leonard," the second trucker said.

"Claude."

Leonard saw his eye in the light and tossed him another. "Here, Claude, you look like you need this more than either of us do." The second was gone as fast as the first. "Whoa, I'd slow down and enjoy the moment. That's gonna hit pretty hard after it hits your stomach."

"I can handle it," Claude said.

"Where you off to?" Chuck asked.

"Headed back home, or what's left of it."

"Where you been?"

"Went out to California to, uh, check on some things."

"Wife left you and ran off to California, huh?"

"What? How'd you know that?"

Leonard laughed, "You're wearing it hard, man."

"Wearing…Hey, I don't like people buttin' into my business," he moved chest first toward the men.

"Calm down, little man," Chuck said standing. He was a big man. Massive arms rippled out from under the seam of his t-shirt. Claude stepped back.

"Ain't quite over it," he said.

"Well, we got another six-pack that might help," Leonard said, pulling another carton from a sack on the ground between the two truckers.

"Yeah, that's what I need."

Claude slowed down his pace but still ended up drinking six of the twelve beers. The two men laughed as the alcohol began to show its effect on Claude.

With all the beer gone, Claude weaved back to the car and climbed into the backseat. His head was spinning. He lay down and pulled his hat down over his eyes. Soon he was asleep.

Frank finished up cleaning the store and bathrooms, the tank of gas his reward. "Do you thank you could throw in a couple of quarts of oil? She's about burned out all that I had left," he asked the clerk.

The clerk agreed and Frank headed to the car with his reward. He never looked in the backseat, just got in, started up and pulled over to the pumps. With both engine and tank full, he looked for his dad. "Dad!"

The moan from the backseat was unexpected but welcomed as he glanced in to see Claude there. He got back in and drove off.

Texas came quickly and with it Sunday morning. Frank drove until he couldn't stay awake any longer. He had tried several times to rouse Claude but had less effect on him than the alcohol. At a roadside park he pulled over beside an 18-wheeler and stretched out on the seat.

Too tired to drive but now too tired to sleep, Frank lay there, listening to the night sounds coming through the window and from the backseat. He adjusted his position and soon had joined his dad to sleep away the rest of the night.

Early in the morning the trucker fired up his diesel. Both Frank and Claude shot up. Daylight had just broken and rush of adrenalin from being startled by the noise had them wide awake.

"Let me out, I gotta go," Claude said.

Frank stepped outside and pulled the seat forward as Claude stumbled out. He started down the path to the restroom. His one wide-opened eye blinking feverishly to try and focus him on which door was for men. Frank followed.

On the way back to the car, Claude stopped and stretched. "It's gonna take me a month to get over this trip," he said.

"May take me a bit longer," Frank replied.

"Shoot, boy, you're too young to worry about stiff joints and worn out backs."

"Ain't my joints and back that's bothering me."

"Look, I ain't in no mood to talk about how you feel about all of this."

"And I ain't in the mood to talk about it neither."

"Good then."

"But just tell me one thang."

"I knew it."

"If Momma had left you and took me away would you have come after us like you did them other ones?"

"That ain't the same thing. First of all, we're talking about two different women. Your Momma wudn't have done anything like Flo. And she wouldn't have left me."

"But if she did, would you have come looking for us?"

"Frank, you don't know nothing."

"I thank I'm beginnin' to."

"Your Momma was too good a woman for that. She knew her place and…she loved me."

Frank was looking down, now he looked back at his dad. Claude gazed out toward the open pasture land. "Flo didn't. She never did. If your Momma hadn't died…Ain't no reason she had to go off and do that."

"God says there's a reason for everything."

"God. God! There can't be no reason why God would take away a Momma from her kid and a wife from her husband. I ain't got no use for a god like that."

"But, Dad…"

"Let me tell you what. I've…people have called on God and still had the same mess in their lives. What they didn't want to happen, happened anyway, so what they got ain't made no difference."

"But that ain't all they got. It ain't just them. Dad, having God means something special. It makes it easier…"

"Easier? Life ain't supposed to be easy! It's hard, boy, and it makes you hard. The sooner you learn that the better off you'll be. That's how you get through. You do whatever it takes. If you need help, you help yourself. You can't count on nobody else. Whatever works. You go with it. Then…you just numb the pain."

"Numb? Numb?"

"Whatever works."

"That ain't right. That just don't feel right."

Claude spun about and stared deeply into Frank's eyes. "Feelings don't matter none. You got that? Feelings don't matter nothing!"

Frank blinked rapidly and looked away. "I wish," he mumbled as he walked back to the car, nine years of feelings tracing down his cheeks. He wiped the tears and got in the car. The ever-present silence returned and the two of them drove on toward sunrise, but sunrise was blackened out by dark clouds covering the eastern sky.

The rain had become monotonous. When it began it was a welcomed break from the hot summer, but now, it was too much too soon. Puddles had long past grown into ponds that connected and flowed forcefully down the creeks and into the Mulberry River. Manny had a rule for the ladies due at her house for birthing class to never try and come if the weather turned bad. Today definitely could be considered bad.

Though no one knew it, a hurricane blowing up from the Texas coast had veered directly toward Pine Hollow. At the same time a high-pressure system had moved over from the mid-west and was pushing against the storm, holding it still over western Arkansas.

Dearl drove his truck up as close as he could to the house, got out and sloshed up the steps. He was drenched. Though the roof was on the new shed at the mill, with no sides, he and Ernest had spent the last two hours fighting howling winds and straight-line rain, tying tarps over the equipment.

The coupe roared down Highway 66. The wide-open plains of Oklahoma and the drone of the engine teamed up to put Frank in a hypnotic trance. He fought hard to stay awake, adjusting the side vent, slapping himself in the face, jerking his head. Claude had long given in and was asleep in the backseat. The explosion of the right rear tire blowing brought them both quickly back to the moment.

"What was that?" Claude yelled.

"Blowout," Frank shouted back. The rear began to fight for control as it slid toward the ditch. Frank slowed the car and pulled off to the shoulder. Dust swallowed them up and poured into the open windows.

"Of all the stupid…what'd you run over?"

"Nothin' that I know of. Just blew." Smoke drifted out from the fender well.

"Well, get out and fix it," Claude ordered.

"Can't."

"You ain't got a spare, do you?" Claude asked.

"Uh, nope."

"No!" Claude screamed.

"I was gonna…"

"Well, gonna ain't helpin' us none!"

"We ain't too far to the next town," Frank said. "I'll take it in and get us another one."

"Blast it, Boy! I ain't in no mood to be traipsing around in the middle of nowhere, rolling a torn-up tire."

"You can stay here. I said I'd do it. It ain't no big deal." Frank began to remove the hot tire.

"No big deal! This is gonna add a whole 'nother day. I told Creighton we'd be home tonight."

"We ain't got enough money no how. I used up all but a couple of bucks gettin' gas back there. We're gonna have to get some work."

"Ain't got time for this. If you've messed up my job…"

Frank grabbed up the hot tire and started off. "Sign said Pleasanton was down the road a bit," he said. "Closer to go there than back to where we got gas."

"How far?" Claude asked.

"A couple of miles or so. Don't matter. Gotta go however far it is anyhow."

"Well, I ain't stayin' here for that long."

"You comin'?"

"Yeah, but I ain't carryin' that thing."

The tire was too shredded to roll. Frank began by carrying it in his right hand then traded off for the left. Soon it was back in the right. "Aw, heck, give it to me for a while?" Claude said.

"No, you said you weren't carryin' it." Frank shifted it to the other hand. Claude took the tire and carried it a few yards then set it down. "Let's sit here and let you rest a while," he said.

Claude sat facing west. He squinted as he saw a pickup coming over a rise. He stood to flag them down.

Bud and Bea Vernon were farmers who made a weekly trip into town for church every Sunday morning. They had been as faithful to their church as they had each other and hadn't missed in sixty-two years. The old '51 Chevy hummed along at its forty-five mile per hour maximum. Bud wore his standard red plaid, long-sleeve shirt and bib overalls. Bea had on her summer dress. She wore a scarf to keep her hair the way she had fixed it earlier that morning.

Bud was a slight-built man, weathered hard by the Oklahoma sun, his leathered face and arms darkly tanned from years of exposure. The parts usually covered up still pale.

Bea shook, not from the rough ride in the stiff truck, but her hands trembled, and her head wobbled beyond her control. The doctor suspects Parkinson's but thinks it could have other causes since nervousness made it worse. Bea was the first to see Claude and the crevices in her brow deepened. Bud noticed her agitation and looked and saw Claude for himself. He let off the gas.

"Nope, nope, nope, don't you be stopping for them fellas there. They're strangers, you know."

"Now, Momma, didn't you see that car back there, jacked up and all? It surely belonged to these fellas. They need help and we're gonna help them. It'll be alright."

She huffed. "You don't know where they've been?"

"Don't think that matters none. Let's just stop and see what the matter is."

"The matter is they've got a flat tire. No need to stop and find out what you already know."

Bud pulled up beside the two. Bea looked straight ahead through the windshield. "Your car I passed back there a mite?"

"Yes, sir," Frank said.

Claude carried on from there. "Got ourselves a flat here. Think you could save us some wear and tear by giving us a ride into town?"

"Don't see why not," Bud said. "Throw your tire and yourselves in the back and I'll haul you in. What's your names?"

As Frank placed the tire in the bed of the truck, Claude stood at the window. "I'm Claude Massey and this is my son, Frank."

"Bud and Bea."

"Good to meet you folks. Thanks for the help."

"Where you headed?"

"Well, northwestern Arkansas. Little place called Pine Hollow, that is as soon as we get this tire fixed."

"Well, that tire's gonna need a lot more than fixin'," Bud said. "You pretty much blew it to heck."

"Yeah, may have to rustle up a job to buy a new one," Claude said. "The trip's done ate up our money some time ago."

"No working on Sunday, young man," Bea said. "This is the Sabbath, you know."

"Yes 'em, but don't this count as having your ox in a ditch?" Claude said.

"Yes, I believe it would," Bea said, never taking her eyes from looking down the road. "I believe it would." She adds, rocking to her shaking.

"She okay?" Claude asked.

"Bea? Shoot yeah. Just hop in and let's get going," Bud said, placing his hand on her leg. She slowed the rocking.

"Don't want to cause you any trouble," Claude said.

"No trouble at all, right Momma?"

"No trouble at all," she said.

Bud headed them off toward Pleasanton quickly reaching his maximum of forty-five. Every couple of minutes Bea would quickly turn and glance out the back window then, as quickly, jerk back and stare down the road.

"What's wrong with that lady?" Frank asked.

"Don't know, just a bit nervous. Don't matter none, as long as we don't have to walk any further."

Frank handed his wheel to the attendant. Across the street from the gas station, the smell of fresh bacon wafted out of the open door of a café. Claude and Frank were instantly captured by the smell. "You fellas had breakfast?" Bud asked.

"Naw, sir," Claude answered. "Tell you the truth, we ain't had much of nothin' for a couple of days."

"Let's go take care of that," Bud said.

"We can't…" Frank began. Bud waved him off. The four walked across the street and into the aroma of the café.

Bea sat very upright, her white cotton gloves far from standard dress in the cozy diner. She cut her eggs and biscuits with her knife and forked everything in in some preset order.

"So, why'd you fellas start off on this trip to California and back?" Bud asked.

"To get my family back," Claude said, followed by a large bite of buttermilk pancakes.

"How long had they been gone?"

"Just left. We got up the next day and took off after them." He drank down the last swallow of his coffee and held it up for the waitress to refill.

"Did you have any warning they were going to leave?"

"None that I could tell."

Bea wiped her mouth with her napkin. "Every camel has its last straw," she said.

The waitress filled Claude's cup. He looked at Bea as he swallowed his first sip.

"Well, I'm sure if you had seen it coming, you might have been able to do something," Bud said

Claude waved his hand. "Thank we might talk about something else," he said. "This don't matter no more."

"That simple?" Bud asked.

"Yeah, if she don't want me, I don't want her. It's that simple."

Bea finished her meal. She removed her gloves, rolled them neatly and placed them in her purse. She slipped her arm through the straps of her purse and stood. Bud stood. Frank cleared his throat at Claude. He looked up and the two of them stood as well. The watched Bea walk toward the ladies' room.

"You sure she's okay, Mister?" Claude asked.

"Bea's just fine."

"But I ain't never seen nobody eat with gloves on before," Frank said.

"Son, we've been together for sixty-two years. Bea eating with gloves on ain't nothing."

"And you just put up with it for all that time?" Claude asked.

"Reckon I don't see it as puttin' up with it, Claude."

"Toleratin'?" Frank asked.

"Naw. When I tied my knot with Nellie, I figured whatever I got just came along with the whole package."

"I, uh, I can't take stuff like that from no woman. If I don't like somethin' then they gotta change."

"How many times you been married, Claude?" Bud asked.

"Fire!" The scream from the startled cook caught everyone's attention. The flames shooting out of the kitchen had everyone pausing, preparing to run outside.

"Throw some baking soda on it!" yelled the waitress.

The cook grabbed the box off the shelf, tore off the top and doused the flames with the powder.

"And open the back door!" she yelled again.

Soon the wind coming in the front door was blowing the smoke and excitement out the back.

"Uh, three or four," Claude laughed. "Ain't rightly sure no more."

"Ever stop to figure out why?"

"'Cause after they all left me, and I didn't like being alone."

"My momma didn't leave him," Frank added. "She died."

Bea came from the restroom and stopped by the cash register and spoke with the young waitress.

"I'm sorry, Frank," Bud said. "But Claude, you want to know why me and Bea's been together so long?"

"Well, she loves you, I guess."

"Yes, she does, but that ain't the reason. It's because when the preacher asked us if we promised until death do us part, we both said we did. And neither of us have died yet, so the promise is still good."

"Well, that's good for you, for both of you."

"Claude, marriage takes work. You gotta accept who you got. It ain't one-sided. It ain't all about you. It's about the both of you."

"Well, I guess you're just more of a man than I am."

"More? I figure you either are or you ain't. Look at them cows out there in Justin's trailer. They're either cows or they ain't. Ain't one of them more of a cow than any of the others."

"Alright, you've made your point. Maybe next time."

"Maybe so," Bud said. "Hey, looks like Bubba's got your tire fixed and ready. We better get you back over there before he starts charging us a parking fee."

"What about our meal?" Frank asked.

"Oh, Bea's done taken care of it." Frank looked at Claude. Claude shrugged.

The tire was in the bed of the pickup. Bea was in the front seat as before, sitting tall, staring out the windshield, her scarf tied tightly around her head.

"Gotta ask the guy to let us come back and work off the bill," Frank said as they walked up to the station.

"Oh, Bea's done taken care of it."

Claude looked at Bud, then at Bea. "This don't make no sense. You don't know us from Adam. Bought us breakfast and now a tire. That just don't seem right. We cain't pay you back."

"Don't expect you to," Bud said. "Get in the back."

Claude and Frank climbed in and sat on the new tire. "Dad," Frank said. "We can't pay them for this."

"I know," he said. "I know. He said he don't expect us to."

Bud headed back to their car. The forty-five mile per hour trip was made even faster by all the thoughts flying through Claude's mind.

"We're gonna head on back into Pleasanton to church. We still got time to get there. Ain't probably missed nothing yet. Hope you fellas get along alright."

"Bud, wish we had money to pay you," Claude said.

"Just promise me you'll consider what I told you in the café. That would be payment enough."

"I will. Who knows, may make a difference. Thanks for everything."

They stood watching the old black Chevy drive back toward the town. Claude sighed and thumbed for Frank to get the new tire on. "That rain's moving in pretty fast. You better hurry up."

# Chapter Thirty-one

BY THE TIME THE RAIN HAD SPREAD TO PLEASANTON, IT HAD covered half of Arkansas and Oklahoma. It was moving slowly but would be into Missouri and Nebraska by nightfall. Because it was taking its time on its wide arch toward the northeast, much more rain was falling than could be absorbed by the ground. The run-off was rushing down toward every low spot, filling sloughs, streams, creeks and rivers. The land was being pounded by hard, vicious water pellets driven by howling winds, stripping off leaves and toppling large trees as their roots lost their ability to grip in the soggy soil.

Frank tightened the last lug nut and rushed back into the car. His back was totally soaked with water. "Man, that came up fast," he said.

"Must be a hurricane," Claude said. "Coming up like that from the south. Must have left a mess on the coast to still be that strong up here."

The Ford started up and resumed its familiar rumble, but with the rain pounded hard on the roof, as if a dozen percussionists joined the song. The winds were driving the rain straight across the highway. Frank struggled with the coupe as the winds steadily pushed it out of its lane. As soon as he leaned the tires toward the shoulder to hold into the wind, the blast would let up. The car would head toward the ditch. Frank would cut back to the highway and another blast would push him into the opposing lane.

"Want me to drive?" Claude asked.

"Don't thank you can do any better," he answered. "This wind is somethin' fierce. Maybe we ought to wait it out in Pleasanton."

"Naw, I want to get back. Just keep us between the ditches."

"I can't even see the ditches. These wipers can't keep up with all this rain."

"Then stick your head out the window. I don't want to stop."

As they drove through town nothing was as it was before. The gas station was shut down and across the street, several people were huddled behind the plate glass of the café watching the rain pepper the windows. No one stirred outside as the gale pounded the town. They continued on.

The city limit sign seemed more of an ominous warning than a designation of boundary. Frank watched it as they passed by. The sudden blast of a wall of water pressed the car to the left. Frank jerked the wheel back to the right. The rear wheels came around and the coupe spun a complete circle in the middle of the highway. When the spinning stopped, the front of the car faced a small, white building with a tall steeple over the front porch.

"That's it for me," Frank said. "I'm going to church." He put the Ford in first gear and splashed through the puddles in the parking lot.

"No way! You just need to change your drawers and we can keep going. I'll drive if you're too scared."

"Dad give it up. It's just too bad to go on. And goin' to church is probably the best way we can wait out this storm. Maybe Bud and Bea are in there."

The two water-logged travelers stood in the vestibule puddling on the floor. An usher rushed over and handed them each a towel which absorbed most of the loose water. He gave them another one to place on the pew to soak up the water saturating their clothes. As he did, he offered them his ebony hand and smile to welcome them inside.

The crowd was sparse but active. They had spread themselves around in the small chapel and clapped and swayed to the singing of a hymn. The lady leading stood just right of the pulpit which took its prominent place in the center of the platform. The choir behind her followed every movement of her hand and head. The pastor stood, centered behind the pulpit, singing with arms raised and eyes tightly closed. Frank's heart was captured, and he quickly joined the song. Claude stood beside Frank, folded arms across his chest, watching.

"Well, Sister Beulah May," the pastor said, "That one put a smile on the face of God, I can guarantee it." The congregation laughed.

"Amen, brother," shouted the usher standing in the back behind Claude. Claude tightened but kept himself from jerking around.

"Alright now, let's tell the Lord what He wants to hear," the pastor began. "Yes," he said softly. "Yes," the congregation repeated. "Yes," he said louder. "Yes," they repeated. "Yes," he shouted. "Yes." They matched his volume. "Yes!" he finally roared. "Yes! Yes! Yes!" they sounded back. Then, everything went quiet and the pastor spoke, "Lord, You've heard our answer. Now tell us what you want us to do."

The organ cranked out the introduction to another song. Beulah May turned to the choir and pointed at an older man in the back on the top row. Jewel Johnson opened his mouth and began singing. "Living below in this old sinful world/Hardly a comfort can afford/Striving alone to face temptation's call/Where could I go but to the Lord?"

The choir and congregation joined, "Where could I go/Oh where could I go/Seeking a refuge for my soul? /Needing a friend to help me in the end/Where could I go but to the Lord?"

The song pounded hard at Claude's chest. He felt a tight discomfort he was unaccustomed to. It wasn't a pain. No fear of a heart attack. It was deeper, touching a point within his very soul he usually numbed with whisky and beer. He shook his head and quickly thought of the rest of the trip remaining, of work awaiting him back at Creighton's Mill. He flashed to the confrontation with Stanton, then to the café with Bud and Bea. Soon the song was over as was the rumbling within his chest. He breathed rapidly, then took a slow, deliberate breath and stared blankly at the pastor.

"Oh, Lord, You are so good to us," the pastor prayed, arms raised, head back, eyes closed tightly.

"Amen," voiced the congregation.

"Lead us, Lord. Not like some dumb mule you have to whack on the head to get his attention. Not like some stubborn jack donkey you have to wait on for him to decide to carry your load. Not like some pack of dogs you have to fight to prove yourself worthy of leading. Lord, lead us like sheep. Sheep who want Your green pastures, who want Your still waters. Lord, only You can restore our souls. Lord, only You can anoint our heads with oil. Lord, only You can place before us a feast. Lord, only You can walk with us through the valley. Lord, only You can grant to us mercy and goodness. Lord, truly, because of You, our cups overflow." He paused.

The moment was growing a bit uncomfortable for Claude. He looked up and saw the pastor looking directly at him. He continued, "Lord, You are our shepherd. We are the sheep of Your pasture. With You we got everything we could ever need. Help us to be smart enough to stop looking as soon as we find it. Amen." The congregation replied. Claude looked down.

"Let's all have a seat and see what the Lord has for us today," the pastor said. Everyone sat and opened their Bibles. The pastor looked back at his chair and under the pulpit. "Well, now, this is interesting," he said. "Seems in all the rush to get in here out of the storm I must have left my Bible in the car." The usher in the back of the room stood and started for the door. "No, Brother Curtis. No need for you getting all wet because of my mistake. Got something else on my heart anyhow." Curtis sat back down.

"Ever felt rejected?" the pastor began. The congregation nodded and spoke their agreement. "Sister Beulah, ever felt rejected?" "Yas, suh," she said. "Sister Faye, ever felt rejected?" "Amen to that," she said. The Pastor paced across the platform pointing his finger at members. They nodded back. He pointed at Claude. Claude looked down.

"Ain't nothing hurts like rejection," he continued. "It hurts deeper and lasts longer than most any other kind of hurt. You can cut your arm off and one of these days its gonna quit hurting, but you get rejected and it's gonna stay with you like a haunting you just can't shed."

"And when you done been rejected by somebody you needn't have been rejected by, somebody you'd been counting on not to reject you, it hurts the most. Take Jesus right before he was crucified. Two men rejected Him. One, Judas, sold Him outright. The other, Peter, denied he even knew who Jesus was. Both rejected Him. Which one do you think hurt Him the most?"

"Peter," the congregation shouted.

"Peter. 'Cause Peter had already said who He was to him. He said He was the Lord, the Son of the Most High God. To know somebody close and still reject him is the biggest kind of hurt you can do."

"Come on," the elder on the front row shouted.

"When somebody's supposed to love you and then turns their back on you, that hurt goes deep. Y'need that love to last. Y'need to count on that love every day. And when that love gets taken away or, worse, refuses to be given, it leaves a deep hole in your heart and a darkness in your soul."

"Been there," shouted one voice.

"Yas suh," shouted another.

"Each day it will dig a little deeper, a little wider. Every day we feel that moment of rejection as freshly as if it had just happened. And do you know what'll happen?"

"What's that?"

"Tell us."

"That hurt will turn into anger. We'll be mad at who hurt us, mad that we hurt and mad at ourselves for feeling this way. Then blame God that it happened."

"Alright."

"Hear me now. That anger will turn into hatred that will become a barrier to healing. Only one power can heal that kind of hurt—forgiveness. But forgiveness can't work if we'd rather hate. Gotta quit the hate to let forgiveness do its thing." He stepped down from the platform to the main floor. Claude pressed back in the pew. Everyone else leaned forward.

"Love plus forgiveness gives life," he said. "Love and hatred can't live in the same house. Love and hatred can't dwell in the same heart. If we ever want healing from the hurt of rejection, we gotta forgive. To be able to forgive we gotta chase off the hatred."

He paused and scanned the faces in the crowd, nodding at each one. When he looked at Claude, he stopped nodding. Claude could not maintain eye contact and looked down. The pastor kept his eyes on him. Claude looked back up. The pastor smiled and nodded. "Well, amen. That may be the shortest sermon on record, but I'm done. And speaking of done, believe we *done* got some fried chicken waiting for us in the parlor. Sister Beulah May, sing us out of here."

The organ began. Beulah May raised her hand and the choir sang, "Some glad morning when this life is o'er/ I'll fly away…" The congregation rose and danced out the side door, into the parlor. Frank moved out to follow.

"Whoa there, son, we're not staying here any longer. We need to head on."

"Not me, I'm gonna get some of that fried chicken."

Frank followed the other folks toward the food. The organ stopped and Claude was the only one left. "Shoot," he said and headed into the parlor.

The spread was bountiful. Piles of fried chicken overflowed their large platters. Bowls of mashed potatoes, green beans, gravy and corn crowded in for the rest of the space on the table. A separate table was covered with pies and a huge bowl of banana pudding. The feast was set. Everyone stood patiently waiting for Pastor Holliday to pronounce the blessing.

"Before I ask the Lord to bless our food and fellowship, I'd like to welcome our lighter-skinned brethren today. It's not often we are blessed by such variety in color." The folks waiting for their meal laughed politely. Frank smiled. Claude looked down.

"Anything we might add to our prayer for you fellas?"

Frank took in breath to speak. Claude elbowed him in the ribs. He shook his head when Frank looked over at him. Frank stared hard, took another breath and began to speak. "I'd appreciate it, Pastor," he said, turning his attention now to the preacher. "My dad and me, we're heading home from a trip to California. Life's gonna be a bit different when we get back. Guess I'd hope the Lord would help us out."

"A worthy petition. Let's pray, folks. Lord, You are no respecter of persons. You've made that clear. We ask you to help these two white brothers to find what they're lookin' for. Help them to know when they've found it and help them to be content with what they find. Amen."

"Pastor, the food," whispered Beulah May.

"And, Lord, bless this food and the chickens that gave their lives to fill our bellies. Amen."

"Amen to that," laughed Beulah May.

"Come on fellas," the pastor said. "You get to go first with me."

The home cooked food hit taste buds that hadn't been touched since they left Pine Hollow. Southern cooking, real food, no pretenders, just genuine fried chicken and all the fixings. The first plateful went fast, too fast for conversation. Pastor Curtis nodded to Frank to go for a refill. Both Claude and Frank made a second pass.

"Tell me about this trip, Frank?" Pastor Holliday asked as Frank settled his refreshed plate on the table. Claude was still refilling.

"Dad's wife, Flo, left him and took her two girls and their son and left Pine Hollow," Frank began. "We left the next day but didn't find them till we got all the way to California. The man where they were staying hit my dad and we left. Been making our way back since then."

"So, this wasn't your momma?"

"No, his momma died when he was eight or nine," Claude answered, as he set his plate in front of his chair.

"Seven," Frank said.

"I ain't good alone," Claude said. "I was a mess when his momma died and then Flo came along a few years later. She kinda took over. Wasn't like any other woman I'd ever been around."

"How's that?" the pastor asked.

"I don't know. She was just something."

"In a good way?"

"Not really. She moved in and just took over. Not that the place didn't need it. She brought her two girls then we had Jack."

"How'd that work out?"

"Didn't," Frank said.

"I'm telling the story," Claude fired. Frank shrugged and resumed eating. "Guess it was too much for her, so we sent Frank to live with his Aunt Alma."

"She beat me till I ran away," Frank said.

"That's enough," Claude said.

"When did she leave?" Pastor Curtis asked.

"A couple of weeks ago," Claude answered.

"Another man?" the pastor's wife asked. She had sat silently beside her husband. These were the first words she added to the conversation.

"No," Claude indignantly replied.

"What did you do?" she asked.

"I didn't do nothing," Claude snapped.

She snorted and rolled her eyes.

"Listen, Flo was a hard woman. Probably more of a woman than a guy like me can handle."

"Strong?" Pastor Curtis quickly cut into the conversation.

"Mean."

"It's better to dwell in the wilderness than to live with a contentious and angry woman," the pastor said.

"She's both of those alright. But it weren't right for her to just pack up and head out like she did."

"Unless…" offered the wife.

"No! It's not." The Pastor asserted. "I wish you God's best on the rest of your journey, Claude."

"Thanks, we'd hoped to be home tonight but with this rain it probably won't be till tomorrow."

"That's good, but you never know where a journey like this is gonna take you," Pastor Holliday said.

"What you mean by that?"

"Meaning, before you're done you may have to go a whole lot deeper inside yourself than you might want to."

"Preaching's over, ain't it, Preacher?" Claude snapped.

He clapped his hands together and brushed them apart. "Preaching's over. How about some of that dessert over there?"

The storm was still raging when the finished. Pastor Curtis walked them back to the front door, took a handful of dollars out of the offering plate and slipped them into Claude's hand. "No, no. I can't take this. I ain't never taken money from a…"

"Preacher? It ain't much but maybe it'll get you a little closer to home."

"You know I've been around a lot of dark folk. Work a lot of them at the mill. You're probably the whitest I've ever met."

"It ain't the color, it's the heart of a man, Claude. Color don't make one man better or worse than another. Good or bad, color ain't the difference. *As a man thinks within himself, so is he.*"

"Proverbs 23:7," said Frank.

"If a man is good, it shows," the pastor said, looking at Frank. "If not…" He looked back at Claude.

"You sayin' I ain't a good man?" Claude asked.

"Ain't sure, Claude. But you got a good boy here in Frank."

"You ain't been around him any more than you have me. And you thank you can tell all that about us?"

"It's the embers."

"Embers?"

"What flies off a log when it burns."

"I know what embers are. What's that got to do with anythang?"

"Claude, you're burning up. We all are. And as we do, we sent off embers."

"So?"

"Some of those embers just fly off to who knows where. Some land on those around us."

"You talkin' about my drinkin'?"

"I'm talkin' about your embers. It's the embers that cause the trouble."

"Trouble?"

"Where do the embers that hurt others come from, Claude, but from the trouble in our own lives."

"So? Ain't nobody perfect."

"Claude, you got a problem with your manhood."

"Ain't nothing wrong with my manhood!" He moved closer to the pastor and stood looking up at him. The Pastor Curtis had him by six inches.

"Think about it, Claude. It's one thing for you to not feel good about who you are. It's another to cause someone else to feel the same way. I'm done. Lord bless and keep you." The pastor placed a comforting hand on Claude's shoulder. Claude jerked away.

"Thanks for the lunch and money," he said as he turned and rushed into the downpour and back in the car. Frank shook hands with the pastor.

"Sorry, Pastor," he said.

"Son, don't be sorry for somebody else's actions."

"I thank I'm beginnin' to get that message," he said and followed his dad out into the rain.

# Chapter Thirty-two

"THIS RAIN IS RUINING EVERYTHING," MR. CREIGHTON SAID. "Oh, it'll quit before long," Dearl replied. The Sunday afternoon meeting at the Mill office was unusual. Mr. Creighton tried not to take the men away from their families on Sunday afternoon, but with thousands of dollars of new equipment rusting away under a shed because of rain, wind and lack of use, a meeting seemed justified. Why should he carry the burden by himself?

"Dearl, look out that window," he said. Dearl turned in his chair and looked out at the rain pelting the glass, the trees in the distance bending and twisting to the ferocity of the winds. He knew what the ground looked like, having just driven through the puddles and sloshed across the grass leading into the mill office. Rain like this was a disaster to the logging business.

"It's bad," Dearl said.

"Bad! How long do you think it's going to be before we can get the mill back operational?"

"Well, the logs are soaked, the machinery's soaked, the roads in the woods are mud bogs. We can't get in and if we got in, we wouldn't be able to get out. We're shut down."

"But, for how long?"

"Soon as this storm passes through, it's gonna take probably a week or so to dry out."

"Weeks?"

"A week or so," Dearl repeated.

"Do you have any idea what that's going to cost me?"

"No, sir."

"Plenty, that's what. All these men, doing nothing. Logs ruining. All that equipment just sitting there. Do you know I've got a payment coming up in a month? A big payment and we aren't doing anything to help me make that payment? This is the worst thing that could ever happen. Why on earth did I ever listen to Claude Massey wanting to expand operations?

Mr. Creighton got up from his desk and walked to the window. A gust of wind blew a bucket of rain against the pane. He flinched back. "You'd think a church-going man like me would get better treatment than this," he said.

"Ain't sure that's got anything to do with it," Dearl said. "You know it rains on the just and the unjust just he same."

"Well it should. It's how I'd run things. You do good, you get good. You don't do good and you get a flood."

"Be tough to be the one to measure good, don't you thank?"

"Humph." He turned back to Dearl. "Just doesn't make any sense."

"It's just a rain storm. Probably a hurricane up from the gulf. Doesn't have anything to do with us. It'll pass on through soon. I'm not worried."

"That's because it's not your money on the line."

Sara Beth looked like a drenched dog standing at the door. "Sara Beth, what on earth are you doing out in this storm?" asked Billie Nell. She grabbed a towel and opened the screen door. Sara Beth melted in a flood of tears more torrid than the storm.

Manny rushed in from the bedroom. "Sara Beth, what's wrong, Baby?"

"Momma won't wake up," she sobbed. "And Daddy just sits there looking at her. He won't say nothing. I'm scared, Miss Manny. Scared something awful."

"Billie Nell get my bag. I'll go see what's wrong. Sarah Beth, you stay here with Billie Nell."

"What?" Billie Nell asked.

"Keep her here with you. It's best for now."

"But…"

"No buts, Billie Nell. Keep her here."

Manny wrapped one of Dearl's extra raincoats around her and rushed out into the storm. The winds blew her faster than she could run and tossed her onto the soggy ground. She got up and forced her way down the trail.

The dog run seemed deserted. The front door was closed to keep out the rain. She looked through the window and saw Luke sitting in the rocking chair staring at Sally as she lay on the bed. Her eyes fixed toward the ceiling. Manny opened the door.

"Luke?"

He just rocked and stared.

"Sally?"

She just laid there, eyes fixed.

"Oh, Dear God," she said. She rushed in and looked for the other children. They huddled on their pallet in the corner. She approached the bed. "Sally," she whispered. "Sally, can you hear me?"

Manny touched Sally's face. It felt cold and clammy. She jerked her hand back and held it against her chest. She trembled as she frantically looked around the room for an answer, any answer. She pulled back the sheet covering Sally's lower body. Blood had fully saturated the bed. Manny looked up into Sally's lifeless face and wept. She pulled the sheet back over the stains and turned to Luke.

"Oh, Luke, I'm so sorry," she said. "I didn't know this would happen. With the storm, I couldn't…I should've come over anyway. I'm sorry, Luke, so sorry."

Luke didn't move. He just stared at Sally. Manny got his raincoat off the hook by the front door and wrapped it around the older ones. She took the twins and hid them underneath Dearl's coat. "I'm taking them to Annie Mae's, Luke. Then I'll be back." Luke just sat there.

The load of the twins, the torrent of rain and pounding wind made the trail nearly impossible. Manny kept praying, "Lord, get me there quick, please."

"Annie Mae!" Manny shouted when in sight of the shack. The rain and wind drowned out her voice. She kept coming. The door opened and Annie Mae came out on the porch.

"Lord, have mercy!" she shouted when she saw Manny and the girls. She rushed off into the rain and grabbed up the two older girls. "I just felt I needed to go outside," she said. "Lord, have mercy."

"Floyd, get some towels and dry these young 'uns off," Annie Mae shouted. "Hope, get over here and help your daddy."

Once everyone was dry and distracted, Manny turned to Annie Mae. "We lost Sally," she said.

"Lost her? How we done lost her?"

"She bled out too much, I guess."

"Miss Manny, she was fine when I left her before the storm started. Luke came in and I thought I ought to get on home. I wouldn't have left if I'd a known…"

"Ain't your fault, Annie Mae. If anyone's to blame, it's me. I knew I should've gone over and checked on her, but this blasted storm…"

"Ain't the storm's fault," Annie Mae said.

"I know, if I'd only…"

"Ain't no *if I'd only's* fault neither. It's the Lord who giveth and the Lord who done taketh away."

"Ain't there yet, Annie Mae. I still thank I should've done something."

"And what, took away God's right to be God?"

"Just you keep the young 'uns and I'm gonna go to the mill and get Dearl then go back over there and see what I can do."

"Yas 'um to all that except Hope'll watch the chil'uns. I'm goin' with you."

"Whew," Manny sighed. "Thanks, I really need you. I don't know what in the world I'm doin'."

"You and me both, so's we better put this one in the hands of the Lord." Annie Mae took Manny's hand and stopped time. "Lord don't know what's goin' on or why or what you plan on doin', but we know nothin's done 'til You say it's done. So, Lord, we're asking for a miracle for Sally." She shook Manny's hands. "Amen."

They both darted off the porch and out into the rain. The path to the mill was well worn but slippery when wet. Today it was a slosh pit. They ran, skidded, slipped and fell, holding each other to help steady the treacherous trip.

Dearl had told Manny he would probably stay at the mill most of the day. Once the meeting with Mr. Creighton was over, he said he'd spend the rest of the afternoon securing the grounds around the mill. All the machinery was tarped, and the loose tools gathered up, but the rain was just too hard and steady for a run to the truck and a desperate rush home, only to be drenched again when he got out. He and Ernest sat in Ernest's shop and listened to the new tin roof getting dented by hail and debris.

"This ain't like no thunderstorm I ever saw," Ernest said.

"Probably a hurricane," Dearl suggested. "A thunderstorm would have been done and gone by now. This thang doesn't seem to be going anywhere for a while."

"We had a typhoon when I was in Korea," Ernest began. "That was the worst I ever saw. They said that was the same thing as a hurricane back home."

"Yeah? What was that like?"

"Like three days of solid, hard rain. Everything got wet. Couldn't dry out our clothes so we wore the same ones every day. Got the jungle rot. That was the worst thang I ever got. Like to never've cleared up."

"So, I guess the war had to let up till the storm was over."

"Naw, they didn't stop that for nothin'. They did shut the tanks down for the time. They could still run in the rain, but them boys kept gettin' stuck in the mud. Me and Dutton built a tractor out of some left-over tank parts and spent most of the time going out and pulling the real tanks out of the mud."

"I thought tanks could go through anything."

"Yeah, until they sank up to high bottom. They ain't goin' nowhere then."

"Did you like your time in the Army?"

"Weren't that bad. Missed bein' home, but it weren't that bad with Dutton there."

"Mr. Creighton told me about your award some time back for saving those people in that helicopter. That makes you a hero, you know."

"Aw, Dearl, I didn't do nothin' you or nobody else would've done. You just see somebody needin' help and you go help them. Ain't no big deal."

"Ain't what I heard but I'm proud of what you did. Probably some helicopter guys were pretty proud, too."

"Except that one I couldn't get to before the thang blew up."

"Naw, I'd expect him to be glad you got his buddies out. I know I would."

"Huh, never thought nothing like that. Maybe so."

"Ernest! Ernest! Where's Mister Dearl?" Annie Mae yelled as she approached the shed. She nearly collapsed from the strain as she and Manny ran into the garage.

"Annie Mae, what on earth…" Ernest said.

"I'm right here," Dearl said. "Manny? What's goin' on?" Manny melted both emotionally and physically into Dearl's arms. She couldn't speak as she gasped for breath.

"Mister Dearl…you gotta come quick…Miss Sally…dead or dying…Miss Manny needs you…" Annie Mae said.

Manny collected herself. "Dearl, I thank we lost her, and I don't know what to do." Dearl pushed the ladies back out into the rain and toward the truck.

"Need me to come?" Ernest asked.

"Naw, I don't know what's goin' on but if I need you, I'll come get you. Get in the front Annie Mae and let's go."

The truck slid around in the parking lot, splashing up giant gushers and spraying mud and water on everything behind it as Dearl headed off to the Johnson's.

"Alright, somebody tell me what happened?"

"Don't know," Manny began. "Bled out, I guess. She was alright when we both saw her last. Something must have gone really bad."

"You sure she's dead?"

"She looked dead and felt cold," Manny said.

The rain continued to pelt them as they pulled up in front of the house. Manny was pushing Annie Mae out the door even before the truck fully stopped. They both rushed up the steps and reached the door at the same time. Annie Mae stopped and let Manny go in first. Sally was still on the bed but rolled on her side. Luke was sitting in the rocker staring at her.

"Luke," Manny asked. "How did Sally get turned on her side?" Luke just stared. She asked again breaking his line of sight to his wife. "Luke! How did Sally move?"

He looked up at Manny and said, "She asked me to move her."

"She talked to you?"

"Yeah," he said. "She kinda woke up for a minute and now she's gone again."

"Luke, she ain't gone," Manny shouted. "Dearl! We gotta get Sally to the hospital."

"Luke, let's go," Dearl yelled. Responsive to his boss's command, Luke shook his head and looked at the whirlwind going on around his wife. He pulled up his boots and jumped out of the rocker.

The nearest hospital was in Lathrup Springs, thirty minutes away on a good day. With the storm, they knew it would be an hour. They wrapped Sally in a blanket. Luke carried her to the truck and held her in his lap. Manny squeezed in the middle and Dearl cranked up the motor. Annie Mae waved them off, closed the house and headed back home in the rain.

Frank had traded off with Claude and was in the backseat trying to catch a nap while Claude drove. His dreams drifted to a familiar scene, one he had caught only glimpses of from time to time. He saw himself as a child, not more than seven sitting on the floor in the kitchen playing with clothespins. He'd connect them together to make horses and have single pins become soldiers riding them. Behind him was Marissa, a young Mexican lady who served the family as housekeeper. She was washing dishes. She reached over, took a dishtowel and turned toward him, drying her hands. A red mark on the side of her face bore a hand-print. Her eyes were wet with tears. He just looked at her. She blew her nose on the towel and tossed it onto the table. She stooped and tussled his hair, then walked into the bedroom.

In a moment he heard a gunshot blast. He got up and walked into the bedroom. Marissa was lying across the bed. Her feet were hanging off on one side. He walked over and shook her feet. She just lay there. He went to the other side of the bed. Blood covered the side of her head and was dripping onto the floor. A pistol was on the floor beside the pool of blood.

The screen door slammed against the wall as Hattie, a large, black woman came in the house screaming. She scooped him up from behind and held him tightly burying his face in her chest. "God Almighty! God Almighty! God Almighty!" she kept repeating.

As she rushed him outside, Claude and Lou came in from the front porch. "Frank!" Lou screamed.

"Frank's alright, Ms. Massey," she said. "I'll take him to my house." Hattie rushed out the back door and down the steps. The screen door slammed hard against the frame. Hattie rushed through the back yard, kicking chickens out of the way as she ran. "God Almighty! God Almighty! Get out the way, chickens! God Almighty!"

The blast from a diesel truck's horn startles Frank awake. "Stupid trucker," Claude said.

"We alright?"

"Of course. Stupid trucker don't know how to drive."

Frank lay back down and quickly was back asleep and into an earlier moment of his familiar dream.

He was in bed, woke up and walked down the hallway to his parents' bedroom. It was the middle of the afternoon. He heard sounds from the bedroom and opened the door. He stood at the doorway and looked at the bed.

"Frank, get out of here!" his dad shouted. "Get out of here and close that door!"

As he backed out of the room and was closing the door a fast-moving form rushed past him and pushed it hard against the dresser.

"Frank!" Claude yelled. He looked up from the bed and jerked the covers up over him. "Lou?"

Lou was a tall lady, dressed in a flower-print dress that showed the bulge in front indicating she was heavily pregnant. She reached behind her and slammed the door shut. Frank could only hear muffled shouts and screams, then a crash. The door opened. Lou turned and shouted, "Thought I wouldn't be back so soon? You idiot." She rushed past Frank and out the front door.

Claude was hurriedly dressing as he stumbled by Frank. "Frank, go in the kitchen and play." Marissa followed closely behind Claude and grabbed his arm.

"Marissa, leave me alone. Don't you see the mess I'm in?"

"But you promised," she said.

"I ain't leaving Lou for you," he said. "You got that."

"But…" *Whack!* The slap knocked her back into the bedroom.

"Marissa, get out of here. Go home. And don't come back." Claude yelled as the rushed out the front door. Marissa ran into the kitchen and began washing her face. Frank saw through the screed door his mother was sitting in the car, crying. Claude stood beside the closed window. "Lou, I'm sorry. This don't mean nothing, Honey." She looked up at him and screamed. He opened the door and took her by the arm. She pulled back. "Lou, please, come out and let me explain."

She suddenly stopped crying. "Explain! You can explain this?"

Claude noticed Frank standing at the door. "Frank, I said get back in the house. Go play in the kitchen. He turned and went back into the kitchen, took out his close pins and sat on the floor. He looked up as Marissa reached over, took up the dish towel and began to wipe her hands.

He woke again and lay still on the back seat, staring up at the headliner. He began to breathe hard. His heart raced fast within his chest. His breaths came quickly. He raised up off the seat. "Augh!" he groaned.

"Frank, what the heck's wrong with you," Claude said. "Nearly scared me to death. What's the matter?"

Frank stared hard at his dad. Through the rearview mirror Claude could see the fire in his eyes.

"Finished the dream," Frank said, climbing over the seat to the front.

"Bout time."

"You want to know how it ends?"

"Sure, I guess."

"You were with Marissa."

"What?"

"You were with Marissa before she shot herself."

"What are you talking about?"

"You were with Marissa in the bedroom and Momma caught you."

"'That's' stupid. It's just a dream, Frank. It ain't real."

"Momma came in and caught you in bed with Marissa. Y'all

fought in the bedroom then went out front and fought some more. Then Marissa killed herself."

"You're out of your mind."

"All this time I never knew what had happened. But it was you all along."

"That's enough."

"Then Momma died right after that. All because of you and Marissa."

"Your Momma died giving birth to your little sister."

"I don't have a little sister."

"No, you don't. They both died during delivery." Claude pulled underneath an overpass and turned the car off. "Frank, I ain't proud of what I did. But I did it and I carry the guilt. Your Momma had gone to the doctor for a checkup. She had been having a hard time carrying your little sister so we couldn't...you know."

"So, you and Marissa..."

"I told you I ain't proud of none of it."

"Momma should'a left you in a heartbeat."

"Your Momma was better'n that. She forgave me."

"No, she didn't."

"Yeah, she did. Shouldn't have but she did. With Marissa dying and all the hurt I'd caused, she knew I was sorry. She forgave me."

"When?"

"In the hospital, right before she died. Guess she knew I needed it to get over thangs."

"You got over this? How can you get over this? I ain't over this!"

"Don't have nothing to do with you, boy. This was between me and your Momma."

"Don't have nothing to do with me? All my life I've wondered what I did to make Marissa do that and that God was punishing me by taking Momma away. I've fought with that guilt every day and begged God to help me."

"Well, there's your answer."

"Just like that."

"That's your answer whether you want it or not." Claude slid over to the passenger side. "I'm tired of driving. You drive for a while." Frank climbed over the seat and settled behind the wheel. He stared out into the storm, breathed deeply and turned the key. The eight cylinders roared out the anguish in his soul. The wipers slapped to the pounding within his heart.

# Chapter Thirty-three

FIFTY-THREE MILES TO LATHRUP SPRINGS. ALMOST THERE, THEN *thirty minutes more to Pine Hollow,* he thought. The sign brought a measure of relief to his wearied face. Frank now realized how important it was he had gone with his dad, but now couldn't wait to be out of the car and out of his life. Home, he knew, would be Aunt Alma's house. He was done with Claude.

The wipers labored hard to squeegee off what rain it could from the windshield. Frank strained hard to see the stripes dividing the roadway. They were his only reference when the heavy rains and winds blotted out the rest of the road. Frank fought the wheel as the winds blew the coupe into the opposing lane. He'd bend it back, leaning into the gusts and then loose his line when the winds let up.

"What's going on?" Claude snapped. He wiped the haze off the windshield and leaned forward to see through it. "Can't see a thang, can you?"

"Not really."

"Then pull over and let me drive."

"You ain't gonna see any better than I can."

"Naw but I got more experience than you, so pull over."

"I can't even see the edge of the road on your side. How you expect me to pull over?"

"There, under that light. Pull in at that gas station and switch out with me."

The Ford splashed through the potted drive and underneath the awning of a deserted gas station. The brake drums were soaked so the shoes had little effect on stopping the car where Frank intended. He ran past the cover and had to back up. He knew he didn't want to see his dad's expression, so he kept his eyes on the mirrors.

The rains pounded and water blew from all directions. "Yeah, I'd definitely say this is a hurricane," Claude said. "Too much pounding to be a thunderstorm." The cover of the awning began to creak and sway. The next gust took it from its poles and flipped it across the road. The coupe again was taking the full brunt of the storm.

Claude adjusted himself and pulled the car back onto the highway. "Turn up the wipers," Frank strained.

"They're up."

"No, they ain't. They got another speed."

"No, they don't. These cars didn't come with a higher speed."

"Me and Ernest put one on. Just turn the knob one more click."

The wipers began slapping hard against the sides of the pillars. "Huh, ain't bad. I still can't see worth a flip, though."

"Hope you can see when we get to the river bridge. That thang ain't wide enough to be all over the road like we are."

"I'm just hoping it ain't flooded too bad. That's all we need."

The bridge was coming up quickly. The warning sign gave Claude only a few hundred feet to take aim between its steel-trussed frame spanning the Arkansas River. The water had risen to its base and was splashing up on the roadbed. A house dislodged from its foundation was fast approaching in the swollen current. In the twilight it appeared as a huge boulder rolling down black asphalt. Halfway across, the house crashed into the side of the bridge. The steel bent to the power of the flooding water pounding the house into its truss. Claude had no warning, only the strange awareness that the road was turning sharply when it should have continued straight.

The support gave way and the bridge broke in half, taking the coupe with it into the raging water. The car dipped hood-first into the depths then began to tumble end over end. The forces threw Frank into the backseat. Claude lost his grip on the steering wheel and was tossed down onto the floorboard.

The car twisted sideways and began to roll. The force brought Frank back to the front. Claude was head-first under the steering wheel and Frank forced down into the floorboard of the passenger side. His door opened and the suction pull him out into the water. He fought to find the surface. His lungs burned and his water-filled eyes flamed with panic.

He tightened everything in his face and thrust his hands toward the surface. He flailed his arms and legs in all manner of effort to reach air. He broke through and gasped, drawing in a gulp of precious life. He slapped about on the water until his lungs assured his mind they had enough oxygen, then he calmed and looked for the car. Nowhere. "Dad!" he yelled. He spun to look upstream, along the banks. Nothing. He turned back to where the current had driven him. No dull-black, 1940 Ford coupe anywhere. He settled into the disbelief and drifted with the current but swimming hard toward shore. He grabbed hold of a low branch and pulled himself to the bank. He lay out, peppered by the constant rain. He raised up and looked again at the river. No sign of his car or his dad. He fell back to the bank.

Carl Murphy saw the bridge collapse. He had been out in his tow truck anticipating trouble. He had braked just in time to avoid joining Claude and Frank in the river. "Hey!" he shouted. "You alright?" He was fixed on where Frank had gone on the bank but couldn't see if he was still there or had gone into the woods. "Hey! Fella, you alright?"

Frank raised again and looked back toward the bridge. He waved his hand, got up and started following the cow trail beside the bank. Carl came down to meet him, his bright yellow raincoat blocking off most of the rain.

"Man, that was some tumble you took there," Carl said. "Wasn't sure you'd get out of that one alive."

"Don't think my dad did," Frank said.

"What?"

"My dad, he's still in the car, wherever that is."

"Aw, I'm sorry, kid. That current is pretty strong even without the floods but now, there ain't no way he's gonna survive that."

"Thanks, that's real encouraging."

"No, I'm sorry, I was just talking. Didn't mean to…"

"Hey, don't worry about it. Guess we'll find him when the waters go back down."

"Yeah. Come on, let me get you into town." Carl led off back up the trail to his truck. "You want some cover from the rain?" He opened his coat and offered a portion of it to Frank.

"Naw, I'm already soaked. Don't thank I can get any wetter." He brushed his hand through his hair to get some of the water away from dripping into his face. As he pulled his hand back it was red. "Ow," he said. "Guess I hit something during all that and busted my head opened."

"I got a dry towel in the truck. We'll wrap it up and I'll take you to the hospital."

The sixty miles back to Lathrup Springs took forever. Carl was overly cautious and kept the speedometer somewhere between thirty and forty the whole way. He kept glancing over at Frank, waking him each time he closed his eyes. Frank felt his head go light and soon he was out.

Dearl and Manny watched as Luke paced about in the small waiting room. A candy-striper appeared at the door. "Any word yet?" Luke demanded.

"Sir, I'm just a candy-striper," the young girl said. "I brought y'all some coffee." She came into the room pulling the cart of coffee behind her. Dearl was up before she parked the cart. Luke wasn't sure what he wanted. Dearl insisted and placed a cup in Luke's quivering hand.

"Got any sweetnin' and colorin'?" Manny asked.

"Yes, ma'am," the girl answered. "What do you want in it?"

"Oh, here, let me do it," Manny answered. "I need to get up and move around anyhow."

With freshly brewed coffee in hand the three sat back down and resumed the wait. Most said Doctor Bradley was too good to be working in Lathrup Springs. "He should be down in Little Rock," they'd say. But having him in Lathrup Springs, on call at this very moment, should have brought great comfort to Luke and the Thomsons. However, being from Pine Hollow, anyone with M.D. behind his name was considered more than adequate.

As Luke was raising himself back up to continue pacing, Doctor Bradley came in. All three stood. "Please sit back down," the doctor insisted. Manny looked at Doctor Bradley as if they were waiting to hear from God. The doctor began, "Well, though we're not out of the woods yet, I believe you got Mrs. Johnson in here just in time. Any longer and I'm not sure we could have helped her." The three stared at the man.

"I'll not use all the technical terms they taught me in medical school, so let's just say, after the miscarriage, some things didn't close off like they should have. She probably formed a clot that came loose and after that the bleeding never stopped. The reason you thought she was dead at first was because of how much blood she lost. When the body gets stressed like that it starts to shut down to stay alive. Being awake was not as important as keeping the insides working."

"So, is she gonna be alright, Doctor?" Luke offered.

"We had to go in, clean up some stuff and fix some other stuff. We had to give her a lot of blood. Normally, it takes the body a day or so to start to come back after something like this, so we'll just have to wait and see. She'll be staying here for the time being."

"I sure thank you for saving my wife," Luke said.

"Actually, Mrs. Thomson, here, was the one who did the saving," the doctor said. Dearl put his arm around Manny and squeezed. She began to cry. "You done good, Girl." No word of thanks could come out of a throat squeezed closed to keep from crying. Manny just nodded.

"Can we see her?" Luke asked.

"Not for a couple of hours. We have her in recovery and need to keep a sharp eye on her for a bit. You can see her when she's in her room."

"Okay."

"And Luke?"

"Yes, sir?"

"No more kiddos," the doctor said.

"Yes, sir."

"No, I've made sure. I had to remove some of the stuff where babies come from to be able to fix the other problem."

"So, we can't...you know?"

"No, you can still, you know, but you won't be making any more babies."

"I can live with that," Luke said. "Bet ya Sally can, too."

Carl came into the parking lot at the same speed he had been driving the whole way in. Slowly on the highway, way too fast in the parking lot. He set on his horn and flashed his lights as he skidded up to the curb at the ambulance loading dock. Frank was still unconscious and unresponsive to Carl's yelling for him to wake up.

Carl bolted from the truck and threw back the doors going into the emergency room. "I need some help out here!" he shouted. An admissions clerk yelled back from behind a desk.

"That's enough shouting in here, young man," she insisted. "Now come over here and fill out these forms."

"Ma'am it ain't me. It's the fella in my truck. He's dying on me. Maybe dead already. Get somebody out there or get up from there and come help me get him in there!"

From behind a closed door an orderly pushed through with a gurney. Carl opened the exterior door and rushed him to the truck. The two men scooped Frank up and placed him on the gurney. The orderly pushed Frank through the double doors directly into the treatment center. Carl watched as the doors closed behind. He stood on the dock, then realized he was getting peppered by the rain. He shook off the wet and headed back into his truck, driving off into the storm, ready for the next crisis.

"Doctor Bradley, E.R., STAT," the loud speaker sounded. "The only words Luke, Dearl and Manny knew were *Doctor Bradley*. Their hearts raced as they all three imagined him rushing back to Sally. They sat again and Luke began to pace.

"What do we have?" Doctor Bradley asked, donning a clean smock.

"Car accident victim, we assume," the nurse said.

"Assume?"

"Well, a tow-truck driver brought him in and just left him here. Until he's conscious I'm not sure what we're dealing with. He's got a pretty good gash on the back of his head, probably a concussion."

"Well, let's find out," Doctor Bradley said. He turned Frank over and peeled back the scalp to examine the gash. The blood began to flow again. "Let's irrigate this wound and sew him back up. Mary, you wanna be the barber?"

"Sure," the nurse said. She took the clippers and cut back the hair around the wound. Another nurse placed a syringe beside a tray holding a small pail of saline water. Doctor Bradley filled the syringe and squirted into the cavity. He pulled up the flap and ran his finger around the edges and across the soft tissue.

"Good," he said. "No debris. I think we can put this young man back together." He gently maneuvered the top layer until everything lined up. Mary handed him the suturing needle and he drew the skin up tightly around the edges. "Okay, let's clean these sheets up and turn him back over."

Though Frank was still out, Doctor Bradley lifted his eyelids and flashed his light onto the pupils. "Well, Nurse Mary, I believe your diagnosis was correct. This young man has a concussion. Let's wrap him up and get him in observation until he can wake up so we can see what kind of damage all of this caused."

An aid was in the corner of the ER pealing papers and pictures apart from Frank's wet billfold. "Looks like his name is Franklin Massey," she said. "He's got a rural route address. I think it says Pine Valley."

"Well, start calling people in Pine Valley and see if any of them know a Franklin Massey," Mary ordered.

"Alma?" Manny asked the tall, middle-aged woman walking past the waiting room. "What're you doing here?"

"Oh, Manny," she replied. "Somebody called and said Frank was in a car wreck and they had him in here somewhere."

"Well, we've been here for an hour or so and hadn't heard nothin' about that. Uh oh, maybe that was the big announcement for Doctor Bradley to go earstat, or whatever that was."

"Yeah, they told me at the front desk to go back her to the ER but I can't find it. I just need to talk to somebody. Find out what's goin' on. They didn't say nothin' about Claude. I don't know if anything happened to him either."

"Come on, I'll help you find it and we'll see what's goin' on," she said.

The attendant at the ER desk sat fixed, staring at an open notebook. The two ladies stood in front of her, waiting for her to look up. "Excuse me," Manny strained. The woman slowly looked up from her trance. "This is Alma Anderson. Somebody called her and said her nephew was here. Can you find out for us?"

The attendant paused then asked, "Sorry, we don't have anyone named Anderson in the ER."

"His name's Frank Massey," Manny replied.

The woman slowly closed her notebook and placed it on the desk. The reached into a stack of papers and pulled out a tablet and ran her finger down the list. "No Frank Massey either," she said.

"What?" both replied.

"There's a Franklin Massey."

"That's him," Alma said. "Where is he?"

"Says here he's in treatment. You'll have to wait over there." She pointed to a row of well-worn vinyl chairs pressed back against the wall. She turned her attention back to the notebook she was studying before they came in, and the romance novel hidden within it.

"They didn't say anything more?" Manny asked Alma.

"Naw, just that they had a Franklin Massey who had been in a wreck. That's it."

"Ma'am?" Manny asked the attendant. She ignored her. "Ma'am?" The lady looked up, slowly, solemn and uncaring. "You don't happen to have a Claude Massey on that list, too, do you?" she asked. The Lady smirked, took up the stack of papers again and glanced through them.

"No," she said.

"I wonder what happened to Claude?" Manny asked.

"How should I know," the lady replied.

"No, I wasn't really asking you. I was just wondering out loud."

The double doors opened, and Doctor Bradley came through. "Mrs. Thomson? he asked.

"Hey, Doctor Bradley. This is Alma Anderson. They told her her nephew, Frank, was in the ER but we don't know what's going on and nobody will tell us anything."

"Yeah, I just finished up with him," the doctor began. "We don't know any details, but it seems your nephew was in a wreck of some kind at the river bridge and ended up in the water."

"Is he okay?" Alma asked.

"Well, he had a pretty good cut on the back of his head that we fixed up, but he has a concussion. We're going to keep him here for observation till he wakes up and we can see how things look then."

"He ain't conscious?" Alma asked.

"No. That's not that unusual with an injury like he had, but it's not best. We'd rather him be awake but since he isn't, we're just going to have to keep a close eye on him. I don't see any reason why everything won't be just fine."

"Oh, thank the Lord," Alma said.

"I do, every day," Doctor Bradley said. "Now, if you'll excuse me, I need to go check on Mrs. Johnson."

"Can I see Frank?" Alma asked.

"Not much to see. He's just sleeping it off. Why not wait until we get him in a room, say in an hour. Then you can stay in there with him."

"Okay, thank you Doctor," Alma said.

"Are you coming, Mrs. Thomson?" the doctor asked.

"I can see Sally?"

"Don't see why not."

"Are you okay, Alma?" Manny asked.

"Oh, sure, Dear. You run on and I'll wait here until I can see Frank."

# Chapter Thirty-four

THE COUPE STOPPED ROLLING AND WAS DRIVEN UP ON THE bank beyond where Frank or Carl could have seen. As the water drained out from the doors, the only thing left behind was mud and a crushed suitcase. Far down stream, a weak and disoriented man clung to a section of wall from the house that had crashed into the bridge. The current was too strong for him to do anything but ride along with the debris. Claude had pulled himself on to the boards and submitted to wherever the river might take him.

The flow was strong and swift. As Claude drifted in and out of consciousness, time became immaterial. The narrow bridge at a bend in the river near Little Rock caught the debris and forced it onto the bank. He lay there, still and detached from who he was, where he was and why he was cold, wet and groggy.

Blanche McDonald was running late for work. Her shift at the Pulaski County Hospital in Little Rock was starting in ten minutes and she was twenty minutes away already. She needed an excuse. Being late three times in a row was getting her too much attention with the scheduling nurse.

As she crossed the bridge the debris pile was an obvious addition to the usual scene and caught her eye. Seeing a man lying on the pile was enough for her to stop the car and investigate. Now, she would really be late, but also now, she had gotten her reason to be late.

Her white uniform was completely out of place surrounded by

the mud and moisture left over from the storm. It had passed only a couple of hours before but left its reminders everywhere. She made her way down the slope and to the debris pile. "Sir? Sir, can you hear me?" she shouted.

Claude opened his eyes. His body lay still. He looked into the sky then followed the voice toward Blanche. "Ma'am," he said.

"Sir, are you hurt anywhere?"

He looked back to the sky. "Don't rightly know," he said. "Ain't wanting to move nothin' to find out."

"Do you think you can get up if I help you?"

"Maybe so."

Blanche placed her hand underneath his neck and began to raise his head. He followed her effort and sat upright. "That's good," she said.

"Why's ever'thang spinnin'?"

"Just wait a minute and that should clear up."

He sat and looked around. "Where are we?"

"This is the Arkansas River and you're just outside of Little Rock."

"Little Rock? How on earth did I get down here?"

"Looks like you road on that pile of wood. Do you remember where from?" Claude shook his head. "Can you stand now?" She wrapped her arms around him and pulled him tightly to herself, then lifted him from the ground.

"You're mighty strong there for a lady," he said.

"I do this every day," she said. "You gotta be strong to do what I do."

"Some kind of nurse?"

"Yes, if I don't get fired for being late. Let's get you up this hill and to the hospital."

Blanche drove fast and covered the distance quickly. Claude kept awake but rested his head on the back of the seat. She pulled up at the emergency room entrance and rushed in for help. The orderly wheeled out the gurney as Claude got out of the car.

"I don't need no bed," he said. "I can walk in." The orderly left the gurney and hooked his arm underneath Claude's to walk him through the doors. Claude staggered wildly.

It was a quiet morning in the ER, so Claude was taken directly to treatment. Because he was alert, he took off his own clothes and put on the flimsy gown. He was sitting on the bed when the doctor came in.

"Blanche, that's four," Mrs. Mackey said. She was not a lady to trifle with. You either were late or you were not. Why, was not her concern.

"Yes, ma'am. I'm sorry."

"And your uniform is atrocious. Do you think you can come in here filthy and help take care of patients? What are you thinking?"

"Yes, ma'am. I'm sorry."

"This will go into your records and be brought under review. If we were not so short of good nurses, this would be your termination. Do you understand?"

"Yes, ma'am. I'm sorry."

"Now, get yourself a clean uniform and get to work. You'll be working overtime to make up for being so late."

"Yes, ma'am. I'm sorry."

"Well, I take it I didn't die," Sally said weakly. She looked up at Manny, Luke and Dearl coming into the room. "These sheets are clean enough to be in heaven, though." The clean, white sheets and pristine floor were far removed from the modest, lived-in cabin back in Pine Hollow.

"You gave us quite the scare young lady," Manny said, brushing Sally's hair back from hanging across her face. She leaned in and kissed her forehead. Luke pulled a chair near to her bed and took her hand. He pulled her hand up to his lips and kissed it, then began to tremble.

"I'm alright, Luke. You ain't gettin' rid of me that easy."

Dearl rested his hands on the footboard of her bed and smiled. "Doc Bradley said you'll be just fine," he said.

"Shoot, I was hoping for better than just fine, but that's better than what I could have gotten, I guess. Are the rest of the babies alright?"

"Yep, Annie Mae's got 'em all at her house," Manny said.

"Man, what a house full. I'd better hurry up'n get myself out of here before she and Floyd go slap-dab crazy."

"Billie Nell's there, too, so I figure between the three of them they've got ever'thang under control," Manny said. "Let's just take it easy and not rush this too much. You've been to the edge and back, or at least that's what Doc Bradley said."

"I know. Ain't sure why, but I know."

"Well, me and Dearl are gonna leave you two alone and go check on Frank."

"What's happened to him?" Sally asked.

"Some kind of car accident or what not," Manny said. "Ain't sure what happened to Claude. Hope Frank'll wake up soon and maybe we can find out something."

Blanche couldn't take a break until late morning, a whole hour beyond when she typically sat down for a cup of coffee and decompression. The strain of working during a nursing shortage compounded throughout the day. The power of the calling to care for the sick and infirmed was strong each morning but by lunch, the thought of spending another minute with whiney and needy people was overwhelming. Nancy Lutcher had reached her limit by ten o'clock. She had changed uniforms twice already from an artery explosion and projectile vomiting but being bumped into by a candy striper carrying a full bed-pan was her final straw. She screamed and stormed out of the main doors, into her car and drove away.

Blanche heard the call and rushed in to help the candy striper clean up the floor, the wall and several pieces of equipment that got in the way. The extra hour pushed Blanche's break to eleven, too close to lunch, but necessary anyhow.

Instead of the break room, though, she found herself standing in the doorway watching Claude sleep. She saw a peaceful man, not one riddled with rejection and loss. She saw confidence in his face, relaxed from the tensions of the pressures which intensified his need to escape his life through the bottle. She saw a man who needed a woman like her, a woman whose capacity for love and empathy were beyond any he had found thus far. She saw a new life with a man she knew nothing about but was willing to learn.

Would he, could he be drawn to her? She decided then, in a fifteen-minute break, not to leave his side, at least not until after her shift was done.

# Chapter Thirty-five

"CAN I GO SEE FRANK IN THE HOSPITAL?" BILLIE NELL ASKED AS she got into the truck with Manny and Dearl. With all the children asleep, the long day at Annie Mae's and Floyd's was over for Billie Nell and the Thomsons were ready to get back home.

"Well, I guess you could go back with us tomorrow," Manny answered. "We're gonna go check on Sally and Luke in the morning so I don't see what it'd hurt."

"Is he still sleeping?"

"Yeah. Doc Bradley said he might sleep for quite a while. They just don't know. He has a concussion. That's a ..."

"He got his brain bruised," Billie Nell said. "We learned about that in science last year."

"Well, it's something pretty serious. At least the doctor seemed worried a bit."

"You know, Frank ain't as bad as everyone makes him out to be," Billie Nell said. "He's just trying to be funny most of the time. Still gets him in a lot of trouble, though."

"He'll probably be alright," Manny said.

The house was dark and damp from all the rain. Though it was mid-summer, Dearl lit a fire in the fireplace just to draw out some of the moisture. Even before the fire was fully ablaze, the three were asleep. Nubbin found her comfortable place in front of the hearth.

Morning came quickly and the smells from coffee and bacon drew

Billie Nell and Dearl to join Manny for breakfast. The trip back to Lathrup Springs went quickly. Billie Nell chattered incessantly.

The hospital was slow to awake. The waiting rooms had a few people sleeping on chairs pulled together. The halls were deserted, except for the occasional nurse flitting from one room to another like hummingbirds seeking nectar. The air was chilly and antiseptic.

The door to Frank's room was open so they walked in. The man in the first bed looked up and pointed to the second bed by the window. The curtain separating the two beds blocked them from seeing Frank. Manny slowly led Billie Nell and Dearl and peaked around the curtain. Frank was asleep. They didn't know if he was still comatose or just resting.

"Frank?" Manny whispered. No movement. "Well, I guess he's still out. I thank I'll run down and check on Sally. Y'all coming with me?"

"Yeah," Dearl said.

"Naw, I thank I'll sit here with Frank for a while, if that's okay."

"Suit yourself," Manny said. "Might get lonely if he don't wake up. We'll be down in 113 with Sally and Luke when you want to come down there."

"Okay."

The room was dim. The florescent light aimed up at the ceiling was all that made the room not totally dark. Billie Nell pulled back the heavy drapes and suddenly the room was alive with morning. She turned back and Frank was squinting, though his eyes were still closed. He moaned and cracked his eyelids just enough to see someone standing beside him.

"Hey, sleepy head," Billie Nell said. "'Bout time you woke up."

He blinked and pulled his eyelids open from the inside until there were large enough slits he could through. He looked at Billie Nell and smiled. "Hey," he strained.

"How you feelin'?"

He breathed deeply through his nose. "Don't know. Tired. Sore. Head hurts. Throat, too."

"Well, from what folks say, you done been in a car wreck of some sort, but nobody knows nothin' about it." She offered him a sip of water. He raised his head and she slipped her hand underneath his neck. She saw the blood on the pillow. Her eyes widened and she quickly looked back at his face to make sure she was putting the cup where he could drink. "You remember any of it?"

"Yeah, prob'ly, some of it. How's my dad?"

"Nobody's seen him. They were hopin' you knew what happened."

"We went in the river and everything got tumbled around. I got thrown out, nearly drowned. Never saw what happened to Dad."

"Oh, I'm so sorry, Frank."

"Yeah. Me too."

"Need more water?"

"Yea, thanks. And thanks for bein' here."

"Thought you might need a friend." Frank lifted up his hand toward Billie Nell. She took it and wrapped both of hers around it.

"Can I ask you something, Billie Nell?"

"Sure."

"I know it ain't the same but maybe it sorta is."

"What?"

"Well, I heard you had it bad with your mom and dad, so you moved in with the Thomsons."

"Yeah?"

"And your dad hurt you."

"Yeah?"

"Are you over it yet?

"Oh, it quit hurtin' after a while."

"No, I wasn't talkin' about getting' over the hurt on the outside but the inside hurt."

"Well, Manny told me the only way I'd get over it was to forgive 'em for all of that stuff they did."

"Did you?"

"I've said the words and I meant 'em, but ever now and then I thank about it and it hurts again, not as much but it still hurts to thank about it."

"I thank I need to do that with my dad."

"Did he hurt you?"

"All...my...life," Frank said deliberately. "I never knew how or why till we made this trip. After what I found out, I ain't so sure I'm not glad this wreck happened."

"Frank!"

"You don't know what he's done."

"Yeah but being glad somebody's dead ain't good neither...if he is dead."

"I know. But the stuff I found out...he's...was...a bad man."

"Frank, ain't nobody a bad man, they're just somebody than ain't met Jesus yet. That's what Preacher Dutton says."

"Well, if he ever did meet Jesus, it was just to shake hands. It sure wasn't to have Jesus come into his life and show him how to live," Frank said, straining to swallow. Billie Nell placed the cup back up to his lips. He swallowed hard.

"Manny said the only way to get over thangs like this is forgiveness. You're gonna have to tell God you forgive him and mean it—God knows whether you're lying or not—and then try not to thank about it. That's when it bothers me the most when I start thankin' about it again."

"Ain't sure I can even say the words right now, much less mean it. Maybe later."

"That's what I had to do. It took me a couple of months. I was afraid to say it till I really meant it. Didn't want God mad at me for lying to Him."

"Nobody could ever be mad at you."

The curtain flew back. Billie Nell let go of Frank's hand and drew hers back to her chest. She quickly looked at the nurse smiling at the end of Frank's bed. "So, we decided to wake up, did we? Did your girlfriend kiss Sleeping Beauty and bring him out of it?"

Both of them looked up at the nurse. "She/I ain't my/his girl-friend," they said together. Frank turned to Billie Nell and smiled. She smiled back.

"Well, she's not your aunt. Young lady, could you excuse us for a few minutes? I need to check your…friend out," the nurse said.

"Yes ma'am," she said. "I'm gonna go tell Manny and Dearl you're awake, Frank. We'll be back in a bit." She rushed down to Sally's room.

Manny and Dearl came back with her to Frank's room. The nurse came out as they went in. "How is he, nurse?" Dearl asked.

"Fine, as best as I can tell," she said. "The doctor will be making rounds soon and he'll tell you more."

Frank grinned when the Thomsons came in. Manny reached over to hug him. "Watch out for the back of his head," shouted Billie Nell. Manny jerked back her hand, then gently placed her cheek beside his and patted the other. Dearl extended his hand. Frank shook it firmly.

"Frank, do you remember what happened?" Manny asked.

"They went off the bridge into the river and Frank was thrown out. He don't know nothin' about his daddy," Billie Nell said. Manny and Dearl looked at her. "Well that's what he told me."

"How you doin', son?" Dearl asked.

"He's…" Billie Nell began but stopped when everyone turned to look at her. She nodded at Frank to continue.

"Fine, I guess. Kinda stiff and sore but I've felt worse. Mr. Thomson, do you thank they'll find my dad?"

"Let's not worry about that now. I'm sure they're looking for him, but maybe he'll probably turn up some place. You're dad's a tough old goat."

"Dearl!" Manny snapped.

"He's right, Mrs. Thomson," Frank said. "They say the good die young. Dad ought to be around for quite a while. Anyway, if I got out, he probably got out, too."

"Well, right now, you just worry about you gettin' better and get-tin' back home," Manny said.

"Home?" Frank said. He shook his head and looked out the window. "Don't know much 'bout what that means right now."

"Your Aunt Alma's place is alright, ain't it," Manny said.

"Yeah. I'll probably stay with her till I can get out on my own. Dad's house belongs to the mill so I can't stay there. Hey, Mr. Thomson, do you thank I could get a job doing something at the mill somewhere?"

"Well, we can always use a good hand, but let's not worry about that just yet," Dearl said. "You just get out of here and get your strength back. Once you're up to speed, I'm sure Mr. Creighton'll have something you can do. Maybe something out in the woods with me, in time."

"Or with Ernest?" Frank asked. "I'm a pretty good mechanic, at least that's what Ernest says."

"Or with Ernest. In time."

"Yes, sir. In time."

# Chapter Thirty-six

THE YEAR HAD DRAWN TO A CLOSE. THE FINAL CONCERT BACK
in New York marked the end of a remarkable journey for the
young boy from Arkansas. Leland was used to limos. He settled back
in the seat and pressed his head back onto the head-rest. The trip from
the Little Rock airport would take longer than the flight from New
York. A nap, hopefully, would shorten the time.

Ralph had never left Leland's side the entire tour. Perhaps as much
a desire to protect his protégé as to honor the commitment he made
to Dearl and Manny, he shadowed Leland's every move. He occupied
the space on the seat with Leland, absorbed in a tabloid of musical
interest, but with a lead story about a cellist and his gift.

It seemed like half the community of Pine Hollow was in Dearl's
and Manny's small house, spilled over onto the porch and filled
the front yard. The last postcard Leland had sent said, *be home by
dark-thirty Saturday.* Now a year since a chance meeting with Ralph
Watkins at the drug store in Lathrup Springs had taken Leland from
Carnegie Hall to performances across the nation, it was now over and
time to go home.

"When'll he get here?" insisted Billie Nell.

"Billie Nell, you know as much about it as we do," answered
Manny, more annoyed that she didn't know the answer than she was
that Billie Nell kept asking.

It was moving into evening when Frank Massey came running

around the bend in the driveway. "They're coming! They're coming!" The house cleared quickly as everyone rushed into the yard.

"Would you look at how long that thang is!" exclaimed Dearl as the lights of the black limousine came into sight. "That's gotta be the fanciest car I've ever seen."

"This will be close enough," Ralph said to the driver, which really wasn't necessary since all the people surrounding the car kept him from moving any closer anyhow. The cheering was deafening.

"Back away so he can get out!" shouted Manny, her voice piercing above the noise of the crowd.

As the door opened, out stepped a young man resembling the boy who had grown up there. The crowd went silent. "It's just me," the familiar voice called out from within the stylishly dressed body. Again, the crowd cheered. Out from between the press of bodies lunged Billie Nell, whose embrace nearly knocked Leland back into the limo.

"Well, Leland Thomson, don't you have something to ask me?" she asked.

"Well, yeah, in a minute," he replied.

"No, sir, you wrote me that the first thang you wanted to do when you got back was ask me, so ask!"

"Kinda thought I'd do it, you know, privately. Just in case."

"Just in case what?"

"Just in case you might turn him down," shouted Frank.

"Turn him down?" Billie Nell shouted back.

"She's gettin' mighty riled, there, Leland," Frank said. "She might actually turn you down for spite, just for takin' so long. I'd get on with it if I were you."

"You shore might better, Leland Thomson," Billie Nell said. "But the only turnin' down I aim to do is turnin' you upside down if you don't ask me to marry you right now! So, yeah, you better be gettin' on with it."

"Thank she might mean it, son," warned Dearl.

"Well, aw right," Leland began and paused. "Billie Nell, I was wondering…"

"What?" she shouted.

"Aw right! Will you marry me?" He shouted back. She jumped into his arms and kissed him all over his face.

"How's that for an answer?" Frank said.

"Does this mean yes?" Leland asked back.

"Of course, it means yes! Yes! Yes! Yes!" she said, kissing him with each answer.

*Two weeks later. . .*

"Well, that was one ceremony for the books," Maestro Cacucci said.

"I told you, things were quite a bit different up here in the Hills," Ralph replied.

"But their ages," Cacucci continued, "they're, what, seventeen, eighteen."

"She's fifteen and he's seventeen," answered Dearl, stepping into their conversation. "That's how it is up here. You get born, grow up, get married, go to work in the Mill, have kids and watch 'em do the same thing. Worked for my daddy. Worked for me and his momma; it'll work for them."

"Mr. Thomson," Cacucci began, "It's no small thing to say that Leland has had a remarkable year touring. I'm just wondering how he'll handle living back here in the Hills after he's been to the places he's been. Has he said much about wishing he could continue touring and playing?"

"Naw, he'll be too busy being home to miss any of that stuff. I got him a job out in the woods. Don't want him to lose any fingers in the Mill."

"Oh, I can't even imagine," shuttered Cacucci.

"Think you'll ever get your house back to normal, Dearl," asked Ralph.

"Oh, when all the food's gone, the varmints'll start disappearin'."

"Time to cut the cake!" announced Manny, directing everyone to clear a path to the kitchen table.

"Shove it up her nose," shouted Frank.

"Franklin Massey!" rang the unmistakable voice of Miss Ida Mae Grubb.

"Yes, ma'am. Never mind, Leland."

"Watch and learn, Frank," Leland said, taking a napkin and wiping the corner of Billie Nell's mouth after she had eaten her piece.

"Humph," pouted Frank.

"Hey, Leland, are y'all gonna move to town and become all high-falutin' and all?" asked Sara Beth.

"Nah, I spent a whole year bein' one of them. Ain't no big deal. Just as soon stay here and be what I always been."

"Didn't it make you feel like a somebody?" she asked.

"We ain't nobodies here, Sara Beth," Leland said. "Bein' aw'right with what you are ain't as bad as bein' all cruddy with thanking you oughta be somebody else. I'm a Hills boy. It's what I was; it's what I am. I'll always be a Hill's boy."

"And that Hill's boy is *my* Hill's boy," Billie Nell added, smothering him again in kisses. The crowd cheered.

"Well, Ralph, obviously Mr. Thomson was right," Cacucci said. "Looks like your miracle boy might be hanging up his fame and fortune for good." He took a bite of cake and chased it down with a sip of coffee.

"Believe it or not, I really did expect this all along," Ralph smiled.

"What we had was the fulfillment of a grand experiment. It was the dream of a young boy from Pine Hollow, Arkansas, to see what was calling out to him from beyond the hilltops. Added to that was the passion of a refined music lover from New York to discover a remarkable talent. Then include the clamoring of a world longing for the kind of inspiration that comes when you realize greatness in the most unassuming places and people. And, regardless of of the fact, that it was only one year, this year of Leland Thomson was without doubt the finest I have ever lived. A boy with a gift and a cello gave the world incredible music."

"And what about you?" Cacucci asked. "What did it give you?"

"A desire to believe again," Ralph answered. He, too, took a bite of cake and followed it with a sip of coffee.

The unmistakable strands of an Irish jig coming from a well-worn cello came from the front porch. Soon it was joined by a band of guitars, jug and fiddle. Couples drew together and followed the urging of their hands to pat, their feet to bounce and their arms to swirl. The dance lasted long into the evening, well beyond the cake, punch and coffee, for in the Hills the feast is more than what was spread out on a table. It was the joy that came when who you were and what you were doing matched, a moment that both satisfied and surprised, and always left you with good memories of what a big time you really had just being you.

Billie Nell came in from the outside, leaned over and whispered into Leland's ear, "I got something I want to show you."

"What's that?" he asked, never missing a note.

"Just wait," she said. She went to the door and soon returned with a tightly swaddled newborn in her arms. She stood in front of Leland. Leland looked at the baby, then at Billie Nell, then back at the baby. He never stopped playing.

"Billie Nell, you done already had a baby?" he asked.

"Leland Thomson, we *just* got married."

"Well, whose is this, yur momma's?"

"Naw, this is my cousin Mable's. Guess how she got here?"

"Uh, the stork?"

"*Yur* momma!"

"My momma? My momma had yur cousin Mable's baby?"

"She brung her into the world, Leland Thomson! She's Aunt Nora now." Billie Nell stated proudly.

"She's what?"

"Yur momma is Aunt Nora now."

"Huh? Where'd Aunt Nora go?"

"Aunt Nora cain't do it no more. She made yur momma the birthin' lady now. Said she had the gift. That's why you were their only child."

"Thought I got the gift."

"Guess there's more than one to be got," Billie Nell said.

"Yep, prob'ly so. And my momma's Aunt Nora."

# Chapter Thirty-seven

"SO, YOU QUIT SCHOOL?" LELAND ASKED FRANK.

"Yeah, same as you. Figured I got enough education for what I need to do." The lug bolt on the old Dodge field truck creaked as Frank broke it lose from the axle. The years of water and caked-on mud had rusted the threads. Ernest had told Frank to soak it with penetrating oil, let it set, then get some leverage on the end of your wrench, bump it and it'll break free. Waiting for the oil to work gave Leland and him time to catch up.

It had been about three months since Leland had returned to Pine Hollow from his national tour as solo cellist with the New York Chamber Orchestra. It also had been three months of marriage with Billie Nell, who now shared his bedroom as they lived with his parents. After a week of honeymoon, which consisted of a few days camping and the rest hanging out at the house, he was put to work at Creighton Mill, working with his dad in the woods. Today's assignment: take the Dodge to the mechanic's shop at the Mill and have the front two tires replaced.

To save money on expendables like tires, Ernest, the chief mechanic, would go down to Lathrup Springs and buy used tires from the various service stations. As long as they weren't worse than what he was replacing, they were usually an improvement and would give a few months of good use. Any tire, new or used, would only last a few months in the woods. Too many stumps, pot holes and misplaced equipment, shortened the lifespan of whatever was put on the vehicle.

"How you likin' married life?" Frank asked.

"Ain't bad, but tell you the truth, living at home…it don't feel like we're married too much. Kinda like it always was when Billie Nell would hang out over there. Only she don't go home at night."

"That ought to be pretty good, huh?"

"Well, yeah, but…well, a little privacy would be nice."

"I hear that."

With the wheel off Frank began breaking down the old tire and forcing on the new. He lay in the new inner tube and finished mounting the tire. He worked fast, not at all distracted by his friend.

"Hey, what's the latest with your dad?" Leland asked.

"Still no idea. They found the car but never found him. He may have gotten run up under a limb or root or something and is stuck somewhere under the water. May have just floated off downstream. May never know."

"Does that bother you?"

"Nah, not really. I'd like him found and all but it don't bother me he's probably dead."

"That don't seem right."

"I know, but he told me stuff on our trip that kinda put out the fire of me caring about him."

"I know y'all ain't always got along, but he's still your dad."

"Yeah, weird, huh?"

With her shift over, Blanche McDonald rushed to her car and headed home. Home, now, had new meaning and a larger purpose. Home now included a new life, a new love. Gone were the old days of dinner alone, evenings alone, sleeping alone. She now shared her life with a man who showed her compassion, tenderness and understanding.

Claude Massey had dinner prepared when Blanche pulled into the drive. Though modest, to Blanche it was a banquet since she didn't have to prepare it and her man met her at the door. While Claude was in the hospital in Little Rock, Blanche would spend the time from the end of her shift until he fell asleep sitting with him in his room, talking and falling in love. In his quiet moments during the day, Claude considered life back in Pine Hollow, the possibility of going back, and the embarrassment of everyone knowing of his failure as a husband and father. Blanche gave him another option.

With what he had learned on the trip, the words from Pastor Johnson, the example of Bud and Victoria, and, ultimately, the rejection by Frank, Claude wanted a new life. He remembered the old instincts and replayed the pounding messages that drove them. He saw the points of failure and the dishonesty that kept him bound. He looked at Blanche and saw a new life. He could talk with her, and she would talk *with* him, not at him. He enjoyed listening to her and found himself eager for her to get off work and come through the door. He trusted her enough to tell her things no one else knew. He told her everything. And she still loved him.

"Okay, Dearl." Mr. Creighton blew out a large cloud of cigar smoke. "I don't seem to have any other choice than to rely on your judgment." The meeting had dragged on for two hours. Scenario after scenario had been laid on the table to determine how to run the mill without Claude. Finding a foreman with experience from another mill made sense but the timing was way off. They needed someone now, someone who knew the business and the woods, not a new hire a month from now.

"I just thank it's worth a try," Dearl said. "I believe I can run the mill for you and Luke's able to run the woods. He's got a good handle on how everything works. I thank it's doable."

"Alright. I'm just tired of trying to run all this by myself. That blasted Claude. I never should have let him go on that wild goose chase to California."

"Well, if he hadn't died on that trip, something else would have happened around here. When your number's up, that's it. Don't matter where you are."

"Yeah, I guess. But it sure did mess things up." Another cloud of smoke left his lips and hovered above his head. "Well, Mr. Mill Foreman, have at it."

"Alright, then. First thang I want to do is have a meetin' with all the men and let 'em know we ain't changin' how we been doin' stuff, just who'll be pushing to get it done. I'll meet with Luke and Ernest this afternoon, then get all the men together in the morning."

"Sounds like a plan."

"Mr. Creighton?"

"What else, Dearl?"

"Wondering if Manny and me might move into Claude's house and let Leland and Billie Nell have our place?"

"You two moving in is fine. Let me think about the other. It rightly should be Luke's. Then Leland could move in their house. I'll let you know."

Luke and Ernest were sitting in the mechanic's shop drinking a couple of Nehis when Dearl walked over. "Saved you one," Luke said. He lifted the cap off the bottle and handed it to Dearl. "Did you and Mr. Creighton get everything worked out?"

"Pretty much," Dearl said. "I'm stepping up to take over Claude's job."

"Crud, I knew it. You get the job and somebody new comes out in the woods and messes up the whole operation. He ain't gonna know nothin' about who we are or how we do thangs. Gonna mess up the whole thang. Dang it."

"You done?"

"Yeah, I guess."

"I'm stepping up to take over Claude's job and you're gonna step up and take over my job. Thank you can handle it?"

"Uh, me? Well, yeah, I guess. If you thank I'm ready. You mean it? Really? You thank I can handle it?"

"That's what we decided. You've apprenticed well. You know the men and the woods. Yeah, I thank you can handle it. And if not, I'll kick your rear end up between your shoulder blades."

"Wow. I don't know what to say."

"That's a first," Ernest said.

"I'll still be here to help out if you need it, but you gotta ask. I ain't plannin' on running the mill and nurse-maidin' you."

"No, I got it. You thank the men'll be okay with that?"

"We'll find out in the morning, but they should pretty much expect it. You've been working under me long enough."

"Well, alright then. Mercy. Sally ain't gonna believe this." And with the last few drops of grape soda downed, the meeting was over.

Sunrise could not get here quickly enough for Luke. He had been up since four thinking about what he'd say to the men and fearing what they might say back. Until now he'd had no issues with anyone. Primarily, he figured, because Dearl had his back. Dearl was a man of high integrity. The men knew that. They also knew that he expected the same thing from them, even though many lived far beneath that goal.

He wanted them to give their best, take care of the equipment and do what they were told. If not, they knew they'd face the back side of his integrity, the harsh reality of justice above mercy. They would do what was expected or they wouldn't have a job. Luke wanted to do the same, but he wasn't Dearl. All he had was a few years learning why Dearl had those rules and how he'd enforce them. He wasn't planning to change a thing.

The men began to draw into the clearing in front of the processing shed. Everyone was to be present by six each day. Dearl and Luke stood together as the men collected in front of them.

"Alright, got some news for you today," Dearl said. "You know Claude's gone and we've been limpin' along while Mr. Creighton figured out what he wanted to do. Well, all that's been decided. I'm gonna take over Claude's job." The rumble spreading out among the men unsettled Luke. He looked over at Dearl. Dearl shook his head.

"And since we don't want ever'thang changing and going to pot around here. We ain't hiring a new woods foreman from outside." The men rumbled again. Luke began to shake. "Luke, here's gonna step up to my job." The men cheered. Luke almost fainted. He forced a quivering smile, then broke out to a full grin. "He's the best man for the job. So, from now on, he's your boss. You do what he says and if you have a problem you go to him to straighten it out. If he hires someone, they're hired. If he fires someone, they're fired. Don't come runnin' to me to help you work thangs out with him. He's in charge of the woods. He's in charge of your life. Ever'body got that?"

The men nodded and mumbled a *yeah*. Luke was in. He knew he'd be tested by some of them, but Dearl had made it clear who he expected to win. And with Luke being six-four, and powerfully built, Dearl knew most of the challenges would be resolved before things got physical.

"Alright, hit the woods." Dearl ended with his usual final command to close the meetings and release the men to their work. The men just stood there, looking at Luke. Dearl conceded.

"Alright, men, hit the woods," he said. The men cheered, shook his hand, patted his back and then headed to their trucks.

"Mr. Dearl, can I talk with you a minute." Preacher Dutton, though commanding from the pulpit, knew his place in the mill.

"Sure, Dutton, what's up?"

"Mr. Dearl, with Frank helpin' Ernest out in the shop, I was wonderin' if you really need me 'round here much anymore?"

"Well, Dutton, that's Ernest's call, not mine. But just because we brought Frank on to apprentice under Ernest, your job is still safe."

"Oh, naw, suh, I know that. It's just that I'd been thanking quite a lot 'bout the church and wishin' I could give more time to it."

"Oh, I see."

"Yas, suh, I thank I'd really like to cut back here and do more there. Now I'd be able to help out if'n ever Ernest ever needed me, you understand. But me and Sister Mary don't need much now with Irma married off and got the twins and all."

"So, you want to quit."

"Retire sort of. I ain't through, just changin' my work schedule."

"Well, let me talk with Ernest and see what he says. If he thanks Frank can handle your load, I ain't got no problem with it. You're gonna have to move out of the mill's house though. Ain't nothin' I can do about that. But I'll see you get enough time to find you another place."

"Sure, appreciate it. You're a good man, Mr. Dearl."

"Well, I don't know about that, but I do know you're more important around this community as a preacher than a mechanic's helper anyhow."

"Thank you, Mr. Dearl. Do you thank Mr. Creighton would let me buy some land up by the church to build me and Sister Mary a house?"

"Let me work on that for you. For now, get on to the shop and do your job till we get all this worked out."

"Yas, suh. Thank you again, Mr. Dearl."

Dearl's second policy change, after appointing Luke foreman of the woodsmen, was to have a whistle blow at lunch time so all the men at the mill proper could shut down operations and have their lunches at the same time. He had designated a space just behind the new ripsaw shed to have some tables made to accommodate the men.

Ernest was to join him at his table. Dearl had already instituted the practice in the woods, so Luke simply continued what the men were accustomed to. Ernest met Dearl at the table underneath the spreading oak.

"Dutton came to me this mornin'," Dearl said.

"Yas, suh, I saw him talkin' to you."

"Know what it was about?"

"I figure it was about him takin' off so he can give more time to preachin' and all."

"You okay with that?"

"Yas, suh. Dutton's good help and bein' my brother and all, we get along just fine, but that Frank's somethin' special. That boy's a lot like me when I was his age. I can do without Dutton now that Frank's here."

"Okay, here's what I want to do. I talked with Mr. Creighton and the mill's gonna give him a place to build a house up by the church and we're gonna help get it built. Won't be his, none. It'll still belong to the mill, but he can live there as long as he's the preacher of the church. Then when he leaves the next preacher can live there."

"Sounds alright to me."

"And the mill will let him stay where he's living now. When we get the new house built, he'll move up there. Till then, he can work for you whenever you need him but he's free to do his church work full time if he wants. Mr. Creighton's gonna keep payin' him till the church can afford to take over. Thank he'll go for that?"

"Like a buzzard to a dead 'possum."

"So, it's your call if you need him to work. You bring him in. If you don't need him, he's a full-time preacher. You explain that to him?"

"Yas, suh." Ernest grinned, drank down a swallow of iced tea from his thermos. "Mr. Dearl?"

"What?"

"You're a mighty good man. Mr. Claude wouldn't have done none of this." Dearl nodded and took the last bite of his sandwich.

# Chapter Thirty-eight

"No, Lucy Marie, it ain't bring, brang, brung. It's bring, brought, brought," Billie Nell strained.

"But you said it was sing, sang, sung," Lucy Marie said. "Sing and bring rhyme so they ought to be the same, huh, Billie Nell?"

"No, Lucy Marie, it ain't bring, brang, brung!"

"Billie Nell!"

"Oh, sorry Miss Ida. It *isn't* bring, brang, brung. I know it don't make no sense, but that's just the way it is."

"Billie Nell!"

"Oh, sorry again, Miss Ida. I know it *doesn't* make *any* sense, but that's just the way it is."

"Boy, Miss Ida, I tell you what, English is a whole lot harder speaking it than it is talking it."

"Well, a teacher has to know the difference and must speak it correctly so the children can learn from your example."

Though Billie Nell was finishing up her last year, Ida Mae Grubb, was using her as a teaching assistant with the younger children. Billie Nell had always shown a love for education and a greater appreciation for Miss Ida being there than Ida had for herself. Allowing Billie Nell to help would help lessen her load.

Leland was working in the woods. Dearl wanted him to get a broad appreciation with the sawmill business. He showed him no favor but did have a plan to help him move up the food chain. Working with Elwood would help him develop patience with some of the fringe workers, men who had minimal skills and a limited future with the mill.

"Leland, go around on the other side and grab that chain tied onto this cable and hook it under the frame." Elwood had tossed the hook of the chain over the logs to secure them to the trailer.

Leland ran to the other side slipping in the mud. The hook had sunk into the mud. He traced it out. "Got it."

Elwood began jacking the come-a-long to tighten the cable. It jerked out of Leland's hand and caught in a nub on the bottom log.

"Hey, Elwood! Wait! It ain't hooked to the frame yet!"

Elwood pulled one more time on the come-a-long and the bottom log shifted. From the top of the pile the last log loaded began to slip to the side. He felt the cable go limp and yelled, "What happened over there?"

The rumble was unmistakable. The stack was higher than the side rails and the logs rolled. Leland stood watching. Elwood came around the truck. "Run!" he shouted. Leland turned and looked at him. The top log hit the edge of the truck and bounced into Leland's chest. It knocked him back into the mud and pressed its massive weight across his body. He stared up at Elwood, his eyes full of questions, his head twitching, his body shivering in response. Leland couldn't move. He just kept quivering and looking into the sky. Barely able to breathe, blood began to run from his mouth and nose.

"Leland, you okay, boy? You stay there and I'll go get help."

Elwood got into the truck and fired it. Its tires fiercely spun mud as he forced the truck down the narrow trail. The logs began to fall from the trailer. He skidded out onto the main road. The side rails broke, and the rest of the load littered the highway. He sped into the Mill and slid to a stop in the clearing, his hand blaring his horn. Dearl came out of the shop, looked up and saw Elwood's face. He knew. He threw the pad he was holding into the mud and turned to get into this truck. Elwood shut off his engine and ran over to Dearl's truck. "He's hurt, Dearl."

"Get in!"

Dearl spun around in the clearing, splattering mud on everything and everyone standing there. The engine roared, trying to gain traction. "How bad?" he asked.

"Bad."

Leland was still conscious when they pulled up. Though it was much too heavy for one man to handle, Dearl picked up the end of the log and spun it off Leland. He knelt into the mud. "Leland, you alright?" Leland looked up at his dad, his blank stare sent a cold chill through his dad's heart. "We gotta get you out of here." Dearl ran his hands under the soft mud till he could feel Leland's neck with one and his lower back with the other. He lifted his son up and held him against his chest. Leland groaned. "Okay, okay. Gotta get you into the truck." Elwood stood watching. "Elwood, help me stand up!" The logger grabbed Dearl from behind and lifted as Dearl strained to stand. "Now, open my door." Dearl got into the cab with Leland and sat holding him tightly in his lap. "You drive but take it easy! Don't want to jostle him anymore than we have to."

Once on the highway, Elwood opened the truck up to full speed making the hour-long trip to Lathrup Springs in half the time. He pulled into the emergency entrance, blaring the horn. Attendants came out and took Leland from Dearl and placed him on a gurney. Dearl got out. His arms and legs caked in mud.

"What do you want me to do, Dearl?"

"Go get Manny and Billie Nell and bring them down here," he said. Elwood hurried back to the truck. "But don't tell them how bad it is. You understand that? Just tell them he got hurt, but don't tell them how bad."

"Yes, sir." He paused at the door. "Dearl, I'm sorry."

"Now ain't the time, Elwood. Just go get my family."

The door opened. Doctor Bradley's white smock was splotched with blood and mud. "Thomsons," he called. Dearl, Manny and Billie Nell stood. "Sit back down," he said as he approached. "Well, we've got a pretty bad situation here."

"How bad?" Manny asked. Billie Nell grabbed Dearl.

"Well, Manny, your boy's been hurt really bad. That log crushed his chest and, well, he's losing blood from somewhere inside. We need to operate but two of our main people are off at a convention today. We can't get replacements until late tonight or early tomorrow."

"So, you'll do it, then?" Billie Nell asked.

"As soon as we can. But I can't promise you Leland can wait that long."

"What are you saying?" asked Dearl.

"I'm saying…I'm not sure your boy's gonna make it."

"No!" Billie Nell and Manny screamed together. They both draped themselves around Dearl. Dearl pealed them off and handed them to each other.

"What do you mean, my son's gonna die?" Dearl stood, standing and brushing his chest into the doctor.

"Dearl, calm down. I don't know. If I could do anything I would, you have to know that. He's losing blood faster than we can pump it in."

"Cain't you do this without them other two?"

"I wish we could. You just can't do surgery without an anesthesiologist."

"So, you're gonna just sit around and let him die?"

"Dearl, it's not like that."

Dearl spun around and walked outside. He looked up into the sky and screamed, "God! What's goin' on here? This cain't be happenin'. Please don't let my boy die. Take me instead. Right now! But please, God, don't take Leland! Don't do this."

Manny and Billie Nell rushed out through the door and embraced Dearl. They wept.

"Mr. Thomson, Mrs. Thomson," a nurse softly called from the door. You can see Leland now, but only one at a time.

Dearl looked at Manny, they both looked at Billie Nell. "Y'all go first," Billie Nell said. "I'll wait."

Dearl looked back at Manny. "Go ahead. I'll wait with Billie Nell," Manny said.

Dearl rushed back inside and followed the nurse through heavy, double doors, past the nurses' station and into a small, private room. As Dearl's eyes adjusted to the dim light, he saw his son, clean and resting on crisp, white sheets. "They done cleaned you up right nice," Dearl said. Leland dropped his eyes from the ceiling to his dad's and smiled, then raised them back to the ceiling.

"Ain't...doing good...am I?" He strained to breath.

"You've done better."

Dearl sat on the edge of the bed and stroked Leland's hair. He felt the hot sting burning in his throat. He cleared and said, "Well, your Momma and Billie Nell want to come in here, so I guess I'll go back outside so they can see you."

"Am I gonna make it, Dad?"

"Don't know, son. Guess you're in God's hand now."

"Well, I can thank of worst places to be." Dearl reached over and kissed Leland on the forehead.

Manny was next. She followed the nurse, sniffing to keep the moisture in her nose from dripping onto her lip. "Try not to upset him," the nurse said, handing her a tissue. Manny nodded.

The room was stark. Only a bed, a dresser and one chair pulled back in the corner. There was a monitor hanging on the wall flashing out Leland's heartbeats and a pole handling a bag of fluids trickling into Leland's arm. Manny stopped at the door, trying to embrace her courage to enter. The nurse placed her hand on Manny's shoulder. "You can do this." she said.

Again, Manny nodded. She took a deep breath and walked into Leland's room. His eyes were closed. She grabbed the nurse's arm. "He's okay, just resting. See that monitor there. He's just asleep. Let's come back later."

"Can I just sit with him a while?"

"Sure, but don't try and wake him. Let him sleep."

Manny sat on the bed beside him and watched the face of her son. Memories flooded her thoughts. He just turned seventeen and was a husband; he was four or five, hiding behind her apron when visitors came to the house. He was an eight-year-old holding up his first squirrel he ever shot. He was ten romping around on the floor with Nubbin. He was beside the fireplace playing his cello. He was standing on the stage at Carnegie Hall. She bit her lips together but couldn't stop the tears from flowing down her cheeks. She leaned over and kissed his forehead. He opened his eyes and smiled at her, then closed them back. She began to tremble, got up and rushed out of the room. She embraced the nurse in the hallway and cried.

The walk back to the waiting room took longer than the trip to his room. Billie Nell stood, looking out of the window. Dearl sat with his head in his hands. "Billie Nell," Manny said. "He's asleep but you can go on in. They said not to try and wake him up."

Billie Nell got up slowly. She had loved Leland as long as she could recognize the emotion. The thought of losing him had no place in her heart. She followed the nurse into his room. He opened his eyes and looked into hers as she came near. She forced a smile at him.

"Leland Thomson," she said. "Now why couldn't you have just lost a finger or two like everyone else?" She began to cry. He smiled at her and looked back at the ceiling. His lips began to quiver, and a tear trickled down his face. She sat with him, stroking his hair. In a couple of minutes the nurse came back.

"Mrs. Thomson, he needs to rest now."

"Okay," she said, sliding off the bed.

"Get…my cello," he said.

"And do what with it?"

"Bring it…to me."

"You ain't gonna play it in here. This is a hospital. They got rules against stuff like that."

"Just bring it…okay?"

"Okay. Let me go tell your Daddy."

"His cello?" Dearl asked.

"Why on earth?" Manny added.

"Don't know. He just said bring it."

"Alright. Elwood, go back to the house and go on in. Over by the fireplace is Leland's cello. It's in a black case. Get it and bring it back up here. And get Ernest to follow you down here so he can take you back home."

"Yes, sir."

"And be careful with it," Billie Nell added.

Leland looked up as Billie Nell walked in with his cello case. "Hand me…my cello."

"But Leland, you might hurt yourself. The doctor said to lay still and not move around."

"I need…my cello."

"Did you hear me? I brought it so you could see it, not play it. What are you gonna do with it?"

"Billie Nell…please…just get…my cello…lay it…on my stomach…and put…my bow…in my hand."

"You're gonna get me in trouble."

He slowly drew his hand from his side and painfully followed the neck to set his hand into position. Billie Nell placed the bow in his right hand. He turned it then tried to raise it to the strings.

"Help me…set the bow…on my strings."

"Leland!"

"Billie Nell…do this."

She lifted the bow and his hand. He played a simple, note-by-note melody of *Amazing Grace*. Though his vibrato was missing, and the beat was much freer than Newton intended, the message was clear. As his life hung precariously to the threads of eternity, Leland affirmed the gift, the Giver and the grace that had sustained him. Suddenly the door opened and the charge nurse rushed in. "What is the meaning of this? What are you doing? Who gave him that cello?" She reached to take it from him. Billie Nell stepped into her path.

"You ain't touching that cello."

"Why are you doing this, son? And why are you letting him play? Don't you know how dangerous this is? You ignorant..."

"Ma'am, if you have to ask those questions, you probably ought not be in here right now."

"I'm in here to help him."

"Then get out and let him play."

The nurse glared at Billie Nell, then at Leland, then back at Billie Nell. She stormed back out of the room, leaving the moment as abruptly as she had intruded. She brushed past the door, leaving it open. Leland continued to play. The notes left the room and traveled down the hallway, past the nurses' station and all the way to the waiting room. Manny took Dearl's hand and wept. Leland completed the phrase and the sustained the final note.

The monitor went straight. His heart beat stopped, but the sound held on long past the point when he released his last breath. Everyone stopped and listened. They knew what it meant. They knew it was over. The note ceased. The music went silent. The bow dropped to the floor. Leland was gone. Billie Nell took his cello and set the instrument back in its case and placed it in the corner. Then she got into the bed and held her husband.

# *Chapter Thirty-nine*

THE CHURCH AT PINE HOLLOW WAS PACKED. PEOPLE STOOD outside, straining to hear through the opened windows. Paul Persky went to the chair set for him on the platform. He took up Leland's cello and quickly tuned. He looked out at the crowd and said, "One thing I learned from Leland, that regardless of what goes on, God never changes. He isn't faithful one day and unfaithful the next. We can't judge God based upon human understanding of how things look. We trust, we believe, and we live with a confidence that somehow in all this, good will come out.

"His ways are higher than our ways and His thoughts are higher than our thoughts. I don't know why this happened, but I do know, beyond any doubt that God isn't finished. In a concert, the audience doesn't clap between movements. You wait until the orchestra is finished and the conductor drops his hands. Sometimes there are two movements, usually three, occasionally four. If you clap too soon, you'll miss how everything turns out. Leland may be gone, but God isn't finished."

He pulled the cello in tightly and began the familiar strain of *Great is Thy Faithfulness*. Gertie Roberts, the church song leader, began to sing. Soon the woods were alive with praise. Paul left the melody and added embellishment as Leland had the first time Paul heard him play. The concert, indeed, wasn't over.

The Thomson house seemed empty, though the small living room was crowded. Ralph, Paul Persky, Dearl, Manny and Billie Nell sat around the table. Nubbin lay in front of the dark fireplace. Ralph sipped his coffee, set it down and expressed his loss. "I thought I had found fulfillment in the amazing things I had accomplished. I rated my life high because of my knowledge and experiences. I admit, I even felt superior to just about everyone I knew.

"When I met Leland, I felt inferior for the first time in my life. I couldn't put my finger on why he made me feel that way. Obviously, his ability…gift, placed him into an extremely small club of musicians. But more so, here was a sixteen-year-old boy from Arkansas with more grasp on what was valuable in life, with more perspective on who he was, with more intentional faith than any person I had ever met.

"He cast a huge shadow over my life. I either had to have what he had or get away from him. For the first time in my life I pitied myself. Me, in all my refinement, came undone. Here I was, a man in my sixties, wanting to sit at the feet of a teenager and have him teach me how to live. So, I did. And he told me what I needed to do, as straight forward as if I were asking him directions to the next town. And in a matter of seconds I left my life behind and entered a new existence. An existence where God could be my God as He was Leland's. And the amazing thing is, it happened, just as Leland said. I called out to Him from a place within my heart so deeply suppressed I didn't even know it existed and my life changed. At sixty-four, I started life all over again. Had it not been for Leland, none of that would have happened."

Ralph took up his coffee cup and drank down the remaining liquid. "Because of Leland Thomson, I am, forever, a changed man. The year of Leland Thomson was not about him playing at the most prestigious concert halls in the country, being lauded with the highest praise of highly appreciative audiences, being extolled as the greatest living cellist in the world today. It was about me. None of that mattered to Leland. He remained the young boy from Pine Hollow.

"But burned into my memory, was that smile, or better, that grin. The grin that said, *I know something you don't.* That same grin he'd given each time he finished playing he gave to me the moment I opened my eyes after calling out to God. There he was, grinning. He knew. And I knew he knew. Manny, Dearl, thank you both for allowing me the privilege of having your son be a part of my life's story."

Manny had no words. Dearl kept wiping away the tears. Billie Nell just stared at Ralph as this portly man shook while he wept before them.

As the day closed, Ralph and Paul excused themselves and headed out to the car. Billie Nell leaned in through Paul's window. "Mr. Persky, you said you don't clap till the orchestra stops playin'. I remember that from our trip to New York. You sayin' the Lord maybe ain't through yet, just because Leland died. That there might be something more to come?"

"Yes, that's exactly what I said, Billie Nell. We often look at events—things that happen—and try to judge what's going on because of that moment. We think life stopped. Life doesn't stop. It goes on. And until it's over, we need to anticipate something more to come."

"So, my life ain't over?"

"No, not by a long shot."

"Okay." She reached into the car and kissed him on the cheek. Ralph backed the car into the yard and drove away into the darkness. Billie Nell and Dearl headed back into the house. Manny stayed. "You comin' in?" Dearl asked.

"In a minute. I'm gonna just sit out here on the steps awhile."

The night was too still. The silence too loud. Even the crickets, locusts and tree frogs usually singing from the trees were quiet. It was as if the music had ended. Manny stared into the sky. The stars were still there, speckling the darkness as they had forever, but she wasn't looking at the stars. Her vision strained beyond. Her heart soared further and further away. *Where is Heaven? Where is God? I need to have a word with Him.*

She adjusted her posture, sat up straight as if presenting herself more properly. She took a deep breath and began, "I know You don't do nothing for nothing," she said. "But…Leland? I'm havin' a hard time not getting' mad at You about this. He's the only one I ever had or ever will. You know that, don't you? I ain't sayin' You don't have the right…but why?" The flood of tears blurred away the stars. Manny covered her face with her hands and bent to touch her hands to her knees. Her grief came rolling out in bursts of sorrow. She looked up again, face stained with tears and screamed, "Why!"

Dearl rushed back outside and pulled her up and hugged her tightly. They both heaved heavy sobs. He said nothing. "This ain't fair, Dearl," she said.

"I know."

"Ain't no reason for it."

"I know."

"Does God hate us?"

"Not that I know."

"Well, what *do* you know?"

"I know that this hurts more than anything ever hurt, ever. I know that I don't care if tomorrow comes or not. I know I want to wake up and it all be a dream. But I know it happened and we somehow gotta keep goin'."

"Don't think I can."

"You can. You will. We both will. Somehow."

"Why ain't God payin' attention to us?"

"He is. You know that. Remember, His eyes on the sparrow."

"Well, He should of quit looking at them stinkin' birds and watched Leland better. Now, I need Him to watch me. I just don't feel like He's doin' a good job at bein' God."

"Manny!"

"I want to know why did He this?"

"Probably ain't never gonna get an answer to that one. But I haf'ta still believe He's good. He don't do bad. So, I ain't gonna say He did it. I ain't gonna start blamin' Him. I need Him to get me through this. Not get mad at us for not trusting Him."

"I gotta blame somebody."

"Manny, stuff happens. God don't make it happen; it just happens."

"He could of stopped it from hap'nin'."

"Yeah, I guess. But since He didn't there must have been a reason."

"Then tell me the reason!"

"We don't know the reason!"

"And you can just go on not knowing why?"

Dearl breathed deeply and closed his eyes. He looked up at Manny. "If we gotta know why to everything, we ain't trustin' Him to be good."

"Well I ain't there yet."

"I know."

She pulled away, out from under his arm, and walked back into the house. Dearl watched her go then followed her up as far as the porch. He stopped at the door, turned and sat in his chair, took out his pipe. He picked up the stick he had been whittling away at and stared out into the darkness. Nubbin pressed her nose through the door and joined him. She lay on the porch beside him resting her chin across his shoe. She, too, stared out into the darkness. The 'coon walking across the yard attracted neither of them. They both stared out into the night, beyond anything they might see, sending their thoughts as far away as they could.

From inside the house he could hear Manny sweeping the floor hard and deliberate. She stayed in the same spot long after any evidence of dirt remained. Billie Nell lay on her and Leland's bed. Her grief had wearied her to sleep. The silence of the evening and the constant scratching of straw on the floor were the only things speaking. Joy's curtain had been drawn.

# Chapter Forty

MORNING CAME LATE. THE WEARINESS OF YESTERDAY'S GRIEF had drained them all and they slept hard and long. Billie Nell was first up but found herself outside heaving away any remains of last night's meal. Manny heard her gagging and went out to check.

"Something not agreeing with you this morning, Billie Nell?"

"I've sure been feeling sick in the mornings lately." She wiped her mouth and headed back inside.

"Really? Probably from how upset you've been."

"Yeah probably, I guess, but it started even before Leland died."

"Really?"

"Manny, can I ask you a woman question?"

"Sure."

"You know the womanly way we get each month. Well, I didn't get that this month."

"No?"

"Is that a bad thang?"

"Oh, my Lord. Billie Nell!"

"What?"

"You and Leland done made a baby."

"A baby? How do you know that?"

"Billie Nell?"

"Oh, okay, you ought to know."

"God didn't take Leland away from us without leaving a part of him behind. It ain't over. You're gonna be a momma. And I'm gonna be a grandma."

"Guess that's why you don't clap till the orchestra's done, huh?"

Frank came up the trail and up the steps. Nubbin ran out onto the porch, hair bristled on her back and a low growl in her throat. When she saw it was Frank her tail started wagging and she ran out to welcome him. Dearl met him at the door. "Frank?"

"Hey, Mr. Thomson. Thank I could see Billie Nell this morning?"

"That's up to her," he said. "Let me check. You wait out here on the porch."

Billie Nell pushed past Dearl and stood in the doorway looking at Frank. "Hey, Frank."

"Hey, Billie Nell. Thought I'd come by and see how y'all…well, how you been doin'."

"Well, we're doin' alright, I guess. Don't really know how we're supposed to be doin'. Ain't never done none of this before."

"Wanna sit out here and talk?"

"Sure," she said. They sat on the porch and looked off down the trail. "Don't seem real, you know. I still expect him to come up that trail any minute."

"Leland was a good friend."

"Yeah, I know."

"He's probably the closest thing I had to a brother. That's why what I want to tell you may not seem right, but the way I see it, it is. I'd like to help you out if I could."

"Help me out?"

"You know, talk to you, listen to you, cry with you. You know, help you out."

Billie Nell looked hard into Frank's eyes. She saw the glimmer of moisture building up. She knew it was best to look away so he could wipe the tears about to trickle down his cheeks. "Frank, I appreciate the friendship, but, well, you can't help me out of this."

"What?"

"I'm pregnant."

"What!?"

"Well, that's what Manny thanks."

Frank shot up and began to pace about the yard. He stopped, turned and said, "Then, Billie Nell, I want to marry you and help you raise Leland's baby."

"Frank Massey, I ain't looking for a husband. I just buried one. I ain't ready to talk about stuff like that."

"I ain't asking you to say yes right now. But Leland was like a brother to me. Well, a brother that didn't have the same parents or house or—well you know what I mean. We've been growing up together the whole time since we were born. We ain't always showed it but I thank we were the brother neither of us ever had."

"That's nice, Frank."

"And in the Bible whenever one of the brother's died, the other brother would marry his wife and raise up his kids. That's what I want to do."

"You want to raise Leland's baby?"

"Not by myself. Thought we might could do that together. 'Cause I don't thank a kid should grow up without a daddy like I did."

"You had a daddy."

"Don't thank my dad ever made it to be a daddy. And anyhow, I'd never have a kid as good as you and Leland would have. I'm afraid it might turn out like me, or worse like my dad. I know I wouldn't be his father, but I could try real hard to be his daddy, the kind Leland would have been."

Billie Nell got up and walked out into the yard where Frank was. She faced him said, "I thank Leland would'uv liked that. I thank you'd make a real good daddy."

"What about you? Thank you'd ever like something like that?"

"Well, maybe. We'll see."

"And do you thank, in time, you'd ever love me?"

"Like I did Leland?"

"Yeah, you know, when you fell in love with him."

"Never knew a time I didn't love Leland. We knew from little kids we'd someday get married. It always felt the same—it was right. I never had to fall in love with him; I just was. So, I don't know what that feels like—falling in love."

"My dad used to say it was like an itch you cain't scratch."

"Ain't felt that way before. I just never saw nobody else as my husband, just Leland. So, I guess I'm gonna haf to learn what it feels like to love somebody else some day. Ain't sure I know how, but I guess it starts with feelin' right somebody. Kinda like I do with you. That's somethin', ain't it?"

"Yeah, that's good enough for now."

"Frank, losin' somebody tears a hole outa your heart, like somebody done stuck their hand inside my chest and pulled out a chunk of it. I ain't never hurt so much, ever. And I don't know if I'll ever not hurt about this, but you bein' there's gonna help. And me hurtin' over Leland don't mean I won't care about you."

"Alright. I can live with that. But Billie Nell, if it's alright with you, I'm gonna love you with all my heart till yours gets well, and then someday we can love each other the same from then on. Alright?"

She reached out and pulled him in close and hugged him tightly. "Alright."

CFS

Printed in the United States
By Bookmasters